By Joseph Olshan

THE WATERLINE
A WARMER SEASON
CLARA'S HEART

THE
WATERLINE

THE
WATERLINE

a   n o v e l   b y

JOSEPH OLSHAN

DOUBLEDAY   *New York   London   Toronto   Sydney   Auckland*

PUBLISHED BY DOUBLEDAY
a division of Bantam Doubleday Dell Publishing Group, Inc.
666 Fifth Avenue, New York, New York 10103

DOUBLEDAY and the portrayal of an anchor
with a dolphin are trademarks of
Doubleday, a division of Bantam Doubleday Dell
Publishing Group, Inc.

Excerpt from "The Divided Child" from *Collected Poems 1948–1984* by
Derek Walcott. Copyright © 1972, 1973, 1986 by Derek Walcott.
Reprinted by permission of Farrar, Straus and Giroux, Inc.

Library of Congress Cataloging-in-Publication Data

Olshan, Joseph.
The waterline : a novel / by Joseph Olshan.—1st ed.
p.   cm.
ISBN 0-385-26505-0
I. Title.
PS3565.L8237W35   1989
813'.54—dc19   89-31153
CIP

Designed by Guenet Abraham

October 1989
FIRST EDITION
BG

They melt from you, your sons.
Your arms grow full of rain.
—DEREK WALCOTT

FOR MY MOTHER AND FATHER

S U S A N

T H E   N I G H T before we learned of the drowning, I dreamed that Billy couldn't breathe. I dreamed that he was lying in an iron lung. The steel cylinder, shaped like a polished torpedo, suddenly began whirling around him. His eyes rolled back, his cheeks drained of color and his mouth kept popping open like a fish suffocating in an aquarium. Frantic, I pushed my hands like brakes against the lung, which continued to smother him despite my efforts to stop it. Then the floor ruptured beneath my feet, and all I could see around me was the cold night sky.

I awoke in a sweat, my nightgown clinging to my back. My husband, Michael, was asleep next to me, his eyelids fluttering in response to what surely must have been a more pleasant dream. Afraid to check on Billy all by myself, I fought the urge to wake Michael. Finally, I got out of bed and went down the hallway to my son's room.

The door was closed; his air conditioner was on. I opened the door. Billy was lying on his back, completely still. Despite the coolness in the room, his face was flushed. Pearls of sweat had gathered at the top of his forehead, dampening his thick, tortoiseshell-colored hair. Holding my breath, I went and put my ear against his chest. When I felt his body rising and falling, I began weeping in relief.

His air conditioner had begun ailing recently and we had ordered him a new one. The blades of the faltering compressor were making sounds like a warbler whose weakened heart was giving out. Suddenly worried that a faulty part inside the motor would fail and start a fire, I turned it off. From somewhere deep in his sleep, Billy registered the absence of sound and woke up.

"Mom." He stared at me in the midst of a terrific yawn. After the drone of the air conditioner, the sudden silence in the room between us felt accusatory, made me feel ill at ease. "Why did you do that?"

I bent over him. His eyes shone in the hallway light that slashed into the room. "Because, Birdie." I called him by his nickname. "It sounded worse than usual tonight."

His sleepy face, stern for a seven-year-old, continued to question me. "It won't break," he said. "And besides, we're getting a new one, aren't we?"

I was afraid to tell him the air conditioner could start a fire and burn down the house, for then my fears might be contagious. "All right, then, I'll leave it on," I managed to say as I went over to the air conditioner. When I turned it on this time, there were no heart murmurs, just a sturdy, resonant hum.

I sat down next to Billy and combed my fingers through his mop of hair, splitting tangles, feeling his scalp for bumps and imperfections. "Why are you up, Mom?" he asked after I had stroked his head for a while.

Suddenly nervous, I said, "Because I had a bad dream."

Billy smiled. Up until now we had only dealt in his bad dreams. Whenever he had bad dreams he'd come wake me up, recount what had happened, and then I would judge how bad the dream was, how long he could stay in our bed before he had to go back and sleep in his own room.

"You can sleep with me," he now offered.

I shook my head. "No. I'll go back to Daddy. Shortly. I just wanted to see how you were."

And yet, I was reluctant to return to my own bedroom. For although I had awakened from the nightmare feeling frightened and confused, my thoughts were now clear. And as they were liable to do in the quieter bands of the night, worrisome issues fell to nagging at me: my sister, Tina, who had just recently left her family in Galveston to enter a private mental hospital in New York State, a hospital that she had chosen in order to be near me; Michael, whose working marathon hours left him too exhausted to spend enough time with Billy.

It saddened me to think that Michael and I hadn't made love in ten days. I used to count the number of occasions we made love in a given week, thinking that the frequency of our lovemaking was also the barometer of our feelings for one another. And yet, I knew this was a particularly busy time for him. A budding theatrical agent, Michael often had to stay late in Manhattan. That month, June of 1962, he was particularly busy, beset by complications for a play that was supposed to open up at the Long Wharf Theatre in New Haven, a play whose premiere he promised we'd be able to attend.

The next morning, before I knew it, Michael was up and in the bathroom, leaving me to scheme how I could seduce him. I considered climbing into the shower and sucking him hard or waiting until he was shaving, hoisting myself up with the shower-stall railing and wrapping my legs around him. I was still lying in bed, conjuring fantasies, when he suddenly emerged from the bathroom, a blue towel wrapped around him, the hair on his chest matted luxuriantly with water.

"I've got to write something down or I'll forget it," he said. "Where did I leave my pad?"

I was pretty sure he had left his pad in the study.

He crossed the bedroom, imprinting the carpet with wet foot marks. I got up, put on my lime-green bathrobe with its print of roses and followed him. I was hoping to entice him and perhaps lure him back to bed. I stood at the door of the study, watched him pluck a pen from its well and pick up the pad. Then he put down the pen for a moment to wrap the towel even tighter around his hard middle. The front panel of the towel took on a strong impression of his genitals. I felt a twitch of lust, beginning at the back of my throat and threading down through my body until it bloomed into a circle of warmth between my thighs. Indolent with desire, I allowed the flaps of my bathrobe to fall open, a view of my nakedness, my nipples tingling and swollen. But instead of noticing me, Michael spied what was underneath the pad: envelopes with plastic transparent ovals sealing the name Mrs. Michael Kaplan, the markers of charge accounts. I shuddered as he noticed the first bill and opened it, water from his armpits dripping on the paper, leaving blots.

He flipped the first bill behind the second, read the column of numbers, shut his eyes and pinched his forehead. I sensed what was coming. "Susan," he said, his eyes still closed, "you spent seven hundred and fifty dollars on one dress?" Then he opened his eyes. "Are you out of your mind?"

Recently, I had driven two and a half hours to the psychiatric hospital to visit Tina for the first time. The visit had so depressed me that to make myself feel better I had gone out and bought the gown on impulse. "Don't I need a formal dress?" I asked weakly. "Don't we have to go to that play opening?"

"But seven hundred and fifty dollars?" Michael croaked. "You could buy a dozen dresses for seven hundred and fifty dollars. How am I supposed to pay for it?"

"They told me we could pay them one hundred dollars a month on installment."

"Oh, great," Michael said, shaking his hair and shedding more water. A drop splattered on the crystal coffee table. A drop hit me in the throat. There was no chance now we'd make love.

"Do you want to see the dress?" I asked. "I'd like to show it to you."

"No, I don't want to see it. I just want to know why, why you're spending money so irresponsibly," he growled.

I started to weep. I don't cry easily and Michael was surprised to see me break down. "Honey," he said, still cross, although his voice had cooled, "you don't have to cry. It's not the end of the world. Ah, come on, you know I hate to see you cry."

I shook my head. "It's not the dress," I managed to blubber out. "I'm not crying about the dress."

"Then what are you crying about?"

I hesitated. "I'm crying . . . about Tina." Her illness made me feel powerless, as powerless as I felt being unable to seduce Michael.

When I had gone to visit Tina at the hospital, I had seen a woman whose features were similar to mine: a broad face, flinty blue eyes and a well-defined chin that quivered under any emotional stress. But when I looked at Tina more closely, I noticed her cheeks were puffy from the combination of salts and sedatives she had been taking on a regular basis, her rheumy eyes hazed with drugs. She was wearing a housedress with a faded yellow print of chrysanthemums. I recognized the dress as having once belonged to me. I had given it to Tina a few years before when she started gaining weight due to all the drugs her

doctors were prescribing. Shortly after my arrival at the hospital, Tina quite proudly led me to a small room equipped with
wires and gauges and clamps and a doctor's table fitted with
canvas restraints. "This is where you get shock," she said, a smile
wriggling its way across her face. "We call it the zap-'n'-zoom
room."

After I had met her roommate, a dangerously thin, dark-
haired woman in her early twenties who suffered from anorexia,
Tina led me outside for a stroll through the asylum's beautifully
manicured grounds. The compound was populated with stands
of pine trees, a massive stone fountain that produced only a
gurgle of water, great long beds of white azaleas and fifty-year-
old lilac bushes. The beauty of the place struck me as ironic; I
wondered if here most people swung too far from their own
minds to be able to appreciate the simple pacifying pleasure of a
lovely landscape.

As we walked I felt a painful silence grow up between us, and
I tried to conjure up a subject of conversation that would be
neutral. We entered a wooded section of the compound, where
the silence deepened as birds wheeled above us, mocking one
another. We could hear the rustling of ground animals.

A squirrel darted out from the underbrush and stood facing us
on its hind legs. When I bent down to coax it with an open
hand, I heard Tina say, "Don't get too close to them, Susan.
They're dangerous."

I drew my hand back. "Really?"

"People get bitten. Although it doesn't make much difference. Everybody around here is already rabid."

Still perched on its hind legs, the squirrel held me in a beady,
hopeful stare that made me think of Billy when he implored
with his eyes. "But he looks so sweet," I said.

"God, you sound like some of the nuts I know around here.
Around here," Tina said, "the nuts feed the squirrels."

I was allowed to take Tina out for lunch. She wanted to go to a Friendly's and sit in a red vinyl booth. I ordered a grilled cheese sandwich, and she ordered French vanilla ice cream with caramel syrup, specifying to the waiter that she wanted to eat her sundae with a long, slender spoon. I'd forgotten that as children we'd always eaten ice cream this way—the longer the spoons, the longer the caramel sauce seemed to last. Whereas my weight had always fluctuated, Tina, until she got sick, was always thin. Now, when she walked her thighs and buttocks jiggled: fleshy lithium dividends.

"It feels strange to be going out to lunch after living at the hospital," Tina said. Up until this point, the conversation had lagged while she focused intently on mining veins of caramel sauce from her vanilla ice cream.

"How so?" I asked her.

Her forehead screwed up as though she were trying to multiply numbers without pencil and paper. "It just doesn't feel like I should be here in this restaurant. It doesn't feel appro . . . priate." She had trouble uttering the last word.

"If they allow you to come, then it's appropriate," I said.

After another silence plagued us, I asked Tina if she had any idea how long she'd have to stay in the hospital.

"It'll all depends on the doctors' evaluations."

"When do they evaluate?"

"Every week I get sessions with a psych." Tina's expression grew murky, but then clarified. "I actually like it here," she said with a trace of arrogance.

My throat closed. The clattering of restaurant dishes grew louder and I suddenly wished we had not gone out to eat. Leaving the asylum was obviously provoking Tina to make strange remarks. "What do you mean?"

Tina carefully placed the long spoon by the side of the ice-cream dish. I glanced down at my uneaten grilled cheese sandwich. "They treat me well," she said. "Give me everything I want. Three good meals. I never have to cook or worry about—"

"But, Tina," I said, "you're making it sound more like a hotel than a hospital."

She looked placid, her eyes focused so distantly I felt she was peering inside herself. I had never seen her skin so pale. "It's nice," she went on in a dreamy voice, "to have a nurse tuck you in bed every night. I really like that, being tucked in every night. Although I miss Rachel."

As I drove the two and a half hours back to Hartsdale, I grew more and more depressed. Even though Tina had wanted to commit herself to the hospital, I never expected her to enjoy living there. Perhaps they had tampered with her, the shock treatments somehow altering Tina's perception of her needs so that now she would never choose to leave. Perhaps the drugs Tina was taking had helped her acquire a taste for the place, provoking a false affinity for the sterile surroundings like a serum that induced the telling of lies.

After I finished explaining everything, Michael drew close to me and pressed his chest to my face. I breathed his morning shower and his toasty scent from being in the sun on weekends. "I think maybe I should come when you go visit Tina the next time."

Although I hardly heard him, I said, "Okay . . . Michael, I can pay for the dress."

"Don't be silly." He began massaging my shoulders. "Just don't wipe us out. The simple fact of the matter is I can't afford to keep you in that kind of clothing. Not yet, anyway," he said with a grin. He obviously felt guilty for yelling at me.

"That job at the boutique that I was offered. I could take that, save from my earnings and pay you back."

"I don't want you to pay me back."

"Well, maybe I'd feel better if I paid you back," I said.

"Well, I wouldn't feel better." Michael planted a kiss on my ear. He glanced at the brass desk clock on his desk. "I've got to hurry up or else I'll miss my train."

I watched him leave the room, his black wavy hair bouncing damply. The carpeting still bore impressions of his wet feet.

I will always remember what Michael wore that day, because what happened later transformed each detail of that twenty-four-hour period into something photographically permanent. I will always remember him returning from work that evening, strolling up the cement walk that resembled so many other cement walks in our quiet tract neighborhood, hewed out of the combined property of two large estates that had been sold to land developers. Michael had the compact body of a man a lot younger than one in his thirties. In the semi-darkness, his blue eyes glowed like icy coals against his suntan. He had no idea that just an hour before our driveway was packed with police cars, unmarked detective cars, journalists parked haphazardly up and down the street. He had been in and out of his office all afternoon, and I had been unable to reach him.

Billy had a friend named Peter Freed who lived down the street on the bank of a man-made lake that was stocked with carp. There were maybe fifteen split-level houses built around the lake, which fed gluttonously on ten good years of rainfall between 1952 and 1962. Until Billy learned how to swim, Michael and I had forbidden him to play anywhere near the water, which was semi-polluted and murky. The previous summer, I had discovered that Billy actually had been playing by the lake with Peter, and when I found out about it, Billy was severely punished. Determined to keep playing with his friend, however, Billy insisted we get him swimming instruction, which Michael and I finally agreed to. A year had passed since the first lesson. He had learned well. I had an arrangement with Peter's mother that whenever Billy was fishing by the lake, he had to be within view of the Freeds' house, where an adult could keep an eye on him. Wading was not allowed; in fact, he was strictly forbidden to go beyond the waterline.

There was another family, the Rosens, who lived across the street from the Freeds. I had never been formally introduced to them. I had seen Harriet in the Shopwell; she played bridge with one of my tennis partners. I said hello whenever I saw her but we had never spoken at any length. Her husband worked for IBM and must have done pretty well for himself, as they were able to afford a housekeeper as well as a nurse to look after their two children: Mark, who was two and a half, and a baby, who was just a few weeks old. I distinctly remember seeing Mark being wheeled through the neighborhood in his stroller. He was a swarthy child with green eyes.

Peter and Billy knew Mark as a little kid. He was five years younger, a rather vast age difference for them. As far as I knew, Peter and Billy had associated with Mark only when the neighborhood kids swarmed together to share a lawn sprinkler, taking their turns leaping over the wands of water that flew across sodden carpets of Kentucky bluegrass and caught the sun, prisming into rainbows in the midst of a sweltering afternoon. I do remember Billy telling me how Mark's nursemaid once took Mark down to the lake to watch a bunch of kids fishing for carp. There, he had misbehaved and thrown somebody's bait into the water. He had been scolded and promptly taken home.

I can still picture the stainless-steel pail I bought Billy to hold the carp he caught with bread balls and then kept in a gallon of lake water. I can see the bright orange-and-gold lozenges fanning slowly back and forth in their captivity. I had done some volunteer work in White Plains for part of that afternoon and was leisurely driving home when I heard fire engines pursuing me on the two-lane road. I pulled over, rolled down the window and watched them roar by. Although it was quite warm outside, I could feel the trucks generating heat from their engines, a heat that mildly seared my face. I could smell the pungency of melting macadam and motor oil mixing with the heady smells of June. I began driving again but had to pull over a second time, to be overtaken by a police car; the same thing happened again with an ambulance, which turned down my street.

When I saw the ambulance, I began to worry, as any mother might worry, thinking: Did I forget to turn off the toaster? Did I put too many plugs in the outlet? Did Billy leave his air conditioner on all day? I was relieved when I pulled into our driveway—no fire trucks and ambulances and police cars to be seen. The tragedy was happening elsewhere, if at all. I figured maybe some kid went to the firebox at the corner and pulled the lever, which had summoned this mad procession to a counterfeit event. If so, there was a way the police could track down the culprit; the area around the lever at the firebox was laced with a transparent goo that showed up on the hands under ultraviolet light. Then I noticed an eerie quiet embracing the neighborhood. No children were playing. The houses appeared empty, windows shuttered against the blaze of the early summer afternoon. Not a single lawn sprinkler ticked against its water flange. The stillness was suspicious.

There seemed to be lots of false alarms in the neighborhood, but few fires, a burglary now and then; you hardly ever saw red-and-white ambulances. Ambulances were fashioned out of Cadillacs, as were hearses, and to me they shared the same death coefficient. Death was supposed to be an uncommon occurrence in such a young neighborhood. Parents were all in their early thirties, children of elementary school age. The homes were created from similar designs, plumbing and electrical systems were modern and efficient. It was as if this uniformity suggested that all our parallel lives would flourish equally well. Unfortunately, dark things bubbled up and broke through the surface of this radiant lie. Mindy Bernstein, a nine-year-old who lived down the street, was diagnosed with leukemia. Dorry Snyder, cruelly abandoned by her husband, took advantage of her spacious garage by starting up the family's two cars and asphyxiating herself amidst the potent whispering of V-8 engines. As I pulled into our driveway, I remembered how Billy made me promise that if he ever got sick enough to warrant an ambulance, I would ask the driver to hush the siren while he was being driven to the hospital. Billy was unnerved by the sound of sirens.

It was just shy of 4 P.M. Mercedes, our housekeeper, had just gone off on some personal errands and I was completely alone. I remember looking at the thin black hands on the kitchen clock, which marked the time against quadrants of bright enameled flowers. The house was chilled, a welcome respite after the hot outdoors, where the sun blazed through the eggplant-colored leaves of the Japanese maples, glinting off Billy's set of swings, making a black pool of shadow on the patio beneath the barbecue. I had just poured myself a glass of orange juice, added a dash of vodka, when the phone rang. It was Norma Freed, Peter's mother.

Her voice was shaking. "Susan, I'm glad I got hold of you." I could hear the sound of screaming children in the background.

My breath caught. "What is it?"

"Hold on a second, will you." Norma muffled the phone and yelled, "I'm talking to Mrs. Kaplan, so would you leave me alone!"

I was suspended and then plummeting hard and fast. I wanted more than anything to retrieve the moment of balance before Norma Freed had dialed my phone number and left me open to all sorts of possibilities I felt I could never face. It was like being suddenly shoved out of an airplane and into the harrowing instant before gravity takes over and establishes free fall, believing it's possible to climb back up to the fuselage, that an invisible ladder exists if only one knew where to find it. Suddenly, the kitchen seemed to come alive: the polished tea kettle hummed without a flame underneath it, dangling pot holders ejected pinwheels of colored air, the refrigerator whined like a ghost. Billy's blue cereal bowl stood alone on the spotless counter.

"Hi, I'm sorry." Norma came back on.

"Norma, are you calling about Billy?" I stammered.

She hesitated before saying, "Well, yes."

My throat swelled shut. The rings on my fingers seemed to be encasing a stranger's hands. I now knew that all the machinery and manpower that flew past me on South Street had been called —something had happened to Billy; he had been burned or blown up somehow—and in the short interim between my driving home and this telephone call they had done whatever they could to save his life, and had failed. At the moment of his death I was actually having myself a screwdriver. I began to feel faint.

"Was there an accident?" I gasped.

"Yes, but it's not what you think. It's . . ."

And then arrived a moment of complete unreality as the front door opened and slammed and I recognized the pattering footsteps. How could this be? Was my mind playing tricks? I looked once again at the cereal bowl on the counter. Then Billy raced into the kitchen, sobbing. I looked at him in a way I never had, the way I might study myself if I were walking down a street and caught my own reflection in a sliver of mirror, to make sure that it was me whom I saw and that I was actually there, that I existed. He was still alive.

"Mark fell in the lake," he sobbed, throwing himself upon me. And I thanked God for sparing my son, as yet without a clue that now an ordeal of a different order was about to begin.

In the midst of Billy's commotion, Norma Freed said, "Mark Rosen somehow fell in the lake. I don't know how. Billy was fishing. . . . Peter and I weren't home. . . . My daughter didn't see anything."

"Is Mark okay?" I asked.

"I can't tell. The firemen are outside trying to resuscitate him. . . . Hold on a second. Would you leave me alone for one minute, Peter!" she yelled. "I'm sorry. I don't know what's going on. It's crazy here. The whole neighborhood must be outside in the yard. Last I heard they said it was touch and go."

"Oh my God, Norma," I said. "I'll be right over."

When I got off the phone, I enfolded Billy into my arms. "But you're drenched." My first thought was that he had fallen in the lake as well, but then I realized he was soaked in sweat. He was crying steadily now. "Don't worry, it will be all right," I soothed him. "Shhh. I'm taking care of everything now. Let's go upstairs and get you changed."

I took Billy's hand and led him up to his bedroom. Before leaving for the lake, he had positioned squads of lead army men all over his floor and had neglected to put them away. Sniffling back his tears, he looked up at me, expecting to be scolded. Instead, I stroked his head. I stripped off his tee shirt and rubbed his back with a fresh towel, and as I looked at his fleshy body, I was so glad to have him there with me. I kissed him softly between the shoulder blades. We went back downstairs and I sat him down at the kitchen table, poured him a glass of apple juice and gave him an oatmeal cookie. Then I sat where I usually sit during dinner, folded my hands in front of me and as calmly as I could asked Billy to tell me what had happened.

Refusing to touch his snack, he shook his head. I reached over and began stroking his arm and said, "Come on, honey, a lot has happened now and we need to talk about it."

"I told you what happened."

"I need you to tell me how it happened. You were there."

"But I don't know," he said, averting his eyes.

"Billy, this is a very serious thing. Your father will be home soon and we're going to have to tell him everything."

At the mention of Michael, I could see panic cross Billy's face. He both adored and feared his father. Then his face crumpled in horror and the tears gushed forth again.

"Something's wrong, Mom!" he cried out, startling me. "Something's wrong!"

"Please tell me, or else I won't be able to help you."

"Do you promise to fix it?"

"I hope I can fix it," I said.

"You have to promise."

"I can't promise unless I know what it is."

"Why?"

"Because I'm not God, Billy, that's why."

Billy grimaced. And then he wailed in frustration.

"Take a deep breath," I said, "and try to relax."

"Okay," he said. "Okay." He shut his eyes for a moment and I looked at his reddened cheeks.

"I caught all these fish. I got carp and sunfish and he wanted to see them."

"Where was he?"

"He was standing on the street. He asked and I told him to come with me. Was that bad?"

"Was there anybody watching him?"

Billy shook his head.

"Are you sure?"

"Yes."

It amazed me that a two-and-a-half-year-old child wasn't being looked after. "All right, so then what happened?"

"He asked me if the fish were going to sleep. I didn't know what he was saying. I was trying to catch more. But he stayed there, looking in my pail. And then he took my last piece of Wonder bread, ate some and threw the rest in the water." Billy started speaking quickly, his breathing running shallow as though the telling was winding him. "I told him to go home. And then all of a sudden a fishhook got stuck in my finger and I was bleeding and I had to get a Band-Aid from Connie. Mark was supposed to leave . . ." Billy broke off, squirming in his chair.

"But he didn't," I said.

Billy scuffed his sneakers against the linoleum floor. Something within me wondered if he had just withheld something. "Go on," I said.

"And then . . . when I got back outside I didn't see him, so I thought he went home. But then I saw something floating. First I thought . . . it was an old man or something and then I saw it was Mark." Billy started shaking and I moved my chair closer and held him to me. His cheek against my shoulder, he continued: "He was trying to swim but he couldn't. So I ran and told his mother and she went down to the lake with her bathrobe on and swam out and got him. And then his nanny came and they tried pushing his back. And then I saw this white stuff coming out of his mouth. It was my Wonder bread—"

He broke down and cried harder than he did before.

"It's okay, it's okay," I soothed him. "Let's just sit here for a bit and quiet down." My mind, however, was racing. I was afraid. I looked at my watch. It was four-thirty.

"Is it my fault?" Billy suddenly asked me in a shaking voice. "Did I make him fall in?"

"Of course not," I said, rocking him.

"But I let him come down to the lake."

"Yes, but he was too young to be playing across the street without somebody watching him. God knows, they have enough housekeepers and nurses for one family."

"Are you sure?" he implored.

"Yes, I'm sure."

"But this is different," he said, which I knew to be true. It

was different, unlike anything that had ever happened to either
of us before.

"It has nothing to do with you," I reassured him again, although I was afraid something else had happened, something he
was hiding from me.

Mercedes had not yet returned, so it was impossible for me to
leave Billy at home while I drove to the lake. "We've got to go
now, sweetheart," I told him. "It's time to drive over to the
Freeds'."

We walked outside to the car. The neighborhood was even
more still than before, as though all its blood had rushed to the
wound. When Billy climbed in the front seat, I didn't force him
to hook his seat belt. He sat very still, a veil of dried tears on his
cheek. He was waiting to learn whether or not Mark Rosen
would live.

I started the car, put down the electric windows. I drove my
Buick Skylark, which Michael had once gotten up to 145 miles
per hour. Now I wanted to drive the four blocks to the lake as
slowly as possible. I wanted to prepare myself to confront whatever might be there. I figured I'd be consoling to Mrs. Rosen in
whatever way I could, would discuss the event in greater detail
with Norma Freed. After all, I was the fortunate mother whose
son did not fall in the lake; it was my duty to aid these people.

As we approached the lake, we could see signs of activity.
Lured to the incident, people were scurrying across the contigu-
ous green lawns. Housewives in Bermuda shorts and sleeveless
tops—hair wound around plastic rollers and webbed in hairnets,
carrying babies, frantically pushing strollers—reminded me of a
pack of vultures. The air streaming into the car was warm and
fetid. Eventually, we could hear the motors of the fire trucks,
caught a whiff of heavy diesel fuel. We glimpsed patches of the
lake through the trees. The water looked calm and impervious
to any tragedy.

There must've been two hundred bystanders milling behind

the blue police barricades that were erected on the lake side of the road. I didn't recognize most of the people; I honestly don't know where they all gathered from. I parked near the corner, took Billy's hand and walked toward the scene. It was difficult to know exactly what he was feeling just then; I was so over-whelmed by the commotion, by our connection to it, wondering what would be demanded of us. A group of neighborhood kids, Peter Freed among them, already had gotten wind that Billy was involved; as soon as he appeared, several of them surrounded him and eagerly asked what had happened. Peter was particularly keen. He had a round, Nordic-looking face, cold mocking eyes, a shock of white-blond hair. Billy began to recount, his crystalline voice going over the details carefully. "And then he came to see my carp. He ate my last piece of bread, so I told him to go home. When I came back to the lake I saw him floating."

I left Billy with his friends for a moment and went to find Norma Freed, whom I spotted standing by the side of her house. Norma was a homely woman, never did much with herself. Her hair was an overpermed mousy brown and her arms were fleshy and pockmarked. She was speaking to a fireman in a black rain slicker with fluorescent yellow stripes on the cuffs and collar. The fireman had obviously just said something upsetting; Norma was putting her hand to her forehead and seemed to be groaning.

"Norma, Norma," I said, "what's going on?"

She looked bewildered. "He's still alive. They're taking him to the hospital."

"Did they say if he'll make it."

She winced and shook her head. "They still say it's touch and go." There was a small crowd of people separating us. I tried to get closer to her but unfortunately was wedged in. "I've got to take something to calm my nerves," Norma said, edging away.

"I'll come with you," I said.

She looked at me fiercely. "They could sue me," she cackled. "The Rosens. It happened on my property. They could sue the pants off me so I'd have to sell my house and move out of this neighborhood. They could sue me!" she cried out. The din of the anticipatory crowd died down for a moment to gauge her outburst and then swelled again. Norma scurried toward her front porch. I was flabbergasted. I didn't know what to say. Was she inferring that what had happened to Mark Rosen on her property was Billy's and my responsibility? I wanted her to clarify what she meant. I pivoted toward the lake. A cloud was masking the sun and there was a blush of darkness on the water, whose surface looked suspiciously sober, as though suddenly it had grown ashamed of its unconscious killing power. Hugging the lake bank was a group of perhaps two dozen firemen and policemen. They were flanking a square metal machine with tentacles of blond rubber tubing that was pumping: some sort of resuscitating device, I figured. There was something achingly familiar about the scene—then I remembered my dream of the iron lung the night before. I continued to scan the group of men. Somewhere in the midst of that cluster must lie Mark Rosen. Touch and go, I mused. Touch and go. Suddenly frightened to be among so many strangers, I searched the crowd for someone I knew, finally recognizing a mother who lived two doors away. "Where's Harriet Rosen?" I queried.

"She's hysterical," said a man standing a few feet away. "She's in her house. They put her under sedation. Aren't you Mrs. Kaplan?" he asked. "The mother of Billy Kaplan?"

Their names suddenly had taken on such significance. Mark Rosen. Billy Kaplan. I looked at this small wizened fellow, who wore a pair of crooked black glasses, hands too large and hairy for the rest of his body. He held a small pad and a Bic pen with only a millimeter of jet ink left in its cylinder. "I'm Tom Morgenthau, reporter from the *Dispatch*. Could I ask you some questions?"

"There's nothing I can tell you," I said absently.

"Well, but your son—"

"What about my son?" I interrupted.

The man hesitated, then continued: "Your son was involved."

I felt the words first in my solar plexus like a tight, cruel punch before I heard them. The reporter sensed something. Whatever that was I would pound it into nothing. I raised my chin and glared down at him. "My son was not involved. My son did not drown!"

"But he was there. He was the last person to talk to Mark Rosen."

Ignoring him, I looked back toward the lake at the tangle of policemen and firemen. Their formation had just broken up around a white stretcher mounted on a gurney. There was an indentation of a small body beneath a sheet, the face exposed, the nose and mouth covered by an ominous-looking black mask that fed into a large rubber tube. Even though he was overwhelmed by all the equipment, which certainly gave the impression that it suffocated rather than revived, I could recognize Mark Rosen's wan face, his black hair plastered down, as though with Brylcream, his eyelids fluttering long, dark lashes. A pale stalwart woman in white, obviously the nanny, was absently stroking his forehead, her face wreathed with anguish. She was the one who should have watched him, I thought angrily, the reporter should be questioning her! A group of firemen lifted the stretcher while a hospital attendant wheeled the resuscitating machine, all of it a rather slow procession in the midst of such urgency.

"Mrs. Kaplan, could you just answer one question?" persisted the reporter.

"My son had nothing to do with it," I repeated. "That's all I've got to say. Talk to Mrs. Rosen. Talk to their nanny, for Christ's sake!"

Afraid the reporter would seek out Billy, I began searching

for him. The group of kids were no longer standing where they had been, had dispersed into the crowd, probably disseminating Billy's story along with their seeds of doubt. I finally spotted him. He stood rigidly next to a blue hydrangea bush in the yard of the neighbors who lived adjacent to the Freeds. As Billy watched the firemen's procession, a lone tear slipped down his cheek. Then another. I went and put my arms around him.

"Is he going to be all right?" Billy asked.

I pulled him close to me, hugging him tightly so as to stop him from shaking. But despite my comfort, he still quaked in my arms. "I don't know, Birdie," I said. "I guess it's in God's hands."

"Then maybe we should go home and pray for him," Billy said. "Maybe if we go home and pray, God won't let him die."

T I N A   W A S   born during the Los Angeles earthquake of 1933. Although I was only two years old at the
time, I clearly remember the occasion. My father always said
that my recollection of Tina's birth was distilled from stories
that I had heard later on, but I know the range of my memory
dates back to a much earlier impression: my mother carrying me
through our bungalow-style house in Redondo Beach, California, passing the hallway mirror, where she stopped to fix her
hair. Mother has always been a vain, beautiful woman; even
now, at the age of eighty-five, she still keeps a stately, elegant
appearance, with a prominent jawline and a scroll of shiny silver
hair. That day she held me tightly in one arm and with the other

pulled her charcoal-dark hair out of the schoolmistress knot she wore and gave her head a few side-to-side tosses until, no longer captive, her hair turned into a storm of unruliness, slapping me gently in the face before cascading down her muscular white back. I remember looking in the mirror and seeing my own reflection, which was startling, and somehow I knew it was the image of no one else but me. I was wearing a blue romper embroidered with white bunnies. In later years, when I described the outfit, my mother claimed that I outgrew it at eight months of age.

When the earthquake began we were having dinner at a noisy steak restaurant in Redondo Beach which was only a few blocks away from the two-bedroom house we were renting at the time. My parents were celebrating my father's promotion to regional sales manager of a company that sold doughnut-making machines. Mother was in her eighth month of pregnancy; Tina wasn't expected for three weeks. I was perched in a high chair provided by the restaurant, peering down at the sawdust-covered floor. Only a moment before the wooden floor planks began undulating and buckling, some instinct within me seized up in anticipation, and I threw my fork along the aisle of tables, startling the patrons of the restaurant. I watched the weather in my mother's expression change from annoyance to alarm, as her eyes jerked to the ceiling and in utter amazement followed the spectacle of a crystal chandelier swinging perilously above us. The dining table pitched forward. Liquid rocked higher and higher up the sides of the glasses until they upset; father's wine was quickly drunk up by white linen. Then there was a strange roaring that sounded as though the ocean were bursting through the back of the restaurant. "Get out of here," people shouted, bolting from their chairs in order to flee. My mother stood and snatched me out of my high chair. "Come on, David," she ordered my father. "Before the place caves in."

In comparison with everyone else, my father was amazingly

composed. That night, as always, he was immaculately dressed, wavy hair pomaded to a sheen, moustache waxed perfectly, his merry blue eyes bright and mischievous. "Nothing doing," he said, moving his head in a singsong way as he sliced into his rare steak and put a bite-sized morsel into his mouth. "I'm not going to leave this wonderful meal for an earthquake," he blustered.

"You're a fool, David!" Mother cried, prodding his elbow.

"I told you, Rose, I won't leave my dinner. I'm paying good money for it. The place won't fall down," he said, glancing up indifferently at the doddering chandelier. "I've been in worse shakes than this."

In fact, he hadn't, but Mother sensed he wouldn't budge. Besides, she had little patience for his stubbornness. And so she grabbed me and hurried outside. I remember resting my chin on her shoulder and looking back at the mass confusion of waiters and busboys and patrons scurrying to follow our example, fascinated by the dinner carts with untouched food moving waywardly on their own wheels, abandoned tables lurching every which way. Glassware rolled off the tables like balls; falling pots sounded like gongs. And there was my father, sitting all alone in the dining room savoring his steak. After that night my father would always say that by refusing to recognize the danger of the earthquake, he had protected the restaurant from collapse, the fate of most of the other buildings on the street.

After the first shock died down, and while mother stood holding me on the sidewalk, she was attacked by terrible stomach pains. She motioned to a waiter and asked him to go back inside and tell my father she was in trouble. Luckily, by then he had finished his meal. He emerged from the restaurant, full of boldness and grinning pride at not having been spooked by an earthquake. Mother, in the meantime, had put me down on the sidewalk, clutching my hand while doubling over. She explained to my father that it was time to go to the hospital, and while helping her straighten up, he apologized for not leaving the restaurant.

"I hope you had fun, David," she hissed.

"I'm sorry, honey. I just wanted to finish my dinner. That's all."

"Well, what about us?" Mother demanded. "We could've been hurt."

Father looked around at the mass confusion of people exiled from damaged buildings, listening for a moment to their cries of confusion. "I didn't realize it was going to be like this," he said. "But don't worry. I'll take care of everything. How are you feeling now, sweetheart?"

"Just take me to the hospital!"

"There, there," he said, encircling the both of us with his great arms, kissing her on the cheek, and then Mother started to cry. "Now let's just walk slowly to the car and we'll be there in no time."

"If the car is still there."

"It'll be there," Father said. "The world hasn't ended."

I remember that crazy drive. Two-story stucco buildings had pitched into rubble; others appeared on the brink of collapsing, bearing angry cracks along their walls. People gathered around what remained of their homes, sidestepping the wreckage in a state of numbness. Palm trees had been uprooted, roads ruptured, broken apart and separated like a great opening jaw. Fallen electrical wires sizzled and jumped like snakes on fire. It took us forty-five minutes of maneuvering down streets blocked with debris to get to the hospital, where injured people with make-shift bandages and blackened faces were lining up outside the Mediterranean-style buildings. Mother began fretting that the earthquake victims would make it impossible for her to get medical attention before the baby was delivered, but Father was able to slip inside and charm one of the nurses into coming out and helping. Tina was born of a quick labor shortly thereafter in a small anteroom to an operating theater in the hospital; she was delivered by the nurse whom Father had charmed. Tina was red and wriggly with a mass of dark hair on her head, her freshly cut umbilical cord protruding from her belly like a cone. She would grow into a prettier child, her skin smoother than mine with more of an olive complexion, her hair a darker umber that made a more startling highlight of her flinty blue eyes—my eyes were more of a reddish hazel.

While we were still young, Father kept getting relocated. The doughnut-machine company was owned by his uncle, my great-uncle Isaac, who kept sending us to different territories all over the country. And because we kept traveling, it was difficult to forge lasting friendships with other children. Mother thought that the lack of geographic continuity was bad for Tina and me. She could only grumble, however, for she too was bound to the business, collecting a small salary from Uncle Isaac for helping Father with the backlog of paperwork and accounting that accumulated as he sold and serviced various doughnut-maker accounts. I remember Mother staying up late at night, working in these enormous leather ledgers that unfolded into airplane wings. She would unwind her hair, which would spill over the complicated grid of columns and boxes that made up every page. She tallied orders and balanced accounts, her entries written in a painstaking, beautiful hand. Sometimes, while Mother was out of the house, I would unfurl the ledgers to hear the crack of leather and to take pungent whiffs of the books. To me, they smelled like the cologne of a strange, exotic man. And when I looked at the rows of numbers she had written, they appeared wonderfully complicated and arcane, hieroglyphic counterparts of the business language she and Father spoke between themselves and to those handsome, charismatic salesmen who came over for Sunday dinner.

Constant moves made Tina and me closer than most sisters. At each new school, we clung to one another, preferring to spend free time in our own company. Whenever I was invited for a play date after school with girls my own age, they were always miffed by my insistence that Tina be allowed to come along. Some of these girls had younger sisters Tina's age and would never dream of allowing them to horn in on their friendships. Tina and I preferred to walk to and from school together. We liked to meet at lunchtime and trade stories about morning classes. In every city and state that we lived in, we witnessed or heard stories of best friends betraying one another, breaking confidences. It made us wary of other people. And besides, our personalities complemented one another. I was a sunny child who lived intensely, got completely caught up in the emotions of any given moment until they burned out and I was rid of them. Tina burned at a lower intensity, stewing over things for a long time. She was far more serious and tended toward dark moods and brooding, internalizing everything that was said to her, moping for days if someone in the family had slighted her. When Tina got into one of her smoldering moods it was up to me to say something lighthearted—but not so silly as to make her angrier.

Luckily, throughout most of her life, music would always be an outlet for Tina's floating anger as well as her moodiness. It was quite obvious to everyone in the family, as well as the teachers who guided her talent in the various cities we lived in, that Tina was extraordinarily gifted. Had we stayed in one place and had she been schooled in the style of one master, she might have been able to gain the rank of a concert pianist. As it was, we kept moving and she got all kinds of instruction—some of it less helpful than others—and her technique ended up being a patchwork. She had an amazing recall for learning music, an uncanny ability to imitate the style of a performer. She could memorize a ten-page composition overnight, could listen to a recording of Vladimir Horowitz and then mimic the accent in his playing.

Oddly, Tina never really entertained notions of being a world-class performer; she was more practical than her peers at the music conservatories, who had far less chance of distinguishing themselves and yet still dreamed of renown. Instead, Tina aspired to write sonatas and, eventually, symphonies, and as soon as she was able, she began to compose. Even her very first efforts impressed her teachers—she wrote études and nocturnes—and at the age of thirteen won the Grand Prize in a national competition for teenaged composers. We were living in Seattle at the time, and when the local news station came to interview her, she seemed relatively unfazed by the success. After that burst of publicity she refused to enter her compositions in any more contests. When we asked why, Tina claimed she hated competing with other people. I always thought, however, that the prospect of being famous frightened her.

Whenever we had to move to a new city, Tina would be impossibly irritable for weeks before and after. She would have just gotten comfortable with her piano teachers, would have performed in recitals and garnered a quiet reputation for originality and brilliance, and now we were relocating in another city. There she'd have to start from scratch by ingratiating herself with the new instructors—and who knew how competent they were?—while trying to wangle scholarships; our parents were unable to afford the kind of training Tina needed. She worried that she'd be unable to get the same quality of guidance in music theory and composition, worried about having to once again ship her upright Baldwin piano, which might be damaged in transit. Venting her fear and frustration, Tina picked huge arguments with our father over her unwillingness to pare down her belongings and to help with the general packing up of the household.

"You were supposed to box up all the dishes and the silver," Father complained the time we were moving from Seattle to Kansas City. It was a Saturday morning in 1947, two days before we were due to vacate our rented house, and Tina had spent the morning holed up in our bedroom, clipping photo portraits of war heroes out of *Life* magazine. "I'll get to it," she kept saying, her eyes flaring at Father and then continuing to peruse the magazine.

"You'll do it now!" he finally said. "It's your responsibility. Spoiled rotten," he said under his breath.

"Spoiled rotten," Tina mocked him angrily, as she began tearing whole pages out of *Life*.

"You're ruining it!" Father hissed.

Tina ignored this and continued to pull apart the magazine. "Maybe I'm spoiled rotten, but at least I didn't avoid my duty." Father's not having served in the war for "medical" reasons was a sensitive issue with him. More than once he had been called a coward in the bars he frequented and had gotten into brawls. His left pinky had been mangled in a childhood accident, which exempted him from the draft. But he had hardly been disappointed by the Army's rejection, having had a strong suspicion that Mother and he were on the brink of making a fortune with their doughnut machines.

"You know, Tina, we don't have to take you with us." Father cracked down. "We can very easily leave you behind."

Tina tossed aside the magazine. "Fine with me," she said, challenging him. "I'll get along perfectly fine. Me and my piano."

"You can't stay by yourself in Seattle." Mother overheard the conversation and butted in. "You're fourteen years old and you're coming with us." She turned to my father. "Don't let her get to you, David. Just leave her be. She's in one of her moods. She'll get everything packed that she's supposed to."

"I won't have it!" Father said, fuming. "I won't have her talking to me that way. I'll throw her goddamned piano out into the street." He turned to Tina. "Then see what you have to practice on."

"You do that and I'll change my name!" Tina screamed back at him. "You hear me? I don't need you."

Shocked by her nasty remark, Father stormed away.

As it turned out, Tina punished him by not getting around to packing until there was little time left. Assuming she'd eventually accomplish her chores, I didn't realize what she was doing until the evening before we were due to leave. When I discovered she had done nothing to prepare for a 9 A.M. departure, I knew that I would have to double up on my own duties— helping Tina load boxes with dishes, silverware and wall paintings—as well as help pack her clothes. Normally I would have argued with her, but I realized that Tina was despondent about something other than leaving her music teachers in Seattle.

Father had allotted each of us two moving cartons in which to pack all our clothing; anything we were unable to fit in was to be left for the Goodwill. I found Tina raking through a pile of sweaters, trying to winnow them down to a few that she would bring with her. "Tina, what is going on with you?" I finally asked. "What are you so angry about?"

Tina stopped what she was doing and turned to look at me with concern. "I just don't want to go live in Kansas City." Kansas City would be our first midwestern home.

"You afraid you won't get another scholarship?"

She shook her head and threw off a sigh. "No," she said. "That's not it at all."

"So then, what is it already?" I said.

Although I was standing still, she looked at me as though I were making all sorts of violent gestures, and then blurted out, "I don't want to leave . . . Paulie."

I was flabbergasted. "Paulie!" Until his recent dismissal, Paulie Mason had been one of my father's best salesmen. "But he hasn't even been around."

"Yes, he has."

"Tina," I said. "Have you been seeing him without Mom and Dad knowing?"

Tina frowned at the pile of sweaters and then eliminated one the color of dusty rose and then a navy-blue solid. The dawning of Paulie into our conversation suddenly seemed to diminish the dilemma of what to take and what to leave. "Yes," she said finally. "I've been seeing him."

"But where? Where have you been seeing him?"

She shrugged. "I've met him for sodas and, you know, we've gone for rides in his car and sat by Puget Sound."

"When have you been doing that?" I said in a whisper.

She looked at me unwaveringly. "After school. When I was supposed to be at the conservatory."

I couldn't believe that Tina had spent time alone with Paulie. She was only fourteen. He was ten years older. I was jealous. She had finished dividing up sweaters and was now packing white cotton underwear into the bottom of another moving carton.

"What's going on between the two of you, Tina?"

"What do you mean?"

"You know what I mean."

She turned to me. "Father shouldn't have fired Paulie. He had no reason to."

"Is that why you've been deliberately picking fights with him?"

Tina's shoulders tensed as she looked at me. "No."

"Is there something between you and Paulie Mason?" I asked, feeling humiliated.

"I don't know," Tina said. "I guess so. I guess we've been dating."

"Tina! Has something happened between you?"

She was standing stock-still, peering at me with a hollow look in her eyes, and I had the sense that something in her had shut down to me. It was the first of many secrets she would keep from me, the beginning of her drifting away from our confidence. "No, not really," Tina said flatly. "All we've done is kissed a little." I felt she was lying to me, that she had done more with Paulie than she admitted to, but I dismissed the notion simply because it would have been too difficult to swallow: I was too eager to believe that my fourteen-year-old sister had not learned about sex before I did.

"What does he feel like?" I couldn't help asking.

Tina described Paulie, his cologne that smelled like the inside of motorcars and lemons and how it felt to have his breath tainted with nicotine tickling her neck. His touch made her feel like Passover nights, when our parents allowed us each a glass of Manischewitz wine.

Now that it was spelled out that Tina was in love with Paulie, the ride from Seattle to Kansas City became a sullen excursion. She refused to talk to anyone but me, and spoke little at that. Still angry with her comment about his cowardice, Father remained in a sour mood. Mother kept herself busy by being the navigator.

As far as I knew, Tina never got any letters from Paulie in Kansas City; nevertheless, she claimed to have kept in touch with him. And a year later, when she was fifteen, she approached me with a plan and asked me to back her up. She had just told our parents that she was going away for the weekend with her friend Lorna, whose family owned a cabin on a lake in central Missouri. In reality, she was going to spend time in a motel room with Paulie Mason. He was coming by train all the way from Seattle to see her, and, Tina added, she was planning on losing her virginity to him.

Although I was shocked by Tina's audacity, I didn't try to stop her. The plan already seemed to be in gear; she was not the sort of person who could be dissuaded from something once she made her mind up. I decided to be supportive and agreed to back up her story should our parents suspect anything. And yet,

I was consumed by my disadvantage: she had Paulie and I didn't; she was going to lose her virginity before me.

They allegedly ended up staying in a garish motel room with red wallpaper and flocks of gold and got drunk on a bottle of blackberry wine. Tina told me how Paulie had put a scented red candle on the night table and lit it, how he stood in front of her and slowly undressed. Paulie looked like a 1940s version of Robert Redford with a shock of wheat-colored hair that fell like a shade into his face, and a sheepish, wide-toothed grin. His body was tanned and hard from exercise, covered with fine blond hairs, and his penis jerked with excitement as he undressed her himself, his fingers deftly removing her clothing. The first place he touched her was the small of her back and that first contact sent a delicious shivering jolt through her, like ice cracking in warmth. She told me how when he went inside her, the first stroke of his penis that penetrated her and took her virginity made her feel dizzy and caused the room to spin. As she told me this, I could truly imagine him inside me; and the composite feelings of sharp love and fear and tenderness that she described seemed so true. I was in awe of her confidence, her daring; she actually had enticed this beautiful man from Seattle halfway across the country to make love to her. When I first made love to a man several years later, on a one-night stand I had hopefully arranged in order to capture some of the raw pleasure that Tina had described, the loss of my virginity was nothing like she had said, but rather was clumsy and dissatisfying.

After that weekend with Paulie, Tina lied to our parents in order to date as many men as she fancied. During her last two years of high school, which we spent in San Diego, she deceived them continually. She'd claim to be visiting a girlfriend's house when, in fact, she'd be going off on a date. She would tell me about each one she got involved with, her stories of heavy petting and—occasionally—going all the way as wonderful as the tale of her first encounter with Paulie. If a guy lasted more than a few weeks, he became, at some point, "the man of my dreams," taking on godlike proportions until she found someone else, thereby perpetuating a pattern of end-to-end love affairs. Her compulsion troubled me.

But then Tina failed to get a scholarship at the only reputable music conservatory in San Diego. At one time she'd spend hours at the piano in feverish practice, scribbling and revising her compositions on staff paper, so much so that we'd have to drag her away for meals or to do her homework. Now, the moment she got a phone call from a young man, she'd skip out of the house without giving a second thought to practicing. When Father threatened to stop contributing money to her training, Tina received the news with a shrug and said that she refused to beg for lessons and would continue practicing on her own. Mother was inconsolable; she'd always hoped that Tina would —even if she wasn't going to be a concert pianist—at least carry on composing and perhaps eventually make her reputation as a songwriter. Without a conservatory, however, it seemed to the rest of us that Tina was throwing away her considerable talent.

She was stubborn and proud and sacrificed the long-range possibility of a career for the more immediate: personal freedom. And I believe that later on she regretted having done this and, in a way, was never able to forgive herself.

But Tina was being driven by something, and I never really learned about it until one Friday evening when I came back to San Diego from Los Angeles, where I was in my second year of college. When I arrived home my parents seemed to have gone out. Tina was doing some entertaining on the back patio. She was there with a girlfriend of hers, a leggy blonde named Linda. They were surrounded by all these gorgeous guys whom I recognized from Black's Beach. After a half hour, during which I had a series of disjointed conversations, I realized that the lack of focus on the part of the men was due to the fact that their attention was more or less constantly fixed on Tina. Wearing tight black jeans and a white sleeveless top, she was giving off an air of detachment.

After prompting from some of the guys, she left her chair, wriggled through the sliding glass patio doors and then opened them wide. She sat down at the baby grand piano (she had recently made a down payment on it with money she made working part-time at a beauty salon) and began playing. From where we all sat, the view of her was soft and blurry and she resembled a wraith making music rather than a young woman.

As Tina continued to play, I looked at the company scattered around the patio. Pink and green spotlights were on, painting everyone an absurd ghoulish color. The flagstones were studded with ceramic pots filled with large cactus. We all sat in these metal-frame deck chairs whose backs were wound with plastic tubing. Some of the men seemed on edge, nervously undulating their hands in and out of the chair backing until their fingers eventually were immobilized, restrained in the plastic. There was quite definitely an air of anticipation.

Finally Tina finished playing. She came outside and stood in the middle of the patio. There was a strange rapturous look on her face, so rapturous, in fact, that she almost seemed impervious to everyone and everything. Then she arched slightly, placing her hands behind the small of her back, where I remembered she claimed Paulie Mason had first touched her. Her breasts strained ever so slightly against her blouse. As she did so the various threads of chitchat conversation pulled together into a taut silence. The men perked up, ensnared. Tina was sending out the signal. She wanted one of them to make love to her. It was as though a tuning fork had been struck and the night filled to its saturation point with her vibration.

But no one made love to her that night. She sent them all away, with the excuse that I rarely came home from college and she wanted to spend some time with me. As the men were leaving, however, I did notice her whispering to one of the more beautiful ones, a guy nicknamed Spotty—apparently, Tina told me a lot later, he was called Spotty because his penis had this huge freckle that had formed when he spilled some coffee on his crotch and got burned.

I went and unpacked and then stopped by Tina's bedroom. She was poised before her mirror. She had put on a white plastic hairband and was in the act of threading its teeth through her fine dark hair toward the crown of her head, the strands pulled back tightly against her scalp. She was tanned a golden color, her eyes luminous. Then she took a tortoiseshell brush in one hand and with the other divided her hair into two parts and brushed it along the sides of her scalp down onto her shoulders. She finally caught my eye in the mirror and stared at me blankly for a moment before smiling.

"You meeting that boy later, the one you were talking to before?"

"You mean Spotty?"

"I guess that's what his name is."

"Yeah, I'm meeting him," she said.

As I entered the room, I caught a whiff of salt air that came through the open window laced with the fragrance of orange blossoms. "Sometimes, Tina," I said, "I don't understand you."

She nervously began collecting hairs tangled in the bristles of the hairbrush. "Why is that?"

"Well, for one thing I don't understand why you can never be alone."

Tina recommended brushing her hair, in what now seemed like an absent, superfluous gesture. "There's nothing wrong with wanting to be around guys."

"Except when you change them almost every week. Like linen. I think there's something strange in that."

Tina's eyes locked with her mirror image. She put the brush down carefully on her vanity table, which was bare except for a cobalt-blue jar of Noxzema skin cream. Then, placing her hands on her hips, she turned to me. "I guess I like different guys . . . because I get depressed a lot. A new guy distracts me."

"What do you mean by depressed?"

She shrugged and sat down on her canopy bed, placing her hands between her tightly clad thighs. She looked at me, suddenly helpless. "I . . . always feel like something terrible is about to happen to me; the feeling that kind of swells and shrinks depending on how much I distract myself from it." She sighed. "Problem is, once I get to know a guy too well, he begins to remind me of what I'm trying to forget about."

"What are you trying to forget about, Tina?"

Tina turned away and leveled her eyes out the window. "Oh, something I really can't control. Something that has its own will."

"What?" I said.

"I told you, I get depressed. I can't put my finger on it," she said.

I suddenly grew suspicious of the entire conversation, which Tina seemed to be making intentionally enigmatic.

"What about the earthquake?" I found myself asking.

Tina looked at me, as though I had suddenly spoken in gibberish. "What about it?"

"You were born during an earthquake."

"So?"

"Maybe that's where you get those terrible feelings. A certain memory you have before you were even born."

"That explanation is a little obvious."

"I don't think so."

Tina surprised me by growing so agitated that she could barely sit still. She shut her eyes and swallowed. "Okay," she said. "Okay. I'm lying to you. I do know what's bothering me."

I looked at her and waited for her to tell me.

Flushing deeply, she looked down at the floor. "Remember

that weekend back in Kansas City when I had you cover for me when Paulie Mason came to town?"

"Yeah."

She now gazed at me intently. "Well, I never spent the weekend with him."

"You didn't?"

"No, I didn't."

"Then what did you do?"

Tina drew a deep, agitated breath. "I spent the weekend with someone else entirely."

"You lost your virginity to a complete stranger?"

"No . . . I wasn't a virgin," she blurted out.

"I don't understand."

Tina shut her eyes, collecting herself for moment, and finally explained.

Back in Seattle, the afternoon our father fired Paulie Mason, she already had plans to see him. When they met outside the conservatory, Tina could tell that he was drunk; a chilled six-pack of Rainier ale rested on the floorboards of his old battered Chevrolet. Her judgment told her not to get in, but then Paulie insisted. "Come on, baby. Come out with me. I'm not tight at all. I just want to be with my baby. Something's happened. I need to tell you." Tina climbed in the car.

And as Paulie drove, slowly at first so that Tina would know his judgment hadn't been altered by drink, he described a disagreement he had with Father just a few hours before and which had ended with his being fired. The money he had saved up would hardly last two weeks; he didn't know what he was going to do. Of course, Tina felt immediately responsible and offered to give him some of what she had saved, but Paulie refused to take any money from her and asked, instead, that she keep him company.

And so they drove through South Seattle to the dock where

the ferry left for Vashon and parked and they talked for a while
holding hands. Paulie cheered up for a bit and spoke of his plans
to get another salesman job and perhaps—like Father—acquire
his own franchise on some popular item and hire his own employees. Then, as a lark, he suggested they take the ferryboat to
Vashon; it was only a twenty-minute ride. They could go for a
short walk on the island and catch the next boat back.

It was four-thirty when they made the crossing. The sun was
slipping down behind the Cascades, inflaming them. Puget
Sound, normally choppy, was hyaline and cut for the boat like
two pleats of gray silk. Tina and Paulie stood on the prow, arms
around one another, Paulie listing against the railing. He finished and tossed overboard the last tall can of the six-pack. As
Tina told me all this, I imagined that to any bystander she and
Paulie must have looked like any young happy couple, although
there was a serious gap of ten years between them.

In those days Vashon Island was almost entirely capped in
forest. Very few beach homes had been built. It wasn't such a
popular ferry run, and only after their departure did they learn
the next boat back to Seattle wasn't for two hours. When the
boat docked and Paulie suggested they go for a walk in the
forest, Tina began to doubt his intentions. But the idea of trying
to find her way back to the dock was more frightening than
being alone with him. And so they walked into the woods,
which were so thick that the daylight was shuttered to near-
darkness. And in the midst of the evergreen silence, he suddenly
began kissing her fiercely. When she tried to push him away,
they stumbled and fell. She begged him to stop, fought him as
he yanked off her clothes. But Paulie nevertheless forced Tina to
have sex with him.

After it was over, when he was feeling more sober and con-
trite, Paulie created an elaborate rationale of why, under any
circumstances, Tina could tell no one—not even me—about

what had happened: he'd get thrown in jail for at least twenty years, she'd probably be disowned by my parents.

"How could you listen to him!" I interrupted her.

"I didn't listen to him," Tina said. "I believed him."

"Then how could you believe him?"

"Susan, he hurt me. I wasn't thinking clearly."

"Of course he wouldn't tell our parents. Because he was the one at fault. He was the one who . . . forced you!"

"He was drunk," Tina said sadly. "He said he loved me. And I wanted to believe him."

"He was a liar," I said. "And what's worse, he made you lie."

Tina's shoulders slumped forward and she caved into herself. "He told me to try to put everything out of my mind. That was the best thing to do. But then he wouldn't see me again."

"Why would you want to see him?"

Tina looked at me, her face drained of color. "Because I wanted him!" she hissed. "He told me I was too young to be having sex with a man like himself and that I should just forget about him."

"But you obviously haven't," I said.

Moments passed, and I soon realized that Tina was not going to contradict me. The breeze coming through the window no longer smelled of orange blossoms, but of something imperceptibly bitter.

Outside everything had been so bright and bursting with crisis. My eyes filmed over with blindness as I threw open your screen door and barged into a house where furniture was tall and spindly and where there were odors of rancid diapers and cooking grease. "Mark, is that you?" your mother called out. I homed in on her voice and found the kitchen, where she had just beaten eggs in a green bowl and was pouring them into a buttered frying pan. When she saw me, she looked distressed, sensing calamity even before I shouted, "Mark fell in the lake!" Screaming, she dropped the bowl, flew across the street and down the embankment and vaulted into the water. As she waded out to save you, her red bathrobe trailed behind her like a skin, and then gathered wetly around her figure as she lifted you out of the water.

---◉---

BILLY AND I drove home. It was the time of day when the sun sinks low enough to set the suburban world ablaze, and the windows of the split-level homes ignite like fiery spades, the time of day when droplets on the newly watered rhododendrons glisten like spit, the time of day when my nerves feel the most frayed. I wanted to sip a cool gin and tonic and let the evening slip into place, for there to be no sounds in the neighborhood except for the quiet humming of air conditioners. I was furious to find two police cruisers parked in the driveway, their rotary lights flashing impotently in the great swath of afternoon light. Two uniformed police and two plainclothesmen stood by my zinnia garden, dragging on filterless cigarettes and blowing smoke up to the searing sky. Each held his hat. That there were four of them suggested force—in case we resisted them. To me their presence immediately questioned Billy's role in the mishap, suggested that he was more than just a witness who had broken the news to Harriet Rosen that her son had fallen into deep water. I suddenly remembered the fire engines swerving throughout quiet Hartsdale and how afraid I had been when I first saw them. I was just as afraid now as I was then.

Across the street from our house, I noticed a trio of mothers gathered informally in the shade of a Japanese maple, whose leaves, normally an eggplant color, under the incredible glare had gone black like a doom tree. I stopped the car in front of our house, switched down the electric window and said to the waiting cops, "Would you mind backing out so I can put my car in the garage. Thank you."

"Sure thing, Mrs. Kaplan," one of them said, which made me angrier. They knew my name, perhaps had even done some research on me.

I looked over at Billy, who sat stiffly on the passenger side, his head resting halfway up the seat, his eyes wide and alert. He was awed by his involvement in what seemed to be a very grown-up situation. I suddenly realized that, for the moment, I was more afraid than he. Because, during the last hour, as I witnessed the scene at the lake, talked to Norma Freed, heard that Harriet Rosen was under sedation, heard that phrase "touch and go," I began to realize that there was now to be a chain of events, people I knew only casually suddenly assuming importance in my life, all of it in an upheaval that would not so easily subside.

I was to be different now, ordained into a misfortune that would interlock at least three families. I glanced once again across the street at my neighbors, acquaintances who knew me but didn't really know me. Cass Greenfeld, my favorite of them, a raven-haired woman who had a girl and a boy both younger than Billy, trilled her fingers at me. I put down the electric window on the passenger side of the car. "Everything okay, Susan?" she asked in a vague tone of voice, glancing toward the policemen, whose presence suddenly clotted our free-flowing suburban artery. When we had first bought our homes we had been told not to worry about our children getting injured, abducted or strangled in the suburbs. "Do you need me to come over?" Cass said, while keeping her distance, huddling into the abundant shade with the two other women. "That's okay," I said.

Cass Greenfeld and Lucille Spanier and Hortense Woolf were all dressed in short golf dresses and sleeveless pastel blouses, their figures trim, their legs hard and shapely, just like mine. I had had tea or coffee with each of them at various times during the five years we had lived in the neighborhood. As I fought the urge to scream that there was nothing to gather out there for, I remembered the get-togethers I had had with each of them, remembered how conversations had begun at the general and gradually wound down to the specific until, after the third cup of tea as the afternoon was being reeled into evening, we'd finally begin to hint at the confinement we felt: the boredom of city women shoved into these homes that we bought from a model we had first visited, a model that had since been demolished. Now that I had refused Cass Greenfeld's halfhearted offer, I watched the three women visibly relax. I knew they were glad to be uninvolved, just the way I was relieved at first when I pulled down my street and saw there were no fire engines. They were unscathed by the incident. Death had skirted their yards and had fallen instead like a scourge upon a neighbor. Their own lives suddenly must have felt protected and hallowed.

In the meantime, the two police cruisers had backed out of my driveway, traveled in reverse down the street and parked in front of Cass Greenfeld's house. Seeing where they intended to stop, she sprinted over and practically threw herself against the hood of the first car. "Could you please not park here?" she complained. "Park in front of the Kaplans' if that's where your business is."

"We could, but we're not moving again," answered one policeman with annoyance.

Good, I thought. Let her house attract some attention. As the four officers got out of their cars, Cass pivoted to face them, widening her stance. "But . . . what am I supposed to do? My husband is coming home soon and, I mean, what will he think when he drives up and sees—"

"Lady, does he have a heart condition?" asked one of the uniforms.

"No."

"Lady, go home and calm down. Have a drink or something. Stop being so hysterical," said one of the detectives, a short, stocky fellow with greased-back wavy hair.

The men approached me and politely introduced themselves. In the preliminary conversations out there in front of my house, they didn't seem to be well acquainted with one another. The other plainclothesman, who ended up doing most of the talking, was called Mr. Chambers. He was taller and fairer than his partner. The knot of his tie was pulled askew. He had a soft voice that begged you to relax. He asked me how long Billy had known the Rosens.

"Why don't you come inside and we'll talk about this," I suggested, glancing at the women across the street. "I'd prefer it if the whole neighborhood didn't know my business."

"Certainly. We understand. Sorry," Chambers said.

Mercedes, our Guatemalan housekeeper, had in our absence returned from her errands and was now ironing Michael's shirts in the den. As soon as she saw me entering the house with policemen, her plump arms stopped their circular movements, her sad eyes bulged fearfully. "What is wrong, Miss Kaplan?" she gasped. "What happened to you?"

"Be careful or you'll burn that," was my answer as I jockeyed the policemen toward her. "In fact, Mercedes, why don't you leave the ironing for a while and go start dinner."

"Yes, Miss Kaplan," she said, shutting off the iron, yanking the plug the way I had taught her. The steam continued to pour from the iron. Cowering, Mercedes squeezed past the collection of men, who filled the antiseptic den with the smell of nicotine and perspiration.

As I invited the policemen to sit down, I noticed Billy was perched by the front door, staring fearfully at the visitors. "Come here," I said gently.

He held his ground. "I'm going upstairs to my room."

"I'm sorry, but you can't go upstairs right now. These men are here to ask some questions."

"Why?"

"Because it's part of their job," I explained. "Like Daddy has a job."

"Where *is* Dad?" Billy asked.

"Honey, you know where Dad is."

"Can't they talk to Dad about me?" Billy asked, squirming into himself.

Mr. Chambers held up his hand to me, to indicate he'd try to talk to Billy. He began slowly: "Billy, your dad has been at work all day today. He wasn't at the lake and he didn't see what happened. You're the only one who saw what happened and that's why we have to talk to you."

"But I didn't do anything," Billy protested, beginning to cry. I began moving toward him, to comfort him, when Chambers stopped me. He turned to Billy. "We know you didn't do anything, Billy. And that's not why we're here. We're here because . . . Why, do you know that you're a very brave young man?"

The compliment from a stranger had an immediate effect. Billy stopped weeping and stared curiously at Chambers.

"How old are you?" Chambers asked.

"Seven," Billy said sheepishly.

"Most kids your age wouldn't have thought to go and tell Mark's mother something happened to Mark. Let me tell you, Billy, you did the right thing. A lot of kids wouldn't have known what to do."

"Yep, that's true," seconded one of the policemen.

"Here, here," said the detective with the greased-back hair.

"So why don't you come and sit down and tell us exactly what happened. So we can get our work done and go home to our families just like your dad is probably on his way home to you," Chambers said.

"Are you married?" Billy asked.

Everyone laughed.

Billy ended up sitting on the sofa between Chambers and his partner, the two uniformed policemen occupying easy chairs. I asked them to hold their questions for a moment, while I tried to reach Michael, who I was sure would want to monitor the interview long-distance and tell me what to interject if he felt the policemen were straying too far into our personal affairs. I took the phone extension off an end table next to the sofa and, dialing as I walked, carried it into the hallway that led to Mercedes's bedroom. Michael was still out of the office at a meeting. When his secretary asked for a message, I wondered what sort of message I should leave—that it was urgent? But then I reasoned that, sensing something wrong, his secretary would blab to the whole office that there was some sort of crisis, and the word would be out even before Michael returned from wherever he was. And by the time he would call me, the policemen already would be gone and he would have been unable to make any difference in the course of their questioning of Billy. Taking a deep breath, I glanced at my watch: it was 5:25. "Just tell him to call me as soon as he returns."

Billy told the policemen the same version of the story I'd heard, except that now he embellished, gave more details: the water in the lake felt quite cool, Mark was wearing a blue-and-white-striped shirt. At one point I worried that Billy was enjoying the attention and had completely lost sight of the fact that it was a tragic thing to have happened.

Then one of the policemen raised his hand. First he glanced at the others, as though soliciting their silent approval, and then asked, "You mind if we smoke, Mrs. Kaplan?"

I shrugged. "No one does in this family, but sure, if it'll make things easier."

"We won't if it disturbs you," Chambers said.

"No, go ahead," I said, getting up. "I'll go get some iced tea." I had made a fresh pitcher that morning. As I left the room I noticed puffs of steam were still leaving Mercedes's iron.

She had done little else in the kitchen but set a large pot to boiling. She was standing by the window that viewed the backyard, where a set of swings we had bought for Billy cast spindly shadows into the rhododendrons. She jumped when she saw me. "God in heaven, Mrs. Kaplan, what has happened?"

I explained to her that a boy from down the street had fallen into the lake and that Billy had been a witness.

"Lord have mercy," Mercedes said as she crossed herself. "What misfortune has come to this neighborhood."

I said nothing.

"I'm just about to get dinner, Mrs. Kaplan." Mercedes excused her lack of activity. I had sent her upstairs to the kitchen nearly twenty minutes before. Normally I'd be annoyed by the delay.

"Don't worry." I made a feeble dismissal with my hand as I went to the refrigerator and brought out the aluminum pitcher full of iced tea as well as a lemon, which I cut into thin rings. I got four tall glasses out of the cupboard. I put a lemon ring in the bottom of each glass.

"And you say that after Mark annoyed you, you told him to go home?" one of the policemen was asking Billy as I reentered the room with the sweating pitcher and the glasses on a tray. I stopped abruptly to hear his answer. Since I had left, the den had accumulated a blue haze of cigarette smoke, which lent the room a feeling of hard-boiled interrogation.

"I even told him to go back to his mother. That she should be taking care of him," Billy said.

"And that was when you pricked your finger on the fishhook?" Chambers said.

"No, I already pricked my finger. I pricked my finger after Mark threw my bread bait into the water."

"And then you went to the Freeds' to get a Band-Aid."

"Yes."

"And the next time you saw him he was already . . . in the lake?" Chambers asked gently, stabbing out a cigarette.

Billy nodded.

"How far out in the water would you say he was when you discovered him?"

"Pretty far," Billy said. "I didn't know how he could have gotten out so far. Even if I was swimming I'd never swim out so far."

"Could be a current," one of the policeman interjected.

"Delzio, not in a man-made pond," said the other detective.

"Could have struggled his way out there, somehow," Chambers said, more to himself than to the others, and then glanced at Billy. His probing expression softened and a subtle smile graced his lips. "Well, that looks good enough for me. How about you, gentlemen?" he asked the uniformed policemen.

"We're fine for now," said one of them.

"Some iced tea before you go?" I offered. By now my hands were shaking, the glasses rattling against each other.

"Sorry, but we'll have to forgo that, I'm afraid," said the other detective.

Chambers shrugged. "Hope we haven't inconvenienced you, Mrs. Kaplan."

"It won't be an inconvenience if everything that's happened is made clear," I told them.

The four men stood up simultaneously, awkwardness suddenly generated. Now that their business was concluded they appeared unsure of themselves. They seemed to be acutely aware that they had intruded harshly upon the privacy of my house, leaving the scent of cigarettes and their nervous bodies. As they shuffled out of the den, one of the policeman grabbed a glass of iced tea, downed it in a gulp and then grinned at me as he put it back down on the tray. His partner scowled at him, as though he had just broken some cardinal rule.

"I'd like to talk to you, however, Mrs. Kaplan," Chambers said. "If you could accompany us outside, I'd appreciate it."

I handed Billy the tray of iced tea and told him to take it upstairs to the kitchen. He held his ground, as though desiring to answer more questions; he even seemed to lament the policemen's departure.

Several unmarked cars had lined up in front of the house; men in business suits wearing wide-brimmed hats had assembled on our side of the street. "Reporters," Chambers said of the men after a quick glance. Across the street, Cass Greenfeld and Lucille Spanier and Hortense Woolf had been joined by several other mothers, some of whom I recognized as living down near the lake. Random words between the two groups were being exchanged.

"What do *they* want? Can't they leave us alone?" I complained.

"I honestly suggest you talk to the reporters," Chambers said. "Otherwise they'll interview those ladies over there, perhaps get wrong, inflated information and use words like 'according to' and 'apparently' in their article. You and Billy should just tell them what you've told us. He comes out completely clean." Chambers smiled broadly at me and his smile almost seemed like a leer.

"But they could still twist what Billy says."

"Okay, here's what you do," Chambers went on. "Once we leave, tell them you'll grant an interview, but only if they'll listen to your statements and agree not to question you other than to clarify the information you've given them."

"Maybe I should wait until my husband gets home before talking to them."

He paused. "You seem pretty collected. I'm sure you can handle them."

In the meantime, the other policemen had returned to their cars in front of Cass Greenfeld's house. I could see her making frantic shooing-away gestures. I would have nothing more to do with Cass Greenfeld. Her selfish behavior, her lack of compassion damned her permanently in my eyes. If the situation had been reversed and she were in my position, I never would have hung back the way she did. In a moment of self-righteousness, I remembered how I had appeared at the Bernsteins' door with a tuna casserole when we found out about Mindy's leukemia. And I was always the one the other mothers called upon when their ovens caught fire—I kept a fire extinguisher and knew how to use it. "Okay," I said.

"There's just one more thing," Chambers said uneasily. "Unofficial." His eyes focused on the knot of people at the edge of the lawn and then locked with mine. "I've never dealt with a drowning before. I mean, the next-closest body of water is Long Island Sound, which is Rye jurisdiction. Still, I've seen fires, explosions and other things. And people in these kinds of situations, well . . ." He paused, flattening his hair back, pressing on the hat he had been holding in his left hand since I had first seen him blowing out cigarette smoke by my zinnia bed. "They tend to look for someone to pin things on."

"But this situation is different. What happened *is* clear," I said, probing the detective's face for some crease of suspicion that Billy might have hidden something, a bitter exchange between himself and Mark, or even some sort of violent gesture.

"Look, I'm not making predictions, I'm just saying I've seen it go on. And unfortunately, when kids are involved, other parents talk among themselves and their children hear and blab what shouldn't be said."

I shrugged and looked down at the lawn. I felt miserable, hearing this. "All right."

"Now, I may need to borrow Billy tomorrow for a couple more questions."

"Okay."

Chambers shook my hand and trotted toward his unmarked car. As soon as he climbed inside, the reporters began advancing.

I did exactly what he suggested—summoned them over, stated my rules for the interview. I then asked the reporters to go around to the backyard, where we would not be ogled by any of the onlookers clustering across the street. I ducked inside and asked Billy if he wouldn't mind telling the story one more time. When he agreed, I led him out to the backyard through the kitchen door. The whole interview took twenty minutes; his third rendition of what had happened was less inspired than his previous account. And Michael arrived home an hour later.

Throughout the ordeal of facing the police and then the reporters, whenever I tried to imagine Michael's arrival I pictured myself collapsing into his arms and weeping over what had happened, while allowing him to take command as the husband and the father. Both Billy and I heard the tail pipe of his El Dorado rake the lip of the driveway as the car pulled in. The slamming of the driver's door detonated throughout the neighborhood. We were waiting in the foyer when he walked through the front door. As soon as I saw Michael, however, for some reason I found myself wanting to be vigilant over his reaction to the events of the afternoon. It was as though I instinctively didn't trust him to show enough support or compassion for what Billy and I had just been through. Immediately sensing there had been other males in the house, Michael stiffened. "Smells funny," he muttered. I had forgotten that I had allowed the policemen to have cigarettes. "Who's been smoking?"

"There have been detectives here," I told him.

Michael's briefcase slipped from his fingers. He braced his arms over his chest and stood there gaping at Billy and me. "Okay, what happened?"

"Didn't you get my message? I left word for you to call."

Michael looked bewildered. "Yeah, but you didn't say it was anything urgent. I figured I'd . . . What's going on, Susan?"

"Mark Rosen fell in the lake," Billy whimpered.

Frowning, Michael glanced at me. To him, Billy's remark sounded like a non sequitur.

"Is he all right?"

"We don't know," I said. "Last we heard it was touch and go."

"But what does that have to do with the police being here?"

"Because Billy witnessed it," I said.

"In what capacity?"

"They were playing."

Michael knelt down. "Come here, Birdie," he said. Billy ran over and hugged his father.

"Don't be mad at me, Daddy, please?"

"I'm not mad at you, Billy." Michael shut his eyes for a second, and when he opened them, they were flicking back and forth, as though charting the beginnings of a scheme. Still clutching his son, he glanced at me. "Who has Billy told about this? Who knows?"

Everybody but you, I thought. "As I said, the police were here. And the reporters."

Michael released Billy, stood up and stepped back, facing me.

"Jesus Christ, Susan! You mean you already talked to reporters without my being here?"

"The police said that we should talk to stop the reporters from questioning other people. Because, you know, of hearsay."

Michael rubbed his face. Billy was looking on, wide-eyed. "That sounds like a bunch of bullshit to me."

Billy moaned.

"Michael, now listen to me!" I spoke sharply, finishing the rest with a dagger look that meant we shouldn't make it appear to Billy that we were going to wrangle over what I should have done.

Michael bobbed his head in acknowledgment and then squatted down to Billy's height and gently held both of his arms. "Birdie," he said, "can you leave your mom and me for a while so we can talk about something?"

"But I want to hear," Billy insisted. "I know what you're going to talk about."

"I know you know, you smart little guy. But your mom and I need to figure out some things about what happened. And as soon as we figure them out we'll come upstairs and tell you. Promise."

Billy looked skeptical.

"And I'll take you to Playland this weekend."

"You said that before and you never did," Billy accused him.

"I know I didn't. And I'm sorry. It won't happen like that again. You've been a really good guy. Don't worry, we'll definitely go to Playland," Michael said.

Billy filled his cheeks with air, wrinkled his nose and then reluctantly turned and trudged upstairs. As I watched him leave, I suddenly worried that what happened might affect him in ways Michael and I would never see.

Michael waited until Billy had gained the top of the staircase and then drew closer to me. His eyes were hard and fearful. "So, you talked to the reporters."

"Michael, if you'd been here and seen all the commotion you'd have talked to them too."

"I just wish you'd called me."

"I did. Your secretary said you were away in a meeting and couldn't be reached."

"You should have said it was an emergency."

"I decided not to. Because I didn't want her to know. I didn't want your whole office to find out something was wrong before you did. I didn't think you'd want that."

Suddenly, Michael got a better grasp of the situation. "This is not the time to disagree." He came close and wove his arms around me. "I'm sorry I reacted so strongly at first. I guess we really have to stick together and figure out what to do."

I sighed heavily and slackened into his embrace.

"I think I need a drink," he said.

"How about if I make us some martinis?"

"All right. And we'll go outside and figure this out."

We were soon sitting on the back patio in the ebbing daylight, watching the yard vanishing into an envelope of shadow. We were sitting in lawn chairs at a white wrought-iron table that was covered by a round sheet of glass. Mercedes hadn't cleaned the glass in a while and several rainstorms had soiled it to near-opacity. Michael had taken off his sport coat and his tie, unbuttoned his shirt halfway and rolled up his sleeves. A fine gold chain hung from his neck, fell across his clavicle and glowed in the early darkness. He practically guzzled down his martini as I told the story of Mark falling in the lake and the policemen's arrival. And then I told him Billy felt that he had participated in the accident, because Mark had followed him down to the lake on his invitation, and if Billy had not been there in the first place, Mark never would have ventured anywhere near the water.

"But he told Mark to go home."

"Right. And Mark refused to leave."

"Well, I mean, legally there's nothing to it. No negligence. Everything inadvertent. Nothing premeditated or deliberate."

I hesitated and then I lowered my voice. "Michael, when Billy was telling me what happened I got this strange feeling there was something he wasn't saying."

"What do you mean?"

"He clammed up at one point."

Alarmed, Michael glanced stealthily at the house and then looked to me. "What are you suggesting, Susan? That Billy could've pushed him in or something like that?"

"No, I don't think it's that at all. But something else might have happened that makes him feel . . . I don't know, more responsible."

"Like . . ."

"Michael, I don't know."

Michael looked at me with eyes cool and beautiful in the soft, dimming light. "Maybe Billy shouldn't play by the lake for a while," he suggested. "Maybe the lake will be too much of a reminder."

"Michael, we can't restrict Billy on account of what happened. Then he'll only think we're punishing him for it."

"Maybe he won't want to go there anymore."

"Of course he will. Peter Freed is his best friend. And Peter Freed lives on the lake."

Michael clattered the ice in his nearly spent cocktail.

"Want another?"

He shook his head. Then he reached for my hand and squeezed it. "I'd rather we just sit here for a while and consider everything. Be with each other. Do nothing else." He blinked several times as he looked at me; his eyelashes were incredibly long. He suddenly looked so vulnerable. I was wondering if what had happened, the ordeal of it, might bring us closer, when I heard the phone ring. I reacted and Michael told me to let Mercedes answer it. We listened to it ring five times.

"Where the hell is she?" he complained.

"She's supposed to be cooking dinner."

Then the ringing ceased. Billy stuck his head out of an up-stairs window. "Mom, it's Mrs. Freed," he said ominously.

"Why couldn't Mercedes have answered the phone?" I exclaimed as I got up.

"Are you coming in soon?" Billy called down.

Michael peered up at him and said that we were. Then he looked at me. "I'll come to the phone with you."

As I followed Michael through the sliding screen door into the den, I heard the downstairs toilet flush. Mercedes had been in the bathroom. What bad timing. Already waiting for us upstairs, Billy had answered the phone and knew it was Norma. Just as I bent over to get the receiver, Michael embraced me. "I love you, honey," he murmured.

The room was murky and the only light filtered in from the twilight outdoors. I could barely make out Michael's features, but he seemed so potently handsome to me. And for a moment I knew a happiness of being safe with him, protected, and was grateful for that. "I love you too, Michael," I said, and picked up the receiver. "Hello, Norma."

There was noise in the background, like a dishwasher or an eggbeater, something clearly domestic-sounding, although unidentifiable.

"You alone?" she asked.

"No," I said. "Michael's here."

"Right there with you now?"

"Uh-huh."

She drew a sigh.

"Tell me already."

"He didn't make it." Norma stifled a sob. "His heart stopped in the ambulance. They couldn't bring him back."

"I see," I said, turning to Michael, shaking my head.

"Damn," he said, and drove a fist through the air.

"How's Billy doing?" Norma asked.

I hesitated. "As well as can be expected. How's Peter?"

"The little idiot thinks it's a big joke," she said angrily.

"Well, they're young, you know. They don't really put it all together."

The appliance in the background shut off. "I'm sorry about yelling at you earlier," Norma said. "I'm just crazy about getting sued." She was breathing unevenly, and I realized that she had just lit a cigarette.

"Well, I don't know if this will make you feel any better, but on that account, if you need any advice, there's a lawyer at Michael's agency whom he could get—"

"Sure thing," Michael seconded me immediately. "Anything I can do."

"Well, fine, but let's not talk about this right now." Norma hesitated. "Although, if I do seek legal advice, it doesn't seem to me, considering the circumstances, that Michael's attorney would be the right person."

Now what's that supposed to mean? I wondered. "I see," was all I could think of to answer.

"What'd she say?" Michael mouthed.

"I'll tell you. Wait a second," I mouthed back. "Have you spoken to the Rosens yet?" I asked Norma.

Norma hesitated and took a pull on her cigarette. "I spoke to Larry. Harriet is completely out of it right now. To be honest with you, I don't know how she's going to make it through the funeral. I mean, on account of their being Jewish, doesn't it have to be the next day?"

"Usually. Unless there's a holiday or the Sabbath. And then they wait until the holiday is over."

There was a pause and then Norma made several attempts to say something. "Uh . . . I was wondering . . ." Finally, she blurted, "Were you planning on calling them?"

"I was waiting to hear from you first, Norma."

"Well, maybe at some point you can call them, but don't for a while. Better to write them a note."

My face suddenly looked afflicted and Michael got concerned. "What is it?" he whispered.

I held up my hand to silence him. "Why are you saying this, Norma?"

"Because . . . of course, she's distraught right now, but, well, Larry specifically asked me to ask that you and Michael not call."

"Meaning what?" I demanded.

"Meaning she might say the wrong thing to you."

"The wrong thing?"

"You know?" Norma hedged.

"You mean about responsibility?"

"I wouldn't put it exactly like that."

"But she must know that the nurse was negligent."

"What?" Michael hissed.

"Of course she does, but I'm just telling you that Harriet isn't herself and she's been saying a lot of different things."

"Well, then," I said in a low voice, "if she says anything about Billy being involved, it's complete slander. She has a fucking nurse who's supposed to be watching the kids!"

"Susan, I won't listen if you talk like that," Norma complained.

"Okay," I snapped, realizing I also had to be careful so that Billy didn't overhear anything from upstairs. "But Harriet better not implicate him. She better look at herself!"

"Damn right," Michael said.

"Would you stop jumping to conclusions? I'm just saying that right now she's deranged and it's better not to call her. That's all I'm saying. I'm trying to do you a favor and save you further upset over this."

"Then let's just drop it for now," I said in a smoldering voice. "Okay? And we won't plan on going to the funeral either."

Norma sighed. "I really think that's the wisest decision."

I was shaking when I put down the phone, and Michael sat me down in order to be comforting. He felt that we should assume that Harriet Rosen was probably too out of her mind with grief to even begin facing her own mistake. If she had mentioned to anyone that Billy had something to do with what happened, which we didn't know for sure, she probably was just trying to deflect her anguish in order to keep her sanity. In time she would come to see the clear-cut truth. But until then, to guard against rumors scattering through the neighborhood, we had to stay close to one another and protect Billy. Hopefully things would clarify in a few days or weeks, however long it took, and the Rosens would better come to terms with the death of their child. But while I allowed Michael's words to soothe me, I felt differently. I felt that things would not get better any time soon. I remembered Mr. Chambers's warning. I remembered what happens when a stone is cast toward the middle of a pond and how the shock waves radiate until they collide with the shore.

After deciding how we'd break the news to Billy and what to say, Michael and I left the den and went upstairs. We passed the brightly lit kitchen, where Mercedes was grilling veal cutlets and chopping fresh vegetables for a salad. She was humming to herself.

Billy had been pacing up and down the hallway, waiting for us to come tell him if Mark Rosen had been saved. He stopped in his tracks when he saw his father and me. "Come here, pal," Michael said, and he ran to us.

"Is he okay? Is he all right?" Billy's face was anxious and hopeful.

We both knelt down and put our arms around him. "He decided to go to heaven," Michael said.

The padding of words did little to buffer the news. Billy immediately burst into tears. "How do you know?" he sobbed.

"How do you know he decided . . ." He broke off. "To go up to heaven? How do you know he didn't decide to go to the bottom of the lake?"

"Because children always go to heaven," I said. "That's the way it is."

"Who says?"

"God," Michael said, massaging Billy's back. "Suffer the little children to come unto me."

"Why couldn't he have lived?" Billy said. "It's not fair."

"It doesn't seem fair to us," I said. "But we just have to try and accept that and think of him as happy in heaven."

"I don't think he's happy."

"It takes time to accept and understand."

"No," Billy said, pushing us away. "It's because of me that he went to heaven."

"No, it isn't," Michael said too quickly.

"He chose to go to heaven, Billy," I said. "And his choice had nothing to do with you. You just happened to be the last person to see him before he decided to go."

"Dinner!" we suddenly heard Mercedes calling.

The three of us looked at each other. The idea of having dinner suddenly seemed foreign, intrusive.

"Why don't you come with us downstairs and have something to eat?" I cajoled Billy.

Billy shook his head. "I'm not hungry. You go with Dad."

"Ah, come on and eat," Michael said.

Billy pulled away and looked at me severely. "Mom, why was I the last person to see him?"

There was no answer to his question, but I knew I had to find one. I shut my eyes for a moment and asked the part of me that sometimes finds unexpected inspiration. I looked at Billy. "Maybe so that you can know how lucky we all are to still be alive."

But Billy was dissatisfied with my explanation. He turned and ran to his bedroom and slammed the door. Michael would have followed him if I hadn't suggested that we just leave him alone for a while.

TINA'S HOSPITAL room was painted a semi-gloss robin's-egg blue. I found the color a bit stark, and wondered if a more soothing tint might have been used, an earth tone, for example. I mentioned this to her, but she said studies had shown blue to be the most healing of colors. It suddenly seemed wrong that a hospital stay with electroshock and daily sessions with a psychiatrist could actually lift someone's depression. To me, these difficult treatments tested Tina's mental endurance, and only by contrast made living in the outside world appear to be easier.

There were two walk-in closets; the door to one of them, presumably her roommate's, was ajar. Aligned with the cinderblock wall was a set of metal dresser drawers painted that same therapeutic blue. From steady use, paint was flaking from the drawers, and each chip took with it preceding layers, so that the bare metal of the drawer was exposed: rusted orange—certainly not a healing color. I thought of houses I had been in where paint had peeled, and how the cosmetic decay, revealing each layer of color, was like an X ray through the decades down to the bones of walls.

Tina was wearing a pair of baggy blue jeans and a burgundy gauze shirt that hung loosely around her hefty midsection. She sensed something amiss the moment I entered her room. I actually believed I would be able to hide from her what was going on at home. Sure, I had wanted to share with her what I felt about the drowning of Mark Rosen, my fears of how it might affect Billy, but I had been advised both by Tina's husband and by the hospital psychiatrist to shield her from disturbing news. As it was, two months before, our father had undergone spinal surgery in San Diego, and even though he recovered, Mother still felt that Tina shouldn't know he had been ill. I abided by Mother's wishes, although I disagreed with her and Marty and the doctors. To my mind, preserving Tina from the truth reinforced the idea she was not well enough to cope with life.

"You don't look so great, Susan," Tina said in her blunt manner after we had embraced and she had pulled back to arm's length to look me over. "Did you lose weight or something?"

I shrugged. "I don't think so." I realized that despite my efforts to conceal it, I must've been wearing a look of misfortune.

She put her hands on her ample hips. "Think I shed any excess baggage?" she asked, laughing before I could answer.

"Hard to tell."

Her eyes drank me in again and then narrowed in suspicion. "Boy, Susan, you really look like you've been dog-whipped. Now, for Christ's sake, what's wrong?"

And so I told her about Mark Rosen and Billy's part in what led to the drowning.

Tina was not so shocked to hear about the tragedy as much as she was saddened by it. "You know, Susan," she said after an appropriate pause, "I always thought it was weird they put a lake smack in the middle of a bedroom community. When they did that they were really asking for trouble."

"The lake's been in for nearly ten years," I pointed out. "And this was the first mishap."

"But if it wasn't there, one child would still be alive," she pointed out. "Why don't you sit down," she suggested, leading the way to her bed, which was covered with a green checker-board quilt I recognized as belonging to us when we were children. Suddenly, Tina looked wounded. "I wish you had told me sooner."

"The night it happened I almost called you. Really. But then I thought you're not supposed to be up here worrying about everybody else."

"Who says so?"

"The doctors have said so all along."

"Screw them," Tina said. "What else am I going to do?"

"Get better," I said hopefully.

She smiled dismally.

And then I told her how from early in the morning until when Michael and I went to bed, the drowning pervaded my thoughts. I told her how I surveyed the neighborhood for tell-tale signs of unfair accusation, that it might be my imagination but I thought I saw cars decelerating as they passed the house, people behind steering wheels gawking at our windows. I had become acutely attuned to changes in people's attitudes. The friendly manner of the Haitian man who worked at the dry cleaner's seemed curiously clipped and disgruntled. In the super-market I thought I saw neighborhood mothers frown at the sight of Billy, who wandered through the aisles ahead of me, making his various sales pitches to me for foods like Ring Dings and ice-cream sandwiches, products I normally did not buy and which I knew he had eaten in abundance at the Freeds'. Inquiries from people who knew about the drowning and who were supposedly sympathetic never ventured any further than innocuous questions: "So, Susan, is life more settled down? Have things gotten back to normal yet?" It was as though the drowning was viewed as a stigma on the pristine face of Hartsdale.

Tina asked how Billy was handling things, and I told her that for the time being he had continued to play with Peter Freed. Significantly, however, on each of the three days following the accident, Peter had suggested they get together at our house. Ordinarily, the two played a lot more in Peter's neighborhood, fishing by the lake.

"I'm sure it's his mother's doing," Tina said. "What's the name of that bitch again?"

"Norma."

"A dreary bitch," Tina amended. "I'm sure she's trying to appear neutral in front of the Rosens by keeping Billy out of the neighborhood. Politicking 'cause she's afraid of getting sued."

"Billy probably feels unwelcome now," I said.

"Undoubtedly," Tina agreed.

During Peter's most recent visit he had acted unusually polite. Normally he and Billy would ransack the cupboards and make snacks without my permission. Now, suddenly, Peter was asking for a glass of water and deferred to me when Billy suggested they eat something. I feared that it was only a matter of time before Peter stopped calling. On the previous afternoon the boys were playing army in the living room, had set up platoons of soldiers, when with a swipe of his hand Peter mowed down the carefully arranged leaden troops. Ordinarily, Billy would have stood up to Peter and argued, but now he looked at him balefully and meekly asked what was wrong. Peter shrugged and said he had gotten bored. He seemed to realize that he suddenly held the card to Billy's happiness, that with a word he could reduce his best friend to despair.

Tina sat stock-still as she listened to me, her eyes burning into mine. "I never liked that Peter Freed," she finally murmured in disgust. "Whenever I saw him he gave me an uncomfortable feeling."

"Peter's actually okay," I said, trying to be more positive. "He's just the product of his mother's fears."

"It amazes me what parents do to their kids," Tina said. "I mean, that's why I tried so hard . . ." She broke off with a click of her tongue.

"Look, you've done a great job with Rachel," I reassured her.

"Kids can be so goddamned cruel to each other," Tina insisted. I thought that she was referring to the fact that Rachel had been taunted by some of her classmates about her mother's illness, something I'd been told by Marty and which I didn't think Tina knew that I knew. "I guess we didn't really suffer from that kind of shit when we were growing up, did we?" she said. "We protected each other."

"And Mom was so afraid that not having enough friends would make us antisocial."

"Oh, please." Tina stood up. "How about a cup of tea?" she suggested. "I've got kitchen privileges now." She raised her finger for emphasis. "I'm allowed to make you one cup of tea, under supervision."

"I'll come with you," I said.

"Nah, that's all right. Just kick off your shoes. Relax on my bed."

I looked over at the other bed, which, the last time I visited, had belonged to Tina's anorexic roommate. "Will your roommate be coming in?"

Tina blinked rapidly while rubbing her hands together, as

though the room suddenly had grown chilly. "She's . . . not with me anymore. She's gone to another part of the hospital."

I glanced over at the closet that I had noticed when I first entered the room and that now, upon closer inspection, appeared to be vacant.

"Did something happen?"

Tina nodded and suddenly looked perplexed. "You could say that . . ."

"Well, what?"

Tina shrugged and sighed. "She started talking about doing herself in. It made me feel like a rat, but I felt I had to tell her psychiatrist about it, just in case she wasn't just talking. We have the same shrink, so it wasn't exactly like tattling.

"All in all, I don't think he did much about it. Because one evening, shortly after I told him, I came back to the room and suddenly got this weird feeling that something was wrong. Then I noticed that my top drawer was open." Tina pointed to the metal chest. "A pair of my stockings were gone. At first I was angry because I thought Gloria had taken them without asking. So I started looking around the ward for her—I was ready to blast her. I checked the rooms of her friends. Then the rec room. When I couldn't find her I started getting a little nervous. Finally, I found her in the bathroom. She was sitting hunched over the toilet, shaking all over like she was freezing. She'd made a noose out of a pair of stockings and it was draped around her neck."

"You think she was serious?"

"How the hell do I know? When I told her to give me the noose, she scrunched herself up and started hissing like she was a cat. I didn't know what to do, so I started teasing her about giving up and acting psycho. You see"—Tina was looking at me fixedly—"Gloria and I believed that in comparison with everybody else around here, we acted pretty normal, which is why we were rooming together. So I told her that if she didn't get off the toilet, I'd consider her too nuts to be my roommate. That snapped her out of it. I was able to bring her back to the room and put her to bed.

"Then when she was asleep I went and told the night nurse what happened. And they ended up moving her to another ward where she could get more supervision—we call it 'moving down in the world.'" Tina paused. "Gloria was really angry. She spat at me when they came to take her away."

"You did the right thing by telling them, believe me," I said. "She might've hanged herself if you hadn't stopped her."

Tina's face drooped. "I guess so. For now. Although," she said, sighing, "when people want to end their lives they manage to get the job done somehow."

"Have you ever considered it?" I wondered aloud.

Tina didn't answer the question, but rather looked hurtfully askance; I should have known better than to ask. "It's too bad," she said after what felt like a punitive silence. "I enjoyed having her here. She gave me a lot of laughs. Wacky sense of humor. Anyway." She clapped her hands, as though dispersing the momentary gloominess. "Let me get you that cup of tea." She grabbed her room key and proceeded to the door. As she was stepping out, a willowy black woman confined to a wheelchair was propelling herself down the corridor. "Hi, Berenice," Tina said.

"You got cigarettes?" I noticed the woman was missing her right leg.

"How many times I told you I don't smoke?"

Berenice grinned; her mouth was gaping and had only a scattering of teeth. "You coulda taken it up since yesterday."

"Now, why would I do that?" Tina said, and turned to wink at me. "I got enough bad habits as it is."

"You don't got enough," Berenice said. As she continued to wheel herself along, she caught sight of me. "Honey, you got me a cigarette?" she asked me with a hopeful smile.

I shrugged. "Sorry."

Berenice looked disappointed. "You healthy too, huh?"

" 'Fraid so," I said.

"You gonna play for us tonight, Blues Lady?" Berenice asked.

"There's a piano here?"

Nodding, Tina said, "It's God-awful but they keep it tuned. A couple of guitarists live on the floor. One fiddle player. We jam every once in a while."

"They good too," Berenice said.

"Come on," Tina said to Berenice, playfully placing her hands on the handles behind the wheelchair. "You come with me to the kitchen. I'll teach you how to make a good cup of tea."

Berenice shrugged as she was being wheeled off and then tilted her head back and began singing in a haunting soprano, "I'll come back to the good life again. Don't you worry 'bout me none, just be a friend."

The window in Tina's room viewed the inner courtyard of the asylum. I went and looked down. During the last few days the weather had turned a bit cooler and drier, more seasonably suited to the weather of early June. The courtyard was filled with towering sycamore and birch trees, whose branches, from the great height I was at, looked like feathers sprouting from a duster. Just beyond the copse of trees a volleyball net had been pitched and a serious game was in progress. The players were a good blend of men and women, all rather young-looking. I opened the window so as to better hear their cheers and shouts; from the long view—to me, at least—they appeared sane. I suddenly wondered if Tina's difficulties reduced to the fact that she saw and heard too much, was not equipped with the filters most people had to protect themselves from being overwhelmed by what was outside them.

Tina entered the room with a tray of tea service, the glass and crockery clanking from her movements. I looked at her carefully. Apart from the pallor which was a result of her medication and that strange heated-up brightness in her eyes, she looked healthy, self-possessed even.

She had made Red Zinger tea, my old favorite. Tina had always loved serving tea. I suddenly remembered our childhood, her pouring hot water from a thermos during those interminable car trips between far-flung cities. She had now brought along a small blue pitcher of milk so that I could do what she always had felt was sacrilegious: pour milk into red tea, which would blanche it to an abysmal pink. After she served me, Tina sat down on her ex-roommate's bed, which was protected with a plain yellow hospital coverlet. She smiled and asked how Michael was.

"He wants to drive me up to see you on a weekend. He's going to skip tennis."

Tina looked at me skeptically. "That'll be the day, when he skips tennis to drive you all the way up here."

"He'll take me. He's flexible."

Tina frowned at me, as though to say, "Who are you kidding, Susan?" Her attitude toward Michael had never been quite so caustic and I wondered what had triggered her sudden condemnation.

"Does he know you came up here today?"

"No."

"Why not?"

"Because it just didn't come up."

"Why didn't it come up?"

I hesitated and then said, "I got upset the last time I came here . . . he was concerned."

"Why should you get upset?"

"Because you told me you liked it here, that they tucked you into bed at night and that you didn't worry about your family."

Tina shrugged and walked over to her window. She surveyed the volleyball game, her face grim and expressionless. "Well, I did like it the day you talked to me. The people seemed nice. They were treating me well."

"Has it changed?"

Tina shrugged. "Yes and no. I guess I'm getting tired of it. Now they're trying to tell me how to think. Fuck them."

"So then you're not so interested in staying?" I asked hopefully.

"It doesn't affect your life how long I stay here."

"Of course it does," I said. "Because I want you to get better . . ." I hesitated. "I figured you wanted to rest and get better and be with your family again."

"I said I missed Rachel," Tina corrected me.

"I guess that upset me too," I went on. "You didn't seem to miss Marty. I would have thought—"

"Shut up goddamnit!" Tina suddenly flared up.

I looked at her for a moment in disbelief.

Tina left the window and went to sit down on the other bed, facing me. Dipping her head, she tried to compose herself. "What's wrong?" I said.

She looked up at me and the helplessness that riddled her face was frightening. "Marty thinks we should separate," she said quietly. "Now that I'm finally in the bughouse he wants out."

I was so taken aback I couldn't react for what seemed like a long time. I stared at the wall above Tina's head where a round mosaic of black and white stars in an "S" configuration was mounted against the healing blue background. I imagined it had been made in the asylum's craft center by her departed roommate, left behind like a *memento mori* to their terminated cohabitation. "That can't be true," I finally said. "I don't believe it."

"You have his phone number in your Rolodex." Tina laughed humorlessly. "Give him a jingle tonight when you get home."

I slowly moved across the room to where Tina sat on her exroommate's bed and wrapped my arms around her. I could feel her shoulders heaving under a spell of nerves. "Tina, it just doesn't make sense. For him to do this to you right now when you're not well. I mean, you're not there, so what's the difference? At least he could wait until you go home to ask for a separation."

Tina shrugged at my statement. "Ah, come on, Susan. You think it'll make a difference once I'm out?"

"You might be better able to deal with it."

"Nah, it's the same shit. It's not going to be any easier whether I'm in or out of a nuthouse. In fact, it'll probably be worse when I'm out." Tina leaned away from me, her eyes angry. "Bad enough being married to an 'unstable person.' " Tina pronounced those last two words with enmity. "But my being in a mental ward is too much for Marty to live with. I guess I asked for it, since I wanted to put myself in here. He's always thought it was professionally damaging to have a crazy for a wife," she said bitterly. "The latest thing is that Rachel's been getting lots of grief at school from her friends, who've been calling me 'Psycho' and 'Mrs. Norman Bates.' " Tina laughed at the last bit.

"They must have gotten that from their parents," I grumbled.

"Wherever they get it, they call me Looney Tunes," Tina said painfully. "I hate that expression." Her voice wobbled. "It doesn't make sense to me, Looney Tunes. Loons pair up once in lifetime and if they lose their mate they keep searching for them and never mate again. They have this tireless devotion to one another. And that somehow has been construed as crazy."

I looked at her sadly. "The expression doesn't come from that," I said. "I think it has to do with being made crazy by the moon."

"Oh." Tina was genuinely surprised. "Like Clair de Lune."

"Right."

"Except there's no Clair," she said.

"How long have you known about Marty's intentions?"

Tina shrugged. "A few weeks."

"Why did you wait so long to tell me?"

"Did you tell me right away about Billy?" She pointed out.

"I wanted to protect you."

"Well, maybe I wanted to protect you."

"That's ridiculous," I said.

"Ridiculous because you think I can't cope with *your* problems," Tina scoffed. "That I can't think of helping anyone but myself."

"Tina, right now I think you should be concentrating on yourself." I couldn't wait to get home to call up Marty and blast him. No, maybe that was the wrong thing to do. I would have Michael call Marty; they'd always gotten along. Michael would learn the truth of what was going on. I hoped the situation wasn't as bad as Tina described.

"How you doing, girls?" Berenice suddenly called to us from out in the hallway.

Tina closed her eyes, summoning up her patience. "Berenice, why don't you stop by later, okay?" she said kindly. "My sister and I have something to dig into right now."

"You got a cigarette?" Berenice said.

"We don't light up, I told you!" Tina exploded.

As though used to such outbursts from Tina, Berenice made a tssking sound, haughtily raised her eyes to the ceiling and wheeled herself away. "Piano waiting," she called from down the hallway. Tina leaped off the bed and went to shut the door and then stood, uncertain, in the middle of the room. Then she peered at me. "You know how she got that way, lost her leg?"

I shrugged.

"Her husband got drunk one night. Pinned her down and tried to cut it off with a knife. The doctors had to finish what he started." She pinched her shoulders together and then looked down at the floor. "She'd be a lot better off if he'd asked her for a divorce."

After ten years, I thought to myself. After all she had done for him, worked so he could finish graduate school, then picked up and went to Texas on a dime. Raised his child. When they first met, Marty was in his second year of graduate school. A short, dark fellow, he was living in a dive of an apartment with two other grad students in Del Mar, quite near to the University of California at San Diego. He was from Detroit, had attended the University of Michigan. With his entrance exams and scholastic record he had his pick of schools, but chose San Diego purely for the weather.

They met at a UCSD mixer that local girls attended with hopes of meeting college men. The dance was held in the late afternoon in a huge wooden gazebo only a few yards up from the beach and within the sound of the breakers. The way Tina described it, she just stood near one of the open sides of the gazebo and allowed light to surround her like a corona. She was asked to dance several times, but not by the fellow she saw entrenched in conversation with what looked to be a professor. Eventually, however, she caught his eye. She somehow sensed that Marty was from out East, that he was well educated, and by then she had grown tired of the surfer-perfect San Diego boys.

Shortly after they met, she convinced Marty to move out of his hovel and take a one-bedroom apartment several blocks from the beach, which was nearly the same price as his share in the former dwelling, whose oceanfront location had jacked up the rent. When she announced her intention to live with Marty, my father was furious. But Marty placated him by proposing marriage and by offering to have his parents pay for the wedding—of course, in that case, the wedding would have to be in Detroit. My father, who once had risked his life in an earthquake so as to get his money's worth of a meal, agreed. Mother, however, was heartbroken. She had entertained visions of a seaside wedding, a chuppah on the beach and Marty and Tina breaking the wineglass on a bed of sand. The wedding reception was eventually held in a dance hall approximately a half mile from the General Motors assembly plant.

Marty was determined to get his graduate degree in history without taking any extra money from his parents, other than what paid for his exorbitant tuition. Tina agreed they should try to make it on their own, and in order to generate more income got her state certification to teach preschool and kindergarten children. I like to think of those early years as the happiest period of Tina's life. She kept busy taking care of their apartment and teaching while Marty pursued his studies. During that time I completed my undergraduate degree in merchandising and got a job at Bullocks department store in Los Angeles. Even though I was living two and a half hours away from Tina and Marty, I got to see them fairly often, and sometimes spent the weekend at their place in Del Mar, which was due north of the city of San Diego. As Marty was doing research in the library much of the time, Tina and I were given plenty of opportunities to be alone.

During my visits I began to notice that she was often reluctant to leave the apartment, and when we did go out, we never ventured far from the neighborhood. At first, I never questioned this idiosyncrasy. I figured that during the week Tina was consumed by her teaching responsibilities and looking after Marty and was just too exhausted to roam very far on the weekends. It did seem strange, however, that whenever we got together with our parents, Tina always insisted they drive twenty-five miles north from their downtown apartment to where we were.

I particularly remember one Sunday. Partly because it was the last weekend I spent with Marty and Tina before I met Michael for the first time in Los Angeles; partly because it was the first real intimation I received that Tina was having psychological difficulties. It was a hazy afternoon. Marty was out at his on-campus office. Tina and I went to brunch at a cute seaside restaurant five blocks from her apartment. As soon as we walked into the restaurant, a hectic manner came over her. She collapsed on a banquette near the door, saying something about being short-winded. This was odd; we hadn't climbed a hill to get there. Then, during the meal, she kept losing the threads of our conversation while switching subjects and speaking as though under strain. We ordered Mexican eggs and guacamole in tortilla-chip shells, but she barely touched any of her food. At one point I asked why she wasn't eating and she claimed to have lost her appetite, something which had been happening to her lately. However, she downed two margaritas, which, without food, intoxicated her. She had to lean heavily against me in order to walk in a straight line out of the restaurant.

I suggested a stroll along the beach, hoping it would be sobering. We kicked off our tennis shoes, rolled up our jeans and peeled off our tee shirts down to our bikini tops. We joined arms and ambled along the smooth wet tide line, dodging the curtains of foam, the by-products of the clear green waves that broke mercilessly before us.

At one point, Tina turned to me. "Remember that night several years ago when you came home from college and I was entertaining all those guys?"

"Yes," I said, "and there was this one guy named Spotty you were making plans to do it with."

"Right, Spotty penis," Tina gurgled, and we both burst into giggles. "What a dud he was," she added boisterously. I reflected that she didn't seem to think so at the time. In fact, she had told me later on that Spotty was a wonderful, sensitive lover. What had changed her attitude toward him? Was he a dud in comparison with Marty? Marty, I must admit, wasn't the most attractive man I'd ever seen. He had a scrawny build, a departure for Tina, who always went for fair, sturdy men. He had a large mole on his cheek, his eyes were feral-looking; for me, he certainly didn't have a strong sexual appeal. And yet, Tina once told me the homely facets of his looks were what she found compelling and which held her more than beauty itself.

"Anyway," Tina went on, "I know you remember the conversation we had later on after I sent all the guys home." She hesitated, peering out over the breakers, eyeing the line of buoys that had been strung two hundred yards out as markers for intrepid swimmers who took their exercise in the ocean. "When I explained to you why I had to go out with so many guys."

"Have you been going out on Marty?" I asked quickly.

Tina shrugged. "Only a couple of times."

I smirked at her, assuming she thought that a few assignations left her less guilty than many.

"Are you afraid he'll find out you're cheating on him?"

Tina shook her head and looked down the coastline, where along a bend in the distance she could spy the white sprawling monstrosity of the Hotel del Coronado. "No. It has nothing to do with that. Now being with strangers makes me feel even worse."

"Well, maybe that's a good sign," I said.

Tina sighed. "It would be, I suppose. But making love to Marty doesn't feel much better."

Frightened, I closed my eyes. As soon as I became blind to the ocean, the booming of the waves grew louder and louder. Then I focused on Tina, who was looking down at the sand.

"Does he know?"

"No. I let him do what he wants. I go through the motions. But I never initiate anything."

"I thought you told me being married stabilized you. Having someone around made you feel more solid."

Tina peered at me miserably. "No, just the opposite. It makes me feel . . . more conspicuous."

"What are you talking about, Tina?"

"Sometimes I can hardly get myself to go to work. If I didn't have to show up at school and take attendance, I'd probably stay in bed all day. Everything gets so bright outside. I hate being out there. I feel so naked."

"Well, you're okay now," I pointed out gently. "And we're very much outside."

"That's because I'm sloshed!"

A wave swirled in and I quickly sidestepped it. Tina, however, just let the foam douse her feet and ankles. Her white sneakers were now soaked a charcoal gray. "Does Marty know anything about this?" I asked.

Tina shrugged. "Certain things . . . I can't have him know everything. He'd probably leave me if he knew everything."

I stopped walking and looked at my sister, whose hair was blowing wildly from the winds coming off the ocean, who appeared distressed and lovely all at the same time. "I think you underestimate your husband," I said. "He's not going to leave you. He loves you."

Tina shook her head. "Not as much as he used to."

A few weeks later I met Michael at a cocktail party in a house at the top of the Pacific Palisades. He was a young junior agent who had been sent out from New York on some unimportant movie business that, nevertheless, required him to work marathon hours. It was a last-minute fluke that he attended the party as the date of a woman whom he turned out not to be interested in. I was invited as the date of a would-be actor. Among all the jaded entertainment types, Michael and I were the only people who spent any time admiring the panoramic view. There was an instant attraction between us and he invited me to dinner the next night. As he was flying back and forth to Los Angeles a lot in those days, I saw him several times over the next two months. And when he finally asked me if I would ever consider moving to New York, I told him I'd think about it, although I had difficulty imagining myself living three thousand miles away from my sister and my parents.

But then, two days after Michael and I had our conversation,

Tina called me from San Diego. She sounded excited or nervous
—I couldn't tell which. Marty had just received a job offer for a
professorship at a university in Galveston, Texas. The offer stip-
ulated enough money so that she no longer had to work to
support them.

As I listened to Tina speak, I suddenly grew a lot more
serious about investigating life on the East Coast. Galveston was
too far a drive from California; a flight between Galveston and
New York took only three hours. The fact remained, whether I
continued to live in California or if I moved to New York, I
would seldom get to see my sister. "I didn't know you wanted
to stop working," I told Tina. "I thought you enjoyed working
with children. I thought it kept you going," I said, referring to
our last conversation when she told me that if it weren't for
work she'd be tempted to stay in bed all day.

"I do. I'm sure if we were staying in California I'd look for
another job. But each state requires that you pass a test."

"You could pass the test in Texas. How hard could it be in
Texas?"

"That's true. Maybe after we get settled I'll look into it," she
said.

Two days later I received another call from Tina. You would
never know it was the same person. Now she brimmed with
doubts: she didn't want to leave San Diego, or our parents and,
most of all, me. She admitted that Marty took the offer without
consulting her and that she was not crazy about the idea of
living in Texas.

"Why did you suddenly change your mind?" I asked.

"I didn't change my mind. Marty was right there breathing
down my neck. He wanted me to call you with the good news."

According to Tina, people who lived in Texas had a reputation for being a lot more conservative, less open than people in
California. She went on to attack the weather in the Gulf of

Mexico. "I hear in the summer you constantly feel like a limp wet rag."

"You can put up with it," I replied, wanting to encourage Tina now that their moving was a fait accompli. "You'll use air conditioning. And you'll find the right people to associate with. There are always good people wherever you go."

A static silence followed and I began to suspect something more was going on when Tina said, "It's funny how after that conversation we had on the beach you're still not getting it."

This sentence was uttered with a noticeable slur, and I was thrown back to that moment on the beach, which I now recalled with a certain spin of unreality. It was late morning and I got a strong feeling that Tina had been drinking. "What do you mean, I'm not getting it?"

"You're not as bothered by changes the way I am. Things crawl right under my skin that don't faze you. Everything that's unfamiliar is like culture shock."

"Tina," I said, a lot more frightened than I let on. "Then you should talk to Marty about this."

"I already told him I'd do it," she went on manically, speaking so quickly I could barely understand her. "How am I going to stand in his way? What excuse could I give more than not wanting to leave you and Mother and Father and not wanting to leave California? Those aren't good reasons for a scholar in a competitive field who's been offered a professorship. I'm supposed to be supportive, not demanding."

There was a short, electric pause, during which I suddenly realized that she was two hours away in San Diego and I couldn't just rush over to help her. Then, in a half-sob, Tina confessed. "Don't you see? I'm afraid of going anywhere. For Christ's sake, afraid of being away from my center."

Bewildered by the sudden swerve in the conversation, I said hesitantly, "And that's going outside?"

"When I go outside, I panic if I have to go very far." Tina now sounded breathless. "I thought you realized that."

"I thought it was depression you felt. Not panic."

"Don't be a jerk. I feel both."

"Tina," I said. "It's all right. I understand. Don't be upset. I love you no matter how you feel or what you decide to do."

"I gotta be careful," she insisted. "I can bring it on by just thinking about it. Luckily, things are close by. I mean, I can get shopping done. Order in if it's a little too far. The school is within range. The other week, remember when we went to brunch?"

"Yes," I said.

"And I made such a big deal of saying the restaurant had the best brunch. That's 'cause I hate to go anywhere much farther than the block we're on."

"Tina, honestly, why haven't you discussed this with Marty?"

"I have a little, but it's hard . . . it's hard to admit."

"You should think seriously about getting some help," I said.

"Help means more bills."

"Who cares? If you need it, you need it. I understand some doctors have sliding scales." Tina was unresponsive for a moment and then I said, "Are you sure that you're not . . . somehow exaggerating?"

"Susan." Tina sounded even more breathless. "Once I had to pick up Marty at the airport. Around fifteen miles away. While I was driving on the freeway I got so scared, it was like I didn't even know who was driving anymore. For all I know, I could've been somebody else steering the car. I was so nervous I'd forgotten what to exist was, I nearly passed out. And I'd taken two Valiums an hour before I left. So you can understand why I'm anxious about moving to Texas, if I nearly faint driving across town."

"You've got to go for help, Tina!"

"Yeah, and what if they end up committing me?"

"They're not going to commit you."

"How the hell do you know?"

"They'd only commit you if you were a danger to yourself or to other people."

"You don't know shit about that, believe me," Tina said.

"Okay," I conceded. "Maybe I don't. But tell me this: how will you get to Texas?"

"We have to drive! I'll go crazy, but we have to drive!"

I then suggested that, for the short-term, Tina should see a psychiatrist, who'd prescribe strong enough tranquilizers so she could keep steady on the way to Texas. Once they got there, she could start long-term therapy and eventually would get accustomed to being in Texas. "It would become your center." I borrowed her earlier expression.

After a considerable lull, during which I figured Tina was pondering my suggestion, she finally disappointed me. "Look, Susan, I've got to get off the phone. Marty left a notebook behind and I told him I'd bring it to him on campus."

"But isn't campus too far away?"

Tina actually laughed and then in a dismal voice said, "It's really just at the very edge of where I can go."

After they'd been living a few years in Galveston and Tina had been getting consistent treatment, her psychiatrist suggested that having a child would help to ground her. And Tina ended up being a great parent. From a very young age, she treated Rachel like an adult and, with all her fears and phobias about her own stability, ironically was not nearly as overprotective as I or other mothers I knew.

However, as soon as Rachel turned five and began to show more of the independence her mother had encouraged, Tina slipped backward again. She suddenly found the house oppressive, often unable to leave her bedroom, much less leave the neighborhood. It was all she could do to muster up the nerve to pick up Rachel at school. And sometimes she just couldn't bring herself to go out at all and in frustration would start drinking. When this would happen, Rachel got rides from the sympathetic mothers of her friends and would arrive home to find her mother passed out on her bed with a vodka bottle in her hands. The most recent incident of Tina's neglect had occurred while Marty was away at an academic conference in Michigan. She holed herself up in her bedroom and refused to come out. After two days of neglect, Rachel finally called her grandparents in San Diego to complain that she was hungry and not being properly fed.

Tina was now looking somber. She dusted her hands together in a gesture of finality. "He'll probably get custody of Rachel," she said solemnly.

"Let's take this slowly," I said. "Let's not jump to conclusions."

"Especially when they're foregone," Tina said bitterly.

I shook my head. "But you're improving all the time. You'll get out and you'll have your daughter." The words, even as I said them, sounded unconvincing.

"No, Susan, I won't have my daughter. Because I'm not fit and because it was my decision to come here, to commit myself," she reminded me. Now, in light of a possible divorce, I realized that Tina's nearness to me would make it even easier for Marty to let go of her.

"Well, then you'll never be alone," I said emphatically. "You'll always have me to take care of you."

"Come on, Susan, you've got your own family."

"Come on, Tina," I said. "You *are* my family."

She shook her head, got up from the bed, scrupulously collecting the cups and saucers and tea bags before stacking them on the tray. She picked up the tray and then gazed at me meaningfully. "Now, maybe, you understand why I said I liked being here," she murmured as she walked toward the door.

A N A R T I C L E about the drowning had run in the
local paper the day after the incident, and Billy's account
of what happened had been written up. But then, the day after I
went to visit Tina, a follow-up article was published under the
headline "Drowning Raises Questions of Safety in Suburbia."
Surrounded by text like a raft by water, ran a picture of the lake
in a state of quiet, including the sight of a large weeping wil-
low. The writer described the trend of young urban couples
moving to the suburbs, escaping the dangers of street violence,
but unwittingly exposing themselves and their families to the
new dangers that came with living in more rural areas. Exam-
ples were given of people being hit by cars, falling from train

trestles, children getting injured playing with dynamite caps found in housing developments. The drowning of Mark Rosen, at the eye of the piece, was presented as one unchaperoned two-year-old child who had hazarded to play with a seven-year-old fishing alone by a pond.

"Now, when those reporters came here you told them the Rosens had all that extra help, didn't you?" Michael asked as he was reading the article—several hours after I did. The fact itself was not mentioned in the piece.

"Of course I mentioned it to them," I said.

Michael shook his head. "Imagine having two women work-ing for you and something like that happening."

He was sitting at the wooden kitchen table, leaning forward while reading the paper, his tie making a pile of polka-dotted silk on the pale yellow tablecloth. I was standing behind him, glancing over his shoulder. Raw linen place mats were set with matching salad and dinner plates that were glazed with a depic-tion of turquoise mallards. At the edge of his place mat stood a tall crystal tumbler that had just come out of the dishwasher. A roast broiled in the oven and I could feel its crackling sounds with all my nerves. When Michael finished reading the article, I told him I felt that between the lines seemed to be a suggestion on the part of the writer that Billy should not have been fishing alone.

Michael glanced up at me sideways with his iris-blue eyes framed by his long lashes. "I must say that thought went through my mind. Although"—he glanced at the newspaper—"all it says here is that Billy was fishing by himself, which you could take to mean that he had no companion. Mark is the one who's described as unchaperoned."

Considering it further, he rubbed his forehead with his thumb and index finger. "However, to make ourselves feel better, why don't we send the guy a letter and let him know we think he's

insinuating and that we don't like his insinuations. We can draft
it on lined paper and I'll have my secretary type it up."

"I'll bet you he doesn't even have children of his own."

"You're probably right."

I leaned on Michael's shoulders, feeling the tensile strength in
his muscles, and sighed. "I guess I do have my doubts about our
allowing Billy to fish by the pond."

Michael threw aside the newspaper, held one of my arms and
gently drew me around to him. I loved his hands, which were
wide and veined and had a soft fleshy underside, especially below the thumb. His gold wedding band shone against his skin,
whose tan would deepen as the summer progressed. "Susan," he
said, "we both made a decision a year ago to let Billy go fishing
when he learned how to swim. He's shown us that he's reliable,
that he doesn't need to be monitored, that he can be responsible
for himself."

I shrugged. "But you see, even though we allow Billy to fish,
at the same time he's not really old enough to know that other
children are not self-reliant enough to be by the water."

"Listen," Michael said, looking at me intently. "They have a
housekeeper and a nursemaid. I ask you this: Where the hell
were they? How come they weren't around? The nursemaid fell
asleep. How else could a two-year-old get out of the house and
cross the street by himself? Now, would you have done that
when Billy was two, allowed your attention to drift long
enough for him to wander out of the house?"

I shook my head.

"So," he said, "leaving off practical matters, let's take it as a
case of law. There are some states whose statutes are so strict that
mothers lose custody if they leave their children unattended. In
Britain, if it's proven that a woman has left a kid in a bathtub
for two minutes she can be deemed an unfit mother and actually
have to give up her child. And Harriet Rosen"—his voice by
now was booming and I had to ask him to lower it—"didn't

even realize her two-year-old son had left the house and roamed across the street!"

Michael paused, and the mood on his face suddenly shifted, as though a whole different feeling were percolating through him. He smiled sadly at me. "I know this has been really difficult for you, Susan. But you've been handling it all beautifully."

"Michael, I don't know if I'm imagining or not, but I think I see people whispering when I go to the supermarket and other places. It really gets to me."

"You don't think maybe you're looking for it?"

"I don't think I am."

"Well, then, just ignore them. We've got nothing to be ashamed of. We've done nothing wrong."

"I'll try."

He leaned back his chair and cocked his arms behind his head. His rib cage pushed through the oxford cloth of his shirt, and I noticed a few chest hairs poking over the knot of his tie.

"So, how's Billy doing today?"

"He's okay," I said. "Pretty well, considering."

"Considering?"

I told Michael what was going on with Peter Freed, how after insisting that he and Billy play at our house, Peter had been acting a lot bossier than usual.

"Well, there could be a simple explanation for that. Peter could be jealous that Billy has been in the limelight."

I looked at Michael strangely. The thought had never occurred to me. "Are you serious?"

"Why not? It makes sense."

"I think Peter's behavior has more to do with whatever Norma's been saying to him."

"I'm sure she adds to it."

"The woman is really paranoid."

"By the way, did you hear anything about the funeral?"

"Apparently they were both a mess."

Thinking about the Rosens wracked with grief subdued both of us for a while. Finally, Michael looked at me curiously. "How'd you hear about it?"

"Cass."

"I thought you were never going to talk to Cass again?"

"She called me."

Michael glanced at his watch, which prompted me to look at the enameled kitchen wall clock. It was just after eight o'clock. I suddenly felt resentful of the fact that he came home from the steady structure of his employment to try in a half hour to place things in a more secure perspective. But I knew right now I had to rely on him; the things that I always had thought were unshakable—my own judgment on how to raise my son, my understanding of parental responsibility—had suddenly been impugned.

"Do I have time to go up and play with Billy before dinner?" Michael asked.

I nodded.

"He's already eaten?"

"Come on, Michael, it's after eight o'clock. Don't ask the obvious. He's had hamburgers and potato chips. The roast is for us."

"Um. Good. I love the way you roast," Michael said, winking at me as he got up from the table, grabbed his suit jacket, slung it over his shoulders and began loping across the kitchen toward the stairs. His polished brogans clicked on the linoleum.

"Do you have any news?" I asked him.

He pivoted toward me, frowning.

"Did you get any long-distance phone calls?"

Michael raised his eyebrows. "Oh. I left for a meeting at three-fifteen. I hadn't up until then. I'll go upstairs and call the night receptionist and have them check my message box."

"Please," I said. "There's a time difference."

Michael had been equally surprised by the news that Marty

might divorce Tina. Two days ago he had tried calling Marty and left word with Marty's department at the university, but so far there had been no return phone call.

"It's not unusual that it takes him a few days to call back," Michael said, still hesitating by the kitchen door.

I shrugged.

He walked over, put his arms around me and squeezed.

"Suki," he said, "you really do have lot of things on your mind these days."

"Don't call me Suki," I scolded him gently.

"Suki-duki."

"What do you want now?"

"Why don't you come with me to see the Bird?"

"You go see the Bird by yourself and I'll be along."

"Okay," he said.

He took his arms away and went upstairs and I felt more alone than I had felt before he touched me. It was always like that with Michael. In the wake of tenderness comes a hollow feeling that seems as though it will never be filled. We had gone nearly two weeks without making love. The drowning was the latest event to postpone it; although it was true, during the last few days, the lapse of interest had been more on my part. There, in the loneliness of my empty kitchen, I tried to make myself feel luckier by feeling compassionate for Tina in jeopardy of losing her husband and possibly losing her daughter. I wondered what she was doing right now in the hospital, if she had been putting on civil appearances for me and actually had been feeling a lot more wretched than she let on.

"Honey," Michael called down from above. "No message from Marty."

"What about Uncle Marty?" I heard Billy ask. Oh shit, I thought, how would Michael explain? I hoped he had the sense to keep Tina's latest difficulties from Billy. I heard Michael answering Billy, but I couldn't make out what he said.

Not really knowing where I was going, only that I was searching for something to comfort me, to satisfy me, something that would be akin to sex, I turned the oven down and climbed the staircase. As I passed Billy's room, I saw Michael on all fours leaning over Billy, who lay on his back on the carpeted floor with a look of rapture. I myself had rarely seen such a look of pleasure on my son's face. He really adored his father. When Michael noticed me standing there he mussed up Billy's hair, which fell back onto his head like straw.

"So, why did your teacher do that?"

"Because kids would stop talking."

"Did you fall asleep?"

"No way. I waited until she said we could take our heads off the desk. We each had to say we were sorry."

"Were you one of the people who were talking?"

At this point Billy rolled his head around, noticed me and clammed up.

Michael looked at me too. "Don't worry, nobody's going to punish you."

Billy gathered up his legs and put his arms around his knees. "Peter and I were."

"So, I hoped you learned from that. Not to talk during the lesson. You have to get a good education. Go to Princeton like your old dad."

Oh, please, I thought.

"Dad, we're going to Playland this weekend, right?"

"Does it have to be this weekend?" Michael asked.

Billy puckered up his face. "You promised."

"I know I promised. I promise I'll take you. But what happens if I have to go into work—"

"Do your work at home," Billy said. I looked at Michael awry. He had postponed this obligation enough times. If it came down to it, I would absolutely insist that he take Billy to Playland on Saturday.

"All right already, all right," Michael said finally. "I'll take you to Playland."

I left them and continued on down the hallway. I reflected that they both seemed relaxed and easy with one another. I was glad. I just wished Michael took more opportunities to spend time with Billy. Too often he bypassed his son's room and Billy had to seek him out. Look how much love there was between them. Why weren't they together more often? Why did Michael have to go off weekends and do other things? I knew Billy missed him and felt excluded from his father's recreational activities. It pained me that there was so much feeling but no strong connection between them. It was like heating a bedroom in the winter and never sleeping in it.

I continued on to our bedroom and shut the door behind me. I opened the door to my closet, which had a full-length mirror on the back, and shoved wooden hangers aside until I was staring at the dress I had bought for seven hundred and fifty dollars and which had been eclipsed by all the commotion of the last few days. The dress had been displayed in the window, and the moment I saw it from the street, the summer sun beating down on me, I knew I had to have it—no matter what it cost. I now took it off the hanger. It was like a designer's pastry: puffed out with tiers of black organdy and taffeta, fringed with artfully arranged rhinestones. I held it up to my shoulders. It certainly was beautiful. When I had first tried it on in the store I had caused quite a sensation. In one of the glass accessory cases had been a black turban with a large paste sapphire inset like a third eye, which I put on as well. Ooing and aahing, several of the salesladies kept saying the dress was made for me and that I looked like Elizabeth Taylor.

On a whim I stripped down to my bra and panties. I unzipped the back of the dress, got into it, zipped it up and chose an appropriate pair of shoes from my shoe box, put them on and stood in front of the mirror. The dress, all ruffles and flounces, cinched and flattered my waistline, shaped my bust. For a moment I imagined myself attending the play opening on Michael's arm, looking stunning and self-possessed. I saw myself much admired, envied. But suddenly I began to feel foolish. And then sad. My mind was a muddle of conflicting desires. I wanted to wear the dress. I wanted to believe that certain things would come to pass: that Billy would be unscathed by the death of Mark Rosen, that Tina would be able to keep her daughter. And I wanted to comfort myself for an inner loneliness that no one, not even Michael, could reach. But it just wasn't possible. Wearing the dress surely wasn't going to do it for me.

Later on that evening, after we had put Billy to bed and had a quiet dinner, Michael and I sat in our bedroom watching television. Edward R. Murrow was narrating the events of the Battle of Britain to coincide with some rather grim-looking footage of coal-black smoke churning up from various firebombings of London. People scurried to shelters, carrying sacks of provisions they had waited hours to buy. A history nut, Michael loved documentaries and normally sat glued to the television. Tonight, he kept jotting notes on a canary legal pad, jumping up and down to take care of little annoyances: to fetch the toenail clipper, to make certain he had not mislaid the claim check for a pair of wing-tipped shoes he was to pick up the following morning at a repair store near Grand Central Station. He wore only his boxers and his penis kept flopping out. As he tucked himself back inside his shorts he'd glance at me sheepishly—I felt that if he was thinking about sex he'd at least throw me a leer.

Faces of wartime women were tilted upward, scouring the boding skies for errant bombs. I told myself they had been too caught up with survival to be concerned with getting a satisfying quotient of sex from their husbands. Shouldn't I be more satisfied? I cast my mind back over the eight years of our rela-

tionship—was the seven-year itch they talked about now coming on a little late?—and tried to remind myself that his desire
to make love came in fits and starts. For most of the years of our
marriage Michael's appetite had been enormous. Often we'd do
it twice a day and then following our double sessions I'd catch
him masturbating in the shower. He'd look at me, chagrined,
and explain that he was afraid of overwhelming me with his
lust. It was only lately that he'd begun to lose interest. We made
love infrequently, when he wanted to, and I wished somehow I
could alter the pattern and have my way sometimes. Again, I
thought of the drowning and what it was requiring of me. The
drowning made me like one of these wartime women; the quan-
tity of whose sex wasn't so important as quality. But the more I
tried to diminish my longing, the more it ripened. Michael
finally settled down and took my hand as he got reabsorbed in
the program. I knew that today he had dealt with a multitude of
pressures at the office and the television was helping him to
unwind. But I just felt such an incredible distance between us,
which was only accentuated by the fact that he was lying close
to me and could be so much closer. Then I tried to punish
myself further by thinking of Harriet Rosen. I saw her lying in
a shuttered room, a cold compress on her forehead, her painful
grief blurred by a slew of mood-altering drugs.

The next thing I knew, I felt my stomach curdling. Pinpricks
erupted all over my body as I began sweating. I suddenly felt
nauseated and vertiginous as though the room were flattening in
on me. I jumped off the bed. Michael frowned at me. "Honey,"
he asked, "what's the matter?"

"I'm sick to my stomach," I muttered, stalking into the bathroom.

"Is there anything I can do for you?" he asked.

"Nothing." I slammed the door. I peered at myself in the
mirror with the same intensely abnormal scrutiny I turned on
Billy the day I feared he had been killed. Why do I feel sick

suddenly? This is crazy, I told myself. Then I got hit by another breaker of dizziness and the nausea grew worse. I knelt down and clutched the lip of the toilet bowl and vomited until there was nothing left in my stomach. I had never done that before— grown nauseous from thinking too much. When I stood up again, I felt a lot better. I washed my face with cold water, patted it dry with a towel and then scrubbed my teeth. I cracked the bathroom door to see if Michael had been worriedly looking on. But he had completely forgotten that I'd been feeling sick and was totally absorbed in his program. He was tensing and relaxing his toes. So much for caring, I thought as I reentered the bedroom.

His face painted in black-and-white-television hues, Michael watched me walk back to my side of the bed. "You okay now?" he asked mildly, obviously having no idea that I had just retched my guts out.

"I got really dizzy. But I'm all right."

His eyes held to me. "I'm glad you feel better."

I sat down on my side of the bed, my back toward him, gathering the folds of my robe around my knees. Still turned away, I craned my neck to look at him. "You seem so preoccupied tonight."

He shrugged. "Sometimes it's hard for me to unwind. I guess there's a lot of stuff going on here."

"Well, I'm sorry," I said, "if we're not the happiest family on the block."

"Don't be sarcastic, Susan," he said. "I'm not trying to be disagreeable. Give me a break."

"Why should I give you a break? Because you came home tonight and took a real interest in us for once. I should give you a break because for once you're making your son feel loved."

He peered at me in bewilderment. "I don't know what you're talking about."

"Why are you trying to wriggle out of taking him to Playland this weekend? You promised him."

"Susan, you know sometimes I have to work weekends."

"That's an excuse. And Billy's right. You can always juggle work. For some reason, you'd rather not take him."

"I'd love to take him. I just have certain things I need to get done."

"You mean *want* to get done, Michael. There's nothing you *have* to do this weekend. Except take our son to Playland. You have a responsibility to him. And to me. We're raising him together. I'm not raising him alone."

"I can't be at home as much as you. I don't have as much free time."

"So when you have free time, spend it with your son."

"I can. I do."

I gave him a look to mean this was not true and he knew it was not true.

Michael in the meantime stretched out on his back and stared at the ceiling. "Susan," he said, "we have to go on. Our lives are still intact. There's been no death here." He paused. "I don't know what you meant the other night when you said something else may have happened that Billy didn't tell us. But I think that worry is weighing you down. I think it has to do with why you think people are gossiping behind our backs."

I hoped Michael was right that it *was* in my mind, for suspecting an omission on Billy's part had certainly affected my self-confidence. And yet, much as I wished it were otherwise, I perceived what I perceived. "Michael," I said, "there is just something in the way Peter treats him that makes me think he's heard certain things from Norma, things we don't know about."

"Kids are nasty. Their allegiances are pretty flimsy, if you ask me. Maybe Peter's just acting a little wary of Billy because his mother is climbing the walls, worrying whether or not she's going to get sued."

"Okay, Michael, understood. But your son's affections are serious. He doesn't take things lightly. If Peter rejects him—"

"We can't live in fear of Peter Freed. We'll have to try and explain to Billy that Peter has been brainwashed by his mother."

"But, Michael, I think Billy is reading the drowning into whether or not Peter Freed continues to be his best friend."

"All right, then we'll just have to do what we can to reassure him he had nothing to do with it." Michael reached across the bed and hugged me. "Let's not talk about this anymore to-night," he said. And as we embraced, I stifled the urge to weep.

We held each other while the television droned on about the high morale of the British and how everyone pitched in to help the war effort. But our embrace did not progress into lovemak-ing, and finally, despite myself, I asked, "Why don't we have sex anymore, Michael? It's been two weeks."

There was a short ponderous silence following my question, and with a desolate instinct I knew what it meant. He'd been sleeping with another woman.

I could feel a change in his body chemistry that had mingled with someone else's, the fear of his being discovered now suffo-cating us. He gave some half-baked excuse about working late and things not coinciding and that it couldn't have been two whole weeks. Something told me to withdraw, to rein myself in now or else I'd get slammed with the truth. The desire to make love to him began shriveling within me. The next thing I knew his hand had left its resting place around my waist and was now traveling down in between my legs. My longing for him surged back, but now I clamped down on it. Michael suddenly must have felt the compunction to make love to me out of guilt, to prove to me and probably to himself that nothing between us had changed. But I just knew he had been elsewhere. I plucked his hand away.

"I don't necessarily mean that I want to make love to you

right now," I said in an aloof tone of voice. "I was just wondering why it's been so long."

Michael sensed my change in attitude, which only spurred him on. "You're right, it's been too long," he said, reaching for one of my breasts.

This time I gave in and made fierce love to him. I thought: Even if Michael had been sleeping with another woman, why should I deny myself gratification? If there was to be a confrontation about infidelity, it needed to occur in a different arena. I was so intent on channeling my anger that I concentrated on taking what I wanted from him rather than trying to please him. And when it was all over and we were both lying on our backs, my hand under his buttocks, his arm curled around my neck, I felt as though, in some way, I had triumphed.

I've tried to imagine what it's like to drown. You thrash around for a few minutes, trying not to breathe, but you have to inhale sometime. Finally you just give up and your chest caves in with a choke that ruptures everything inside you. I used to put butterflies in closed jars with cotton soaked in alcohol. They skittered around until their wings froze and their veins of color deepened with a stain of chemical death. I remember how your mother laid you on your stomach, water bleeding out of your clothes, how each time the nurse pressed down on your back I was afraid she was killing you. But then your eyes fluttered open, looking far away at heaven. You jerked as white fluid jetted from your nose, which made me cry because I knew this was my bread that you had eaten before I tried to send you away.

L ATER THAT night I awoke on instinct and rushed to Billy's room, where I found him sitting up and sobbing in bed. He was not weeping like a child in that steady stream of tears and wailing that comes as a result of a scolding or a fall from a bicycle or from fear of what might lurk in a closet that should be scoured every night for monsters. His body heaved and quaked in anguish that reminded me of the sufferings of someone older. "Was it a bad dream, Birdie?" I asked, enveloping him with my arms and hugging him tightly to me. He managed to nod against my shoulder. I hushed him and spoke soft nonsensical reassurances.

"Is it still dark out?" he muttered.

"It's just gone on one o'clock in the morning."

"Not later?" he asked, his voice grasping each syllable.

"No," I said, stroking his sweat-dampened head. "It's still a long time until morning."

Billy's sobbing slowly began to subside. Finally, in a sniffle, he said more clearly, "I want it to be morning."

"If you fall asleep it'll be morning," I said.

"I won't fall asleep."

"Of course you will," I said. "It'll help if you tell me about your dream."

Billy looked up at me with red swollen eyes and shook his head. "I can't," he said.

"Of course you can. And when you do it won't seem so bad."

I rocked him some more, waiting. Usually I was able to calm him down fairly quickly; tonight, however, he was a lot more difficult to reach, and I watched his fear hardening into a more permanent trauma. After stalling a bit more, however, Billy finally began to recount his dream.

"We were standing at the fence next to her house. The fence where the roses grow."

"Who are we, darling?"

"Peter. We were in Peter's driveway, hitting a tennis ball with Peter's bat. I hit the ball and it went over onto her lawn. Peter told me not to go there."

"And then?"

"It was in the middle of their flower bed. I went to get it. And she ran out of the house and started yelling." Billy began crying again. "She yelled," he sobbed, "to get out of the neighborhood. She told me to leave her property. And then her thorns got me."

"That's a very bad dream," I said, beginning to rock him. Billy's nightmares always involved some sort of extreme danger or threat to his well-being and were usually painted in feverish strokes of fantasy: scaly green monsters surfacing from street sewers, being chased by Model T Fords, or being pushed off a tall bridge and falling into angry water. The horror of this dream was quieter, more realistic.

Billy picked his head up off my shoulder and looked at me in puzzlement. "You think?" he asked.

"I think the dream is . . . well, maybe you're feeling badly about what happened to Mark."

"No, I'm not," Billy said emphatically. "He shouldn't be down by the pond if he doesn't know how to swim. He shouldn't be playing by himself if he has a nurse."

"That's true," I said, "but it doesn't mean that you're not going to feel bad that he died."

"You said he went to heaven. You said he's up with Poppy. So that means he's happy, right?"

"That's true," I said. "But you didn't see Poppy die; however, you saw what happened to Mark. So it makes sense that you'd feel differently about it."

"Mark drowned," Billy said in wonderment.

"Uh-huh."

He sighed. "It must be so yucky drowning."

"I don't think it hurts so much, actually. It happens quickly."

"How could it not hurt?"

"Sometimes dying doesn't hurt."

Billy had languished in my embrace and I let him lie back down on his bed. When I did so, his eyes shone with purpose. "Really?" he said.

"Sure," I said. "Like, for example, if someone dies in their sleep."

Billy grinned severely. "That's how I'd like to die. I'd like to die in a way that wouldn't hurt."

"You don't have to think about dying right now."

He looked at me sadly. "What about when *you* die?"

I tamped my fingers against his cheek, which was still feverish and moist with tears. "Chances are I won't die until you're at least as old as I am now."

"Is that a long time?"

"A very long time, Birdie," I said, stroking his hair. "Now, are you ready to come sleep in my bed for a while?"

He nodded. "Okay. But what if I can't sleep?"

"I'll make you some hot milk."

"But will you sing to me?" he asked with sudden pained shyness.

"Of course," I said. "Of course I'll sing to you."

In the morning Michael and I talked while he shaved. He left the bathroom with a salmon towel wrapped around him and proceeded to his bureau of drawers. He reached for his gold chain, cocked his arms and joined his hands behind his neck while he fixed the chain's clasp. His arms in that position swelled his biceps. I couldn't help wondering if another woman had recently seen him completing this ritual of putting on his chain, watching as I did the transformation between the private person and the public one. A few beads of water sprinkled from his head to the carpeting. Once he finished attaching the chain, he came over to me and kissed me on the forehead and then over each eye.

Then the phone rang and Michael moved swiftly to answer it, almost as though he wanted to intercept the call. Indeed, I might have allowed myself to suspect his behavior if it wasn't clearly his office on the line.

"When did that call come in?" Michael asked, rubbing the wet ringlets of hair at his right temple with his free fingertips. "No, it can wait until I get there." He looked at me significantly and I wondered if Marty had finally called back.

But he hadn't.

"Will you do me a favor, Michael?" I asked.

"Name it," he said, darting toward his bureau, where he

unfastened the towel from his waist, allowing it to drop into a pile on the carpeting. He stood there with his white muscular behind facing me as he opened his top drawer and took out a pair of folded ice-blue boxer shorts.

"Would you try Marty again today? He hasn't called you back in three days. Maybe he's decided not to return your call."

"I'm sure he'll call when he's ready," Michael said, turning to look at me as he put on the boxer shorts.

"Michael, I'm surprised you're saying this. You of all people. She's going to have to get a good lawyer to protect herself."

"She'll have time to get a lawyer." Michael went to the closet where Mercedes had hung all his newly laundered shirts and surveyed his choices. "Whether or not he's already filed she'll be allotted plenty of time to set things up for herself." He chose a crisp pink oxford and began putting it on. He marched over to his tie rack and methodically selected a rust-and-brown paisley tie I had given him two years ago as a birthday gift. He draped the tie around his neck and headed for the bathroom. "And I'll get the lawyer for her," he reassured me as he began looping his tie. "Somebody associated with my office would be perfect. A tough-assed guy, if I ever knew one."

On the one hand, I felt reassured by Michael's offer to take care of finding Tina a lawyer, but then I worried that he might take the point of view that Tina needed to fight tooth and nail to get what she deserved. Perhaps a tough, fighting lawyer was not the answer. Such a man might cause more anguish and frustration than someone conciliatory who could get the job done with solid work and smooth, persistent negotiation. Divorce would take an enormous toll on my sister, and it seemed to me that hiring someone sensitive to her needs was the way to go. I would have mentioned this, but then Michael said, "We don't have to start worrying about a lawyer for a little while. It'll be a couple of months at least. And there are plenty of people Tina can choose from."

"Okay, Michael. But I still think you should call Marty man to man and find out what he intends to do."

"Unless Tina's making it up."

"She's not making it up."

"It wouldn't be the first time she's made something up," Michael said as he completed his Windsor knot.

"If she was making it up, then there'd be no reason for him not to call you back."

"You assume too much, Susan," Michael said, leaving the bathroom. "Maybe he's out of town." He went over to his valet, where I had put out his charcoal-gray pin-striped suit. Facing away from me, he tucked his shirttail into his underwear and then put on his pants. His shirt now fit his back as smoothly as a piece of vellum lying on an ink blotter. Finally he stood before me completely dressed and in an aura of self-possession. "All right," he said, "I'll try him again today at . . . how about eleven o'clock. And then I'll call you."

"Okay," I said. I couldn't help thinking that Michael looked more beautiful in a suit, taller, sexier than he did in casual clothing.

First I got Billy off to school. Then I went to the grocery store for a few staples such as milk and Gouda cheese and stopped at the Jewish bakery for a fresh loaf of rye. Mercedes and I would complete the major shopping in a few days. I stopped by the dry cleaner's to pick up a batch of Michael's jackets and a few of my blouses. I was driving home when I heard the local news announce that a memorial service was being held at one o'clock for Mark Rosen at the Jewish Community Center of Hartsdale. I got a terrific pang. I thought of my conversation with Norma Freed the night Mark drowned, when she counseled me not to contact the Rosens for a while, not even to make a condolence call. I felt polarized, shunned from a ritual that others in the neighborhood participated in. The reason: I had been too closely linked to the event itself, the death of a child. And yet, I felt that though the other women would huddle together in the front rows of the temple, only I could really empathize with what Harriet was going through, because for a painful thirty seconds I actually believed what had happened to her had happened to me.

It was in this frame of mind that I arrived home and was told by Mercedes that Michael had phoned from his office and wanted me to call him back.

I went upstairs to my bedroom, dialed nervously and reached his secretary, who asked me to hold; he was on a conference call that couldn't be interrupted. The air conditioner was brewing coolness. A potent curtain of sunlight streamed through the windows. Outside, the morning air was plagued with humidity, cowling the yard in a deathly stillness.

Michael finally came on. "Hi, honey," he said with stiff cheer. I immediately sensed the worst was true.

"You must've gotten hold of him?"

"Yep."

"And?"

"He hasn't filed yet, but he's planning to. And he *does* want custody of Rachel, which makes sense on his part, considering the circumstances."

I froze and looked down at our green-and-blue woven bed-spread. Noticing a tiny hole, I inadvertently began picking at it with my fingernail. So it really was true: Marty and Tina were getting divorced. "I see."

Michael perceived my state of numbness. "Honey, why don't we talk about the rest of it later."

"No, Michael," I said stiffly. I would force myself to hear the truth. "I want you to tell me all of it. Now."

I heard papers shuffling, then a thudding sound like a paper-weight. "He's transcribed conversations he's had with your parents about how they've been concerned that she wasn't well enough to take care of Rachel."

"But, Michael." I heard my voice crack. "That makes it sound like he's been planning to do this all along."

"I asked him, and he said that keeping track of everything was his own way of dealing with it."

"Baloney," I said.

"Did Tina say she knew he'd divorce her?"

I explained that ten years ago, when Tina and I first discussed her difficulties, she had wanted to keep her situation to herself for as long as possible; she felt Marty would leave her if anything she did threatened to block the rise of his career.

"Anyway," Michael said, "apparently the doctors who treated Tina in Texas concurred that she wouldn't be stable enough to take care of a child on her own as an unmarried mother. Don't forget that episode when Marty was away and Tina stayed in bed and Rachel had nothing to eat for almost forty-eight hours."

"Jesus Christ," I fumed. "First the doctors encourage her to have a child. Now they say she can't take care of one. And Rachel had plenty to eat that time. Tina keeps the pantry stocked with Ritz crackers and all that cheese stuff you get in bottles. And canned fruit and bread and plenty of other things so a six-year-old girl won't go hungry."

"Susan," Michael said in a lofty tone. "If Tina couldn't make her own daughter dinner, that's clearly incompetence. And you know as well as I do that wasn't the first time it happened."

Michael's secretary said something over the intercom and he told her rather gruffly to hold the rest of his calls. I could feel the pressure mounting for him to attend to his own work. "Look, honey," he said, "it's probably best for you to, well . . . start accepting the fact that Marty will end up getting custody."

"I don't want to!"

"You think there's somebody else in his life?"

"Did he say there was?" I asked quickly.

"He would never admit to that. But I was just wondering."

Which, in turn, made me wonder about Michael.

"It's just my instinct," Michael went on. "Just before I called you I consulted Dorothy Maizel—you remember her from the picnic last summer. She works for the agency now, but she used to practice matrimonial law."

"What about the killer lawyer you mentioned?"

"Nah, I realized he wouldn't be right for this. Besides, there's got to be a lawyer hired from Texas. That's where they live. Anyway, Dorothy thinks it's going to be really hard for Tina to get custody."

I said nothing. I was furious.

"I know it's a hard lot to get all at once. That's why I wanted to wait until I got home. I canceled a late appointment so I could get home earlier."

His gesture set me off and I started crying. "Okay, what time will you be here?"

"I don't know, four, four-thirty. Five at the very latest. But don't hold me to it. You know how I get unexpectedly tied up. I'll call if anything changes. All right? I love you, Suki," Michael said.

Then things began to escalate. At three o'clock, Billy trudged into the house with a black eye. Butch Meebang, a bully two grades ahead of him, had picked a fight. As I examined the swelling, Billy told me the nurse at school had applied blue ice and had lent him some to use at home. He now dug into his satchel and handed me the ice pack, which had melted and felt like cold gelatin between my fingers. I told him to lie down on the living-room couch and went to get some more ice. Once Billy was resting with my ice pack, I asked him what had caused the fight.

Butch Meebang had run up at recess and accused Billy of pushing Mark Rosen into the lake. Billy screamed back that

Butch was a liar, but the bully kept insisting it was true and finally Billy started swinging. I had heard this much of the story when the phone rang. It was the principal of the elementary school, Dan O'Leary.

O'Leary picked up where Billy left off. A teacher had broken up the fight and hauled both children into the office. After questioning each boy and reassuring Billy in front of Butch Meebang that he had nothing to do with the drowning of Mark Rosen, Dan O'Leary phoned Meebang's parents and suspended the boy from school for two weeks. The punishment might have been even harsher, but O'Leary felt that the parents, who lived in a low-income housing project five miles away from our neighborhood, had fomented the rumor. He then explained to me that the drowning seemed to be affecting children at school. Discussions about dying had been overheard by the teachers in the playground during recess; several concerned parents had called to report that their children were having bad dreams and wandering into their bedrooms in the middle of the night to ask questions about Mark Rosen's death.

"I was going to suggest that you come to school tomorrow with Billy for a private conference."

"Oh?"

O'Leary hesitated. "I was going to give Billy a little more support. And then I was going to make a few recommendations."

"What sort of recommendations?"

"We have a therapist working for the school—"

"Look," I interrupted him. "I appreciate your concern. And I'd be glad to come in for a conference. But at this point . . ." I hesitated, thinking of Tina's predicament, and also not wanting Billy to know what was now being suggested. "I'd like to—he's right here," I clarified for O'Leary, "not get into that right now. It would only make everything more complicated."

"Then why don't you call me when you're alone, Mrs. Kaplan, and we'll discuss it further."

"Not that part," I said.

"Well, let me explain that the reason why we have a therapist here at school is to enable the children to explore their feelings with someone who is objective."

"Look, I understand. And I know you mean well. It's just not a good idea right now. Maybe in a few months. Maybe next fall."

I thanked O'Leary for defending Billy and got off the phone, feeling dazed.

From the couch, Billy had listened to my end of the conversation. When I returned to the living room, he was lying there quite still, holding the bag of ice over his swollen eye. He followed me with his good eye. Normally, a phone call from the principal would have driven him to distraction—to elementary school children a principal's phone call is like getting a call from God—but in this instance, Billy remained quiet. His spirits seemed to be completely vanquished.

I went and stood above him to repeat what Dan O'Leary had said about Butch Meebang.

"What did you say to him about 'a couple of months'?"

"He just wanted to know if you'd feel better talking about it with someone else besides us, someone else besides him?"

"Like who?"

"Oh . . ." I began stroking Billy's head. "Like another teacher from another grade. Mr. O'Leary thought if you talked to someone else you'd feel a little better about it." I paused, trying to bathe him with a reassuring smile before saying, "I told Mr. O'Leary I didn't think that was necessary."

Billy shrugged and rolled his head toward the sofa cushions. "What about the funeral?" he asked in a muffled voice.

"It happened already," I said.

"How come we didn't go?" he said, pivoting his head toward me again and fixing me with a doleful, one-eyed gaze.

"Because, Birdie," I said, thinking hard, "because . . . we don't know the Rosens very well. And funerals are usually for friends."

"But I was the last person to see him before he . . ." Billy stopped speaking.

"Honey," I said, sitting down next to him. "I had no idea you'd want to go to the funeral. I only thought going to the funeral would upset you. Funerals can be very disturbing, so disturbing, in fact, that often parents don't allow children to go to them."

"Well, maybe," Billy said in a croaky voice. "But I think I should've seen it."

"Then I'm sorry," I said.

He shrugged and looked away.

"Billy, I'm sorry about this whole strange week. And I'm sorry that you had to get into a fight. Your dad will be so proud that you stood up to Butch Meebang."

Billy smiled faintly at my last comment and then I suggested that perhaps he should go upstairs and continue to relax.

"Will you carry me?" he asked sheepishly.

"Sure."

I removed the ice pack from his swollen eye, which already was going down, and he raised his arms. I scooped one hand beneath his shoulder blades and grasped his upper arm; with the other hand I lifted his legs and held the crook of his knees in the crook of my arm. While I was lifting him, one of his arms got wedged between the rest of his body and my chest and he cried out, "Ouch. You're hurting."

"What, what am I hurting?" I asked, and noticed that he immediately stiffened. Something told me to put him back down on the couch and roll up his shirt sleeve. On his arm there was a network of red abrasions at least eight inches long. At first

I thought he had gotten them in the fight with Butch Meebang. But when I gently ran my finger along the scratches, which already had scabbed over, something dawned on me.

"Billy," I said, trying to collect my wits, which had just been scattered in many directions. "When did you get this?"

"In the fight," he said, looking away.

His behavior only reinforced my suspicions. I softened my voice. "Honey, did you get this yesterday?"

He lay there completely still. "I told you, I got it in the fight!"

I pressed him. "Did you get it . . . at Mrs. Rosen's house?"

He refused to answer.

In the midst of my sudden panic and rage I tried as hard as I could to think carefully about what to say next. "Did she say the same things to you that she said . . . in the dream?" I asked, giving him the benefit of the doubt.

Billy suddenly began crying. "I told you I had a bad dream."

I took his chin in my hands, tilting his head up until he was forced to look at me with eyes that had gone to slits and were pouring forth a gush of tears. "It's okay, honey," I said. "I know you may have dreamed it. But if this also happened yesterday, I need for you to tell me. Because if this happened, Mrs. Rosen has done a bad thing."

"You said it wasn't me who made him go in the water," Billy wailed.

"That's right, his going in the water had nothing to do with you."

"Then why did she tell me she never wanted to see me in the neighborhood?"

"She said that, did she?" I said coldly. "Well, I guess she said it because she's sad about what happened to Mark, and so she says things she would never say if she wasn't so sad."

"Like Aunt Tina?"

"Aunt Tina would never say anything like that to you!"

"Will Mrs. Rosen have to go in a hospital like Aunt Tina?"

"I doubt it. But I'll tell you one thing. I'm going upstairs to call your father. And when I'm through with your father, I'm going to call up Harriet Rosen."

And yet, as I sat there comforting Billy, my fears mounted. Was I so involved in shielding him that I had yet to learn something other people in the community already knew? Perhaps when she had revived him that first time, Mark had murmured something to his mother. Perhaps Harriet had confided whatever he had said to her close friends, who in turn confided in other people, which was how it seeped down to Butch Meebang.

Finally Billy stopped crying and then I left him lying on the couch and went upstairs to my bedroom in order to call Michael. Luckily, I was able to reach him. I explained what Harriet Rosen appeared to have said, and then told him about the fight and how the principal had defended Billy. He absolutely agreed that we should confront Harriet, but advised against doing it right away. They were still going through death ceremonies, sitting shiva, and he felt she'd be unable to respond to our complaint that she had maligned Billy. "She's probably so out of it on drugs she doesn't even realize what she said to him, let alone remember it."

"Look, Michael," I said. "I don't care if she's grief-stricken, I don't care if she's strung out. She yelled at Billy to leave the neighborhood!"

"You don't know for sure she said anything like that. After all, he's been going through a lot himself and could be exaggerating."

"He's not exaggerating."

Michael went on, amazingly composed, "Why don't you tell Billy you tried to call Harriet but were unable to get through. That they're sitting shiva and not taking phone calls."

"Michael," I yelped, "aren't you angry?"

"Of course I'm angry!"

"Well, you certainly don't sound it."

"I'm angry, but I don't want to lose control. If we lose control I think we'll be worse off in the end."

"But, Michael, don't you see, it's already out of control. Kids are blaming him at school."

"We don't know if Harriet had anything to do with that."

"Of course she did!"

"Susan, when things like this happen, rumors fly."

"Then we should put a stop to the rumors."

"Honey, why can't we discuss everything when I get home?"

"Why? You'll just talk me out of confronting her."

"Susan, promise me you'll wait until I get home."

"All right," I said reluctantly. "But hurry up and get here."

After I put down the phone, I was so agitated I felt I needed to get out of the house. I decided to take Billy shoe shopping in White Plains. In the car on the way to the store it suddenly occurred to me that for the last two days Billy and Peter Freed had not made an afternoon play date. I casually mentioned this, glancing over at Billy in the passenger seat and monitoring his response. "Oh, Peter, he's been going places with his mother," Billy said flatly.

I carefully phrased my next question. "You think you'll see him tomorrow?"

Billy threw me a woeful look, his wounded eye making his face look pitiful. "I don't know," he said. I angrily imagined that while Butch Meebang was picking on Billy, Peter Freed had watched without remorse and didn't have enough mettle, enough loyalty in his cold bones to stick up for his best friend. I almost asked where Peter had been during the incident, but thought better of it, afraid to hear the disappointing truth that Billy had been left to fend for himself.

We got back to the house at five-fifteen. Michael had not yet arrived. I called his office at five-thirty. The secretary said he had left for a meeting. He had said he was canceling that appointment, I informed her. She said she was uncertain what he was doing. I asked if perhaps he'd been planning to come straight home from this meeting. She thought he might return to the office before leaving for the day. Six o'clock passed. I called the agency again; by now the secretary had left and the switchboard informed me that Michael had a pile of phone messages. And that didn't make sense—Michael was compulsive about retrieving his phone messages.

The next hour between six and seven passed as though time had been caught in a traffic jam. My nerves slowly frayed down with expectancy. He should've been home by five at the latest, so where was he? He had promised to call. In light of these assurances his lateness struck me as particularly cavalier. I was so wound up, I could concentrate on little for very long and buzzed around the house, searching for ways to dispatch this period of insecurity. I dusted books, ventured outside into the humid oven of early evening and turned sprinklers on; watered my tree peonies, my early thatch of vegetables. I had a distracted conversation with my next-door neighbor—not Cass!—about tuberoses and a new fertilizer I'd been using. Seven o'clock finally rolled around.

Out there in the backyard, sweat pouring off me as I held my trowel and my weeding fork, I listened to the sounds of blenders, can openers, tinny transistor radios keeping the company of husbands ripping open bags of charcoal that rumbled forth and rang the barbecue grates. I was suddenly beset by a twisted fantasy that Michael had spent the rest of the afternoon in bed with another woman so as not to have to deal with the enormity of our problems. As each significant minute elapsed, I grew more convinced of this, and finally by eight o'clock I was irate. Three hours late, I kept raging to Mercedes, who was unable to fathom why I had grown so agitated. After all this time, she said, I should be used to Michael arriving home much later than he was expected. "But this time he promised to be home," I explained. "He knows what's going on."

"Maybe his meeting last too long," Mercedes suggested.

"Then he should've called."

How could I tell her that my worst fears were about to be played out: that after breaking his promise to be home, Michael would walk in the door and announce that he was leaving me? And, of course, for a younger woman with a body uncompromised by having borne a child, a woman who enabled him to make a complete transfer of affection, so that toward me he was already feeling hollow.

In an effort to compose myself, I went and sat down on the living-room sofa, where, a few hours earlier, Billy had lain with an ice pack, and took deep breaths. I started looking around at the artwork we had collected: a watercolor painting of a California marsh; a six-foot seascape in oils that Michael and I had loved at first sight; twelve-inch-high sculptures of athletes Michael had bought and for which I—reluctantly, since I didn't much care for them—had had the niches in the wall made and installed ceiling lighting that illuminated them from above. On the coffee table was a pewter-framed picture of us on our wedding day, a black-and-white photograph of Michael when he first got out of college and a purple agate crystal that caught the low-slanting sunlight infiltrating the room and incandesced. What was happening to me? I hid my face in my hands, once again trying to quiet my nerves, when suddenly, in my head, I began hearing the words "Get out of my neighborhood!" "You don't belong here!" "You pushed Mark in the lake." The last accusation, which Billy had heard at school, seemed to follow in the progression of commands.

I went upstairs to check on Billy. He was kneeling on the hardwood floor, drawing a picture with crayons. He was so intent on his creation, he didn't hear me enter the room. Glancing over his shoulder, I saw that he had drawn a crude circle and colored it lightly in red. Outside the circle were a few geometric shapes that to me looked like houses. Within the circle were small green and yellow dots surrounding a black stick figure turned upside down. Closer to but well within the border of the circle was another stick figure, right side up, and between the two figures Billy had etched a bold line. I gently touched his shoulder and he sat up quickly, startled, and covered the picture with his hands.

"What's the drawing, honey?" I asked.

He glanced back at me drearily and said, "Nothing."

"What's this?" I said, gently prying his hands away from his depiction and pointing to the line drawn between the upside-down figure and the upright one.

"That's me, me saving Mark," Billy said, looking at his creation from different angles.

I gently put my hands on Billy's shoulders. "It was impossible to save him," I said.

"No, I could've," he said softly. "I know how to swim."

"Not well enough."

"Do so."

I rotated his shoulders and made him face me. "Billy, listen to me. If you had stepped one foot in that lake you would have been disobeying my rule. You did exactly what you should have done. You told his mother."

"She doesn't think so."

"Well, we'll soon set her straight."

For the drawing had banished any doubts I had about my instincts and clarified my purpose. I stood up, opening Billy's closet, and selected a clean white dress shirt, the sort he'd wear to religious services for the high holidays. Holding it, I said, "I want you to put this on."

He looked at me and asked why.

"We're going out."

"Where we going?"

"Just get dressed," I said.

We said nothing during the drive, just as we had said nothing several days before when we drove to the Freeds' after Norma's phone call. In comparison with that late afternoon stillness, when the tract residences, in the blaze of sunlight, looked gloomy and uninhabited, now, in the dimmer band of early evening, the neighborhood brimmed with all sorts of activity. Wives stood outside watering, husbands in cutoff tee shirts methodically Simonized cars, children dressed in bright colors turned cartwheels and played "horsy jump" with yard rakes laid between folding chairs. Cookout smoke rose and fed a blue miasma above the treetops. My hands shook on the steering wheel and I could feel sweat soaking my underarms. I realized I never should have agreed to move to the suburbs. During the last five years, Michael had been around a lot less than when we lived on Seventy-third Street. So many times he would leave his office and not arrive home until hours later, and although it was only a forty-five-minute train ride to and from the city, he would say nothing to account for his delay. Something seemed to get lost in translation and Manhattan felt hundreds of miles away.

Three cars were parked in the Rosens' driveway and several more were lined up on the street in front of the house. In comparison with the other homes on the block, the Rosens' gave no signal of life except for a wan flickering against the darkened bay window of the living room. I decided to park down the street, to be less conspicuous than those who had come to pay condolences.

Suddenly realizing where we were headed, Billy said, "Mom, I don't want to go in there. She's just going to tell me to go away."

"She's not going to tell you to go away." I was emphatic.

"She's going to apologize to you. She's going to apologize to both of us." Reacting to my intensity, Billy fell silent.

He got out on his side of the car. I hurried around and grabbed his hand and we began walking toward the Rosens'. The air outside was just beginning to cool, filled with the reek of fire starter and watered-down asphalt. We passed the Freeds' house, and Billy looked toward it, searching for signs of activity, searching for signs of his best friend, Peter. His hand tightened around mine as, I imagine, a feeling of disillusionment began circulating through him. As we veered off the street into the Rosens' driveway, both of us, hearkening to the same instinct, turned to look across the street at the lake, which was gently rippling, the water a pale amber in the shaded light.

Just before we rang the doorbell an anxiety detonated in my stomach and spread outward like a fluey feeling. For a moment I doubted myself and wondered if I should have heeded Michael's advice and waited a few more days before speaking to Harriet. But then I remembered that Michael had broken his promise to be home early. I remembered my suspicions. And I grew calm in my purpose.

A woman I didn't recognize answered the door and, assuming that we were calling with our condolences, ushered us into the house. Various knots of people stood in the foyer beyond the grimly lighted entryway and it was difficult to judge where to walk. A normal house would have smelled like a mixture of laundry soap and cooking and burning wood, but the Rosens' smelled like a blend of expensive perfumes and tallow and the various fragrances of flowers. "They're in the living room."

As we slipped through the house, I kept my eyes on the hemline of the dress of the woman who led us. Indistinct rooms peeled off on either side of us, so that where we walked seemed like a pathway. Peripherally I was able to recognize neighborhood mothers, several of whom flinched in shock to see us. There were stands of gladiolus everywhere, baskets of fruit cov-

ered with emerald cellophane, trays of candied almonds. When
we finally reached the living room, the cluster of people gathering there suddenly parted. I could feel my heart throbbing. The
blitz of my nerves made it difficult to judge, but it seemed to me
that we were expected, that they knew we were coming all
along.

Yahrzeit candles in clear glasses were burning everywhere in
the room and their watery light made a collective halo around a
half dozen low rectangular wooden stools on which men and
women sat. From somewhere off in the house came an infant's
muffled wailing, which had to be from Mark's baby sister. I
recognized the ashen narrow face of Harriet, who sat hunched
over on her stool. Cloaked in black, she was holding hands with
a pregnant woman who wore a shapeless sundress. When Harriet
caught sight of us, her face first looked vaguely puzzled and
then colored deeply as she realized that we had dared to violate
the shell of her mourning. She keeled back on her stool and said
in a gravelly voice, "Go get my husband." Naturally, the
woman glanced at us, mother and child, who must've appeared
rather harmless, incapable of inspiring such alarm. "Just get
him!" Harriet repeated.

That she so objected to our being there proved beyond a
doubt that she had said what Billy claimed she had said.

The other shiva sitters turned to her. They were obviously
family members who didn't recognize us. "What's wrong, Harriet? What is it? Is it . . . are you feeling all right?" They
regarded us with the baffled weariness of those who are already
shouldering the burden of grief and who are now asked to deal
with something else equally weighty, equally distressing. In the
strange unreality of being there, I knew I should say what I had
come to say before Larry entered the room. For I felt he would
remove us, physically, if we refused to be removed, and if I
hadn't spoken by then my chance to confront Harriet would be
forfeited.

"We're suffering also," I told her. "So why are you involving us? It had nothing to do with us."

Her eyelids quivered, shut for an instant and then popped open. Her eyes were glossed with disbelief.

"What?" she muttered. "I never said—"

"You chased him off your property. You told him to get out of the neighborhood. That's as much as accusing him. And he's allowed to go anywhere he wants. I think you should apologize for what you said."

"You get out of here. My house! Go back to yours, now!" Harriet growled. "You don't belong."

Belong to what? I wondered as I recoiled. To the ritual of death, to the shelter of her home, to the ranks of mothers grieving?

"She's the mother and that's the other kid!" an elderly man piped in. Billy, who thus far had been standing there in a daze, grit his teeth.

Another man came up from behind and grabbed me by the arm. "You're not wanted at this gathering!" he said venomously, his breath smelling of alcohol and garlic. "This is for mourners."

"Shut up, you," Billy told him.

By now I was shaking all over. "But we *are* mourners," I objected.

The electric lights in the room were suddenly switched on and people shrank from the brightness, as though afflicted by it. There stood Larry Rosen, a tall strapping man with a head of prematurely silver hair. When he saw Billy and me, his face contorted in fury. "You. What are you . . . ?" he sputtered. "Who let you in?" he cried out in a voice of such resounding pain that I nearly apologized for our unannounced presence. For I knew at once he had no idea what his wife had said to Billy.

"She blamed my son. Yesterday," I tried to explain. "Outside in the garden. He was chasing a ball."

Larry frowned at Harriet, who now began to scream. Women

huddled around her, as though she needed to be guarded from us. Then Larry turned to me, his eyes registering the conflict. "Mrs. Kaplan, I'm asking you to leave."

And so I led Billy through the gathering of mourners toward the door. I had come there full of purpose, wielding my indignation like a knife cutting at a tumor of false blame. Now I was leaving. I felt vindicated, but vacant in my heart and even somewhat remorseful. I turned around and found Larry staring after us. "I came here . . ." I faltered. "I came here only to ask her to stop blaming him."

MICHAEL

⊙

T H E N I G H T Susan went to the Rosens', the night
I came home a lot later than I promised, she could smell
it on me just like I could smell other men in the house the
afternoon Mark Rosen drowned. I had taken a shower at Sondra's and borrowed her pine bath gel. If I'd been smart I
would've taken the time to go to the corner drugstore and buy
the Lifebuoy soap we used at home. But I didn't bother doing
that. Knowing I was already two hours late, I was reluctant to
be fifteen minutes later. And yet I had to ask myself why I felt
compelled to stop at Sondra's instead of going directly home as I
had promised. I guess part of me was averse to returning home,

where Susan was at the height of her preoccupation with the drowning.

She had listened for my car in order to be waiting for me when I came through the door. She knew the sound of the El Dorado's engine, knew the quiet purr of Cadillac pistons. She and Billy stood in the same spot of the darkened foyer where they had stood several days before to broach the news of the drowning, to explain the arrival of the reporters and the police. In the uncertain light, holding Billy's hand, Susan peered at me with a haggard confusion. Billy was glancing back and forth between us, and when I bent down to kiss him, I noticed his swollen eye.

"What happened to you, Birdie?" I said.

He glanced at his mother. "I got into a fight with Butch Meebang."

"Did he pick on you?"

Billy nodded.

I straightened up again and looked at Susan. "What happened . . . why—"

"Where have you been?" Her voice lingered over the words like a caress; I had expected her to be more strident and demanding.

"I got tied up at an appointment," I said, stowing my briefcase.

Susan and Billy were standing next to a mirror with a mahogany frame that was hanging above a matching rectangular table. On the table stood a raku vase with sprays of indigo delphinium, freshly clipped from the garden. In the mirror I could spy the far side of Susan's face, glistening with tears. I looked down at my feet, and felt weakened by my intention of lying, like a tree drawing acid up its roots and slowly withering.

"Your secretary didn't seem to know where you were," she said.

"She doesn't always know where I am."

"She always knows where you are unless you're out somewhere you shouldn't be and I wouldn't be surprised if she knew that too."

"What's wrong with you tonight?"

Angry now, her eyes bored into me. "How long has it been going on?"

I glanced at Billy, who I hoped wasn't following the gist of the conversation, and then peered contemptuously at Susan, who shouldn't have been carrying on like this in front of him. In response to my silent objection, she now summoned Mercedes, who promptly ushered Billy out of the room.

"Nothing's going on," I said once he was out of earshot.

She gravitated forward and smelled me at the neck, precisely at the place where Sondra sucked on me when I was taking her. Susan's breath caught sharply. I flushed in mortification and shut my eyes. "I figured . . ." she hissed, recoiling, barely managing to utter the words. "You don't smell like you did when you left this morning."

"I passed Bloomingdale's. I got spritzed. Inadvertently."

Susan returned to where she and Billy had been standing. "Look me in the eyes," she said. "Look me in the eyes and say you weren't out making love to somebody else."

"I was at appointments. I told you."

"You're lying through your teeth."

Then she quietly told me about finding Billy's drawing and how they had visited the Rosens, made a beeline through the house, parting the swarm of mourners, and found Harriet sitting shiva. She explained what she had said to Harriet, how Harriet had acted as though she'd been accused of something she had never uttered. Then I lost my temper and started screaming. "What are you, nuts? I told you not to go over there! Thanks a lot. Now you really screwed us up with them!" But losing my temper was my desperate way of deflecting Susan from my own far worse transgression. She sensed this immediately and was hardly intimidated. Trembling with her own anger, she glowered at me and refused to engage.

Later on, I often found myself wondering whether if each of us hadn't acted indecorously that day, things might not have disintegrated so quickly. If Susan had waited for me and not gone to the Rosens', I would have profusely apologized and promised never to see Sondra again. And if I didn't have to admit to philandering, Susan might have immediately conceded to me that she was overwrought and had done the wrong thing by taking Billy over to the Rosens' and demanding concessions from them when it was quite obvious in their state of grieving that they'd be unable to give her what she wanted.

Susan stormed out of the room, and feeling demoralized, I wandered outside to calm myself down. I stood in the darkness of the backyard, listening to the crickets crooning in a thunderous quiet, hating the country for what it had brought me to. By contrast to this annoying tranquillity, my affair and what Susan had done down the street—not to mention Mark Rosen's drowning—all seemed so much more significant here in the suburbs than if they had occurred in the city and Mark had, for example, drowned in the Central Park pond. There were hundreds of such tragedies every day in Manhattan, thousands of betrayals, all of it set against a backdrop of violence and tension. However, as I looked over at the houses of the neighbors, glowing orange with electric lights and peaceful with husbands, wives and children crisscrossing in the carefully executed choreography of suburbia, our misfortunes were magnified by the fact that nothing of much urgency seemed to be going on within a several-mile radius. I was probably the only man in these deceptively well-populated areas who was standing outside looking up at his bedroom window in complete distress, watching for traces of the wife's shadow darting back and forth, listening to the sound of drawers slamming, gushes of water hitting the porcelain sinks, toilets flushing, the medicine cabinet scraping open and scraping shut, knowing she was packing me an overnight bag, that she was in the process of kicking me out.

It amazed me that after all she had been through that day Susan still had the moxie to take a stand and expel me. I figured she would've collapsed in my arms and asked for my immediate support, momentarily overlooking the fact that I had slept with another woman, just so she could lean on me. But no, she was proving capable of withstanding the trying circumstances. I could already imagine, although I was the husband and men typically were able to survive a marriage's faltering better than their wives, who had fewer opportunities for work, for meeting new people, that it was I who might be the first to go under.

And then the screen door opened and she came outside. She had changed into a long-sleeved cotton shirt of pale turquoise that made her skin gleam in the dusk. There was something lustrous at her throat, a strand of pearls that I had given her when we first met. Ten years was a long time. Had she just put them on to mock me with a vivid telltale of our history, or had she been wearing them before she changed and I just hadn't noticed? Susan had a wide handsome face, passionate russet eyes. People always said we were a wonderful contrast, she in her tawniness of skin and hair and I with my black curls and blue eyes.

"I packed you this," she said, holding out the torn leather overnight bag I'd kept since college, once a trusted companion that now was helping her to deny me. "I don't want you to stay here tonight."

I apologized for what I had done. I tried to hug her, but she backed up and told me to keep away. "I want you to go. I don't want to be with you tonight."

"I'll sleep in the den," I said quietly.

"No. I don't want to see you here in the morning. Please go. We'll talk about what you're going to do tomorrow night, tomorrow."

"It's my house too," I complained; I was even tempted to mention I paid for it as well, but I knew that would be the worst possible thing to say.

"Michael, if you don't leave, then I will."

"What would you tell Billy if you left?" I challenged her.

She smiled in agitation. "I'd leave that up to you. You're his father. You're as responsible as I am for what's going on." She glanced away. "The problem is, you forget that."

I noticed that as the conversation had progressed, her posture had grown straighter. Forcing me out was obviously difficult for her, and yet I had a sense that the more we argued and the more I tried to pry her away from what she had already decided, the more Susan would grow determined to resist me. "Look, I'm not the only one who's done something wrong," I said.

Grimacing, she swiped her hand over her face and peered out toward the dark abyss of our backyard. "I'm not saying I haven't done anything wrong. But you've been with somebody else. Tonight of all nights. Tonight when I needed you here, when I needed you more than any other night."

"All right. I know," I said, "and saying I'm sorry probably sounds insulting, but I *am* sorry." I crept forward until I stood a foot away from her. I tried to kiss her, but she flinched away. It amazed me that just twelve hours ago as I was dressing to go to work, she had been so loving, almost seemed reluctant to see me depart. This revulsion was the flip side of that seeming fathomless devotion. Once again I asked to be forgiven and once again she insisted I leave.

That night I never did go anywhere to sleep. For a while I drove aimlessly through the neighborhood, watching the homes grow dark like cinders turning to ash, so that by eleven nearly every residence had perished—it really was a bedroom community. I drove to the lake, left the car idling and kept peering back and forth between the Rosens' house and the bank of the moonlit water, studying the night landscape for signs of the

treachery it had so obviously inspired. But the lake looked as
gentle as a puddle; weeping willows, backlighted by the moon,
cast frosty shadows on its silvered plane. The surrounding banks
were sonorous with choruses of insects. Summer was always
supposed to be a time of exultation, a time people looked forward to. I realized that I hated summer. For one thing, both my
parents died during the summer, each a year apart, my father
from emphysema and my mother brokenhearted from losing
him at the age of fifty-nine. It amazed me that this little spot of
turf, two lawns separated by a quiet street, had set the stage for a
fatal combination of several different events. An irresponsible
nurse had taken a catnap, a child had wandered away and
drowned, another child was being traumatized by the first
child's death. And out of all this had flourished my compulsion
to take a two-hour sexual vacation from my wife that from the
start was doomed to discovery.

A half hour slipped by, and suddenly all the houses on the
street had gone black—except the Rosens', where one light on
the second level was burning. The shiva show was over, I
thought, and they were finally alone with their grief. Up there I
spied flitting shadows that reminded me of the shadow dancing
that had gone on in my own bedroom just a while ago when
Susan was packing me a "get lost" toiletry bag. What were they
saying to one another? By now, certainly, they'd discussed
Susan's violent arrival and had come to some opinion regarding
it. Did Harriet really chase Billy out of the neighborhood like
that? Could she actually be shunting her grief onto a seven-year-
old boy?

I quit Lake Drive for a bar in the heart of town that was
filled with blue-collar workers who gawked at me in my business suit. Few of the other husbands I knew who commuted to
Manhattan would venture out to a local bar during the week.
Could men like me who thought of themselves as rising through
their careers, mortgaging themselves to the hilt in their middle

to late thirties, be more tethered to their wives and children? Usually, once I came home from the city I never considered going out again and Susan wouldn't hear of it. And yet obviously the wives of these men at the bar did not require their husbands to remain at home on weeknights—the molecular structure of their marriages must be fundamentally different.

Oh God, I thought to myself, Susan was only a few miles away and she didn't want me. That was inconceivable.

Here I was caught in the act and having the nerve to feel cheated. And so, to dull the swirl of pain and loneliness, I drank one beer after another. I felt better for a while, detached, heedless. However, the glow of nonchalance eventually grew dull; then I felt a shift and the alcohol failed me. I began to see myself stripped of everything—wife, child, house—and having only my job to fall back on. The fantasy of that loss grew so tangible that I thought somehow I had to dispel it or else it would actually come to pass. So I left the bar, roamed through the deserted streets of the town until I came to an all-night diner. It was just going on 2 A.M.—I realized I'd had nothing to eat since my luncheon appointment. I sat down at a window booth. I ordered scrambled eggs and hash browns. I bolted them when they came and then sadly realized that sating my hunger had no relation to sating my despair.

I finally decided to try to distract myself by working and got a movie contract out of my briefcase. For the rest of the night I nursed coffee from a white mug that seemed to have suffered through the dishwasher ten thousand times, tumbled against so many other cups until it was paved with chips of wear and tear. And as I worked, I often glanced out the window, expecting her to drive up and tell me it was all over and that I could come back home and sleep in my own bed.

I sat working in the diner until six in the morning, when I left for the train station and waited for an early commuter to New York. The sky was cloudless, a soft and warm wind hoisted a smell of fresh earth and heady blossoms from the gardens of suburbia. Summer's here: barbecues; dinners outdoors at the red-wood picnic table; beers in plastic coolers lodged in ice cascades that slowly thawed until the cans submerged in water were as cold as mountain streams; fresh fruit sliced and blended into mash and mixed with Caribbean rum that dulled the coiling worries of the office and made threshing voices in my head: "So what? It's summer. Tonight Susan and I will sleep with the windows open and the night air will rake over our bodies and I'll get hard and stay hard until she climbs on top of me."

I got to the office unshaven, wearing the now rumpled suit I had worn the day before. I might as well have been naked; anyone could see that I was in a crisis. One of my associates corralled me near the copier machine and discreetly palmed me the keys to his apartment, which he suggested I use to shower and shave away my conspicuous state. Susan had packed a fresh shirt, a toothbrush, toothpaste, razor and shaving cream, but had forgotten a clean pair of underwear. I left the office and wandered around until I spotted a Gap clothing store. Once inside I found myself vacillating over whether or not to buy a ten-pack of briefs in a place whose fluorescent lighting only increased my indecision. I finally left the store with the idea that I'd chuck away my dirty boxers and go around without underwear for the rest of the day.

Of course, after taking a shower, which overstimulated me, I was unable to work when I returned to the office. I was completely distracted, feeling lethargic and desperate at the same time. I tried calling Susan, but got no answer. I had my secretary call each of my appointments to say that I had fallen ill. I called Sondra and canceled lunch. Sondra was an ex-model who was now vying for acting jobs, a willowy woman with unruly black hair and waxen skin. She asked if the change of plans had anything to do with Susan. Normally I would have lied and said it was work—a man's work could shield him from just about anything—but today I couldn't bring myself to cover my tracks. Sondra hung up on me. As if she didn't think wives could or should be obstacles to love affairs. I weakly reflected that Sondra, who belonged to various political organizations that extolled women's rights, had on more than one occasion asked if I'd ever consider leaving Susan. Bear in mind that Sondra and I had never declared undying devotion to one another and hardly spent every free moment together. And yet on two occasions—once over dinner and once after we made rousing love—she had suggested that I leave Susan. And each time, I was so taken aback by her audacity I could say little in response. I was amazed that she was so willing to usurp Susan, not even considering what destruction leaving her and Billy might wreak. Were women so used to being thwarted by men that they, despite their own highly socialized compassion for one another, developed a calculating survivalist side of themselves?

I left the office and headed for Central Park. I walked to the middle of a green field, loosened my tie, spread my suit jacket like a blanket, lay down and fell asleep. When I woke up my face was sunburned and I smelled a fresh pile of dog crap not three feet from my head. The nerve of people, I thought, to let dogs shit near sleeping pedestrians. Then I grew aware of a slackness around my rear end and realized that my wallet was not where it should be. I slapped the other pockets of my pants, thinking perhaps I had put it somewhere else. Then I patted the breast pocket of my suit. Nothing. My wallet had obviously been pinched while I was asleep. The sun had left a blotting headache that centered at my forehead, and through the pain I slowly tallied up what had been in my billfold: no credit cards, just a driver's license and two hundred dollars. Then I fell back on the grass, which had taken an impression of my body and was moist with my sweat. I hardly cared about losing the wallet.

When I got back to the office just before five there was a message from Susan. She had called me. She had called to summon me home! When I phoned back, though, Mercedes answered. Susan no longer was there. Mercedes said she'd be home soon, however. I imagined that Susan had discussed the whole situation with our housekeeper. Susan was compelled in that way; when something happened to her she had to talk to someone, no matter whom. So I waited. An hour passed as slowly as I could ever remember an hour passing. I worked on more contracts, returned phone calls; still it was the slowest arc of my life. Between five and six in the summer, the light hardly diminishes in intensity, the way it does in winter when you have the strong sense of night emerging. I suddenly longed for that quick passage of afternoon into evening that occurs in colder months, longed for the visible changes of passing time; it really did seem to stand still. I reflected on so much during that insecure hour. I thought about death and how death at some point has to intervene in the life of every living thing. Living forever would render the sense of time useless and obsolete and greatly reduce the importance of its passing, which, after all, was how time defined itself. So, if everyone dies at some point, then from that overview death at the age of two or fifty-five is relative.

The intercom startled me as much as if it had been a shotgun blasting from inside my desk drawers. My secretary said it was Susan.

"Look, Michael, you can come back home. There'll be dinner for you."

Her words instantly brought tears to my eyes, and as I struggled to speak in a steady voice, the tears dropped onto my ink blotter and were drunk up by the contracts. "I'm sorry, honey," I finally said in a gulp. "I hope you can forgive me."

She had no intention of discussing forgiveness; she wanted to talk about other things, about how we could unload some of the burden from Billy. I told her I'd be willing to do whatever I could.

"You might not be so willing when you hear."

"Try me."

"I'd like you to call Larry Rosen."

"For what?"

"I want you to tell him how damaging this has been for Billy, and how if Harriet could just bring herself to say something to make Billy feel better, it would make all the difference in the world."

I was silent for a moment. As they dried, the tear spots waffled the typed pages. The fear of losing my wife and son had vanished as quickly as it had plagued me, and now my mind clicked into gear, surging ahead, trying like an amoeba to encompass and contain the enormous problem that was threatening to annihilate us. Yes, life went on, I thought. Out over the city the sunlight was showing its softer side, the dimming had begun. It was time to begin scheming for relief.

"We have to be careful to take the right approach," I said.

"I know," Susan said in a surprisingly docile voice. I wondered if spending an evening alone had taken its toll on her as well. "And I know what I said is only going to make it harder to get Harriet to cooperate."

"Let me ask you something," I began. "You think Billy is hanging on whether or not she'll apologize to him for what she said?"

"Absolutely. He's already mentioned it. He's already accused me of breaking my promise that she would. He told me that I've never broken my promise before."

Her voice was wound tightly with the strain of the situation. Nothing yet had been mentioned about my coming home preposterously late the previous evening and how betrayed she had felt.

"Susan," I said after a short silence. "Let's be honest with one another. Anyway, let's try to be."

"Okay," she said quickly.

"What if Harriet holds Billy partly guilty for what happened?"

"How could she?"

"You tell me. You saw her reaction when you went over there. I didn't."

"But I went at the wrong moment. I mean, you were the one who said if I'd waited—"

"Yes," I interrupted her. "I did say that. But I'm not sure that if you'd waited another week she would have said what you wanted to hear. I mean, this is her state of mind right now. If she unloads on anybody but herself or that nurse, it's probably because she's unable to admit the truth. I don't know if that's going to change any time soon." There was the word "time" again. Time passing. The longer it took Harriet to come to her senses, the worse Billy would feel. "Susan," I said, "realistically, if we let up for right now and at some point in the future just ask her to be a bit more civil to him, I think we'll be taking the right approach."

I heard some banging in the background, probably Mercedes clumsily handling cooking pots, sounds which might have annoyed me on other occasions but which now were like wind chimes to my ears because Susan had said it was all right to come home.

"Okay," Susan finally agreed. "We'll wait. However, I do think when it comes time to talk to them you should talk to Larry and not Harriet."

"That seems prudent."

A short perturbed gap in the conversation followed and then Susan said, "Well, I guess that's it for now. I guess I'll see you later." She didn't even ask me at what time I'd be home. Either she didn't really care or else she figured I'd probably grab the next train.

"Aren't you curious about where I stayed last night?" I felt compelled to ask.

"I figured you stayed with her."

"Come on, Susan, you think I'm stupid?"

"I think you're stupid for bringing it up at all."

"Well, I thought you might wonder how I made it through the night."

"There's something called a hotel, Michael. It was invented for people who either need to hide something or else have no place to go."

"I spent the night in the diner working on contracts."

"Are you looking for sympathy?" she asked quietly.

"No."

"Let me set the record straight," she said. "The only reason I'm talking to you right now is because of Billy. Who has gone through enough and now doesn't have to see his parents estranged."

"Okay," I said, defeated for the moment.

"And just so you know, I told Billy we had a fight about my going to the Rosens', that you wanted me to wait because they were too upset and that I didn't want to wait and that you were right. I apologized for taking him there. And I told him you had promised to be home at a certain time and you were much later than you promised and I asked you to leave because we yelled at each other, and that I was angry at you for coming home so late. I explained to him that this sort of thing happens between parents sometimes. I told him you'd be talking to the Rosens yourself. I told him you'd straighten things out."

"So you made yourself out to be more the wrongdoer."

"Do you think we should tell him the real truth, Michael?"

I glanced over at my message light, which was blinking six times rapidly in succession. Six calls had come in since I had picked up the phone, six calls that needed to be returned.

"No," I said. "You're right. We shouldn't tell him anything more for now."

Once I dreamed I had a chance to rescue you. You were still struggling as I swam out to where you were and you cleaved to me. Keeping your head above the water, I was able to tow you ashore. I climbed out first, put my hands beneath your armpits and dragged you onto the grassy bank. Your eyes were open, you were smiling and I was so happy I'd saved you. But then your face clouded over and blood began gushing from your neck. I made two fists and drove them against the pulse, which kept spurting, even faster than before. I couldn't believe your heart would betray you this way.

W H E N I came back the night after Susan discovered my betrayal, the house felt tense and unfamiliar. No one appeared to be at home at first, and as I stood alone in the front foyer, holding my offering of Sterling roses, I imagined that nerves of hostility had spread outward from the marrow of the banisters and furniture and window shades and that my touching anything around me might edge a scream. I yelled "Hello! Hello!" until, finally, Billy appeared. There was a large welt at his neck, an insect bite, which he had scratched into further irritation. While he hugged me I inspected it and told him something antiseptic should be applied. Shrugging off my advice, he looked up at me innocently and asked, "Who are the flowers for?"

"Your mother."

His expression elaborated into skepticism.

"Then did you make up?"

"I hope we did."

"I don't like it when you fight."

"Neither do I. But people who love each other fight," I explained. "That's the way of things. Now, where's your mother?"

"She's upstairs. Setting her hair or something."

"Here I am," Susan said.

I gazed up to where she stood on the second-floor landing. She was wearing a white sleeveless blouse, her hands rubbing her upper arms, as though an unseasonal chill had suddenly trespassed through the house. She slowly descended the stairs and approached me with averted eyes. She offered her cheek for one chaste kiss, then relieved me of my briefcase. These gestures, I felt, had been designed to show Billy we were no longer at odds. For I could feel her cowering inside herself, shrinking from me in fury that I had shared my body with someone else, and if that wasn't enough, shared it at such a crucial time, when she needed my support and didn't have it. "You want your usual red label and soda?" Susan asked as she left the foyer and clicked forth in high-heeled sandals across the brown linoleum of the den to the bar.

"Fine."

"Your dinner is on the warmer in the dining room."

"You've already eaten?" I asked, surprised.

"We ate early," she said, grabbing cubes from the ice bucket with silver tongs and plopping them in a cocktail glass.

"Why didn't you wait for me?"

"Billy was hungry." She flooded the ice with scotch, returned to the foyer with the glass, swirled it once, handed it to me and then went to put my dinner on the table.

I turned to Billy. "Want to come sit with me while I eat?"

He shrugged. "I've got to finish my poster for school."

"What poster?"

"A poster for safety. There's a contest in first and second grade. The best posters get put up in the library."

"You need help?" I asked him eagerly.

"Oh." Billy's face was written in longing, which I took to mean that my help was what he most desired, but then he said, "Mom's already helping me," and reluctantly he began to climb the short flight of stairs between the foyer level and the living room–kitchen level. I followed him, and when he was veering off to take the longer flight of stairs up to his bedroom, I rubbed his hair.

"Ah, come on and sit with me for a while."

"All right," he said, smiling, and scampered off ahead of me into the dining room, flopping down in the chair next to mine. Now, for some reason, the idea of him watching me eat made me nervous.

Lamb chops, a baked potato and asparagus were arranged on a plate, lying on the dinner warmer that was covered by a huge plastic bubble that reminded me of an incubator. It distressed me to see my dinner, long ago cooked, set out to keep warm like that. Susan appeared in the dining room. Registering the fact that Billy was keeping me company, she smiled briefly as she lifted the glass bubble and with a pair of polka-dotted pot holders lifted the plate and put it on a place mat on the dining-room table. I sat down. "I've got some things to do upstairs, if you don't mind," she said.

I shrugged. Billy and I watched her leave the room. Her sandals clicking against her heels sounded like a metronome. "No, no, no," I imagined them saying.

I turned to him. "Your mom is a little sad right now."

"I know."

"Fights make people feel badly."

He shrugged. "Okay."

"It passes, though." For a moment I listened to the cumbersome silence in the house. "Everything passes, eventually."

At this, Billy looked puzzled and began searching the irregular mahogany whorls in the dining-room table, as though they were hieroglyphs of the untold truth. "Not when people die," he said.

"You thinking about that?"

He shook his head slowly; it was obvious that his thoughts were circling like a hawk searching for a place to nest. "You know," I said, slicing some lamb away from the bone, "sometimes it helps to think a lot about things."

He looked up at me gravely and said, "Dad, will you help me with the poster?"

I allowed the conversation to be changed. "I thought your mom was helping you."

"I know, but I'd rather you helped. You can draw better than she can."

"You're the one who's supposed to draw," I pointed out.

"Everybody cheats and has their parents draw for them."

"Okay, then, I guess we should keep up with the cheaters."

Billy grinned.

And then something inside me constricted: what would I ever do if something happened to him? I'd be completely thrown off. I had to strike a balance, detach a little bit so this would never happen. Feeling guilty about these feelings, I forced myself to ask, "You still love your old dad?"

"Yeah," Billy said enthusiastically.

"Good," I said. "I love you too."

After I finished eating, we went upstairs and worked on Billy's poster until he got bored, and then we arm-wrestled until it was his bedtime. Billy was delighted by all the extra attention.

As I was tucking him into bed, he tried to prolong my visit by coaxing me to tell him once again about the time I had met some astronauts.

The brass lamp on my end table threw off the only light in the bedroom. Susan already had slipped under the covers and raked her body to the very perimeter of the mattress. Facing away, she lay on her side like an inverted comma—an inch farther and she would have thumped to the carpeting—and actually stiffened up when I climbed in next to her. I stroked her spine. "You sleeping?" I asked.

"Sort of."

"Will you talk to me?"

"I don't want to."

"Ah, Suki, come on, let's not have a stalemate. Let's try to get through this together."

She said nothing for a moment and then her whole body started to tremble as she began sobbing. I inched toward the warmth of her. "Don't," she said. "Please just let me alone for right now. I'm too hurting."

She was similarly distant the next morning, and the following evening, when I arrived home early at six o'clock, she maintained the same formal attitude of the previous day. She fixed me a drink, had dinner waiting for me on the bubble warmer and once again took her coma position at bedtime. And as I looked at her mummified in sheets, I sadly recalled how she once yearned for me to come home as soon as possible. But now that I was coming home early, albeit in shame, she didn't want me. Then came a several-day stretch when I was obliged to work late and take my evening meal at the office. Nevertheless, I made a point of letting Susan know on what matters I had worked and for how long, and which train I took home, leaving my business diary out on the night table in case she wanted to see written proof of my hours—lest she think that I was spending time elsewhere.

"It's so funny that you're doing this now, when you never used to do it," she said sadly one morning, facing away from me as she got out of bed.

"That's because I'm trying to be better."

She crinkled her long lovely fingers and rubbed sleep from her eyes. "Guilty behavior."

"All right. So?"

"Right now, Michael, I just want us to be quiet, not to argue, to come and go without incident," she said, looking at me sideways through half-somnambulant eyes. I looked at the slope of her back revealed by the plunge of her satin nightgown. That momentary gleam of private skin taunted me to touch her. But she never came close enough and I never got a chance, except, of course, when she gave me the obligatory kiss hello or goodbye.

At this point I would have done anything to secure Susan's forgiveness and I began scheming toward that goal. My first ambition was somehow to rectify the situation between Marty and Tina, not to try to persuade him to reconsider divorce—I knew, as a result of our previous conversation, that was impossible—but rather to suggest that he postpone proceedings until Tina was out of the hospital, thereby diminishing the emotional toll of their separation. Of course, the situation was ironic. Here I was trying to take the sting out of Marty's decision as a means of preserving my own marriage. I tried calling him, both at the house and at his office at the university, leaving word with Rachel as well as the secretary of the history department. It would take him three more weeks to finally get back to me.

In the meantime, I tried contacting Larry Rosen at his office at IBM. Larry was not quite as difficult to reach as Marty, though I had to leave several messages before he finally returned my call. When I told him I wanted to meet and talk, at first he was adamantly against the idea. He said that he and his wife preferred to be left alone in their grief; there was really nothing to discuss. He was furious that Susan had burst into their home and no doubt expected the same sort of aggressive badgering from me. I apologized for Susan, admitting that her sudden visit was very much in bad taste, and told Larry that even she looked back on her behavior with mortification. When I finished apologizing, Larry was quiet, obviously surprised by such a capitulation. I went on to empathize with the suffering he and his wife were going through, telling him, however, that my family was also in the midst of a crisis which was, in many respects, linked to theirs. The very least he could do was allow me to buy him lunch, and the lunch, I promised, would be gentlemanly. I suggested the Princeton Club dining room and he finally agreed to meet me the following Wednesday.

I arrived at the club early and sat down in the private booth I had requested and drank wineglasses of ice water until Larry arrived. I knew we had been introduced somewhere along the way, probably over cocktails in a crowded gathering under the charred haze of a barbecue, which was how everyone who lived in our neighborhood got acquainted. However, when he entered the dining room, I recognized him as someone whom I had met once or twice and had liked enormously but had lost track of. I didn't associate this particular man with being the father of Mark Rosen. I stood up and motioned him with a vague waving hand.

Larry Rosen was several inches taller than I, and had broad shoulders and a keen face that flinched with rapid thoughts and reactions. I remembered having been impressed with his energetic intelligence and his fascinating job on the cutting edge of computer technology; he had intrigued me to the point of wondering if we'd ever meet again. So this guy was the father of Mark Rosen—now, in some respects, my adversary. We shook firmly. His suit, a light gray herringbone tweed, looked custommade to fit his strapping figure. His hair was straight and thick and silvering prematurely. Everything about him was solid, except for the wavering look in his eyes that told all. His eyes were the same silvery color of his hair and darted nervously back and forth like helpless minnows looking for a way out of his head. I couldn't help thinking that if Mark had lived he probably would have inherited his father's stature, and I even began speculating on what Mark might have accomplished in life and how I'd feel if the situations were reversed and Billy had died. I suddenly realized that Larry Rosen must feel a lot of anger and ambivalence toward me, the father of the boy who lived, the boy who knew how to swim.

"I didn't realize you were actually Mark's father," I found myself saying.

Larry frowned. "Oh, I knew you were Billy's father."

In the midst of this momentary awkwardness, we both thought to sit down.

"So then you remember meeting me?" I said.

"Of course."

"Whose party was it?" I said.

"Lucille and Bob Spanier's. Three summers ago. It was even before we . . . had kids." His clear, booming voice faltered as he cast his eyes away. It amazed me that in just three years a child was carried to term, born, nurtured and loved, and that an untimely death had claimed a tragic equivalent to the death of someone who had lived decades longer. I raised my hand to flag the waiter. "Let's make this easier," I said. "What are you drinking?"

Larry smiled grimly. "Vodka rocks with a twist."

"Red label and soda," I told the waiter.

"You got pretty drunk the night we met," Larry informed me once the waiter left us.

I was a bit taken aback by his candor. "Must not have been too impressive," I said.

He shrugged. "We all get drunk on occasion." He seemed somewhat relieved to hold forth on issues extraneous to what lay before us like a meal of indigestible courses. We both knew what we had to get down to, and that left us without pretext. The tragedy was forcing us to meet on common ground, equidistant to our offices, to our private lives. As another waiter handed each of us a leather-bound menu, it occurred to me that the situation might have been similar had we been meeting over the fact that I had taken his wife as my lover and Susan had figured out what was going on and stormed into the Rosens' home to discover me in bed with Harriet.

I ordered a Cobb salad and Larry followed my example. By the time the order was taken we had each sipped half our drinks and the bizarre sensation of our meeting was somewhat filed down. I felt looser about things, although still unprotected.

"So how has it been, dealing with everything?" I asked rather clumsily.

His wide shoulders crumpled at the question and his proud head sagged. "We're still pretty much in shock," he said. "Four weeks yesterday."

"Has Harriet been able to get out?"

"Not really."

"You've been going to work, though?"

Jiggling his vodka, Larry frowned at the liquid disturbance in his hands and then peered at me, one of his eyes narrowing slightly. "I have no choice."

"Work is something to hold on to."

Then he flared up. "Look, Mr. Kaplan, I don't feel right talking to you about this. You told me you had something to talk to me about."

"Call me Michael, please. And I do have something to talk to you about."

"So let's stick to that, shall we?"

"I was just trying to see how things are going."

"Well, they're shitty. There's not much more to say."

"You say you don't feel right talking to me. Would you feel

more comfortable talking to some other father in the neighborhood whom you didn't know well?"

"Maybe I would."

"Why would you?"

He glared at me. "You know exactly why. Our sons were
playing together."

"But don't you think that'd make me sympathetic? That my
son was with your son . . . when it happened?"

Larry Rosen gave a troubled sigh and glanced away. "I don't
know," he said. "I don't know what to think." And then some
thought rattled him—visibly—and his attitude shifted. "It's
weird," he said, looking at me fervently with his silvery eyes.
"When my father died it wasn't like this at all. I mean, he died
suddenly . . . just like Mark did." He spoke the name of his
son with such tenderness, he could have been saying words like
"tranquillity" or "angel." "At least when my father died there
were moments when the grief let up and there was some relief."

"How old were you when your father died?"

"Fifteen," he said, though I expected him to have been older,
to have been as old as I was when my father died. "Your parents
living?" he asked.

"No, actually. Neither are."

He flushed and then leaned toward me, which I took to be a
momentary abating of his fierce self-protection, a bodily display
of empathy, the death of parents something we both could share.
"Oh, really?" he said. "How long ago?"

"Around five years ago," I said. "They died within twelve
months of each other."

"I see. So then you understand what I'm saying. That grief
comes in waves."

I thought back and realized this was true. I had forgotten that
aspect of the pain of grief.

"Well, with Mark dying," he went on, "it's relentless. It
doesn't let up for a second. It's this constant jagged torment:

How can he be gone? How could this have happened to us? What did we do wrong?"

"I can understand that."

"He didn't even know what was happening to him—suddenly surrounded by all that dark water and not knowing how to swim—and that just keeps disturbing us. Then we start condemning ourselves for not monitoring the nurse better, for not realizing ourselves that he could have wandered away."

Larry grimaced and shook his head. I had a sense that even his stiff drink was doing little to unburden him. "Mark was just beginning to speak sentences," he said shakily. "He was just beginning . . ." He shut his eyes and drove back the grief. "God, this is difficult, this blaming myself."

This last admission came unexpectedly, and I blinked and then looked fixedly at Larry. I was reluctant to press him since I really did feel his agony, but the opportunity had presented itself and I'd have been foolish to let it slip by. "But how much do you blame yourselves," I asked very gently, "if you also hold my son accountable?"

There, it was said. And once said, it hardly sounded as provocative as I'd imagined it would sound. Larry didn't explode or flare up the way I expected, but swallowed the words with a grunt. He shook his head vehemently. "I don't think your son is accountable. And Harriet doesn't—"

"Harriet doesn't?"

"She's not herself, she's hardly functioning," he said angrily. "My brother and sister-in-law have moved into the house. Sabrina looks after her during the day."

"Well, pardon me, Larry, but my wife said—"

"Come on," he interrupted me, "your wife was a monster to show up like that."

"You're right. And I'm sorry she did that. But I have to tell you that your wife told my son to leave the neighborhood the afternoon before my wife barged in on you."

Larry raised his hand. "She doesn't remember saying anything like that."

"So you're saying he made it all up?"

"Maybe he's exaggerating."

"Does she claim to have said anything at all?"

My question seemed to ring throughout the dining room of the Princeton Club and in the silence that ensued several men gawked at us. Noticing we had attracted a bit of an audience, Larry scowled at me.

"I'm sorry," I said. "I'm sorry to press you like this. It's just that there are certain things that need to be cleared up."

"At least there's something to clear up," Larry said bitterly. "At least your son is still living."

I acknowledged that this was true.

He took a long swig of his ice water and then quietly told his version of what happened. According to him, Harriet had been walking through her kitchen precisely when Billy had run onto the property, chasing the ball. It was practically the first time she had managed to get out of bed after hearing the news that her son had drowned. And when she glanced out the window and saw Billy, she couldn't believe it. Why was the boy who had brought her the bad news standing in the middle of her yard? "Don't you think it was awful for her to see him there, someone who could now only represent that Mark died? That was when she went outside and asked him to leave the property. She said absolutely nothing about him having to leave the neighborhood."

"I see."

The salads arrived in large wooden bowls, plunked down in front of us by a snippy waiter, who halfheartedly offered to dust them with pepper. Larry shrugged and I declined pepper for both of us. The act of eating and using condiments was now incidental, seemingly foreign. Our salads might be wasted, I thought, the embroilment has depressed our appetites.

Larry resurrected the conversation once the waiter had departed. "Look, I understand why your son feels implicated. But how can you expect a woman who's just lost her son to be civil to, even sympathize with, the boy who was playing with her son right before he fell in. I mean, even though she knows Mark wandered away, she knows that he saw Billy and was attracted to him and followed him down to the water."

"And then to make matters even worse, your wife comes barreling into our house and demands that she apologize. Apologize for what?" He raised his voice for the first time since the conversation began. "Apologize for asking the kid who brought the bad news, the kid who was the last one to see our son alive, not to play in front of our kitchen window, for Christ's sake, so we can have a little peace? Come on! You're not looking at our side of it. I'm sure it's traumatic for Billy. But he got himself involved. They were playing together. Can't you explain to him that he reminds us of our son's death? Maybe if he understands that, he'll consider playing on the Freeds' lawn and not running over onto ours. We don't blame him, Michael. But we associate him. When we see your son, we remember that ours didn't make it."

What could I say to that? However, I managed to get Larry to promise that whenever he or Harriet saw Billy in the neighborhood, they wouldn't do or say anything to make him feel responsible for the drowning. I, in turn, would persuade Billy to stay off their property by explaining that he reminded the Rosens of their son's death because he had been the very last person to see him alive.

Later that day, Susan made tall gin and tonics flavored with sprigs of mint she had grown in her vegetable garden, and mindful of being overheard by Billy, we stole out to the back patio. I played back the entire lunch conversation for her among the blaze of crickets and the sputtering of electric mowers powered by the fathers who habitually arrived home earlier than I.

"I figured he'd say that," Susan remarked stonily. "That he'd deny what she said."

"So you still don't think Billy was exaggerating?"

Susan looked at me painfully. "I can see that you do."

I hesitated. "I'd like to think that maybe nobody remembers what they said or what they heard."

"It'd make it easier, wouldn't it? For her to deny that she said 'Leave the neighborhood'—or to say that Billy imagined it. Because those three words make all the difference." Susan paused. "But, Michael, I know in my gut that she said them."

Now feeling somewhat defeated in my purpose, I delivered what I felt was the best news: that Larry promised if either he or Harriet ran into Billy anywhere, they would be sure not to act in any way that would make him feel singled out. When I finished telling her, Susan, still clutching her tall drink, lowered her forehead onto my shoulder, inadvertently splashing gin and tonic on my thigh. And whereas I thought at least part of her gesture was forgiveness, she was only just reaching out for help to ground the anxieties whirling through her. She finally withdrew from me. "Well, at least I haven't turned them completely against us."

For dinner that night she had marinated veal shanks in rosemary and wine and made a summer stew. At a farm stand she had picked up a bunch of Chinese snow peas, a yellow summer squash and a brown bag full of fresh ears of corn, which we shucked together on the back steps. I remember looking at her deftly stripping the corn down to its gleaming flanks and thinking that I loved her more than anything and hoping that the sheer force of my love would compel her to forgive my transgressions. When dinner was ready, we called Billy down from his room. Shirtless, he entered the kitchen cautiously. He had grown thinner and paler in the last few weeks. His rib cage appeared more prominent, corrugated, his little boy's potbelly had grown taut like the stomach of an adolescent. His normally fleshy face showed a trace of jawline. He would look just like me, I thought proudly, his hands replicas of mine, his legs short and powerful. He smiled shyly and I figured his shyness was part of his love. And I also thought that no matter what happened Billy would always be my son, and whenever Susan looked at him she would have to see me. He hugged me and I kissed the top of his head and thought I smelled pond in his hair, though that couldn't have been possible; Billy hadn't been back to the lake since the day Harriet had rebuffed him.

"You're not coming to the table without a shirt." Susan glanced over her shoulder and then pivoted around. "You're not Stanley Kowalski. Go upstairs and get dressed properly."

"Ah, come on."

"Move it."

Billy looked at me to see if I would support his mother. This was unusual, in that when one of us spoke vehemently he accepted whatever was said as our collective opinion. I had been an only child myself and knew, although it is assumed that only children are given in to and spoiled, it is in fact easier for them to be kept in check by parents when there isn't another sibling to play off. And so Billy's glance at me indicated that he still sensed discord.

I tipped my head toward the louvered doors of the kitchen entrance, beyond which lay the staircase. "Run along and do what your mom says. She's made us a nice dinner."

He was back not a minute later wearing a yellow tank top with a silk screen of Mighty Mouse in the center.

I mussed his hair. "So what you been doing, Birdie?"

"Nothing."

"Who've you been playing with?"

There was an odd silence and Billy said, "Nobody."

"Where's Peter these days."

"They're away," he chirped. "In Cape Cod."

"Cape Cod?" I asked. "Before school is out?"

Billy stalled. "It was the only time Mrs. Freed could get vacation."

Susan poured water off the snow peas and a cloud of steam rose up from the sink. "Uh, look how green the water is," Billy said, moving beside her.

"If we were smart we'd be drinking that green," Susan said. "That green is good for us."

"I'm not going to drink no green water," Billy said.

"Any," I corrected.

Susan put the pot down on the counter and then arranged the snow peas on an oblong white server with a gold-leaf border. "It's amazing the improper usages he learns at school." She proceeded to the stove and removed the pot of veal shanks.

"It's probably from the other kids, rather than the instruction," I pointed out.

"Perhaps."

We sat down at the table. Billy listening, Susan and I began a stiff conversation about how the plants in her vegetable garden were doing, how the school was having a summer bake sale. She and Billy were going to make a blueberry pie, hence the white cardboard boxes of berries standing on the kitchen counter, with their sticky caul that rubbed shiny and spurted blue viscera when you squashed them. I asked Susan if she had heard from Tina in the past few days, and she shook her head. "She hasn't called me and I haven't called her. She knows we've been overwhelmed. I'm sure she doesn't want to add to it."

"Have you told her about"—I glanced at Billy—"the latest," meaning, of course, my infidelity, her confronting the Rosens.

Susan shook her head. "No. I haven't wanted to."

That was odd, Susan not immediately confiding in Tina. What could this mean? I began hoping that soon these larger issues would shrink away, and normal household crises like coffee getting splattered on the white rug or Billy sneaking a dollar out of my wallet or Mercedes not showing up for work would once again resume their old priority status. Then the phone rang and Susan retrieved the call.

"What can I do for you, Norma?" were the first words out of Susan's mouth into the kitchen extension. Her eyes moved from left to right, her forehead creasing as though she were reading as well as listening to what Norma was saying. "I wasn't aware of that. In fact"—she glanced darkly at the back of Billy's head— "according to him, you're supposed to be in Cape Cod." No doubt feeling her searing attention, Billy smartly faced away, continuing to eat. Then Susan cleared her throat, his clue to turn around, which he refused to do. "Obviously he didn't want us to know," she said, casting him a look full of hurt. "I can come by or you can drop it off. . . . Okay, I'll pick it up then. Thanks for calling. Goodbye."

She put down the phone, her attention focused on Billy, who didn't seem at all curious that Mrs. Freed had called. Formerly he would have perked up and monitored his mother's conversation, squirming with fierce pride that Susan was speaking to the mother of his best friend, the connection between the two women a firm proof that the friendship with Peter would be lasting, inviolate. "That was Mrs. Freed."

"Duh," Billy said.

"Your bathing suit has been lying on their back porch for over a week."

Billy shrugged.

"They didn't go to Cape Cod."

"Well . . . Peter said they were going."

"Baloney."

Billy grunted.

"Norma just told me she hates the beach . . ."

"Honey," I said. "Ease up a little. Consider—"

"I consider nothing," Susan said evenly. "A lie is a lie," she said with forced emphasis, as though Billy was not the only one she was lecturing.

I argued no further, although I disagreed. Sometimes one had to lie. We were lying to Billy by concealing from him that I had met with Larry Rosen—one lied to protect others from pain or needless anxiety.

Susan returned to the table and sat down. "What's going on with you and Peter?" she asked.

Billy shrugged. Often guilty of sloppy table manners, he suddenly had assumed a very careful attitude with his knife and fork, slicing the tender veal into small pieces that he didn't eat. "Peter doesn't talk to me anymore," he said finally.

"What do you mean, he doesn't talk to you anymore?" I asked.

Billy looked up at me. "He thinks I did it."

"Now, isn't that ridiculous!" Susan said.

"Did he actually say you did it?" I asked.

"Not really. But I can tell he thinks it."

"So, then, are you telling us you did it?"

Billy's face reddened and he dropped his fork. "No!" he said in a convulsion of anger.

"Honey, it's foolish for anyone to assume you had anything to do with it," Susan said.

In a voice salted with love, Billy said, "I hate Peter."

"Peter has no father," I said. Peter's father had died when he was two years old, the same age as Mark Rosen. "His mother doesn't know how to keep him in line. Hell, he's probably jealous that you have a father and that's why he says things to make you upset."

"But he means them!"

"But how could he mean them if he wasn't there? You were the only one who was there, Billy. You were the only one who saw what happened."

Susan shot me a look of concern and then said, "Peter and

Billy haven't spoken for over a week. That's why he told us Cape Cod."

This last bit elicited a growl from Billy. "So?" he said. "What do you care?"

"I care a lot," Susan said, gazing sadly at him.

I asked, "Did you and Peter have any kind of fight?"

Billy shrugged and turned his attention to the uneaten food on his plate, the corn ear with one small bite taken from it, looking as though it had been blighted by some insect.

"Did Peter say something unkind to you?" Susan asked.

"I don't want to talk about it," he said.

"Peter's a little punk, is what he is," I said. I reached over and began stroking Billy's head. "And I'll tell you something else. Six months from now you're going to realize what a punk he is when you have other friends who are a lot nicer."

"No one I know except Peter likes to go frog hunting," Billy said.

"I'll go frog hunting with you," Susan offered.

"That's nice of your mother."

The three of us were silent for a while. I noticed that the table was laden with too much food for three people. Billy pushed his chair back and started getting up.

"Where are you going?" I asked.

"Upstairs."

"We haven't excused you. And you haven't finished eating," Susan said.

Billy looked away dismally. "I'm not hungry."

"We won't talk about it anymore," I assured him.

Billy glanced at his mother. "Try to finish your meal," she gently told him.

"I want to go upstairs," he insisted.

"All right, go on," I said, and then to Susan, "We'll just wrap up his plate and put it in the fridge."

.   .   .

"So what do you think?" I asked her once we had heard that
Billy had finished climbing the steps.

"He's been moping around. I thought it was because Peter
was away."

"He obviously misses him."

Susan looked at me, her expression freighted with concern.
"So many things," she murmured. "So many things just . . .
beating away at us."

And I was thinking: You should forgive me, Susan, and life
will be a lot easier if we're together—in the former sense of the
word.

She was peering at me, still shaking her head, and I imagined
she was thinking about my part in all that weighed down on us,
my betraying her. It was as though the pain of one problem had
inspired a sympathetic aching in another. Then she stood
abruptly, the second person to be overcome by the trend of the
discussions. "I need to go outside and do some watering." She
brushed by me on her way to the back door. As she went out
she said uneasily, "Would you ask Mercedes to clear?"

I barely nodded, wishing she'd remain in the kitchen.

I sat there for another few minutes, finally retreating upstairs
to the bedroom. I passed Mercedes in the hallway. She had
discreetly allowed me my solitude and now was prepared to
tackle the dirty kitchen. Once upstairs, I tried reading the local
paper, which hardly relaxed me. I had already read the *Times*
front to back on the way to work and reading the same news
stories again in a different typeface and with slightly different
emphasis felt like watching television reruns. Outside, I heard
water spraying from a nozzle and went to the window. Below
me stood Susan in her yellow gardening shorts and blue tee shirt
with the gold lettering: C A L. She really had a gorgeous figure,
beautiful shapely legs that were slightly larger than most wom-
en's, but which I found sexy. It occurred to me that Susan's legs
might even be as large as those of some of the men with whom I

played tennis. And yet she looked great in slacks or in short golf dresses. She was obviously having fun with her watering, using the ample water pressure—another suburban amenity—to make a jet of spray so narrow and intense that if it were pointed at your crotch it could easily give you a rupture. She aimed straight up at the darkening summer sky. Twenty feet above the house the stream of water fanned into a spout and softly splattered the dark green leaves of the rhododendrons, splintering like beads of mercury, momentarily chasing away thirsty bumblebees, drowning others trapped within clusters of pink flowers. Then she shot at the Japanese maples, whose dark purple leaves made you think that you were looking at the world through a negative, and then changed the ratio in the nozzle. Walking to another part of the property, like a singer dragging the cord of a microphone, Susan misted her tuberoses, her large tree peonies, the crab apple tree, the azaleas and clematis and then took on the vegetable patch.

She had, by far, the best garden in the neighborhood, easily made so by the sheer size of her flower beds, which she had dug herself like a laborer the length of one side of the front lawn and around the perimeter of the backyard. Whereas our neighbors generally planted short swatches of flowers and a few vegetables, Susan had edged the front lawn with perennials, and in the backyard had fenced in a fifty-by-fifty-foot area, planting corn, cucumbers, tomatoes, basil, thyme and oregano. She had learned how to cultivate vegetables in California from an Italian gardener and was the one neighbor the others consulted. When the Japanese beetles had laid siege to American gardens, she had called her friend in California, who had come up with a concoction to ward them off—to think that the previous summer our insurmountable problem had been the Japanese beetle!

At last she came into the bedroom, her forehead lacquered with sweat, her hands caked with dirt, red patches on her arms from exertion. She raised her eyebrows at me and went into the bathroom, where I heard her peeling her clothing away, then turning on the faucet to take a shower. And as I lay there, listening to the water pound the tile, changing emphasis according to the way Susan shifted under the shower jets, I wanted her so badly and yet I was afraid. Everything was at stake, either she took me or she didn't take me, and I couldn't bear waiting another minute to learn how things would turn out.

Finally I got up, tore off my clothes and flung open the bathroom door to an assault of steam that had fogged the familiar landmarks of sink and toilet and wicker hamper so that I had to fumble around to find my way to the shower stall. "Is that you, Michael?" Susan asked, her voice garbled by water. "Yes, it's me," I said as I made my way toward her. Then I saw the fleshy outline of her body, its familiar details obscured by the opaque shower-stall glass, like an unborn creature undulating inside an amniotic sac.

Carefully, I slid open the shower door. As soon as she realized what I was doing, Susan went still under the pummel of water. Before she could respond, I had stepped in facing her, my oily skin beading with wetness until I was as slick as she was, squinting through the veil of water.

"Michael," she said in a sad voice. "What are you doing in here?"

I said nothing, but rather took a step toward her and tentatively caressed her wet belly. She shrank away from me until her back was flush to the metal faucets that jutted from the tiled wall. "Could you let me take my shower?" she said stiffly, without emotion.

"I thought we'd take one together. Like we used to."

Susan stood there under the bleating torrent of water, her arms hanging at her sides, completely vanquished by something she obviously could not express, her wet hair plastered against her prominent cheekbones, her exotic russet eyes more prominent without a crown of hair to surround them. Then she closed her eyes and her whole body shivered. I pressed myself to her and we both groaned. I took one of her breasts in my mouth, tasting her skin and the water, sucking a nipple as purple as the leaves of the Japanese maples. She drew me against her sharply, her arms wrapped around my back like a vise. I pivoted around and we knelt and then sprawled on the drenched tiles, rocking tightly together beneath the pounding jets of the shower.

"I love you," I kept telling her.

"I know you do, I know," she whispered. She came quickly, before I did, and her body jerked and shuddered. But when we were finished and each of us had taken our pleasure, I saw the light die in her eyes. Finally she tapped me on the shoulder. "Why don't you let me finish my shower," she said. And so, wet and feeling rebuked on the heels of making love, I retreated from the bathroom.

Naked and dripping, I went into the hallway and got a fresh towel out of the linen closet. I rubbed myself dry, only to break out into a sweat, and had to keep patting myself. Meanwhile, the water in the shower kept pouring out; I imagined Susan was probably rinsing herself of my fluids. She must have stayed in the shower ten minutes longer, and each moment her absence was prolonged reminded me of the distance there could be between two lovers in a bedroom.

Then the water finally shut off and I heard the stall door sliding open. Five interminable minutes later she emerged from the bathroom, wrapped in a burnt-orange bath sheet that covered her breasts and middle and dropped down to mid-thigh, a smaller matching towel wound tightly around her head. Admiring her supple upper body, I imagined how many other men might also find her attractive. I had to get her to pardon me. I knew I had betrayed her at the worst possible moment, but I had to secure forgiveness.

She frowned at my state of undress, her expression as austere as a schoolteacher's. "Why don't you put something on," she said.

"I'm too hot to do that."

"But you were just in the shower," she said sadly, taking the towel off her head and rubbing her hair.

"I wasn't in for very long," I said as I reached for my boxer shorts and put them on.

"Why don't you go and take another?" she said, bending over so that all her hair plunged forward. With even yanks of her head she swung it up over her shoulders and down her back and then forward again. She did this several times. "There's plenty of hot water left."

"Susan," I said. "How long is this coldness going to go on?"

Silent, she made no movement to betray her answer other than continuing to dry her hair.

"I feel awful."

She finally tossed her towel onto the bed and, glaring at me, muttered, "How do you think I felt the night I knew what you were doing? When you promised you'd come home, you absolutely promised, the night I needed you the most."

"What can I say more than that it was a terrible betrayal? But, Susan, isn't it forgivable?"

Susan glanced down at her feet and then at me. Momentarily forgetting she was trying to discourage intimacy, she angrily stripped the other towel from her midsection and stood before me in naked splendor, dry and tantalizing. Then she turned her back on me and went to her underwear drawer and drew out a fresh pair of panties and a tee shirt, which she put on facing away.

"Can't I do something to make up for what I did?" I asked in a small pleading voice. "There must be something I can do."

"I don't know, Michael," she said, shutting her dresser drawer. "If it had been any other moment but . . ." She turned to face me. "I don't think you realize how bad your timing was."

"Of course I realize."

"I don't think you do. Because it was so bad it seemed deliberate."

"But—"

"Shut up for a second, Michael. How can I trust you? I love you, sure I love you, but how could I ever trust you again after you went and screwed somebody . . . when you *knew* I was at home falling apart."

The truth was undeniable and that only made me feel more desperate. "Well, there has to be a way." I closed my eyes and tried to think of something that she had been wanting to do. "Hell," I said, "you've been after me to take us all to Europe. How about if the three of us go? Make a fresh start of it. Maybe there you can learn to trust me all over again."

She looked at me with a puzzled expression. "Go to Europe? Under these conditions? It'd be ludicrous."

"Speak for yourself."

"I *am* speaking for myself."

"Maybe the trip will change your mind. Sometimes a foreign environment gives you a new perspective."

Susan shook her head. "I'll have the same feelings anywhere else. And"—she narrowed her eyes for emphasis—"the same things will have happened." She began crossing the room on her way to the door.

"Where are you going?"

"To tell Billy to get ready for bed."

As she was about to leave, something occurred to her, and I could almost see a question insinuating itself onto her face. She spun around. "How could you do that to me?" she asked, quietly, almost tenderly. Then she shrieked, "How dare you do such a thing to me! You bastard! You lousy son of a bitch!"

In its wake, her outburst left a formidable silence, not just in the bedroom where I stood, breathless and stupefied, not just downstairs in the kitchen, where Mercedes had been tidying, and in the den, where Billy had been glued to the television, but also in the neighborhood, where it must've been heard like the wail of Harriet Rosen when she heard the terrible news.

Then the inevitable response. "What's going on?" Billy shouted up from downstairs. Then a crash in the kitchen, where Mercedes, frightened, dropped a broiling pan.

Susan had been staring at me venomously, her eyes skittering like sparrows. Later on I would realize that up until then she hadn't completely accepted what I had done; part of her had been engaged in denial in order to deal with the other crises that demanded our mutual cooperation. But now I had pressed too hard for forgiveness. Without another word, she left me alone and went downstairs. She was gone a long time. I lay down on our bed and stared out the window, watching the last of daylight ebbing until I could no longer see the trees.

O N T H E last day of school that year, two of Billy's classmates approached him to ask what really had happened down by the lake. Billy responded the way we had told him to should the occasion arise when anyone—child or adult —questioned his integrity. The facts had been printed in the newspaper; there was no reason to ask anything more. Then not only did Billy arrive home with tales of being approached and challenged; he also bore a note from the library that claimed he had lost three children's novels in the last month, for which he owed sixty-five dollars in fines; a note from the gym instructor said that he had neglected to turn in a yellow team pennant. In her final report, his second-grade teacher wrote that she had been obliged to place him in a lower reading group. Susan and I were surprised that Billy's teacher didn't even allude to the possibility that his schoolwork might have suffered in the wake of his difficulties, but instead offered a summary of his final weeks as though nothing had happened in the meantime. It was then I began to realize that people didn't regard what had happened to Billy, or us for that matter, as particularly traumatic. Sympathy from within the community seemed to be focused on the Rosens, who had palpable reasons for their suffering. And to make matters worse, when Billy arrived home to say that the issue of what happened to Mark Rosen had been broached again, Susan and I couldn't decide whether the children's inquiries had to do with continuing discussions among the neighborhood families or whether, despite Larry's promise over lunch, the Rosens were speaking openly about it among their friends.

In the midst of our renewed concern over Billy, I heard from Marty Friedman. His call came in late one afternoon at the office, catching me at the worst possible time, when my desk was towering with contracts and deal memos that needed careful scrutiny before the end of the day. I was feeling unnerved and frustrated, wishing to get home as early as possible, knowing full well I'd probably have to work until nine or ten o'clock that night. Marty's voice sounded friendly, immediately reassuring, and I probably should have begun speaking openly to him, told him directly what was going on with Susan, why there was something at stake for me in the outcome of our conversation. But amidst the stack of work and message lights flashing, I began a clumsy, long-winded speech about why he should reconsider his decision and wait until Tina was better before filing for divorce.

"Hold on there, wait half a second," Marty objected acidly. "Have you talked to her directly?"

"No, I haven't. I only spoke to Susan about it. As you know, Tina and I aren't the closest." I hoped this remark would gain me some favor with Marty. From our very earliest acquaintance, Tina and I had clashed over everything from politics to parenting. Several times over the last few years, Tina had openly condemned me for working too hard and not giving enough time to Susan and Billy, scolding me for playing tennis Saturday and Sunday afternoons, when, in her opinion, I should have been planning family outings and taking them.

"Well, Michael," Marty resumed, "when Tina and I last discussed it, she certainly wasn't objecting to the idea. She even said she thought it might be better for Rachel."

I was shocked by his statement. "But that contradicts everything I heard from Susan." I hesitated. "You think Tina might have been medicated when you talked to her?"

"Michael, don't be naïve. You're talking to the woman's husband, for Christ's sake! Don't you think I know when she's medicated. And anyway, she and I have spoken about this on more than one occasion."

"I didn't realize."

"Tina's inscrutable, Michael. It's hard to predict what she's going to say, how she's going to react from one moment to the next."

"But why did she think a separation would be better for Rachel?"

"Because her illness has been hard on Rachel. And because it would probably be less harmful overall if I were to have custody until Tina's completely convalesced."

"Well, this is complete news to me," I said. "In fact, I'm beginning to feel stupid."

"Look, Michael, part of the problem here is that you and I are easy targets on both sides."

"Neither sister likes either of us very much," I conceded.

"That's 'cause they were once so close. And I think sometimes you and I stand in the way of their closeness. It's easy for Susan to take sides against me, as it is for Tina to take sides against you."

"You're right. Look, I'm sorry for butting into your business."

"That's all right. I know you're concerned for her. But just remember one thing. It was Tina's idea to go into a hospital, especially one back East. I wanted her just to be an outpatient here in Galveston! But she said she had to go far away to get healed so as not to worry about us coming to visit and seeing her in a bad state."

"I understand."

"You better," he said, and then chuckled. There was an awkward silence. I now realized I'd never be able to mention the phone call to Susan. The issues had drastically changed, the points I'd wanted to make were no longer germane to what was happening. I also realized that after delving into Marty's life, I was somewhat obliged to confide in him about my own difficulties. I did so briefly, and Marty was sympathetic and urged me to try to hold the family together.

One Saturday afternoon shortly after this conversation, Susan, Billy and I were walking through the local shopping center on our way to a pet shop to look at guinea pigs. Billy had wanted a guinea pig for several years and we had resisted buying him one because Susan was allergic to most small animals. Recently, however, our family doctor had informed her there were effective allergy shots available and that morning she had just taken the last of a series of injections.

Billy had fallen into a sort of withdrawal since he had stopped playing with Peter Freed. After school had let out for the summer, he'd made only a few play dates with other children and tended to stay at home a lot, fiddling with lead soldiers in his air-conditioned room, reading *Robinson Crusoe* and Hardy Boys books, intermittently watching soap operas with Mercedes while she did the ironing. We hadn't as yet been able to find out if anything in particular had catalyzed the breakdown in the friendship with Peter, what word or conversation had finally severed them. We knew the simple truth that friendships bloomed and withered between children, who rejected one another with astonishing cruelty. We assumed that, like the kids at school, Peter had probably said something derogatory which rang with some scary truth.

So we were on our way to the pet shop to buy Billy a guinea pig, hoping that having an animal to care for would help to cheer him up. As the three of us were passing the dry cleaner's, Larry and Harriet Rosen came scooting out of the store: Larry tall and dignified, his silver hair gathering sunlight; Harriet, by contrast, wraithlike and rail thin, stooped over almost as though she sought to fold up into herself. They seemed to be in a hurry; there was no way to avoid them. Each was encumbered by at least ten hangers of dry-cleaned clothing entombed in plastic that caught the steady breeze, hissed and sucked. Surrounded by all that flapping, the two of them took on an almost spectral presence. Billy, who had been walking ahead of us, anxious to arrive at the pet shop, froze in his tracks like a night animal stunned by a beam of light. The Rosens stopped too, and Harriet, still wearing black, swept her free hand quickly through her hair, cast her eyes away and managed to say hello. She then muttered a few words to Larry, broke away from his side and began traversing the melting-asphalt parking lot, the envelopes of plastic trailing behind her. Larry remained with us for a moment, in an effort to be more civil. He peered at Susan, then at me, and said, "How are you?" He half grinned, half winced at Billy, but his smile—to me, at least—could not conceal the inner erosion of his distress. At that moment I could feel him yearning for his son back, wishing that it all somehow wasn't true. And then he took off after his wife. Susan and I watched them join up at their Catalina, which was in desperate need of washing.

Billy continued ahead, skulking along the row of storefronts until he arrived at the pet-store window, where he stood in front of a mixed group of puppies frolicking on shredded newspaper. He stared at the moving tangle of dogs. I knew he was consumed in circular speculation about what Mrs. Rosen had said to him—to leave her property, perhaps even to leave the neighborhood.

I turned to Susan, who was looking at me expectantly. "He has a lot to worry about for a kid so young." Forget the fact that he was a child; the combination of events, the varying opinions, our obvious incapacity to soften the blow of what happened, would be overwhelming to someone three times his age. Children are lucky, I thought, in that they have the ability to get distracted from worrisome things, but perhaps they need that ability because they are so easily distraught.

"They could certainly make it a lot easier for him," Susan said, watching the Rosens' Catalina maneuvering its way out of the busy parking lot, stopping and starting, red brake lights nearly powerless in the deluge of sun.

"I think they were okay. I think they're keeping their word. They're not making him feel responsible."

"What are you talking about?" Susan said, indicating with her chin our son standing at the window of the pet store, staring forward but quite obviously looking inward.

"They act strangely because seeing us makes them feel uncomfortable. We automatically remind them of it. But they weren't uncivil."

"Just distant."

"Uncomfortable, I think, is the appropriate word."

Susan clucked her tongue. "She could tell Billy he's welcome to come on her property."

"She could, but maybe she doesn't have it in her." I searched

Susan's eyes, which were caustically narrowed. "Do you think another mother would have it in her? Do you think you would?"

"Yes." Susan hesitated. "I would. And I would reprove myself."

"It's easy to say that now. But you don't know what it's really like to live through something as tragic as this. It must be agony." I looked down at the cement gutter of the parking lot. "Maybe thinking that someone else had a small part to play makes it easier for her."

"I can't believe you're saying this," Susan said with a look of disgust on her face. "You're paving the way for Billy to feel guilty."

I shook my head resolutely. "I'm just saying that when you're in such pain, you become completely self-involved. You take care of yourself in order to survive. I think Harriet is on the edge. I don't think she has the strength to be gracious or understanding. I think she's struggling to stay together."

"Why do you have to take *her* side?"

"I'm not taking her side. I'm showing you a very important angle to all this, an angle I didn't even see until I had lunch with Larry."

Susan swiveled away from me, facing the window of the dry-cleaning store, where an Oriental woman sat next to a black sewing machine with a spool of baby-blue thread on the top. Behind the woman rose a cloud of steam from an ironing board made of two wings that pressed together over fabric like a waffle griddle. I could smell dry-cleaning fluid. The smell had always meant order to me: pants with flat creases, wrinkle-free suits, shirts starched into obedient lines that complemented my ties. Now I was aggrieved by the smell, reminded of the order and unruffled routine of my life several months before this.

"Susan," I said in a tone of forced patience, "we have to stop worrying about their attitude toward Billy. What's more important is our attitude toward him, that we're certain he didn't do anything wrong. We have to make him believe that the reaction he's seeing in the Rosens comes from grief, not from blame."

Susan said nothing in rebuttal; obviously I had finally made sense to her.

In silence, we continued along the row of stores that led to the pet shop, each of us deep in our own preoccupations. Amidst the storefronts, glass doors opened and closed all around us as couples and families did their brisk shopping for summer sandals and tee shirts and six-packs of Coca-Cola bound for plastic coolers bound for the beaches of Long Island Sound. I watched the exultant beachgoers, thinking how lucky they were; no matter how boring or unfulfilled their lives were, they were probably living relatively free of the embroilments of infidelity or feeling implicated in the death of a child. A few times during that short, yet somehow interminable distance between the dry cleaner's and the pet shop, I thought I heard people calling to us alternately, Michael, Susan, Susan, Michael, the names once part of who were together, our collective persona, but now sounding more apart, more autonomous. I had stopped seeing Sondra, hadn't even considered sleeping with another woman, and now more than ever wanted to be with my wife, especially in light of what was happening. And yet Susan was maintaining her distance. She still made love to me on occasion, while managing to keep up a wall. Our conversations were, for the most part, abbreviated; she had even stopped discussing Tina's predicament, though once my opinion about it had mattered so much to her. This enforced distance colored everything, confused my own judgment of how much I really cared about the drowning and its attendant difficulties. It made me doubt myself. Because in the midst of dealing with the Rosens and Billy, I knew that Susan was thinking that my effort to set things right was motivated by my desire to make up with her, to have her back where

I had her before. And I thought to myself that a failing marriage was like when a teacup falls from a cupboard and cracks into what first appears to be only a few pieces. In trying to glue it back together you begin to realize that crucial bits of glaze and ceramic are missing; however, weeks, even months after the broken cup has been thrown away, the lost shards sadly begin to reappear.

We finally joined Billy by the tall plate windows of the pet store. As he caught sight of our reflections looming behind him, his head slowly tilted upward. When I was standing next to him, he slipped his hand into mine. "I like that dog," he said, pointing to a beagle puppy. "Can we get a puppy?" I glanced over at Susan, who was also allergic to most dogs. I didn't want to indicate that she might stand in the way of getting a dog and hoped she would speak of her own accord. I also was aware that Billy might try to parlay Susan's and my concern over him into consent to get a dog, which we both felt was a responsibility neither of us wanted to take on right now.

"You know we can't get a dog." She finally spoke up.

Billy countered quickly, giving me the impression that he already had planned his arguing strategy. "Bobby Cristo was allergic to dogs and he got shots so they could get one."

Susan raised her eyebrows at me. "We're not going to get a dog," I said in sudden exasperation. "You know that. A dog is a lot more trouble and neither your mother nor I am up to that right now."

Billy turned around, the features of his face asymmetrically disturbed by his sudden disappointment. Perhaps I had spoken too sharply. "I'll take care of it," he said, making me feel as though by denying him a dog we were in effect abandoning him.

"We're getting a guinea pig," Susan said. "That's what we decided on and that's what we're getting. "You've talked so much about wanting a guinea pig."

"I changed my mind," Billy said, turning back to the puppies.

Susan threw up her hands in surrender. She glanced at me and her glance was full of challenge. "Why don't you take him inside and look around." "You deal with this" being the gist of it. She was obviously still annoyed over my attempts to represent the Rosens' dilemma. "I'm going to get a cup of coffee." Billy didn't voice an objection to her leaving. She pecked each of us on the cheek, swung her straw handbag in a wide arc over her exposed shoulder and hurried away.

It took us a while to adjust to the lighting in the store. The pet shop was labyrinthine, cages and glass terrariums planted all over the place, many of them lit in dim fluorescence. The rodent section was in the back of the shop, and although Billy was eager to find his guinea pig, he and I indulged ourselves in an almost hypnotic ritual of gazing at the reptiles and the tropical fish. We paused in front of an enormous fifty-gallon tank with a calligraphic sign in front that read "Salt Water." Inside swam fish from an iridescent spectrum of colors I had never seen. I was as amazed as Billy, whose eyes went wide as he looked at the angelfish with their delicate fan tails, electric-blue coral fish, fish shaped like crocodiles, and leopard-skinned rays. "How do they get that color?" he asked.

"I guess they must eat things that make their bodies turn into whatever color they are."

"But they look like lights themselves," he said. "They look like they glow in the dark."

"Some of them do, apparently," I said, studying the chart of fish pasted on a wooden support column that abutted the tank. Each species of fish that glowed in the dark had a small metallic bar affixed to its tinted photograph. I rested my hand on Billy's hair, which was already beginning to lighten in the summer, with various bands of red and blond and brown all woven together. "They take the sun into their bodies and there's probably some process there that lets them keep the light. Which is good, because when they go into deeper water where the sun can't reach, they glow so they can find each other."

Billy abruptly turned away from the huge fish tank, his face partially lighted by a bulb that gave the water the same aquamarine hue I remembered from the Caribbean.

"Are you figuring this out or is it something you know?"

He was doubting me. Once upon a time he had always been eager to believe my explanations, particularly when they were romantic-sounding. I remembered a discussion the three of us had a year earlier, when I had made a reference to some syrupy letters Susan had written to me from California shortly after we met. She had blushed remembering them herself and Billy had suddenly felt left out. He had turned to me and demanded where he had been at the time this happened, and I had replied, "You were still in heaven, Birdie. You hadn't come down to us yet." He had beamed at the idea of his still being up in heaven and then asked what heaven was like and if he was lonely up there. I had answered that heaven was all silvery and soft and there were angels everywhere and that no one was ever lonely in heaven. Since the incident by the lake, however, he'd become a lot more skeptical, questioning my explanations. It was as though he was now expecting to be betrayed by a conspiracy of misinformation.

I nudged him away from the fish and we approached the glass cage of a turquoise iguana. Unlike the constantly moving fish, the iguana was motionless under a spot lamp, and no matter where we stood, its stationary eyes seemed to probe us.

"Iguanas don't swim, do they?"

"No. I don't think so."

Billy stood there a moment longer and I watched his shoulders hunker down.

"Are you okay?" I asked him, once again stroking his silken hair.

He shrugged.

"What are you thinking about?"

"Nothing."

"Come on."

"I told you. Nothing."

"You don't believe me anymore when I tell you things," I suddenly said, venting my own insecurity. "Is that what's bothering you?"

Billy frowned. "I believe you . . . they were just acting so weird."

I sought comforting words that I never did find. "I know. It's true. They were acting strange."

"Why?"

"Because they're sad most of the time."

"Why did we have to run into them?" Billy asked, his eyes still trained on the iguana.

"It's a small town. You're bound to run into people you'd rather not see."

Billy momentarily turned to look at me again, his face now showing a bitter confrontation with the facts. "Great," he said. "They just act so weird," he repeated, as though part of him still couldn't accept that the Rosens would treat him with such stiff formality; he was used to parental solicitude, being shown affection. To a child, I realized, diffidence was akin to punishment.

"It's not just you, Billy," I said. "Believe me, they act unhappy with everybody they see. Their boy just died."

Billy looked up at me. "He didn't just die," he said angrily. "He died more than a month ago."

To a child, a month is a long time, a miniature eternity. For me, it was a flash, a short clip of an endless blur of routine.

"Billy," I began, gently grabbing hold of his shoulders in an effort to lead him away from the gristly sight of the iguana in the direction of the various cages of guinea pigs, one of which would hopefully help to dispel his miserable fixation on details and events and people's unsatisfactory reactions. But he resisted my coaxing, preferring to stay where we were. "When something like this happens, when somebody dies, it takes a long time to get over it."

"You weren't weird like them when Poppy died."

"In the beginning I was."

Billy poked his finger at the iguana and then slowly advanced it until his fingertip kissed the glass. His gradual movement caused the iguana to flinch. "I don't remember you ever being like them."

"That's because I didn't show you how sad I was. I thought that would upset you."

He turned to me. "You mean you cried?"

"Sure I cried."

"You just didn't cry in front of me?" Billy tested the thought out loud.

"Right."

"Oh."

"Let's go look at the guinea pigs," I suggested.

Something, at least momentarily, animated Billy, who dodged between several cages of guinea pigs, imitating their soft whimpering squeals. There were perhaps seventy guinea pigs all told, segregated by color: appaloosa black and white, solid black, solid albino with red eyes and a cage containing what looked like mongrels. Outside that cage was a sign that read "Rainbow Mix." As though lured by a siren, Billy was drawn to the cage of rainbow guinea pigs, and reaching his hand in among the moving fur, he began examining specific animals. He'd lift up each guinea pig, take it out and hold it. He'd turn them over to examine markings and then would smell them. According to him, some smelled distinctly better than others. At school he had been taught by a science teacher that smell was a sign of health. "See, now this one smells bad," he said of one gray-and-white guinea pig, offering it to me. I bent down and took a whiff. At first I could smell cedar chips and then a bitter odor like vomit drifted up from the animal. "Bluuu," I said, turning away.

"Oh, it's not that bad," Billy scolded me. He examined other guinea pigs and finally found one that was mottled yellow, brown and black. "This one smells nice," he said, holding it up to me. I bent down to smell it and he said, "No, keep it for a second. I like this one."

Dutifully, I cradled the squirming animal, whose small claws pawed at me as it got its bearings. Shivering at first, it suddenly grew quiet as though instantly trusting my touch. I sniffed it and could only smell cedar chips. I studied the guinea pig, whose markings were quite exotic. It was the most rainbow of rainbow mixes.

"What do you think?" Billy asked, looking up at me expectantly.

"I like it. It seems a lot quieter than the others."

"Probably smarter too," he said.

"Undoubtedly."

Assuming he was choosing the guinea pig, I waved for one of the employees of the store, who were easily identifiable by the emblazon of PETLAND on red smocks that were tied tightly around their waists. A dark-haired, acned teenager noticed me immediately and trotted over to us.

"You wanna buy that one?" he asked, grinning at the guinea pig, which seemed to have fallen asleep in my hands.

"Yeah. I also need to price a cage."

"Well, we have several. If you'll come to the other side of the store. We have them on display."

"Dad, wait a second," Billy interjected. "Give it to me," he said softly.

As we exchanged it, the guinea pig woke up and began nibbling lightly on Billy's fingers. Billy closed his eyes for a moment. I wished I could fathom his thinking process. Then he looked at me. "Dad, I don't think I want to get one right now."

He turned away to release the guinea pig into the cage. Stunned for a moment to be back in its original surroundings, the guinea pig eventually joined the melee of moving fur.

The teenaged employee looked surprised that Billy had changed his mind. No doubt he was used to overexcited kids clamoring for animals, kids who'd take home ten guinea pigs if their parents would allow it.

"What's wrong?"

"I don't know," Billy said, looking into the rainbow-mix cage, where his guinea pig was now indistinguishable from the others. "I just don't want one anymore."

"Are you holding out for a dog?"

"No."

"We have lots of dogs," piped in the clerk.

"I don't think we need any more assistance right now," I said, and waited until the kid began helping another customer.

I waited patiently for Billy to explain why he had decided against taking the guinea pig. Then I saw something in his face, a puckering up of his soft cheeks, the chin quivering, and then his tears began to fall. I pulled him to me, embracing him while he cried.

Susan was waiting for us outside the pet store, holding a Styrofoam cup full of black coffee. She was taking a sip just as we came out the door. She frowned when she saw Billy's tearful face.

"Where's the guinea pig?" she asked softly as she bent down to him.

"It's inside," Billy told her. "I decided not to get one."

As Susan hugged him, she shook her head. His unspoken reasons were already clear to her; in some way she had already divined the sequence of events that had occurred inside the pet store and understood what had changed Billy's mind. Unlike me, she didn't have to ask if he was holding out for a dog. She implicitly knew what was plaguing him.

BILLY

---•---

I N   T H E   dream I am always searching for you in a
cemetery as wide as a sea, a cemetery without headstones.
The dead, boys like yourself, are standing atop alabaster pedes-
tals. I see them everywhere—thousands upon thousands standing
in straight rows that stretch all the way to the horizon. They are
dressed in gray flannel shorts, white shirts, striped ties. Their hair
is combed, their cheeks rouged and gleaming—they almost
come alive again. I walk among them looking for you. I search
and search and after many hours I finally happen upon the row
in which you stand so still among others who have also died. At
the last moment, however, I find myself unable to look at you.

Mothers brought us rumors that your parents were going to

move. I kept vigil over the streets, alert for moving vans. My mother said that trucks would never come before a real estate sign advertising "For Sale" appeared on your front lawn. I saw those signs on other properties in the neighborhood, impaled like grave markers among grass that needed to be mowed. But one never appeared where you lived.

I hardly understood how your parents could continue living across the street from the lake, which could be viewed from their windows, across the street from a lawn that had been trodden by the grimy boots of firefighters who had tried to save you. But something compelled them to stay on, and as long as they remained, I still hoped that one day they would forgive me.

Even the Freeds moved. They moved just after we did. Mrs. Freed admitted to my mother that she could never forgive herself for allowing her daughter to watch me while I was fishing. Had she been at home, Mrs. Freed would have spotted you down by the water; she would have known that you were not being watched; she would have known to make a phone call and summon your mother.

The last time I saw the Freeds was the day of President Kennedy's funeral, a year and a half after the drowning. School was closed—we were third-graders—and I was helping Peter with math homework. We sat on the carpeting in their living room, drawing circles with a compass and rectangles with a ruler. Mrs. Freed was perched behind us on a cream-colored sofa that was stained from coffee spills, her hair frizzed out in a triangle to her face. She seemed to be conscientiously following the church service, singing the hymns, muttering prayers, a Parliament cigarette in one hand, a glass of rye in the other. Whenever the priest uttered the holy trinity, Mrs. Freed, holding both her drink and the cigarette, crossed herself. "You boys should be watching this," she kept saying. "This is your history. It's more important than math."

Peter lowered his eyelids and swept some pink eraser bits off the graph paper. He had a dried chocolate river at the side of his mouth; earlier he had eaten an ice-cream sandwich. I was surprised Mrs. Freed hadn't told him to wipe it off. "But, Mom," he said, "this homework was due today."

Mrs. Freed glowered at him. "For heaven's sake, there's no school today. The President was shot, you ninny! Now both of you come right here and watch this program with me," she insisted.

Peter dropped the cluster of pencils he was holding and went to sit next to his mother. Stiffening, I stayed where I was. I didn't want to watch a funeral. I was angry. Ever since what happened to you I hated everyone who died when they shouldn't have died. I hated the young Italian grocer who collapsed from a heart attack, the school principal who was killed in a car collision on the New England Thruway. Eyeing me, Mrs. Freed grabbed a bottle of Wild Turkey off an end table charred with cigarette burns and refilled her glass. "Aren't your parents watching this?" she asked.

"No."

"And why not?"

She knew what had been going on between my parents, that my father was making excuses to exile himself to the bungalow in California, where he conducted his West Coast business. Whenever my father called me from California, I could hear splashing in a nearby swimming pool. He would speak to me in a voice as smooth as his business deals, the sound of his icy cocktails rattling against the receiver. "Where's your mother?" Mrs. Freed pressed on.

"At a fund-raising luncheon."

"Fund-raising for?"

"UJA."

She looked at me with hard eyes. "I bought one of those UJA

trees in Israel," she said, slurring the brightness in her voice. "I bought one in Peter's name five years ago from Harriet Rosen."

Hearing your mother's name stung me; I felt it had been mentioned deliberately. Mrs. Freed seemed resentful of the fact that Peter and I had resumed our friendship. Peter used to blame the strain in our friendship on the fact that his mother got nervous about a lawsuit every time I came over and often had to sneak into her bathroom and pop tranquilizers. One day many months after he initially stopped calling, Peter approached me during recess and said that I must've been glad you died; he'd heard from someone how you'd been bugging me that afternoon. A moment later I had Peter pinned to the cold asphalt floor of the playground, my hands throttling his neck, the back of his head pressed against a painted yellow circle. "No. I wasn't glad," I snarled an inch away from his mouth, forcing him to breathe my breath. "But I'd be glad if *you* died." He closed his eyes, afraid of me for the first time. I smelled his house on him, his mother's brand of laundry soap, the wet leaves gathered around the lake. Then I felt terrible for rendering him so helpless and let him up. And after that Peter loved me more than he ever did and called me on the phone all the time. And the kids who had watched me pin him stopped wondering; because I had whipped him, I must be innocent.

I got up off the floor and went to look out the bay window at the lake, whose stilled surface was quilted with fallen leaves. The long, whiplike branches of the weeping willows dangled like legs of spiders. But this was where Mrs. Freed should have stood watching me—watching us—and where I now stood imagining freezing water feeding into my lungs, my arms thrashing hopelessly. I turned and glared at her; she certainly could shoulder some of the responsibility; she was lucky that the Rosens had never sued her. I looked at the television. There, in black and white, rolled the funeral procession: a casket covered with an American flag slowly being wheeled over cobblestones, a riderless horse pawing its way uncomfortably behind it, Jacqueline Kennedy in a black veil fluttering in the wind so that you couldn't see her expression, funerary flowers crushed by the wheels of the limousines. Tears trickled into my eyes. "I have to go home," I told them.

"Why?" Peter asked.

I stared at Mrs. Freed. "Lunch is waiting for me."

"Why don't you stay here and watch with us," she said. "And afterward I'll make you a sandwich."

"No, thanks. I gotta go."

Mrs. Freed's eyes were veined red, rheumy from drinking in midday. They reminded me how once Peter and I had tried frying marbles in olive oil and how the marbles had puffed and splintered from the heat. "He doesn't want my sandwiches," she told Peter. "He used to love them a year and a half ago. Remember when he used to wolf them down?"

"Lay off him, will you?" Peter said.

It wasn't her sandwiches I used to love—their meager contents, usually bologna or processed ham whose oiliness gave it a rainbow like sheen, wedded to white bread slathered with warm mayonnaise—but rather the Freeds themselves, a family who let laundry pile up and who never put butter back in the refrigerator so that it would spread better.

"It's rude to refuse someone's offer for lunch," Mrs. Freed continued to complain.

"I don't care," I finally told her.

Her cheeks pinched and flushed. On the television thousands of military cadets holding bugles were blowing taps. "You will never be invited here again," she said scornfully.

"I don't care," I told her amidst Peter's yelps of protest.

I shrugged them both off and hurried outside into the chill November afternoon. Shivering in my ski parka, I peered across the street to your property. Ever since that day, your house and yard had always looked uninhabited to me: window shades drawn, shingles blistering charcoal-colored paint, weeds thriving between the heavy flagstones of the front walk, several days of rolled-up newspapers littering the front porch like dog droppings. It was as though your parents knew I'd be watching them and made sure never to be outside when I was there. I'd never get the chance to strike up a conversation, to ask for the forgiveness that my parents told me I shouldn't be seeking.

When I arrived home that afternoon I saw the real estate sign flagging our lawn like a banner that marked a house in quarantine. I raced upstairs to the kitchen, where a mug of hot chocolate was waiting for me at the table. My mother was standing at the window and when she turned to me I saw the frosted halo her breath had painted on the cold glass pane. She was wearing an Indian cotton dress of deep indigo adorned with small golden ornamental disks. "What's the sign for?" I cried out. "We're not going to move. No way!"

"Sit down and have some cocoa, Birdie," she said to me.

"Birdie nothing," I hissed.

"Come on." Her voice took on the nervous edge it never used to show before the drowning. I felt angry at you again and tried to swallow my anger whole. Whenever I got angry I was afraid I was going to die. "You know what's been going on between your father and me. You know he hasn't been home a lot. You know why."

"It's because of what happened to Mark, isn't it?" I said.

"It has nothing to do with what happened to Mark. Not everything that happens to us now has to do with what happened to Mark."

"I don't believe you," I said, holding on to my assumption, as I would over the next few weeks whenever I looked down from my window and saw the real estate sign, that because of what happened to you, our family, the guilty family, was being forced to retreat from the neighborhood.

"So what's to happen now?" I asked.

My mother shifted and the golden disks on her dress made a soft clattering. "We'll all move to Manhattan. But your father and I will live separately."

My eyes bulged to hear what I had for so long feared.

"You'll live between both of us," she went on. "Your father has already found an apartment. In a nice building on the East Side. For the time being I intend to live on the West Side with a friend."

"Can't you find a place in the same building?"

She considered this. "I don't think that's a good idea." She looked steadily at me with dewy eyes. "I guess your father and I need to be in, well, different places, so as not to run into each other all the time."

That last part cut into me more than the rest of it, more than the real estate sign planted outside, more than the sickle of pain and worry that had already struck my heart at the idea of entering a strange new school.

That night I remember my parents and I went to the Sawpit, which was our favorite restaurant in Portchester. We ate dinner in this heavy perturbed silence. It was obvious that something was wrong; maybe it was just their knowing that I finally had learned of their decision that made the meal so difficult, made us all more keenly aware of the scrape of knives against battered heavy plates. And as we all cut into our steaks I kept thinking that the three us together was the natural whole, and that divorce was the divider of that whole, its murderer.

But after the house was sold, after my parents had taken up separate residences in the city, there were times when the three of us got together again, usually at my father's place. His apartment—decorated in a southwestern minimalist style of pale turquoise walls with a salmon-colored trim, charcoal carpeting, a modular sofa, halogen lamps with long swanlike necks—was a lot larger than the two-bedroom co-op that my mother shared with another divorcée and which had blond motel furniture covered in worsted fabric. The conversation was always depressing. "Michael, have you seen that new French movie?" Silence. "Not yet." "Susan, you need to talk to the accountant." "I haven't been able to get by. Billy needs three pairs of shoes for school." "Okay." "Do you mind if I put them on the joint credit card." "Fine." And the silences that followed, fractured by clinking glass and silverware, seemed to me as deep and as endless as if I were looking across the lake to another shore where divorce was the norm and marriage the exception.

I was divided equally between them, as equally as the proceeds from the sale of the house and the furniture, the sale of investments and stocks and bonds that had to be liquidated in order to properly dissolve the marriage. I traveled in taxis between the West Side and the East Side, always making my transition at night after being released from the clutches of a private school that demanded much more of my time and effort than the public schools of the suburbs. Since my father had more room in his apartment, I kept the bulk of my belongings there and shuttled to my mother's with clothing and other necessities in a Naugahyde valise. I learned the best routes between their apartments, would instruct the taxi drivers how to go. I imagined myself an astronaut voyaging between solar systems, the tall buildings of Manhattan like the forbidding spikes of hostile space stations threatening my journey. Somewhere between Central Park West and Madison Avenue, I found myself forgetting my name, forgetting that I had a place to go, but rather momentarily believing that home was the No-man's-land between two apartments, my bed the worn back seat of car services.

For a year after the separation, neither of my parents was seriously involved with someone else, and that allowed us to continue being a family. But then my mother fell in love with a man called Ravi, a spiritual teacher who was born in India; and once she met him, the family ceased to be.

In contrast to my father's high-rise apartment, where light flooded in from four sides, Ravi's West Side apartment was sprawling and dark and dankly odorous. Whereas my father's apartment had no smell whatsoever except that of ammonia and lemon wax when his cleaning woman came, Ravi's apartment smelled of sandalwood incense and curry and coriander. Shocked that my mother had taken up with an Indian man, my father hated Ravi on sight. His reaction spread to other people we had known while we were living in the suburbs, people who thought nothing of calling my mother to tell her they disapproved of her relationship with a man of dark complexion.

Had Ravi been white and Jewish, I might have felt guilty about liking him, might have felt that liking him would conflict with my love for my father. But I felt determined to accept him because I imagined that among all these angry people he must have felt as ostracized as I did, and because the situation reminded me of September 1964, right before we left the suburbs, when a new federal law had forced our all-white elementary school to be integrated.

During the weeks preceding the opening of school, mothers in the neighborhood clustered like parched wasps at the boundaries of their lawns, complaining about having come to the suburbs to find a good safe school system and now look what was happening: black children were being bused in. They imagined switchblades being brandished in the classrooms and threatened to investigate private schools in Tarrytown and Ossining. My mother refused to participate in these commiserations. And I had looked forward to the arrival of black students; at least they would not know that I had anything to do with a drowning.

That first morning of fourth grade the classroom was packed to sweltering capacity, whites sitting on one side, blacks on the other, each faction regarding the other with a mixture of curiosity and suspicion. The air smelled of mimeographing ink and overheated bodies. The mood was tense as all eyes were trained on the pale instructor who stood in front of us unable to mask her uncertainty. I arrived late and without a second thought calmly approached an arrangement of four desks, three of which were already occupied by black students. I introduced myself and sat down at the fourth.

Trouble erupted at recess. Some white boys banded together at one corner of the playground and spoke through Butch Meebang, who, two years earlier, had accused me of pushing you into the lake. "Let's go fight the spooks!" cried Butch. And now the black boys who sat studying with me all morning and who had offered their friendship were being summoned to defend themselves.

I looked frantically for a teacher. Two stood conversing near a red door. I waved to them, but they veered away, as though aware of what was about to happen and refusing to do anything to prevent it. This made me so furious that I ran toward Butch Meebang and the other white kids and shrieked, "Get out of here. You're not supposed to be fighting."

"*You* get out of here, you drowner."

And then I took my mother's opinion of Butch Meebang and let it fly. "You just cause trouble because your father's an alcoholic and because your mother neglects you."

It was too much truth for one remark and Butch Meebang was stunned. "Liar," was all he could say to me.

"If you come any closer you'll get beaten up," I said, referring to the black students who were now flanking me.

"Niggers, go back to your old school! We don't want you around here."

Hearing the "nigger" word made everything within me go blind and all I wanted to do was to kill him. Because he had accused me of pushing you in the lake, which had led to my mother finding out that I had lied when I said I had dreamed something your mother actually had said. I lunged for the bully's throat, swung and kicked and collided until I got hold of it. And if the black boys hadn't pulled me off I think I might have strangled him.

Ravi had meetings with his spiritual students in the only room of his apartment that admitted direct sunlight. He'd sit in a carved wooden chair with worn violet cushions, a stick of Tibetan incense burning, and his students sat opposite him on hard oak stools. The room would fill with laserlike wands that permeated his collections of deity statuaries and Chinese porcelains and clear Arkansas crystals, creating a holy light. Students would talk about their daily challenge and Ravi would give gentle practical advice in the veins of truths he blended from the principles of Jain, Hinduism and Tibetan Buddhism, the latter of which he felt personally closest to. Ravi was handsome. He had a strong jawline, a well-trimmed moustache and a lithe physique. His dark eyes were gentle, his skin light brown with a grayish cast, his hair coal black and lustrous. He always spoke carefully and would close his eyes when thinking. Both he and my mother got up early in the morning to meditate side by side in front of an altar of Buddha bronzes as well as a sixteenth-century hanging *tonka,* of a pale, dreaming-looking Tara, that had been the gift of a high Tibetan lama. I never told my father about my mother taking up meditation.

Fluent in Tibetan, Ravi was involved in the political campaign to liberate Tibet from the stranglehold of the Communist Chinese. Phone calls would sometimes come in the middle of the night from Dharamsala, India, where the Dalai Lama was in exile and where the officials seemed to have trouble calculating the time difference. Ravi, however, welcomed these telephone calls. He was a chronic insomniac and did much of his writing at night.

I finally got up the nerve to ask my mother about her feelings for Ravi one night when I was twelve. I had just made my

Manhattan crossing with my Naugahyde bag—as heavy as an anchor on account of all my schoolbooks—in a plush car that had been sent by the limousine service my father used on his trips to the airport. I had left the smell of wet wool carpeting and my father's citrus cologne and entered Ravi's shrine, which smelled of incense and dust and burned ash that was sacred to the living-room altar. My mother brought me into Ravi's study to be hugged good night before ushering me with a cup of bancha tea into a small bedroom where I slept next to the plaintive hissing of a steam radiator. Looking at her, backlighted by the lamp in the hallway, I asked, "What makes you love him so much and not Dad?"

She reeled back from the question into the protective shroud of darkness, where I could see little else but the weary gleam of her smile. She ventured forward again, grabbed my hand and squeezed. "It's not that I don't love your father," she admitted nervously. "I still think about him a lot. I even still have dreams that he's in."

"But you're not with him," I said. "You're with Ravi."

"I know," she said, her voice suddenly hoarse. And then she briefly explained what had happened a few nights after you fell in the water. She explained that my father was supposed to have been home at a certain time and never arrived, not because he was logged with work, but because he was with another woman. And the reason why he was supposed to have been home: my mother was upset that your mother had commanded me to leave the neighborhood when she saw me parting thorny sprays of roses in your garden in pursuit of a ball that had strayed. "That's the beginning of why I'm not with him," my mother said.

I was upset by the news that my father had gone to another woman's bed, churned up the sheets the way he used to do in my parents' bed and made that other woman feel as though she was as important as my mother. "There are other reasons too?" I asked meekly.

"Yes," she said hesitantly.

Suddenly afraid to hear any other reasons, I blundered in the opposite direction. "But what is it about Ravi that makes you want to be with him?"

"There are a lot of things, Billy. Ravi is a life teacher and I feel I have a lot to learn from him. But mainly Ravi makes me feel like I can grow and change, even if growing means that he and I won't be together eventually."

"But do you think that will happen?"

"I hope it doesn't. And if it does, it won't happen for a long time." She paused for a moment. "Your father wanted me to continue being the same person he married, not to change at all. There's something so very remote about your father, Billy. It was hard for me to feel his love. I think you know what I mean by this. And I can remember that when we were together sometimes I felt even lonelier than I did when I was alone."

I usually spent Monday to Thursday morning with my mother and Ravi and Thursday morning to Sunday morning with my father. Ravi gave teachings and lectures around the country, engagements that required him and sometimes my mother to travel. Trouble would erupt between my parents whenever Ravi's schedule dictated that they had to go off in the middle of the week, which meant I had to spend extra nights with my father. My father felt that since he was making a lot more money than Ravi—and was still paying alimony!—he shouldn't be jockeyed around. Whenever this happened, I would wonder if my life had grown to be a burden to them all. By sharing my custody, it seemed, my parents were now freer to pursue their own interests, my mother as handmaiden to Ravi's spiritual work, my father as confirmed bachelor, and no one wanted to have me full-time.

Ironically, it was Ravi who was the first to suspect that I might feel like an accessory. One night before he and my mother were to travel to a lecture in Buffalo, I was complaining that my father, who had been planning to entertain a date at home, had been forced to cancel his plans. Also, whenever I stayed at my father's during the week, I was obliged to take two buses in order to get to school, whereas I took only one bus from my mother and Ravi's apartment. "Billy, in the future I'm going to try harder to rearrange my schedule so that it doesn't conflict with your father's," Ravi said in his reedy, British-sounding voice. "You must never feel that you're a burden in any way. I love having you here." We were sitting at the dinner table and my mother, in the midst of serving curried lamb and saffron rice, was nodding her head in tacit agreement. Ravi glanced at her. "And if rearrangements are not easily made, then I travel alone."

"Absolutely," my mother said, although her eyes lowered and darted with unexpressed thoughts. I knew she would rather travel with Ravi than stay home with me.

"Would you rearrange the Dalai Lama?" I couldn't help but ask.

Ravi giggled like a child. "Well, I honestly don't think that as far as His Holiness is concerned that would ever happen. For, you see, even though he's too modest a man to admit it, His Holiness has perfect timing in that regard. He'd somehow know never to schedule me for anything that would cause conflict at home."

"You know, Billy," my father said to me a few nights after Ravi spoke to me, "your mother is supposed to take care of you during the week, not go off on Ravi's business."

It was Friday and we were standing in his bedroom while he was dressing to go out. I watched him put on a shirt the color of pewter and cream-colored trousers. I noticed, almost for the first time, that his movements were more abrupt than Ravi's. As he studied himself in a full-length mirror, my father suddenly turned to me. "Don't you agree?"

"I don't know," I said. "I mean, Ravi has to do his work, doesn't he?"

"Mumbo-jumbo work, from the sound of it."

"Dad, it's his religion," I said.

My father ceased what he was doing and turned to me, his face afflicted with jealousy.

"You like it there, don't you?" he accused.

I hesitated before saying yes.

"But does it feel like home?" he asked delicately, draping a necktie over his shoulder.

"In a way."

"More than here?"

I hesitated. "Dad, it's nice to see the same person there with Mom," I said, referring to what seemed like a showcase of ladies who liked to visit my father. "I mean, I've been able to get used to Ravi."

For a while my father didn't speak to me. And I got scared in a way I never did with anyone else, the sort of fear that killed my appetite. I thought he was furious at my honesty and suddenly wished I'd said I hated being at my mother's and much preferred living at his apartment. The truth was that although I felt more comfortable being with my mother and Ravi, I was far more concerned about the time I spent with my father, how much it added up to, because I was never sure of how he felt about me. Despite the fact that my mother had gotten involved with another man, her love was tangible. My father's love wasn't and securing proof of his feelings became far more important.

My father had gone into the bathroom, opened the medicine cabinet and selected a gold aerosol of hair spray with the silhouette of a man on its label. Closing his eyes, he misted himself.

Then he turned off the bathroom light, came over and relieved my fears by kissing me on the top of the head. "Your mother has been able to get in a relationship," he said in a wobbling voice. "She's lucky, I guess." He continued after a thoughtful pause: "It's harder for me. I guess I'm afraid of jumping into something and then doing the wrong thing and failing all over again. That's why I see a lot of ladies. I . . . loved your mother very much," he said painfully.

"Don't you think she loved you too?"

"I guess she did."

On those weekend mornings I'd meet strangers in my father's kitchen, where I'd go to pour myself a glass of orange juice. Most of the women my father slept with would borrow his orange silk bathrobe. Shuffling over the white tiles like zombies, they'd put on the kettle and sleepily stir two white mugs of instant coffee. I would stand at the threshold between the parquet of the front foyer and the bright tiles, staring until they'd notice me. Their eyes would look skewed by the overnight smearing of mascara. Some were polite and made chitchat. Some spoke only a little to me, out of what I later realized was embarrassment.

My father warned every woman he dated that he would never remarry. They refused to believe him until it was too late. Sometimes in the middle of the night I'd awaken to his booming voice: "Let's not talk about this now!" But as these women were drawn to wearing his bathrobe, they were also prone to reckoning the limits of his love at an ungodly hour. Breakups tended to occur at 3 or 4 A.M., accompanied by a slamming of drawers, the shattering of a wineglass that left a stain like splattered blood on the walls.

I finally told Ravi all about you one afternoon when he invited me to come and speak to him. I was twelve. We were in the sun room, but there was no sun; the light was produced by

candlelike wall sconces that held wavering electric flames. I told
him how hot it was that afternoon you drowned, how the June
air smelled of pollen and humus; how I caught a fly in my
mouth while I was riding my bicycle to the Freeds'; how the
fish were biting like I'd never seen. I told him how you and I
first met on the street and how you were wearing a blue-and-
white-striped boating shirt and had scraped knees, how the skin
on your arms and face was tanned, how you'd asked me about
the fish I'd caught and how I'd invited you to come and see
them.

Ravi listened to me with hands folded carefully on his loose
turquoise gauze pants, nodding when I said something particularly vivid. And when I was through he told me that your
drowning could very well end up being a blessing in disguise. I
was immediately disappointed. There was no way this could be
possible.

"Look what's happened," Ravi said. "You're sitting here asking questions you might not have asked otherwise. You're going
to learn things you might never have learned. But let's start
from the beginning. The tragedy quite obviously belongs to the
Rosens. They were not paying proper attention to Mark. They
had entrusted his care to a nurse who obviously lacked responsibility. Your being down there by the lake was just incidental to
something that was going on. You were just there watching
what had been set up to occur."

"But if I hadn't invited Mark to see my fish, maybe he
wouldn't have gone to the water."

"Who says? He might have gone anyway. Did you push him
in the water?"

The question startled me and I blushed and grew frightened.
"No," I stammered, worried that he suspected something.

"Did you intend him to drown?"

"No!" I insisted.

Then something in Ravi's eyes fluctuated and he blinked in a

bewildered way. "So honestly, how could there even be a remote responsibility for what happened?"

Then I got the scary feeling that Ravi was gazing through me
at a chart of what had really happened, checking the facts
against what I had just told him. I began to feel invaded and
longed to end the discussion.

"Billy," Ravi said finally, "the drowning might end up making you do something beautiful and humane that brings you a
peace you never thought you'd find."

"Like what?"

"Oh . . ." He smiled brilliantly. "Like teaching small children how to swim."

This felt true to me, profoundly true, but it hardly made me
feel any better. Ravi's smile, however, was soothing to behold,
and I felt more healing from looking at his face than I did from
his well-wrought explanations.

As I grew up, I kept hearing the lake calling for me; it was
like an instinct, like an inner voice, maybe your voice. When I
was old enough I would borrow my father's car and drive out
of the city and through the old neighborhood. I would drive
past our old house, which had been bought by a family named
Kaufman, who, among other things, decided to keep the garish
metal "K" my father had tacked up on the front door. I felt so
strange, so outside myself, looking at the place where we used to
live. It once seemed so unique and special to me, but now it
looked like a normal middle-class split-level, dwarfed by the
ever expanding purple aura of the Japanese maples that my
mother had planted as seedlings. I'd continue driving through
streets lined with similar houses and would end up at your house
by the lake.

I would pull the car several houses past where you lived and
watch from a distance. Your parents rarely ventured outside
while I was spying on your yard. I watched them buy new cars,

install a new sprinkler system, spackle the exterior shingles and paint them a deep, unforgiving blue. So many times I wanted to get out of the car, ring the bell and tell them how much I thought about you. But greater than that longing was the fear that they'd tell me once again to leave the property.

One afternoon I found them sitting outside on folding lawn chairs with an attractive young woman. She had olive skin and long black hair woven into a single thick braid. Puzzled for a moment, I suddenly realized that she was your sister, the baby whose wailing filled the house that afternoon so many years ago when my mother and I had barged in uninvited. How strange that for all this time I'd kept thinking of your parents as bereft of children. Strange too that for so long I'd never seen any sign of your sister: no bicycle parked on its side in the middle of the lawn, pedals still warm from the pressure of a pair of feet, wheels spinning from a recent joyride. I'd never seen any telltale wear-and-tear scrapes on the painted shingles, no cutouts pasted upon the upper bedroom windows. It was as though for all these years your parents had kept her under lock and key like a baby bird grown and raised in an incubator. Where had she been all those summers I'd seen your mother outside tending her garden while your father stood with the hose in the middle of the lawn absently spraying the shrubs? Where had she been when your parents glanced furtively at the water of the lake that was showered in golden light?

A FEW MONTHS before you fell into the lake, my mother and I visited Aunt Tina in Galveston. This was shortly after she had refused to leave her bedroom the entire two days my uncle Marty was away at a history conference in Michigan and Rachel had gone hungry. My mother was concerned, and there was a great deal of unspoken uncertainty in the air over whether or not Tina should enter a hospital.

From as early as I can remember, I sensed something troubling Aunt Tina. When I was still small enough to sit on my mother's lap, I used to listen to conversations between my parents and my aunt and uncle, conversations I hardly understood but whose tones communicated something to me. In the midst of a flow of words from my aunt, my mother would stiffen and clutch me tightly to her, as though something suddenly threatened to snatch me away. I would then peer at Aunt Tina, whose face was flushed, who had broken out in sweat in the hollow of her throat and looked as though she had just realized something awesome indeed.

I particularly remember one night during that last trip to Galveston. We were around the dinner table and the conversation had turned to President Kennedy and his world politics. Suddenly, Tina blurted out, "I don't trust that operator. He's gonna elbow his way right into nuclear war." I noticed that her lips, as she spoke her vehement opinion, fit together with a slight irregularity; they never quite matched. "Don't think the Russians don't know what he's up to—"

"Tina, for Christ's sake," Marty interrupted while glancing worriedly at Rachel and me; the grown-ups weren't supposed to be talking like this in front of us.

"Let me finish!" she insisted.

"Tina honey, we'll talk about it later." My mother tried to place a calming hand on Tina's bare arm.

Tina jerked away from her. "Don't 'Tina honey' me," she snapped. "I'm telling you, if he doesn't watch out it's going to be curtains."

Rachel, who was my age and sitting next to me, ignored the discussion. With a pack of crayons, she was intent on coloring a golden retriever, shading the likeness reverently within the black lines, her dark, closely set eyes appraising the slow progress of her creation. I envied her care—I was the sort of child whose unruly crayons easily strayed beyond the coloring book's boundary. My mother was sitting on the far side of Rachel, dressed in only a bathrobe. Marty was sitting at the head of the table, his tie pulled askew, his balding head moist with perspiration; he had tippled a few too many beers before the meal.

Wearing a Mexican blouse with fancy embroidery, Tina sat next to him.

"So what do you think of President Kennedy, Billy?" Tina suddenly asked me.

Afraid of answering, I held my breath and glanced at my mother.

"Leave him alone, for God's sake," my mother objected. "He's only seven."

"Rachel has an opinion of President Kennedy, don't we, baby?" Tina asked her daughter.

"Uh-huh," Rachel said, not even looking up from her coloring.

"Rachel, your mother is talking to you," Tina said in a soft voice that was spiked with annoyance.

"What?" Rachel said in exasperation, looking up at her.

"I asked you what you thought of President Kennedy?"

"Rachel and Billy, why don't the two of you go upstairs," Marty instructed us in an even voice. Tina said nothing in response to his order. My mother tried to caress her again, which only provoked Tina into making violent shrinking-away gestures. As Rachel and I left the room, I glanced back and saw Tina grabbing a pack of Marty's Winstons lying on the table—she didn't even smoke—lighting one with trembling hands and then inhaling, which set her to coughing. "Wish Kennedy could be more like Roosevelt," she chortled, and then hacked some more. "Now there was a fine President. Who cared about humanity. Kennedy won't melt like the rest of us when they drop the bomb. I'm sure he's got a place to go and hide."

"Cut it out, will you!" Marty cried. "Enough already!"

As Rachel and I left the room, Tina was looking at her husband as though she despised him.

The whole time we were visiting, Tina wore only two dresses: her "happy dress,"—a yellow strapless shift sewn with blue cutouts of planets and stars, and a "sad dress," a gray flannel skirt that she wore around the house often with just a brassiere. She was sad most of the time. When she strolled around the house in her brassiere, I tried to act as though she was wearing a proper blouse and as though I didn't notice anything out of the ordinary. But I couldn't help ogling her breasts, only flimsily hidden by the sheer fabric of the halter. I'd seen my mother in her brassiere; Tina's breasts were substantially larger. My mother felt it was an ominous sign when Tina paraded around the house in her brassiere. "Brassiere," I'd whisper to myself when I was alone. "Brassiere, brassiere," conjuring up television memories where I'd seen men forcefully ripping women's bodices to reveal a brassiere cupping a pair of overflowing breasts. Indeed, I couldn't help hoping Aunt Tina would continue stalking the house in her brassiere; perhaps one day she'd forget to put it on altogether. I'd only seen my mother once or twice without her brassiere. One of those times, when I was six and refused to believe she had no milk to give, I was actually allowed to suck on one of her breasts for a moment.

It was in her gray flannel skirt and brassiere that, a few days after we arrived, Tina grew fixated on windows, complained how even though she'd clean them with newspaper and vine-gared water there'd still be rain spots. But how could there be rain spots when it hadn't rained? She speculated: perhaps neighbors were doing it; perhaps a sprinkler close by was flinging droplets that were ferried by the wind. Saboteurs, it could be Russian saboteurs.

I remembered that the other times we visited Galveston Tina had neglected her housekeeping; now, her home was kept in a state of hyper-cleanliness. She'd spend hours scrubbing—the bathroom, the kitchen—would insist that after I brushed my teeth I had to wipe the basin with a sponge until it gleamed. Perhaps knowing that she soon might be leaving the family for a private hospital, Tina was making a last-ditch effort at being a proper wife and mother.

But that was difficult, as things were continually disturbing her into her fits of anxiety or rage. In the newspaper she'd read the speeches of political leaders, which she'd interpret as neo-Nazi propaganda. She claimed that we as Jews could never shut our eyes completely after what happened during the Holocaust, that the Nazis would always be hovering around us like mushroom spores. A whole society of them might crop up overnight and overrun the United States and then we would all get rounded up and carted off like cattle to concentration camps in remote areas of Utah. One night she woke up the house, claiming she'd spied people out on the lawn dressed in white sheets and peaked hats: the Ku Klux Klan. We all jumped out of bed, fearfully watching Marty arm himself with a baseball bat and high-powered flashlight, which, when beamed out over the property, revealed only darkness. And yet, Tina was the first one to make me aware that there had, indeed, been a Holocaust. Several years later, inspired by her vehemence, I would read the book *Exodus* and learn of the horrors my parents had been somewhat reluctant to share with me.

Unfortunately, Tina's concerns kept her awake at night. She would pace the house like a doomed spirit, whimpering that she didn't feel tired and why didn't she feel tired and why couldn't she turn her mind off? She listened to late-night radio programs like Larry King's, whose interviewed guests often made her so irate she'd call the station in Washington, D.C. She managed to break in over the airwaves only once, with a diatribe against a psychologist who spoke of the ill effects of cold war on children. Subsequently, the directors of the radio show learned to recognize Tina whenever she called and kept her endlessly on hold. On some of Tina's more difficult nights, my mother would get up and brew a pot of Camomile tea. She would sit on the sofa soothing Tina, and the two would eventually fall asleep, leaning against one another.

Despite all of this, I still believed that one day Tina would get completely well. I believed this from having seen another side of her, the creative side that was calmer and saner, never more apparent when she sat down at the piano and filled the house with beautiful music, not only the music of classical composers like Dvořák, Haydn and Mahler but music that she herself had written. She could be muttering and obsessing about anything from cracks in the ceiling to civil rights issues, but was usually able to shed her mood once she began playing the piano. Unfortunately, she never seemed to realize the calming power of her own song. You might suggest to her that she'd feel better if she just sat down and played, but she'd tell you emphatically that nothing in the world could ever make her feel better. Of course, she was wrong.

During that trip I was able to spend a good deal of time alone with Tina, mostly when my mother was driving Rachel places that were more than fifteen miles away. You see, Tina had a periphery of fifteen miles, outside of which she'd start feeling too anxious to travel any farther. It was a strange given that we all accepted, although at the time I couldn't understand what could happen to a person that made them feel nervous once they had passed fifteen miles.

I liked to sit down next to Tina when she played the piano. Even in her most frantic states, she was still able to focus her efforts and scribble ideas on staff paper, refining for hours and hours, muttering to herself. She struggled with the difficult passages, playing them again and again until she made a small change that transformed the composition. I watched her hands gliding over the keys, saw the calmness in her eyes; she always seemed stirred by what she played. She gave so much to her music writing, whereas in other situations she seemed so scattered. I'd wake up in the morning with fragments of Tina's music squiggling like worms through my head. But I always loved the finished piece, a sculpture of notes hewed and polished from a slab of sound.

"*I* want to play music," I admitted to her one afternoon when we were sitting together on the piano bench, after having listened to a soft, thrilling passage.

Tina stopped playing for a moment and sat quietly, head inclined, for once left alone by her perturbing thoughts. Then she smiled at me. "Well, it's time you got a piano."

I was pressed as close to Tina as would allow her to play. She never grew wary of my closeness, and, in a way, encouraged it. I wondered, in fact, what she'd say if I did my old routine, asking whether or not she had milk in her breasts and if I could test to make sure. But fearing she'd mention it to my mother and I'd be found out, I controlled my impulse. Anyway, she was wearing her yellow happy dress, which covered her chest, so there was nothing to peek at.

"My parents won't get me a piano," I said. "They don't think I'm serious."

She looked at me sideways, her eyes shining with fervor. "Of course you're serious," she said. "I can tell just by the way you sit here every day listening to me."

"I fell asleep when they took me to the symphony," I admitted with embarrassment.

"Music is supposed to relax you," Tina said, playing a chord with her left hand and then allowing her wrist to float above her finger position. "It lets you forget. That's one of the reasons why it came about. For Christ's sake, I used to fall asleep sometimes when I went to hear music."

"You did?"

"Sure I did."

Just then I heard a car plunging up the driveway, the motor panting for a few moments and then cutting to silence. Soon my mother and Rachel would enter the house, and the closeness Tina and I shared would be dispelled. "Aunt Tina," I asked urgently, "how come you can't sleep?"

She winced and then swiveled away. Remembering her diatribe at the dinner table, I said, "Is it because you're afraid the world is going to end over Cuba?"

Tina laughed. "That's the least of it."

I was puzzled by this. "But isn't that the worst possible thing that could happen, the world ending?"

Tina drew her lower lip all the way into her mouth and soon her teeth were raking her chin. "I don't think so," she said. "At least if the world ends, we all go together. Worse, it seems to me, is to die all alone."

I tried to picture each fate as best I could. On television I'd seen the mushroom that Hiroshima flowered into after the plane with a picture of Rita Hayworth dropped an atomic bomb. Piles of smoldering rubber, shadow imprints of people burned into the metal girders of bridges that dropped off halfway across a silvery bay. Then I imagined someone alone in a white hospital bed, living off tubes and bottles, head lolling back and forth in agony.

I heard the front door open and saw Rachel come in with large white shopping bags. She announced to us that she had been invited to a birthday party but the party was more than fifteen miles away from the house. Tina took in the news with hardly a reaction. She bowed her head and began playing a slow thundering melody that sounded like a death march. She played louder and louder until she was banging her hands on the keyboard. "Mommy, stop it, please stop playing like that!" Rachel cried. I looked on in horror, imagining that if Tina ceased playing she'd be letting go of her sanity. But then Tina stopped, stood up abruptly and quickly retreated to her bedroom. There she spent several hours agonizing over whether or not to try to extend her perimeter and drive Rachel to the birthday party. We knocked on the door, called for her, but she refused to respond. Finally she emerged from her isolation and asked my mother to take Rachel instead.

However, there was something about being unable to drive

her daughter to that birthday party that perturbed Tina a lot
more than being unable to take her to, let's say, a distant shopping mall to buy new dresses or spiral notebooks or painted
lunch pails. Tina didn't sleep a wink the night of the birthday
party. The following morning, which was a few days before my
mother and I were due to return to New York, she arrived at the
breakfast table with dark blots around her eyes. Marty had already left for the campus. Tina said she had decided to extend
her perimeter to thirty miles, and in the afternoon would drive
to a field of oil rigs approximately that distance from Galveston.
She invited the rest of us to accompany her.

"It's good that she wants to do this," my mother confided to
me when we were alone in the kitchen and I was helping her
clear the breakfast dishes. "Right now, traveling anywhere
seems to be her biggest problem."

Tina had gone back to her bedroom, where, I imagined, she
was plagued with indecision over which dress to wear: the yellow or the gray. First my mother and I cleared the table and
then I watched her slice boiled eggs and chop celery for egg
salad sandwiches. She packed the sandwiches in a Styrofoam
cooler along with a thermos of hot mocha coffee for her and
Tina, two eight-ounce bottles of apple juice for Rachel and me.
She was planning a picnic—hopefully if we reached the oil rigs
—to celebrate the widening of Tina's traveling arc.

"Why does she get like this, Mom?" I finally asked.

My mother turned to me with a bewildered expression.
"Birdie, I wish I could answer that." She shut her eyes a moment and shook her head. "She was never like this when we
were little."

This surprised me. I had always assumed Tina had been born
with her problems. "You mean, something happened to her and
made her change?"

My mother nodded. "Sometimes, and you'll learn this more
when you get older, we start feeling unhappy about ourselves

and often we're really unhappy about things that happened a long time ago when we were children. That's why someone like Aunt Tina will see a head doctor, to find out what happened to make her feel the way she does now."

So people—people like my mother and me—could suddenly change and become like Aunt Tina. This made me nervous. When the four of us walked outside into the chill February afternoon, Tina was unnaturally quiet. She wore neither the yellow nor the gray dress, but rather a pair of army slacks that Marty had given her and a bulky red sweater. She'd first expand her wardrobe, then extend the fifteen-mile territory of comfort to something infinite, and in so doing would become fearless, like the first woman astronaut. She started the car in such an anxious, faltering manner. She was genuinely oppressed by the challenge of thirty miles and the barren lands that lay before us like an endless booby trap.

Throughout the first part of the drive, my mother and Tina kept up a private conversation in the front seat. Every so often, one of them would glance back at Rachel and me to gather how much, if at all, we were eavesdropping. Once I heard them mention "hospital." I shut my eyes from the blurring view of Galveston's outskirts, hoping with all my might that Tina would never have to enter a hospital.

We finally quit the populated regions and barreled down a two-lane road that was etched into desolate terrain dotted with scrub brush and abandoned trailers whose bright turquoise sidings were rusted beyond recognition. Rachel was sitting next to me. Holding a bright green plastic pocketbook affixed with floral decals, she wore a red sweater a darker shade than the one her mother wore, blue stretch pants with elastic stirrups that arched beneath her instep. She was chewing gum and shied away from looking at me directly.

"Do you know where we're going?" I broke the silence between us.

Rachel looked at me wearily. "Yeah."

"Tell me where we're going," I said.

"We're going out to the oil fields," she said with the trace of a drawl. Neither of her parents spoke with any accent.

"But do you know why?"

She turned to look at me insolently, and in the challenge of her eyes I saw a pained acceptance of Aunt Tina's condition. And I remembered that while Marty had been away at a conference, Tina couldn't bring herself to leave the bedroom and make Rachel dinner. What must it be like to know that your mother is unable to leave the shuttered darkness of her bedroom for the kitchen, where cooking dinner is as easy as carving pats of butter and frying eggs?

Rachel sighed, as though having to repeat the truth of her mother's condition only made the idea of it more painful.

"We're going out to the oil fields to see if Mommy can get there."

Just as the words left her mouth, the back seat swerved like a roller coaster rocketing through a curve and I felt us shooting to the side of the road. Accident, I muttered, as I was hurled against the passenger door. The car was soon enveloped by a chalky nimbus, the world outside the window pale and sickly. "What happened?" I cried. "What happened?"

"Nothing!" grunted Tina, who was pitched forward, pressing her forehead against the steering wheel. She battered the vinyl seats. "I just can't do it," she said. "I don't know why, but I can't go any more today. I feel like a milk shake."

My stomach clenched.

"It's okay," Rachel said quietly. "We'll try some other day."

"We've gone nearly twenty miles," my mother informed Tina.

As the dust cleared, I noticed that we were a few hundred yards shy of a service station. The sun was so powerful that the gas-pump islands and the repair sheds and the ellipses of concrete looked grained with black and orange, like photo negatives. There was no one visible at the gas station and for an instant the world seemed to have crashed. Then Rachel leaned forward, worming her way in between the bucket seats, and put her frail arms around the crumpled shoulders of her mother. "Come on, Baby Lu. You can drive it. I know you can," she said cheerfully. "Baby Lu, it's only a little bit farther. Like driving me to Mary Ellen's house. Just think that now we got in the car and we're going to drive to Mary Ellen's. We're gonna stop. We're gonna get gas and then we're gonna go to Mary Ellen's."

Tina turned an ashen, skittery face to Rachel. "But, Mommy Lu," she said, "isn't it a lot farther to Mary Ellen's?"

My mother gasped.

"No, it ain't. Honest, Baby Lu," Rachel said.

"Well, Mommy Lu, it feels that way. I guess I have to keep being a fifteen-mile Baby Lu."

"You're a twenty-mile Baby Lu," I couldn't help correcting her.

"There are only ten miles left," my mother said, her voice cold and reasonable in the midst of this blather. "It's not so much farther. If you want, we can trade places and I'll drive. Maybe that'll be easier for you."

Frowning, Tina wavered for a moment, and then quickly snapped back to herself. She started the car. "I guess I'll just keep going," she said, pressing the gas pedal so hard that the wheels spit gravel off the shoulder of the road until they took purchase on the highway. "I gotta be able to drive Rachel places," she said. "Driving gives me something to hang on to. It's the only space between me and fearing."

"But there's nothing to fear," my mother soothed her as the car picked up speed. "Remember, we're your family. We're with you all the way. You're not alone."

In response Tina shook her head and clenched her teeth.

"What?" my mother asked.

"Why do you always play dumb?"

"What do you mean?"

"That's what made it so hard growing up. You always played like you didn't get what was going on with me."

"Well, maybe I didn't."

"Shit, you were just afraid it's gonna happen to you." Then she smiled wickedly. "Maybe it will."

"Don't be unkind to me," my mother said softly.

Glancing once again at the bitter landscape that surrounded us, Tina shivered and said in a whisper, "Out here . . . just feels so far, Susan. So far. If only you could understand how far it feels. It feels like we're on the other side of the world."

"But we're not," my mother said gently. "We're only a half hour away from home."

"A half hour," Tina said, incredulous. "Do you know what can happen in a half hour."

"What?" I piped up.

"In a half hour you can fly from San Francisco to Los Angeles. In a half hour you can play a whole concerto." Then she took a huge gulp of air and started breathing erratically.

"Come on, now, Tina, breathe like you always breathe," my mother soothed her. "Don't hyperventilate."

"How can I breathe like I always breathe when I'm thinking about my breathing?"

"Well, then, try to keep your mind off it," my mother said reasonably.

"How can I if I know I'm supposed to?" she snapped.

"Baby Lu?" Rachel piped up.

"What, Mommy Lu?" Tina said.

"Remember, Dr. Peterson said you should sing."

"Yeah. All right, then, why don't you sing, Mommy? Shit," Tina hissed, "I hate feeling like this!" She slammed her fist down on the dashboard.

Rachel took a breath and then, in a small clear voice, began to sing: "This old man, he played one, he played knick-knack on my thumb, with a knick-knack paddywhack, give the dog a bone, this old man came rolling home." I looked out at the deadly landscape and felt angry at how strange and unsettled Tina made me feel. We all listened to the lively melody that grew faint and wavering as Rachel got more self-conscious. My mother joined in before she abandoned her singing altogether.

And just as they finished the song, the oil rigs dawned into view. You could see them in the midst of a flat dusty plain, endlessly pumping beneath the weltering sun. In their seesawing motion they resembled mechanical ducks dipping and upending in a dish of water. Some of them were enormous, like dinosaurs harnessed up to milk the crude liquid from the earth. It was an eerie sight, all this groaning metallic movement in the middle of nowhere, like an outstation on an empty planet in some far-flung solar system. No wonder Tina didn't like driving out this far, no wonder she thought it was like being on the other side of the world. "Yippee," Tina said in a deadpan voice. "I made it. I made it all the way."

"And the next time you'll go even farther," my mother said.

"Maybe even a hundred miles," Rachel said.

No one said anything while the car sped closer and closer to the center of the drilling field. The journey had grown so bizarre, I felt that instead of hurtling forward we were flinging out in a circle. Finally Tina turned to my mother. "Don't you care what happens to me?" she asked.

"Of course I do. You know I do."

"Then if you really care about me, you and Marty should let me go somewhere where I can get some good rest."

My mother glanced back at Rachel and me. No! I wanted to cry out. You're not going anyplace like a hospital! Rachel smiled as though they were discussing something as pleasant as cotton candy. "Let's not talk about that now," my mother said.

"Why not? Marty and I have spoken to Rachel. Haven't you spoken to Billy?"

"Yes," my mother said with hesitation.

With that I caught Tina's eye—hazy, opaque—in the rearview mirror. Her glance lingered on me longer than was wise for someone who was driving.

"Do you know where I might be going?" Tina finally asked me.

"Yes, Aunt Tina," I said.

"But do you know why?"

"Come on, don't ask him that," my mother protested.

"I want him to understand. Why should I rely on what you've told him?" she insisted. With that she once again addressed me in the rearview mirror. "Do you know why, Billy?"

"You're unhappy," I hazarded.

"That's right," Tina said. "I'm ludicrous and unhappy."

"Except for playing the piano," I felt compelled to say.

She smiled at me in a funny, almost mocking way. "He's so sweet. He wants to play too," she told my mother. "He wants to play music. Isn't that nice?"

"Yes." My mother was obviously relieved that Tina had decided not to delve any further into a discussion of her illness.

"Nice, just so long as he doesn't let it get to him."

After she said this, Tina braked the car, pulled off the road and the four of us sat in whirling silence. I didn't understand her last remark; I'd always thought playing music made her feel better. And at that moment I felt something passing between us, like a shade pouring from her soul and settling into mine.

Two days later, before the taxi arrived to whisk us to the airport, Tina summoned me to her bedroom. She was still in her nightgown, shadows ringing her eyes from yet another insomniac night. When I entered, I noticed that one shelf in a bookcase had been cleared to make room for an array of medicine bottles whose different heights and widths described a small amber glass city. First Tina gathered me into a hug, carefully placed my head against her breasts, as though she knew all along that here was where I wanted to be. I could smell her talcum skin, her musky sleepiness. "I got you a little something 'cause you've been such a good little sport," she said, gently fracturing our embrace. She stood there so close to me, pushing strands of dark ratty hair out of her eyes.

"You didn't have to," I said shyly, while dying to know what this "little something" was.

"I know. But I thought you needed to get your hands on it right away," she said, walking to a closet. When she opened the door I smelled an amalgam of scented waters and perfumes. From behind a row of dresses she had ceased wearing, Tina yanked out a large black case. Inside it was a nylon-string guitar. I was thrilled. "But now that I've given you this, you're bound to learn on it and play for me one day," were the last words she spoke to me for many years.

Although I did not speak to her, I kept hearing her voice. Again and again, the way I kept hearing yours. When I began teaching myself the guitar, I heard Tina telling me to memorize my chords, to press the strings hard so they'd resound clearly, to master the marking of rhythm with my foot. A few months after we visited, Aunt Tina came back East to enter a mental hospital. My mother told me that she chose a retreat far enough from her family to discourage them from visiting her. Otherwise, my mother explained, every time Marty and Rachel came to visit, Tina would be reminded of how she'd been unable to fulfill her responsibilities as a mother. Of course, I wondered how, if Aunt Tina had difficulty driving-double digit miles, she'd be able to withstand traveling a thousand. Apparently, after that voyage to the oil fields, she had started making longer and longer drives in increments until finally she could log over a hundred miles without losing control of her nerves.

"And of course, if you're flying you can always take a tranquilizer to help stay calm," my mother explained to me.

"But, Mom, if she can travel again, why does she have to be in the hospital?"

"Billy, remember, she has other problems too."

After you fell in the lake, Tina wrote me from the hospital saying how sad she was that I had to be the last one to see you. She told me to be strong, not to blame myself, she promised we'd get together soon. But unfortunately her plans changed and she never remained long enough in the hospital for me to visit her. Shortly after my mother learned that Marty was in the process of filing for a divorce, Tina disappeared from the hospital.

One morning a month later, she showed up at Rachel's school in Galveston, where she had waited on the fringe of an empty playground until recess. Rachel spotted her immediately and ran over. The two ended up talking for a half hour, their conversation attracting the scrutiny of children and teachers alike. Holding Rachel's hands in hers, Tina explained that Marty and she were separating and that he would soon have custody. She felt that being in her father's care was the best thing for Rachel: he would be better able to provide for her and would be more of a stable parent. The two wept and said goodbye; then Tina left her daughter standing alone next to an empty jungle gym and vanished into Mexico.

E IGHT SUMMERS passed before Tina con-
tacted me again, the year I turned fifteen, the year I earned
the rank of Water Safety Instructor. I was teaching swimming at
an old fifty-meter pool in Queens, a great aquamarine vault that
held many more times the amount of water than was needed to
drown. Although I was a competent enough lifeguard, parents
still hovered over my swimming lessons, afraid some mishap
might cause their children to squirt out of my arms, their lungs
flooding with water before I had time to rescue them. While I
was working I often thought of your parents and imagined the
burden they must be carrying. I thought of you gazing at me
through a window that was spotless and clean, a window that

even Aunt Tina would have approved of. Your eyelids were heavy with nearly a decade of sleep, your face, unlike those children who returned to visit the pool in later years, never aged.

In those eight years Tina had severed communication with my family. My mother had repeatedly tried to contact her, had written a slew of letters describing the changes in our lives, never receiving so much as one reply. My mother had received the address of a post office box in a town outside Mexico City from Uncle Marty, who had been mailing Tina divorce and custody documents. Then one day a letter addressed to me arrived at Ravi's apartment. Recognizing her sister's handwriting on the envelope, my mother waited anxiously all afternoon for me to get home. She had forgotten that after swimming lessons I attended team practice and would be spending two hours doing grueling sets up and down the fifty-meter pool, competing against an unforgiving time clock, against other swimmers.

She was standing at the door when I arrived just after seven o'clock that evening. "You have a letter from Aunt Tina."

"Really?" I exclaimed in disbelief.

My mother was blocking the threshold, bare arms crossed over one another, the fabric from a lime-colored caftan billowing like a loose sail in the air-conditioned draft. She pecked me on the cheek. "Phew, Birdie. You smell of chlorine."

"Did you hear from her too?"

She shook her head. "I left the letter on your bed. I'll be in the kitchen. Okay?" With that she briefly raked her fingers through my hair. Her eyes flickered over me and she remarked, "God, Billy, your shoulders are really getting wide."

"Butterfly," I told her.

She murmured something unintelligible as she turned and drifted down a hallway filled with spindly shadows of early evening, the sort of shadows that fluttered along the bottom of the pool. She made a right turn at the kitchen. I watched her for a moment and then headed to my bedroom.

When I saw how thick the envelope was, I grew nervous, wondering why after so many years of silence, of not answering a stream of my mother's correspondence, Tina had chosen to contact me instead. The letter itself was written in a spidery hand on lined notebook paper. The ink ran in places, seemed to have smudged on Tina's fingers; there were noticeable prints on the page. I felt a twinge of recognition, thinking how she had poured out this letter, the only real proof in the last eight years that she was alive.

Tina briefly explained that she was living with a group of Americans who supported themselves by designing and crafting handmade blankets, which they exported mainly to the southwestern United States.

> . . . I know your mother won't understand why I've contacted you first. It's just that lately you've been in my dreams, Billy. Dreams of water. Sometimes we're on this rowboat together. We're trying to cross marshes or lowlands, trying to get to some island, but the boat is leaking and water keeps coming in the floorboards faster than we can bail. Another dream I've had, we're climbing up these really slippery cliffs in the middle of a cataract and both of us keep sliding. I haven't been to a shrink for years now, but I know these dreams mean something because I keep having them.
>
> Marty thinks it's ironic that your parents also got divorced. But I don't agree. Divorces can be signs of health rather than sickness. Marry one person when you're twenty and chances are by the time you're thirty that person might be totally different—and so might you. It used to be that you had to stay with the person you married no matter what. I think divorce is almost as new to the

world as electricity. I think people should get out of their marriages when they find they've changed and relationships are no longer what they were. All this forever-and-forever business is a pile of nonsense. Love burns, dies faster than a lot of other things.

I want to tell you why I chose to come down here. Just like that day we went for that hairy drive out to the oil fields I wanted to explain to you about going into the hospital. I went into that hospital and came to Mexico for the same reason. I knew in my state that being around my family and particularly Rachel was doing a lot more harm than good. A child has to have a healthy environment, understanding and support from parents. Rachel shouldn't be worrying that I might wake up too depressed to drive her to school, unable to cook dinner or whatever. When I knew I could no longer provide the basics was what made me decide to leave.

I left the hospital because they wanted me to let them think for me, which I was unwilling to do. They complained I didn't participate enough in the group therapy sessions even when I told them I had nothing to say. I kept having run-ins with the staff. I used to get so bored I started organizing relay races down the hallways and a couple of patients fell and broke their toes. That made me a real favorite, let me tell you.

Please give your mother my love and when you get a chance send me a picture of yourself so I can know what you look like now.

All my love,
Aunt Tina

I was so captivated by Tina's letter, I hardly realized that I had been standing in front of a roaring air conditioner. The room suddenly felt as cold as a meat freezer and the muscles in my upper back, still warm from the pool, seized up into a spasm. I sat down on my bed, gathered my knees to my chest and began rolling out the grip of the pain, taking deep breaths. I finally felt the spasm calming down.

I folded the lined pages and stepped out in the hallway of the apartment. I heard some faint music, the notes of a recorded wooden flute, escaping from Ravi's library, and figured he was probably having another meeting with a student. I headed in the direction of the kitchen. My mother sat next to the window on a tall wooden stool, leaning with her elbows on a butcher block that was filled with finely minced green peppers and scallions. She had long since stopped her preparations for dinner and was gazing out the window into the dimming light of an airshaft. Sensing my presence, she pivoted to find me offering the letter, which she took from me with a kind nod of her head. She straightened her posture, crossed her legs tightly and read it through without a reaction until she finally fixed me with a bleary gaze that quickly deposited tears on each of her cheeks.

"Mom, don't cry," I said. "I'm sure she expected you'd read it too."

"I know, Birdie. I'm just sad that your aunt and I have become disconnected." She glanced down at her chopped vegetables. "So much has happened to us and I've let her know about all of it and I haven't once gotten a line of acknowledgment."

"Maybe she has a reason for not writing you back."

"The reason is she's angry with me."

I frowned. "Maybe writing you makes her upset."

"It wouldn't make her upset."

"Yes, because you're the person who's closest to her." I reminded my mother that Tina had once selected a hospital far away from Uncle Marty and Rachel so as not to be perpetually visited by the family she had let down.

"No, Billy," my mother said. "*I* let Tina down. The last time I visited her at that hospital I promised her that if the divorce went through she could rely on me for support, that I'd be there for her. But then that summer all those things began to happen to us. And I got so overwhelmed by our difficulties. And I never came through for her."

> *Dear Billy:*
> *I dreamed of you, last night*
> *We were walking by the waterline*
> *The waves were breaking at our feet*
> *The earth had cooled, not so much heat*
> *Our troubles had lifted, it was a happier time.*

That was written on the back of a postcard of Popocatepetl that arrived at my father's apartment six months later, six months after I had replied to Tina's first letter and sent a recent photograph of myself. I was alone when I received the postcard, confused that it had taken her so long to answer my letter in such an odd manner. Now that I was old enough to look after myself, my father had begun going away more, carving from his busy schedule ten-day vacations to St. Maarten and Barbados, prolonging his trips to California several days after concluding the entertainment business that summoned him out there at least once a month.

Although I really missed him, I consoled myself by taking advantage of his absences—as I did that night—by throwing wild parties, providing trysting places for myself, my friends and our girlfriends. My father had a rabbit-skin bedspread, which got a notorious reputation throughout my school as "the place to do it." At my parties, couples would take numbers and patiently wait their turn to make love on the rabbit. I will always remember the thrill of that soft fur rubbing against me in those early graceless fucks, which, if I wasn't getting enough of, at least kept me in frantic fantasy for weeks afterward. I had to hand it to my father, who by this time had developed an artful seduction style. Most bachelors thought they were really with it by installing water beds. My father had built himself a fur den. And the rabbit skin was much more sensual than a water bed— particularly for women who lay against it, feeling it caressing their back. Alexandra, the girl I was dating, claimed that doing it on the rabbit made the act of love feel as though it took place inside an oversized sex organ.

I remember the Saturday Tina's postcard arrived as clearly as I remember the day you asked to see my fish and followed me down to the water. I was throwing a party with my best friend, Gordon, who at the last minute decided to go away skiing for the weekend. He had already invited many people I didn't know very well and one of them was a guy named Corky Sheehan. Tall and gangly, with a fierce wit, Corky Sheehan was heavily involved in a druggy crowd that I had no part of because I was working out with the swimming team. I had told everyone to bring six-packs of Budweiser, but halfway through the evening Corky infiltrated my father's reserve of Glenfiddich scotch, which I—having been busy on the fur bedspread with Alexandra—didn't find out about until two bottles were polished off.

Around eleven-thirty Corky and a bunch of guys left for someone named Benny's apartment, where apparently there was a stash of Quaaludes. I went to sleep. I remember that night you came to me in a dream. I was in the pool, doing sets of butterfly fifties on minute intervals. You were guarding the time clock, sending me off with a "ready, go" each time the second hand crossed the 60. I pushed myself hard and finally got so tired I was forced to quit swimming in the middle of a set. You yelled at me to keep going, and I told you I couldn't. Then you jumped into the water and tried to embrace me, but I refused to let you near me; I thought that by embracing me you'd some- how lure me into dying. I awoke to my own screams, covered in sweat, and it took me several hours to fall asleep again. The next time I woke it was to the scream of the telephone, and when I heard Alexandra's somber voice, my first groggy thought was that she had decided to break up with me.

"Billy, are you there? Are you listening to me?" Alexandra asked.

"Yes."

"Corky Sheehan died last night."

"How?" I croaked into the phone.

Benny lived in an apartment right over FDR Drive. After he and Corky and a couple of other guys took the Quaaludes, Benny conceived the brilliant idea of going up on the roof, where one of the building porters had stashed an enormous bolt of tartan fabric. He got everyone fired on the idea of throwing the cloth off the roof into the middle of FDR Drive, then watching the mayhem it would inflict on the traffic. They all must have been too wasted to realize what they were doing, and in the midst of their folly Corky Sheehan fell with the fabric and landed smack on top of a car.

"A bunch of people are meeting at Jackson Hole to talk about what happened," Alexandra said. "Will you come?"

"No," I said stiffly.

"Why not? You knew him, didn't you?"

"I can't make it," I said, and hung up the phone.

What I'm getting to, Mark, is that something started happening to me in the middle of Corky Sheehan's funeral. Granted it was strange enough, being a Jew at a Catholic funeral, with all the kneeling, the coffin displayed in the middle of the nave, the overpowering fumes of incense and the north, south, east, west sprinkling of holy water that to me looked more like a reproof of us who dared to keep living than a sanctification of the boy who died. I was fascinated how the priest raised this round ivory-colored wafer and, saying it was the body of Christ, broke it into pieces, how the crackling sound could be heard throughout the church. I kept telling myself there was no reason to be upset, as I hadn't known Corky Sheehan very well. But then, as I sat there listening to the organ piping intensely, to his close friends taking the pulpit to eulogize him, it suddenly occurred to me that Corky had gotten smashed on my father's scotch. I heard the words "a freak accident, a tragedy, his life was cut short . . . he didn't live long enough to realize his potential." Something shifted inside me and then a question arose: was I finally attending your funeral, that funeral your parents had forbidden me to witness? I tried resisting the idea, but the more I struggled, the more it overwhelmed me. My thoughts grew so tangled, I lost track of the service and my knees started to buckle. The next thing I knew I was lying on the floor, gazing up at startled faces of strangers who whispered that I had fainted.

One afternoon several months after Corky Sheehan's death, my mother and Ravi and I had a meeting. We sat before their meditation altar on lavender cushions. Ravi was dressed in the vermilion robes I'd seen worn by Tibetan lamas; my mother's hair was twined up into a pile on the top of her head and held with a mother-of-pearl clasp. She folded her hands and began hesitantly: "We want to ask your opinion of something."

"Shoot," I said.

"Would you consider spending your last year of high school in New Mexico?"

"Don't tell me you're thinking of moving there!" I countered. A sudden chill teemed through me and I rubbed my hands together.

"We're toying with the idea," Ravi said, smiling. "To try it out anyway." He went on to say that the place they were considering moving to was outside Santa Fe: Ojo Caliente, New Mexico—hot eye of New Mexico, literally—situated in the midst of mineral springs that people traveled to from miles around.

"Don't you like New York anymore?" I said.

"Well, Birdie, with the sort of work Ravi does it's not as easy to get by in New York," my mother said. "His work is non-profit, remember, and we really can no longer afford to live here. As far as you're concerned, we're basically talking about spending a year in New Mexico. After that you'll be in college."

A surging in my arms and legs felt like poison. I started having difficulty breathing, just like at Corky Sheehan's funeral. Noticing this, my mother said, "Birdie, calm down, we're just having a discussion."

"Okay," I said, gulping the fear. Then, in the midst of it, I managed to glimpse conspiracy. "New Mexico," I blurted out. "You want . . . New Mexico. Tina's already gone to Mexico. Shit, I wonder where Dad'll go—Mexicali?"

My mother reached for my arm. "Billy," she said, "we're not bailing out on you. We're not going to disappear like Tina." She glanced meaningfully at Ravi. "You know us better than that."

"But wait a minute, we've been figuring you'll come with us," Ravi said with a broad toothy smile.

Looking hard at both of them, I said, "I don't want to spend my last year of high school in a new place!"

"There's a great swimming team in Santa Fe," my mother said.

"Mom," I muttered in the midst of a shallow breath. "I won't even consider moving."

"Won't you even try it for a couple of months?"

At this point I would have done anything to end the discussion and retreat to my bedroom in order to be alone with my confusion. "Go ahead, okay? Just go ahead and live out there."

"But that would mean . . . Your father has been around so little lately."

"If you move out there he's going to be around a lot more than you'll be."

"You'd resent us for moving," my mother said sadly. "I can see that."

"Mom, you don't understand something about me. I'd rather have one home in one place with two parents."

"But, Billy, no matter what, that's no longer possible."

"I know. So then don't think anything else will ever be a consolation."

After this, when least expected, I began panicking for no reason at all. It tended to happen when I was on my way somewhere rather than when I was at home. I'd sometimes get advance warning in cool hands and flushed cheeks and my breathing became something I had to concentrate on, to think about. I remembered that ride out to the oil fields and how Tina had grown hyper-conscious of her breathing, her hands shaking at the steering wheel, how she felt as though we'd all been flung to the other side of the world. What could be causing this? I wondered as I combed through the events of the past few months. It was eerie that Tina's postcard had arrived on the eve of Corky Sheehan's death. Did she sense something about to happen? Perhaps she had always known that one day I'd inherit the legacy of her madness, the postcard being the announcement. The thought so terrified me, I was unable to tell anyone about what was happening to me. It was a feeling of coming unraveled, like the way I pictured the tartan leaving the roof of Benny's apartment building.

Whenever I imagined it, I'd be up on that roof with Benny and Corky Sheehan watching the bolt of fabric unrolling in the night air. Its red and green squares would billow out, catching wind like the skirts of a doomed parachute, slowing for a moment, then plunging faster like a bomb. I would hear shuffling next to me, Corky Sheehan dancing drunkenly on the ledge. He'd step off the ledge as lightly as Fred Astaire, as though the air would support his weight. He'd look at me with a shrug of his shoulders, an ember of mirth in his eyes, but then, as he began plummeting, he'd make these frantic climbing-up motions, his eyes bulging in fear. I'd see his body going through all sorts of contortions as he fell and finally he'd end up far below clutching the roof of a moving car like a starfish.

Dear Billy:

You're wrong. I had no idea that you'd ever get panic attacks. Getting my postcard the day your friend died was just coincidence. I happened to write down some verses that were whirling through my head. There's no piano anywhere around here, so instead of writing music I started writing little poems to myself.

I never saw any similarity between you and me except for one thing you don't even know about. I may as well tell you now. Now is as good a time as any, I suppose. Something happened to me when I was fourteen that I've had to deal with too. A man I was fond of, a man who worked for my father, took me on a boat ride to an island. He got drunk during the crossing and when we got to shore he took me into the woods and forced me to make love to him. After he sobered up, he said all kinds of things to make me afraid of telling anybody about it. I thought I was in love with him at the time and that made it even worse. So I kept what happened to myself for several years. Finally I was able to tell your mother. But she couldn't really help—we both were too young to understand what it could mean on the inside. And so I continued trying to deny what happened. Tried to bury it. But the harder I tried, the harder it pushed back. Finally, as I got older I started having difficulties with all the everyday things . . .

Why did she have to tell me about this? Did she think it was going to help me? Here she was trying to say we were hardly similar, and then she reveals her own experience. Jesus Christ, she was raped at the age of fourteen—no wonder she has so many problems.

And yet, once I finished reading the letter I shrank back from Tina's story. The event, told casually, struck me as being as far removed from my life as she, who had now spent so many years out of the picture. I wanted to ask my mother about it, but never got an opportunity, as she and Ravi were busy sorting through their belongings and furniture, packing up to move to New Mexico. But there was also part of me that was afraid to ask, that chose to doubt what Tina had written, because I wanted to block it out.

A year from then, shortly after I entered the University of Vermont, this beautiful woman was pointed out to me, a senior who had been raped as a freshman in an empty lecture hall. She had pale skin, fiery black eyes and long dark hair worn in a tightly twisted rope that draped crookedly down her back. She'd walk around campus hunched over herself like an old woman, discouraging any admiration of her spectral beauty, silently communicating the fact that she felt ugly. I heard that the man who attacked her—like Tina's assailant—got away with his crime. Whenever I saw her anywhere I went, she was always alone, signaling a feeling of helplessness. And it soon began haunting me that Tina had to live through such an experience.

One day, as I was darting across an icy road, I collided with someone—this very woman, who had been trudging along with her eyes cast down and wasn't watching where she was going. She slipped and would have fallen if I hadn't taken hold of her elbow. The moment I touched her, she threw me a piercing hateful look.

A few weeks later, I was sitting on a chartered coach en route to the first away swimming meet of the season. Already anxious about traveling, I was nauseated by the bus's smell of strawberry disinfectant that reminded me of an antibiotic medicine laced in fruit syrup that I was once forced to swallow. The gawky, red-haired backstroker who sat next to me had steered our sporadic conversation down the predictable avenue of "easy lays on campus" and at one point asked, "You know that chick with the long black hair who walks around with her eyes to the ground?"

"Yeah, what about her?"

"I hear it's all a front. I hear she'll lay for anybody who wants to put it to her."

I whirled on him. "You don't know what you're talking about."

"What do you mean I don't know?"

"She's not loose, you idiot! She's frightened of people!"

"How do you know what she is? I heard she was looking for it that time—"

"You're out of your fucking mind!"

"Hey, Kaplan, cool down, will you," said somebody behind me.

"Take a good look next time, you jerk! And then you'll see what it did to her!"

And then suddenly invisible fingers pressed against my throat and I had to strain in order to breathe. I got this feeling like water rising over my head and being unable to rise with it. I bent forward and forced myself to inhale deeply, but despite the effort my breath felt haunted and shallow.

"Hey, Kaplan, I'm sorry, okay?" said the backstroker, who thought he had caused this distress. "I was just talking."

I shook my head and kept tightly curled up.

"Jesus, Kaplan, now what's wrong with you?" he said.

"Nothing," I managed to groan. "Just nausea."

"What, you nervous or something?"

"Leave me alone!"

Why had I gotten so angry? I shut my eyes, sat up and shoved back against the vinyl seat, feeling a current of electricity jumping through me. My fingers turned to ice, my forehead to flames.

Word of my situation snaked its way forward to the coach, a squat ex-military man named Wal, who ducked out of his seat and ambled his way back to where I was sitting on the aisle. "What is it, Kaplan?" he said, resting a large hairy paw on my shoulder. He had a bullet-shaped head. "I hear you're not feeling good."

"I don't know," I muttered, looking down at my legs, which were chattering of their own will.

"What do you mean you don't know? Are you sick or what?"

I turned to the window. The bus had dragged its way through a bleak late autumn landscape of Vermont into even more desolate regions of upper New York State. I noticed a dilapidated farmhouse whose bright red sidings appeared like a surface wound in the grayness of the landscape. I wished I could quit the bus and knock on the front door and beg whoever answered to take care of me, to let me lie down on a bed and be comforted. This rural person, moreover, would know simple remedies to coax back the feeling of control: a drink of molasses and milk, an egg cooked sunny side up, soft cotton sheets that had been washed a thousand times and smelled like woods and mulch from being aired out to dry. "I'm not sick," I finally managed in a quavering voice. "I'm just overpsyched."

"Well, then don't psyche up so much. Psyching up tires you out. You're okay to swim, aren't you?" Wal asked, now in a gentler voice. This bullethead could hardly hide his true concern.

I looked straight ahead and nodded. "Yeah, I'll be fine."

The bus finally entered the rinky-dink campus of our opponents. And when we disembarked into weather that felt even colder than the weather in Vermont, I reflected that if you hadn't died, I might not have been standing there in such arctic temperatures, holding an absurd green-and-gold canvas team bag with a silk screen of a catamount. I had become a strong swimmer mainly to conquer fear.

A representative of the other team led us across the parking lot to a large recreation building, where I spotted a bank of pay phones. I didn't ask permission to veer away, I just started walking toward them. "Where you headed, Kaplan?" the coach called after me.

"I've got to make an important call."

I dialed my mother's number in New Mexico, praying, as two thousand miles were instantly bridged, for them to be at home.

"Hello?" She answered after the second ring. I couldn't help thinking that she sounded cheerful.

"Hi, it's me."

"Birdie," she said. "Where are you?"

"At a swimming meet. In some hick town. And I'm . . ." I began spilling tears all over the phone receiver. "Mom, I've been having these really weird anxiety attacks."

"What do you mean?" she asked nervously.

"Like I start to panic for no reason. I have trouble breathing. I get like I'm going to pass out."

Then I confessed everything about Corky Sheehan and the funeral and the panic I'd been feeling for the past year.

"I just wish you'd said something to us when this started happening."

I nearly spit out: "I would have, but you were so busy moving to New Mexico!" But I merely said, "It's been hard for me to talk about it."

"Ravi is a great help with things like this."

"Look, Mom, I feel like I can't breathe!"

"Billy, now listen . . . you're okay. Of course you can breathe. You're just feeling some pain, I think."

"Why am I feeling pain?"

"Because . . . maybe you're working things out."

I shut my eyes and said, "Mom, I'm so afraid I'm going to end up just like Aunt Tina."

A shocked silence followed. "No, you're not, Billy!" my mother said emphatically, a little too emphatically. "You're you. You're not Tina. You have a hand in how you're going to turn out. Now just hold on a second and let me get Ravi on the other phone."

Although she muffled the receiver with her hand, I could hear her yelp for Ravi. I blew out a plume of frosted breath and waited.

Ravi finally materialized on another extension. "Your mother tells me you're at a swimming meet," he said calmly.

"In some godforsaken place," my mother croaked from her line.

I looked around the uneventful bush-league campus. Godforsaken it certainly was. The last of my teammates were just now filing into the cavernous dilapidated sports complex. Wal was standing at the entrance door frowning at me.

"I'm scared, Ravi," I whimpered. "I'm so scared."

"Of what, Billy?" Ravi said.

"I don't know."

"Try to put it in words. If you can. Tell me how it began."

I explained the discussion of the woman on campus who had been raped. "And then after I got mad at him I started freaking out."

"What's freaking out to you?" asked my mother, sounding more secure now that Ravi was on the extension.

"I guess suddenly feeling like I'm not me anymore and wanting to cry because I'm so scared I'm not me."

"So you're allowed to cry," my mother said.

"I'm not going to cry in front of the team!"

"Go off where you can be alone. Go for a walk around the campus," Ravi suggested.

"It's too cold out. And there's no time for that."

Wal had finally lost his patience and was now stalking toward me. "Oh shit," I said. "Here comes my coach. I have to get going. What should I do?"

"Listen to me, Billy," Ravi said. "Feeling panicked is part of the process of being alive. Unfortunately, most people deaden themselves so they won't dare feel it so strongly. You have to be brave to feel this kind of panic. But just know, whatever happens, the fright will never kill you—"

"No, it'll just give me a heart attack."

"It won't do that. I promise you. But it'll teach you something about yourself if you could just try embracing it. If you keep resisting it, you'll get even more scared. I think you'll be fine for the rest of the trip. You've already put yourself through enough suffering today. Concentrate on swimming a good race. You'll feel a boost from that, later on. Guaranteed."

"And please call us when you get back to Burlington," my mother said.

I put the phone down and hurried to meet Wal in the parking lot. "What the hell's been going on?" he demanded.

"I, I had to call my father," I stammered.

"You had to call him right now?"

"I was supposed to remind him to sell some stock that he had in my name."

"Oh, really? What stock?" Wal asked keenly.

"Something you wouldn't be interested in," I said curtly. "Something altogether too risky."

Strange how I never got nervous during swimming meets. Once I was standing on the starting block, completely dry, my near-naked body hyper-sensitive to the intense scrutiny of silent spectators, of my teammates, a breeze tickling the small of my back, I'd feel an inexplicable calm. And when the gun sounded, my piked entry into the cold, shocking water was as perfect and clean as the puncture of a knife. After an initial gasp, I became a synchronized machine undulating through each stroke.

The 200-yard butterfly is one of the most grueling races. It requires a sustained burst of energy to keep up the crucial rhythm of a stroke that cannot be properly performed unless one has spent years conditioning for it. When I whipped out of the first turn I saw I was already half a body length ahead of my main competitor, who wore a lemon-yellow tank suit, which in the deep blue shone as brightly as a beacon. I pushed the first hundred yards, gaining as much as I could, and then consciously lengthened my rhythm for the second hundred, conserving energy for the final two laps. At the height of each stroke, my arms powered through underneath my body and catapulted me dolphinlike out of the water. I could hear the thunderous cheering of the crowd before my head plunged into gurgling water silence. I kept looking down at the black line painted along the bottom of the pool. It led me along straight and steady, crossing another black line at each turn. The line was my pool boundary and I relied upon it.

When I took the race by several seconds, my teammates jumped up and down, roaring victory. The crowd, however—populated mostly by fans of our opponents—had grown still and twittering at the loss. I went on to capture the 50-meter freestyle, emerging a double winner from the competition, a close contest that was only decided in our team's favor after the last relay.

One particularly dismal evening ten days after the away meet, I made the mistake of mentioning my panic attacks to my father over the telephone. As soon as I told him, I regretted what I had said. Especially when he called back ten minutes later to insist that I fly home for the weekend. But rather than tell him I got anxious when I traveled, I figured I'd use the visit to play down my difficulties and to assure him that I was feeling okay.

Refusing to endure another panic like the one on the bus ride, I copped five Valiums from an insomniac girl in my dorm, two and a half for the plane ride down, two and a half for the trip back. I was feeling pretty sloshy by the time I boarded the aircraft and the forty-five-minute flight went without a hitch. I got to the apartment shortly before my father and met him at the door with two opened bottles of ice-cold Beck's beer.

"Maybe you shouldn't be drinking, Billy," was his immediate reaction.

I rolled my eyes, cursing myself for mentioning anything to him. I followed my father into the master bedroom. He tossed his slim leather briefcase on the black mink throw which covered his king-sized bed—he'd recently graduated up to a more prized fur, whose feel, ironically, was hardly as sensual as the rabbit. "I was a little overwhelmed when we last spoke," I explained. "I'd stayed up the whole night before I talked to you, studying for an exam. Anyway, I'm fine now." I suddenly panicked that the Valium I had for the trip back had dropped out of my shirt pocket—oh God, then what would I do? My frantic fingers finally located them.

"Billy," my father said, taking one of the cold beers, "if you're having difficulties you should get help for them."

"Dad, I told you I'm fine."

My father quickly stripped from his pin-striped charcoal suit down to his boxer shorts. He grabbed a burgundy cashmere cardigan out of a set of lacquered drawers that glided in and out effortlessly and put the sweater on over his bare chest. He was lightly suntanned from spending two successive weekends in early November at a friend's condominium in Santo Domingo, his legs quite dark, in fact. At forty-seven, he was still the picture of physical health, trim and lithe, his hair artfully dyed by a barber. It was as though having failed to hold a family together and resuming his college dating practices had allowed my father to remain younger longer. I, however, felt as though I'd been left in the wake of disintegration, my hair already beginning to leave me in clumps that gathered on the brush, forming small wreaths that clogged the shower drain.

"Let's go into the living room," he said.

"You mind if I finish my beer?"

"Go ahead, Billy. Drink your beer."

Walking behind my father, I noticed that he carried with him a pink square of scratch paper that came from a plastic container on his office desk that held thousands of such squares; he sometimes used them to jot notes for our more important discussions.

We both sat down on the sofa. "I did some investigating," he began.

"Oh shit," I said. "About what?"

He looked at me quizzically. "I'm going to help you. I'm your protector."

"Dad, I'm nearly twenty," I said, belching. "I don't need protection."

"Okay, then I'll be your adviser." With that, he reached for a pair of half-glasses that lay all alone on a huge blood-colored agate with a flat polished surface that served as an end table to the sofa. My father read from the slip of paper, then peered at me above the lenses of his glasses.

"You ever hear of somebody named Gita Romano?"

"No, why should I know her?"

"Well, she's some famous psych . . . I guess it's -chiatrist."

"Is she your latest entry?" I managed to ask despite my deflating spirits.

My father narrowed his eyes. "Don't be a wise-ass."

"You didn't call her up did you?"

"Of course I called her up."

"Fuck! Why did you do that?"

"Why do you think?"

"Fuck if I know."

"Stop staying 'fuck' all the time, will you? I called her on your behalf."

"Thanks for getting my permission."

"I'm your father. I sometimes do things without your permission."

I flushed and for the moment was too angry to speak. I threw my head back and took a deep swig of beer.

"She specializes in late-adolescent disorders."

I belched. "Then the two of you should get along perfectly."

My father squinted at me. "Why are you being such a smart-ass?"

"Because I didn't ask for your help."

"You told me what was going on. I took that as a hint."

"I can see that."

"Well, look what went on with your aunt, for Christ's sakes!"

Wincing, I closed my eyes.

"I'm sorry, Birdie," my father said in soft concern. "I shouldn't have mentioned that."

"It's all right," I said. "It doesn't surprise me."

"Look, I just thought if you could see someone like Gita Romano, maybe you'd nip this thing in the bud. Apparently, she's not like a normal shrink, who just analyzes. She"—he looked down at the pink paper again—"gives pep talks to her patients. Suggestions."

"How come you know so much about what she does?"

"I know somebody whose daughter goes to her."

"I figured as much."

"Billy, come on. I want to help you . . . I want to provide this for you. Especially because I figure I'm responsible for some of what's going on here."

Then I went into action. "Okay, Dad. Let's say I do need to see a therapist. There's a slight problem here."

"Yeah?"

"I . . ." I faltered, knowing that once I explained, it'd be like stepping into a bottomless pit. "I feel really weird whenever I'm traveling," I told him in a shaky voice. "Even short distances."

My father took this in with a surprised fluttering of his eyelids. "Oh?" he said slowly. "I didn't know that."

"So if you want me to get therapy, let me get it up at school in Burlington."

My father tossed me a look to mean that one couldn't get proper psychological help in a place like Burlington, Vermont. "Billy," he resumed, "don't let your problem prevent you from getting the best care." For a moment, he glanced at the bank of windows that viewed the East River. Next to the windows was a marble pedestal supporting a large bronze sculpture of a football player in hiking position. My father crossed his legs at the ankle. "I mean, what would happen if you had—God forbid—some kind of cancer and there was a specialist at the Mayo Clinic. Would you not go to Minnesota because you hated traveling? Of course not. You'd buckle down and get there somehow."

"But in this case I do have a choice. There are plenty of good therapists in Burlington. New York doesn't have a corner on the market."

"Billy, I'm just saying that a large demand induces a finer, a better supply. After all, don't we have the best museums, ballet companies, restaurants, hospitals? So it is that our shrinks are also of the best caliber. Believe me . . ." Yet again he looked down through his reading glasses at the pink paper. "Gita Romano probably has ten other kids who are afraid to drive home from college for the weekend." He grinned suddenly.

"Dad, it's not funny!" I snapped.

"I know it's not funny."

"Then why are you smiling?"

"It suddenly struck me funny. I'm sorry."

Blinking back an urge to cry, I said, "I took two Valiums to get here this weekend."

My father rolled his eyes. "Jesus," he said. "How did you get them?"

"Some girl I know."

"Well, I think you should let Gita Romano decide whether or not you should be taking Valium."

"Dad, this is going to be really expensive. Not to mention depressing."

"Let me worry about that. Anyway, it'll be nice to have you around more often. I'm lonesome without you," my father said with a silly smile.

Later that afternoon I reluctantly took a taxi to Gita Romano's office on upper Park Avenue. I was shocked at how pretty she was. I liked her buttery gold hair, her quiet crystalline voice, the faint accent that perhaps was Swedish. She was dressed in turquoise pants and a yellow blouse that was covered by a loosely crocheted vest.

Gita told me that for therapy I'd be lying down on her couch, a weathered-looking leather affair whose headrest abutted double-pane windows, which didn't quite extinguish the street noise of Park Avenue. The moment she mentioned this I was perched in a stiff, high-backed chair next to her desk. I told her I didn't feel like lying on the couch. She said we'd work up to it. During the third session she asked me to just try it, so I went and lay down tentatively. The leather molded to my body, immediately feeling snug and comfortable, like an old friend, which made me feel vulnerable and then suspicious. Gita asked me how I felt lying there and I told her she had me lie down on the couch because she really wanted to check out my body and my crotch.

There was a curt silence. "Why would I want to do that?" she said, flipping her voluminous hair behind her shoulders.

"Why not?" I said. "You're gorgeous. Don't you flirt with all your patients?"

"Do you think I do?"

"Most of the guys who come in here probably want you."

'What kind of 'guys' do you think come in here?" she asked.

"Fat, slobby guys with little dicks," I said angrily.

"Oh, really? Anyone else?"

I stopped, suddenly feeling stupid and sad about having gone on like this. In the deepening pause, I could faintly hear car horns on Park Avenue, an even more distant cry of a paramedics van, as well as a screeching of brakes. "Children of divorces probably come here."

Over the course of several sessions, I told Gita Romano about the afternoon we met and how you fell in the lake. I told her about what had happened to Tina, the journey to the oil fields and how I was afraid I'd end up like her. I told about Corky drinking my father's Glenfiddich before he fell off the roof of Benny's building and how at the funeral, when I thought of you, panic started plaguing me like a demon. I confessed to my fear of away swimming meets and of flying to New York every weekend and how I copped Valium to make these trips bearable. I felt guilty about my father having to lay out so much money for therapy and round-trip plane tickets between New York and Burlington, funds that would better serve a Third World relief organization.

"Billy, panic attacks are not hereditary," Gita explained to me. "They happen to many people for many different reasons. In fact, they're a relatively common occurrence." She paused for a moment, reflecting. She grabbed a sharpened pencil out of an upright leather cylinder at the edge of her desk blotter and began twirling it between her fingers. "But let me ask you something," she said finally. "How did you used to feel going back and forth between your parents' apartments?"

The question had the unexpected power of a scythe which,

when aimed at the hard trunk of a tree, inadvertently finds a soft spot and plunges to the core. I felt this dark sap of pain rising from somewhere. The feelings were so fresh it was as though they'd just been inflicted by the sight of you floundering in the water and then lying on the ground with white bile coming out of your mouth. "I felt bad," I admitted. "I felt like . . . I guess . . . like if I didn't get there I'd go under," I said, and began weeping.

With a quick flourish that obviously came from practice, Gita Romano flicked tissues from a gold marbleized box at the edge of her desk, stood up and handed them to me. She sat down again and scribbled a prescription for a tranquilizer, which she said had a shorter life than Valium and would only minimally affect my reflexes. I would be able to take it on the way to swimming meets. The prescription would be temporary until she could better understand what was troubling me.

At the end of that weekend, when I got the old anxious flutters on the way to La Guardia Airport, I popped one of my new pills, which came in the shape of a turquoise diamond. If it was anything like Valium, it'd be a while before the drug would take effect. In the meantime I began to feel stranger and stranger, until the sense of who I'd been up until then and the sense of who I actually was now, at this moment, were at total odds with one another. It was shocking to actually be me. Riding in the taxi began to seem more vague than being in the midst of a dream. It was terrifying to feel so removed from myself. But then I grew aware of a leaden sensation in my neck and shoulders. River light glinting through the girders of the Fifty-ninth Street bridge splintered into blades. A voice in my head said, "Who gives a damn anyway, who cares!" I had to admire the stuff; it worked pretty quickly.

---⊙---

I LONGED FOR a relationship. The longing was only made more acute by the fact that in all the years since you departed, not one of my father's affairs had lasted for more than a few months. Dozens of women had slithered through his life like water through a sieve; the only proofs of their existence were cosmetics orphaned to the medicine cabinet of the guest bathroom, cosmetics that added up to a composite woman who used Lancôme moisturizer and Guerlain bath oil, Jean Patou perfume and Prince Matchabelli eye shadow. Many of my father's attractive dates were only a few years older than I was. Veiled, however, with makeup and chic clothing, they easily looked in their early thirties. Most of them were sexy and I dreamed of making love to them. And during those weekends I commuted to New York for therapy, a few openly flirted with me when my father wasn't in the room.

When my father's girlfriends began flirting with me I realized that the power he held over me was shifting, that something else besides position and money could sway the female eye. I toyed with this new pleasure. Whenever I met his dates, I'd purposely wear my tightest University of Vermont tee shirt. A woman might be sitting cross-legged in the living room, and I'd saunter out of the bedroom to talk to her. Having a tendency to speak quickly, I deliberately slowed down my enunciation and stared boldly with a sleepy intensity. I'd wait until my father left the room to refill drinks or replenish the cheese platter and would cock my arms behind my head and stretch catlike so that my tee shirt would draw up and she could see my stomach, with its fine coating of dark hair, rippling from sit-ups and hard sets of butterfly. And then, after I'd taunted whoever it was with my body, I'd excuse myself to go whack off in the guest bathroom, where many of the women bathed and perfumed themselves.

My father knew exactly what was going on. But instead of throwing me a dirty look or excluding me from cocktail hour, he'd retaliate by waiting until we were alone and bluntly asking me if I was "getting any." Although I always said I was—even though most of the time I wasn't—he'd wink at me as if to suggest that he could divine any exaggeration. Besides, there was hardly the glint of the satisfied lover in my eyes, but rather one of hunger; not to mention the fact that my skin remained pale and prone to overnight rashes of acne, which I figured were telltales of an unchanneled, pent-up sex drive. Indeed, the only date of mine my father ever met was a woman named Melissa, whom I invited home for a weekend because I was certain he would covet her.

Melissa was two years older than I, at the top of her class in the English department, an absolutely stunning towering blonde. When my father met her, he blushed deeply and for a few moments could barely speak. But then he recovered his composure and tried to be charming. Melissa seemed to appreciate his wit. I could tell she found him attractive. We went to Gino's, my father's favorite Italian restaurant, where he was chummy with the maître d' and was able to soak up preferential treatment by the staff, who made him seem to be an important person. Halfway through dinner, he discovered that Melissa was a classic movie buff. As the two of them chattered away about films I'd never seen, I watched him leaning toward her convivially whenever he wanted to make a point about an actress or a director or a writer. Suddenly, it seemed that my plan to lord Melissa over my father might backfire, that she'd end up liking him more than me, that by the end of the weekend they'd be together and I'd be the odd man out. Panicked over losing both of them, I was hardly able to speak or eat. I felt helpless the way I did when I first saw you out in the water with no one to grab hold of; I now would be left to flail around for myself. But then the tide of the evening changed. In the midst of talking about all these famous people, my father couldn't help filling Melissa in on his personal connections to many of them. Eventually, she shot me this bored, exasperated look which meant she was far too sophisticated to buy into name-dropping. By the end of the meal, she was treating my father indifferently.

After I'd been in therapy for several months, my father met a woman named Faith, and the ten-year cycle of loneliness threatened to come to an end. I'd arrive home from my Friday session with Gita Romano to smell the same perfume, which turned out to be Chanel 19. In the hallway closet, I began noticing a full-length red fox coat, which clung statically to the surrounding flock of my father's cashmere overcoats.

Faith was of slighter build than most women my father usually dated. She never flirted with me and I never flirted with her. She was the first person in all the time my father owned the apartment who actually took pains to make it feel lived in rather than just a utilitarian hotel suite. During the reign of Faith, whenever I arrived home after seeing Gita Romano, feeling stripped of my secrets and my will, I'd find interesting things, like a spiky pink bromeliad brightly claiming a dusty pocket of the foyer, a new Italian lamp taking up residence on a stark and gloomy end table, baskets of spider mums placed where the sun, streaming in promiscuously through several different windows, could not reach. Instant coffee was replaced with Italian-roasted beans, augmented by a powerful coffee grinder and a French-plunge coffee maker. A Cuisinart appeared on the barren kitchen counter and menus of Chinese take-out were removed from the refrigerator door, where they had been held beneath strawberry magnets. The refrigerator was stocked with fresh carrot sticks and Camembert, cartons of brown eggs, half gallons of whole milk and real butter. The cleaning woman's odor of window cleaner and ammonia was replaced with spring-scented potpourri.

"How's it going with you and Dad?" I asked Faith one afternoon after they'd been together for six months, a record in itself. We were sitting at the glass dining table, me with my beer, Faith with a cup of steaming Italian coffee. She had bought an apple pastry at Dumas and it was laid out on a black plate, cut neatly into quarters. I had formed a habit of telling her about whom I was dating, and if things were going badly, she'd give me fairly sound advice.

She smiled thinly. "You know your father. He tends to be rather vague about commitment."

"So why do you stay with him," I asked bluntly, "if commitment is what you want?"

Two red dots appeared in the pale planes of her cheeks. "Don't you want me to stay with him?" she asked.

"Of course I want you to stay. But I also know my father."

Faith bowed her head, and I stared down at her fair roots and pink scalp. This particularly vulnerable view of her made me feel sad, bombarded by a sense of her fragility.

"Your father said a lot of things when we first met that fell by the wayside. In the beginning he wouldn't even talk about a routine. Now we spend Friday, Saturday, Sunday and Wednesday nights together."

"What about living with him?"

She looked at me keenly. "Of course I want that. But I guess I have to give him some more time."

I looked out the floor-to-ceiling window and spotted a helicopter hovering above its landing pad just down the street from the apartment building. For some reason, I found myself thinking of Corky Sheehan, now dead nearly three years. It hardly seemed so long. I heard Faith take a long sip of her coffee.

Several months later, in mid-November of my sophomore year, I received a call from Faith late one night in Burlington. Her voice was in tatters. A trustworthy friend of hers had spied my father having an intimate lunch with a brunette. "He was kissing her fingers," she confided to me angrily.

"What did he say when you confronted him?"

"He told me that she was an old girlfriend and that he got carried away after a few glasses of wine. He promised me that, besides you of course, I was the only person in his life."

"So, maybe you should take him at his word."

"You think I should?" she said sarcastically.

"Don't ask me. I never dated the man."

Faith hesitated and then admitted that just recently she had broached the idea of their living together and he had balked at the suggestion. "Hence the other woman," she said. "Who is like an escape hatch."

"Maybe you should have waited longer before talking about living together."

"I can't help it, Billy. It's gotten very intense for me. I love him very much," she said. "I need a commitment. I need some security."

"I understand," I said.

I could hear her breathing going jagged and figured she had started crying. "It gets so scary," she said, gulping. "You begin to put up with much more than you'd ever imagine, because you feel so attached to a person. The hurt makes it even more difficult to get away. Sometimes I think scars are a stronger bond than healthy flesh."

"Don't talk like that!" I cried.

"I'm sorry," Faith said.

She must have ended the relationship later on that night; the following morning my father called with news of his breakup. He sounded really upset, which I thought was a good sign. Unfortunately, I had to make a class and was unable to talk for very long.

"Dad, if I were you I'd call Faith and try to make up with her."

"You like her that much?"

"I think she was after a better life. She didn't care about your connections or your money."

"The only thing is, Billy, I do like seeing other people."

"But why?"

"I guess I don't want to limit myself."

"Dad, if you get serious about someone, you don't see anyone else. I don't believe I have to tell you this."

There was a long silence, during which my father sighed. "Well, if I feel like I still want to go out with others, then maybe she's not the right person for me."

"Dad, after all this time, after ten years, there really hasn't been anybody. Shit, I wish I could meet as many people as you did."

My father chuckled. "You'll get your chance, Birdie," he said. "You'll have it all. Don't worry."

"How do you know?"

"What do you mean? You're young, you're not even twenty-one. You're a great-looking kid. You're smart." There was a pause and then my father said shakily, "Birdie. Shit, I really screwed it up, didn't I? I screwed it up so bad! How could I do this to myself?" He spoke as though the person who had booked the table at the restaurant and kissed the other woman's fingers was his adversary, someone over whom he had no control. "Billy," he said, "will you come down to Florida with me for Christmas?"

"Please, Dad," I said. "You know how I hate traveling."

My father and Faith had tentatively decided to spend some part of the holiday in the condominium my father recently purchased in Florida. Faith and I had made plans to decorate a tree, which, being Jewish, I'd never done before. I'd been hoping that for once Christmas wasn't going to be me and my father having dinner in some expensive and empty restaurant, exchanging gifts of neckties and malachite cuff links between the main course and dessert.

"So, you'll just take one of your pills before you go to the airport."

"Dad, can we talk about it tomorrow?"

"Billy, please. I want you to come down there with me," he said. "I hate being alone. Just say you'll come."

"Dad, I have to get to a class!"

"Okay, then I'll let you go," he muttered and hung up without saying goodbye.

The Avalon was a tear-shaped building on the West Palm Beach side of the Inland Waterway. It was the first tall building constructed in the area and stood apart from other high-rise clusters that later on were etched into the skyline. Each resident of the building was allotted a parking space in the asphalt lot that surrounded the building, their name stenciled in large white letters at the head of a painted rectangle that was the approximate size of a grave. Every other day, it seemed, one of the Puerto Rican porters was outside in the sweltering sun with a long-handled roller, a can of black paint and a can of white paint, lining up letter stencils. With such a high death rate among the elderly residents, the apartments kept turning over and names had to be blackened over and redone. As it turned out, our space, "Kaplan," was located almost directly below the outdoor terrace of our two-bedroom apartment. When I got bored, I'd flick orange peels off the terrace, aiming for our parking box.

Waiting for us upon our arrival was a letter from the agent who originally had sold my father the condo. In light of the recent real estate boom, a year later the apartment could now be sold for nearly twice the price. "That's fantastic," my father exclaimed. "If this guy can get me double the price I'll definitely sell."

"Aren't you being a little rash?" I asked. "I mean, by next year maybe it'll be worth three times as much."

"Nah," my father said. "The real estate market is more erratic than that. Chances are it'll level off. Maybe even drop."

"I thought you bought this place for relaxation."

"I did, but I also bought it for investment."

The apartment had just gone through a six-month redecoration process, the headache of which had been borne—ironically, now—by Faith, who had designed the interior. The carpeting was off-white and matched the wicker sofa that was covered in cream-colored raw silk. The sofa was complemented by a black lacquer coffee table. A leafy banana plant flourished in a Balinesian urn, a huge fern hung from a Mexican tile pot. The walls were painted snowdrift white and filled with Art Deco lithographs and framed posters of gallery exhibitions in places as far away as Turin and Rio de Janeiro. The place had a light, airy feeling. Faith had never seen it completed.

"But what will you do if you sell it?"

My father shrugged. "I don't know. Buy another."

"Then what's the point?" I said. "You might as well stay here. You kept telling me how wonderful it was."

"There are other wonderful apartments."

It was now obvious to me why my father was so keen to sell the apartment.

He called the real estate agent early the next morning and gave a listing. "How about if we play a game of tennis?" he suggested once he got off the phone.

"Nah, I don't feel like it."

"Come on, it's good exercise."

"There's supposed to be a fifty-meter pool five miles up the road. I'll take a drive later on and work out there."

"Billy, let's do something together."

"You want to go swimming with me?"

"Not really."

"So then we'll get together later on in the afternoon. Go shopping or something," I said.

"I'll give you a handicap," my father offered, grinning. He knew I was reluctant to play tennis against him; it would mean losing. I reminded myself that after I took up swimming and started working out with a team, my father, who once willingly raced me, refused to compete against me.

"No, thanks, Dad," I told him.

He made a few calls and finally scraped up a tennis game with an attorney he knew who was vacationing in Palm Beach. He invited me to watch, but I declined. I didn't want to wait on the side of a tennis court. The idea of watching a yellow ball bouncing back and forth unsettled me.

My father called at one o'clock to say that he and the attorney were going to lunch. He invited me to hail a taxi to the tennis club and join them. "I'd rather take the car and go swimming," I told him.

"I'll probably be two more hours," he informed me. "Can you get a taxi there?"

"I'll go when you get back," I said coldly.

Two more hours turned into five. Six o'clock rolled around and there was still no sign of my father. What was all this "I need you with me now"? I wondered angrily. A bunch of bullshit to get me down here. Now I was stuck; it was nearly dark, too late to go swimming. I started getting nervous that maybe something had happened to my father. Could he have been involved in a car crash on the Dixie Highway, or worse still, could his car have fatally careered off one of the many bridges in Palm Beach and plummeted into the Waterway? Perhaps the state police were futilely trying to contact the New York address on his waterlogged driver's license. I paced the apartment like a prisoner. The plants and objects that Faith had lovingly chosen began to palpitate menacingly like vital organs inside the body of an enemy. My pulse was racing; I timed it at 125 beats per minute, which was a lot faster than my normal resting 48. Was I getting enough oxygen? You're here, I reminded myself, you're you. I gave myself a little cuff in the face to emphasize it. Seven o'clock came and my father still hadn't returned. Where the hell was he? I stood out on the terrace, sweeping the parking lot in the dusk out toward Flagler Drive, keeping my eyes peeled for his rented Dodge Aries. I looked down at our vacant space. The white letters of "Kaplan" gleamed like phosphorescent algae, spelling my father's name in a grave on the Waterway. I finally couldn't stand the anxiety anymore and was about to pop a blue diamond when I saw my father's car crawling into the parking lot. The door flung open and he jumped out. "Sorry I'm late, Birdie," he burbled.

"Jesus Christ, where were you?" I demanded.

He looked up at me sheepishly while swaying on the balls of his feet. My God, he was plastered. I'd never seen my father

drunk before! "Just driving around, Billy," he said. "Just thinking about things."

Over the next few days there was a parade of real estate
agents and customers. Some of the people who saw the place
were quite vocal about how they'd change the decor and what
the condominium lacked, even though they themselves didn't
appear interested in buying it. I disagreed with most of the
comments and couldn't help but take them as snide remarks
about the failure of my father's relationship.

"I've gotten a couple of offers," my father boasted to me on
Christmas Eve.

We were sitting on the raw-silk sofa that Faith had shipped
down from New York. The sofa faced a wall that was completely mirrored and captured the reflection of the opposite
shoreline as well as a silvered view of the Inland Waterway.
"One of them is in the ballpark at one-sixty-eight. I was expecting one-seventy-five. The guy claims he won't come up any
higher. Think I should accept it?"

"I don't know the value of property around here."

My father got up off the sofa and, placing his weathered
hands at the small of his back, straightened slowly. "Ooof," he
said. "Am I stiff. Getting old, I guess."

"No, you aren't," I told him.

He went to the kitchen to pour himself a glass of freshly
squeezed orange juice. "Can I get you some, Billy?"

"Thanks. I've had enough already for today."

Wishing he would keep the apartment, I went out on the
terrace and took in the panorama of Palm Beach proper: stark
white homes, both angularly modern and traditionally classical,
inset in the deep green fissures of formal gardens, surrounded by
tall private hedges of privet and yellow *Canarium* and cypress
trees, whose squiggling branches looked like intertwined primi-
tive limbs attached to fuzzy clumps of hair. A flux of jet planes
were constantly gliding down to the airport or taking flight

over the water, so many tourists coming and going for Christmas, so many potential condominium buyers, so many happy couples, who years down the line would betray one another and end up selling their vacation getaways.

I turned around finally. My father was standing in the middle of the living room, holding his glass of orange juice as though it were an offering. His eyes, particularly pronounced by his suntan, looked like sapphires. He was steeped in a daze.

"What are you thinking about?" I asked him.

"Oh, just that once I make a deal on this place I've made a deal on ending it with Faith." He looked around the room. "She put a helluva lot of time into it."

"No one is forcing you."

He shook his head and then admitted, "I've been calling her up late at night, after you've gone to sleep."

"I thought she asked you not to."

"I know, but I can't help it." My father expelled a long sigh. "I can't blame her for wanting out. I was lousy. She says . . ." He faltered. "She says she just wants to forget how important I was to her, that each day she's not with me, she feels a little less disappointed, a little more detached." He shook his head. "All I know is I love her."

I was dumbfounded.

"I have to tell you," he went on, his cheeks and lips twitching with unchecked emotion. "I have to tell you that I'm under such strain at this moment that I can't see straight. I wasn't under this much strain when your mother and I got separated."

"You probably don't remember," I said.

"Yes, I do," he insisted. "Yes, I do. And besides, there was so much more at stake then, so many years together, a house, and of course you. Billy, I never really faced up to what I did, to what happened with your mother. I just threw myself into other women, one after another, until one morning I woke up and the ache for her was finally dull. And that makes me wonder if, rather than Faith, it isn't your mother I'm really grieving for."

Moved to hear my father speaking this way, I started crying. "Don't," he said, "because you'll get me started."

"So? What's wrong with that?"

"It'll weaken me. And I've got to stay strong."

I left the living room and went to my bedroom in order to be alone with my sudden rawness. My father didn't come in to comfort me. I listened to the ice clinking in his glass as he sucked up the last of his freshly squeezed orange juice.

For our Christmas Eve dinner we drove to a restaurant in a residential area of West Palm Beach. It was a block away from a gay bar, whose patrons lingered outside, eyeing us as we strolled along the sidewalk, tossing low-throated remarks and hissing appreciatively. My father got nervous and darted ahead, as though afraid to be thought the elder of a homosexual couple. At first I was amused by his easily flappable confidence. But then it occurred to me that, still rather youthful and attractive to most women, he was made aware, by the men's direct and to-the-point appreciation of me, of the graphic truth. I was younger. I was in better shape.

"Why don't you come out with me tomorrow and play tennis," he suggested once we were seated in the restaurant.

"I told you I don't want to play tennis."

"You'll get it back in fifteen minutes."

He was waning. I was waxing. Beating me in tennis would momentarily shade the sharp reality of this truth. "Nah," I told him. "I like my routine."

"All you do is swim and lie in the sun. You're tan enough."

I checked out my arm, figuring I could be a lot darker. I glanced at my father's forearm, which was mottled by overexposure to the sun, but powerful and gristly with veins from years of tennis and golf.

"Why don't you make your old man happy and play a couple of sets. We'll get up early tomorrow and go out on the court before it gets too hot. Nobody will be out there on Christmas."

"All right, all right." I grudgingly gave in.

Then the waitress appeared and we inadvertently ordered the same thing: chilled cucumber soup and stone crabs. I waited until she left and then I leaned toward him.

"Dad, I know you're going through a difficult time right now, but sometimes I wish you just wouldn't press me to do things I don't want to do."

He looked crestfallen. "Look, if you really don't want to play tennis you don't have to. It's just that I'm happier when I'm playing tennis, and out on the court you won't have to see me being depressed."

"Dad, there's nothing wrong with being depressed. I'd be upset if you weren't depressed, because it would mean you didn't really care about Faith."

"Let's not bring her up."

"Why not, if she's the reason why all this is going on? Why you're being so insistent about everything, why you're selling the condo. Come on. Face it!"

My father's face deepened in color, just as the waitress arrived with the first course. "Shut up, Billy," he hissed as a soup bowl was put before him. Suddenly finding herself in the middle of a contretemps, the waitress nearly dropped the other bowl into my lap.

"All right, I'll shut up," I said, once she'd left us.

We were surely a long way from the early days of the divorce when my father and I would go to restaurants and he would try to explain why things were the way they were. Then, due to a lack of practical experience, I had remained silent and played with my food while he droned on and on about the pitfalls of living.

"Don't worry so much about being a downer," I finally told

him. "We've always spent Christmas together. For better or for worse."

He grinned and leaned forward and told me how much he appreciated hearing this, how much better it made him feel. I wished I could have told him how I was afraid he was doomed to fail at love for the rest of his life and how his failure challenged my own ability to form a relationship.

When we arrived home from dinner we exchanged our gifts. I gave my father the leather shell of a date planner; he gave me a submarine watch with a built-in timer. There was a Christmas pageant along the Inland Waterway, and we went out on the terrace to watch a procession of sailboats, masts trimmed with neon lights, gliding past in baroque silence. Motor launches sputtered along, spot lamps trained on their decks where women dressed like parrots in green tights and plumed body stockings danced. Santas, wreathed in tulip bulbs, stood on the prows, waving at a faceless audience of people like my father and me, who stood on condominium balconies watching in solemn privacy. Christmas carols blasted from everywhere, bouncing over the water, so that by the time the sound reached my ears, the familiar melodies were warped.

A heavy cloud cover advanced over the skies that night and Christmas morning was grim and overcast. At ten o'clock my father and I went to play tennis, and by noon he had won in straight sets, 2 and 3 and 1. Feeling woozy from not playing in so long, I struggled not to give up the last set for love. The victory obviously buoyed his spirits, and it was hard to believe that he relished winning as much as he seemed to. After we were through playing, my father dropped me back at the Avalon and then continued on to the real estate office to sign a deposit receipt. The condo was sold; he had finally convinced the buyer to come up $4,000 to $172,000.

I took the elevator upstairs, taking deep breaths full of sweet humid air. I walked through each room of the apartment, thinking how in a few weeks all the stuff Faith had carefully bought and arranged would be ripped out and replaced by new furniture and carpeting. Life here would be repaved, the parking space restenciled with another name. It reminded me of when my parents had sold the contents of our house in a garage sale and I had watched all my furniture being carted away by strangers.

"You're such a brawny kid," I suddenly remembered my father saying to me once. "It amazes me that you got all that anxiety going on inside you." "What does my build have to do with my brain?" I had asked him. "Your emotions aren't just in your brain," he had answered. "They're part of your whole physical makeup."

Maybe he was right, I thought, as I walked out on the terrace, leaned on the railing and stared down at the empty parking space. Maybe my build should make me emotionally stronger. Well, it doesn't, I thought dejectedly as I got shocks of weakness in my legs, feeling simultaneously drawn and repelled by the column of distance that separated where I stood on the terrace and the bold white lettering of "Kaplan" eleven stories below.

I was standing on the balcony, watching rain-engorged clouds scudding across the sky, puffs of black wind skimming the choppy Waterway. I didn't feel anything give way, the way they say usually happens, but something must have shifted. Up until then I'd always been aware of everything that had happened to me, aware of disorientation, aware of fear. But now there must have been some kind of dislocation with a blip for a reaction. I lost track of what was going on. I know at some point I thought of you strongly, and could smell wood burning and then ozone from the approaching storm. I didn't even have a thought to the contrary, some part of myself which said, "Whoa, kiddo, think about this one first." It felt quite natural to climb over the railing and stand on the ledge with my arms behind me, holding the metal grille. I simply got drunk on the distance down to the parking lot. I focused my eyes on our name, "Kaplan," and was going to remain straight-legged and drift forward, flat into the space. Even my heart beat slow and steady the way it did before the start of a swimming race, when I'd bend down, recoil off the blocks and jackknife into an unblemished pool.

The door flew open. My reaction was to grip tight, to somehow hide what I'd been doing, as though caught in the act of masturbating.

From the side I managed to glimpse the expression that seized my father's face; it was as if everything dear to him had been heaped on an islet that was now sinking into the Inland Waterway. I was fascinated at how his mouth gaped, lips and tongue turning to jelly, his strong body suddenly grown frail. God, he must've left the car on the other side of the building. In a high-pitched voice that didn't belong to him, he entreated, "Don't move, Birdie, please don't move, just keep looking . . . at me . . . Dad." Huge droplets fell on my shirt, staining it. I looked down at the dark blemishes and thought they were blood. I looked at my father. I could think of nothing at all to say. Then the skies broke apart in a downpour. My father approached me slowly, eyes boring into me, as though afraid of what I might do. But I just watched him. He grabbed my arm, first gently, then like a vise, and helped me back to the safe side of the railing. And we stood there clutching one another in the midst of the rain.

ONCE WHEN I was younger, before you died, I tried to figure out what death was. I was acting out the Civil War with a bunch of other kids, playing a "killed Confederate soldier." I was lying facedown on the ground beneath an umbrella tree. Trying to ignore my heartbeat, I asked the question: What is death? The answer came: You don't sleep in your bed; you can't wear your clothes; you can't eat your food. You don't care whether you'll ever see your parents again, or that someone else might take over your room. I breathed in the smell of the dirt and lay completely still. So this was death, only you couldn't say it was death, because you wouldn't be able to think it. It would continue forever, but you wouldn't be able to judge how long forever was although you knew it would always be.

Over several therapy sessions Gita Romano asked me to describe what had happened in Florida. As I spoke I was lying on the couch, from where I was forbidden to look at her. I detailed my father's breakup with Faith, the condo's being sold, the depressing conversations over dinner, how after yanking me off the balcony he insisted that I take two of my tranquilizers. Then he called my mother in New Mexico and the three of us discussed what had driven me to the edge of the terrace.

"But, Birdie, what came over you?" my mother kept asking.

"I told you, I was depressed."

"We all get depressed, but why did you have to take it so far?"

"I guess I was trying to see what it would feel like."

"Because of what happened to that friend of yours?"

"No, Ma. I wasn't even thinking about Corky."

"Billy, remember you called me that time from the swimming meet when you were feeling frantic? Why didn't you call when you felt like going out on the balcony?"

"Because . . . I had no idea what was happening," I tried to explain. "I had no idea what was going on until the parking lot was staring at me."

"Jesus Christ, Susan," my father said. "Did you hear that? Do you know what this means?"

"Hold on a minute, will you, Michael!" my mother hissed, and then said to me, "Billy, listen to me, you're of age now. If you do yourself in it'll definitely mean that I failed you. But, honey, it'll also mean that you failed yourself. And that's something you should really think about."

I explained to Gita that now whenever my father and I were to meet at his apartment in Manhattan, the first thing he'd do upon walking through the door would be to call out for me. If no one answered, he'd rush to the windows and begin scouring the streets twenty stories below to make sure that no ambulances were attending my mangled body. As I spoke, Gita seemed less affected by what I said than I had imagined she'd be. And when I finally mentioned this, she asked what I felt her appropriate reaction should be.

"Horrified," I sneered, "like everybody else."

"It doesn't sound like your mother was horrified," she pointed out.

"I don't think she believes I'd actually do it."

"She's entitled to her opinion. She certainly knows you. But do you want her to be horrified?"

"I don't know."

"Because it sounds like you want me to be."

I shrugged. Gita shifted in her chair and then I heard a pen scratching against a piece of paper. "What are you writing down?" I asked her.

"You tell me."

"Horrified," I said.

"A pretty potent word. What does it mean to you?"

"Scared to death," I said.

She waited a few seconds before asking, "Have you ever been scared to death?"

"I've told you."

"Tell me again, Billy."

"The time my mother and I drove with Aunt Tina out to the oil fields."

"Why then?"

"Because she got frightened she'd be unable to make it?"

"What would happen if she didn't make it?"

"She'd die."

"How would she die?"

"She'd get so scared she'd have a heart attack or something."

"I see." Gita hesitated and then asked, "Any other time you've been that scared?"

"The drowning, obviously," I said in annoyance.

"What about the drowning?"

"I've told you about this drowning a million times."

"Every time you tell it, there's something a little different in the story, something that helps us."

I wished I could see the expression on Gita's face. "I guess just seeing him out there in the water and not being able to save him."

"What about that?"

"I was afraid it was going to happen to me one day . . . like punishment."

"Punishment." Gita gently repeated the word as she tilted back in her office chair, which creaked against the strain. A single ring of her phone jarred the frantic stillness like an alarm and I heard the characteristic click of her answering service.

"Can't you turn that fucking thing off while I'm here?"

"So, Billy," Gita said without missing a beat, "I'd like you to tell me if you intended to jump off that terrace."

The question grasped my lungs so that it grew difficult to breathe.

"Just relax. It's only a question," she said. "For goodness' sake, I'm not asking you to get back up there."

"What's so weird is, I'm afraid of heights too."

"All right, we know this. But what do you think you were doing out there."

"I thought we were supposed to be figuring this out together."

"We are. This is your part."

I glanced up at the ceiling, where, in the last few weeks, a blue water stain had burgeoned like an inkblot. "Why can't you cover up that stain?" I scolded Gita. I'd already told her the stain reminded me of the man-of-war jellyfish that frightened people from going in the ocean down in Palm Beach. When she didn't answer, I turned to search the expression on her face.

"I'd prefer that you not look at me," she said. "You know the arrangement."

"But I need to see you."

"I think you need to see me because you're avoiding the question."

"Why do I have to answer it right now? I feel like you're pressuring me." I hesitated. "To get results. Because my father called you up and challenged your credentials."

There was a brief, thoughtful pause on Gita's part. "We have no control over what he does," she said with her inevitable self-confidence. "And he certainly has no bearing on your treatment."

Looking up at the man-of-war, I groaned. "All right." I could hear Gita creaking back in her armchair. "I think I was really waiting for him," I said. "I think I was waiting for my father."

Gita sighed. And when I turned to look at her again, this time she didn't admonish me to avert my eyes. She had a pleased expression on her face. "I think you were too, Billy," she said, just as her next patient rang the doorbell.

"I'm sorry about laying the cost on you, kid," was the first thing Tina said to me the night I returned to school after Christmas vacation, after the Mexican operator had cleared that I'd accept the charges. Her tone was matter-of-fact, as though only a few weeks and not years had lapsed since our last conversation. She sounded exactly the same as I remembered. "I'm just a little tight on moola right now. I should say I'm always tight on moola. And that's *not,* I repeat, *not* a solicitation for funds."

"How did you get my number?" I said, immediately suspicious. "Did you hear from my mother?"

"Billy!" Tina suddenly exclaimed. "You got a man's voice. You're all growed up now! I guess I don't know you anymore, do I?" Indeed, I must have sounded strange to her—a heavier voice, a more adult manner. "I got a letter from Susan," she said in a more sober tone.

"I figured."

"She didn't write me specifically about you. We've been corresponding for the last few months. They finally installed a pay phone near where I live. And I just called her up one day. When she heard it was me she damn near dropped her teeth."

"It's really been a long time," I said. "How have you been?"

"I've been hanging in. I'm now running the blanket-weaving business. Which is doing quite well for me."

"Are . . . you feeling okay?"

"Pretty well these days. How about you?"

"I'm sure my mother told you," I said stiffly.

"A little bit."

"Did she tell you what happened in Florida?"

"Yeah, so big deal."

"Well, then, you know."

"Billy, are we talking at a bad time?"

"No, it's an okay time."

"Are you upset that I called?"

"No. I'm . . . glad you called. But you can't expect me to start spilling out everything. You haven't been around."

"Well, maybe I can help you," she said.

I said nothing in response to this.

"Why don't you try talking to me a little bit."

"Because I don't feel like just talking."

"Give me a chance, Billy. At least for the fact that I've always been fond of you. And after all, this is my particular area of expertise."

"Don't you understand it's hard for me to admit, especially to you, Tina?"

"Why especially to me?"

And then in my cold dormitory room there was a gasp of heat that made the phone receiver feel as though it might melt into a puddle of plastic in my hands. "Because . . . didn't everything start happening to you when you were about my age?" I finally blurted out.

"Billy," Tina said quickly. "I've told you not to compare yourself with me. You and I are very different."

"You said that in the letter. And then you had to go and tell me your own story."

"I thought the story would help you."

"Well, it didn't. It made me feel worse."

"There's no reason for that, Billy. My life has no influence on your life. None whatsoever."

"Except that when I hear about it, I feel closer to you," I said.

My admission ushered in a silence, during which I decided to tell Tina my own version of what had happened down in Florida. She listened to me carefully, and after a few moments of her own reflection, she said, "Look, Billy, if your worry is that you're going crazy, you're not going crazy. You're just an extremely anxious fellow. There's a big difference between the two, believe me. I never worried about going crazy—now there was something to worry about. I believed in everything that was happening to me."

"But I believed . . ." I hesitated. ". . . that I was going to jump."

"I think you were just fantasizing. Let me ask, did the idea cross your mind before you went out there?"

Gita had posed a similar question. "No."

"Had you been serious, I think it would have. Were you on medication that day?"

"Not before it happened." Then Tina wanted to know what I was taking, and I told her.

"Oh, that shit. I was on that shit for a while."

"Did it help?"

"Sure, it helps, but never permanently. Billy, the only way to break through this is relying on nothing but yourself. That was the only way I broke through all the barriers I had, like the time we drove out to the oil fields."

The mentioning of the oil fields made me shudder. And now that we had talked about the essential fear, I was now more forcibly struck by the fact that it had been so many years since I had last spoken to Aunt Tina. "So then if you're feeling well now, why aren't you coming back?" I challenged her.

There was a fuzzy pause and I heard a dull clamoring at the other end, as though Tina accidentally dropped the phone. Finally, she muttered, "Coming back isn't so pressing anymore. For one thing, Rachel has a stepmother."

This surprised me. "So what? That doesn't mean anything. Don't you at least want to see her?"

"Sure, I want to see her. But I don't have the money to pick up and move right now."

"Have you seen her at all?"

"She came down here once. Unfortunately, she got dysentery and Marty wouldn't let her visit after that. I honestly can't blame him. It's not the safest spot on earth. Or the cleanest. But, Billy, Rachel and I write all the time. We haven't forgotten who we are to each other. There's still a lot of love between us. She's my daughter. I'm her real mother."

"No, Aunt Tina," I said. "I don't accept that. It doesn't make sense to me. That you don't feel the need to see her."

"Discussing my life is not why I called you," Tina said sharply and then suddenly chuckled. "Shit," she said. "You got a lot weighing on your mind. I think this must be the payback for when you used to ask me things about myself nobody else would dare ask—except, of course, the shrinks."

"Like what did I ask you?"

"Oh, things like 'Why can't you sleep, Aunt Tina?' or 'Why do you get so depressed, Aunt Tina?' You really had a lot of nerve in those days."

"I wouldn't ask those things now," I said.

There was a significant pause and then Tina continued. "If I came back now I'd only end up hurting Rachel. I'd create a conflict; another woman raised her. I think Rachel would feel she'd have to choose between us. My illness wore her down enough." Tina expired a sigh. "So, Billy, for her sake, *because* I love her, I think that now I have to stay away."

"But that must be so hard on you!"

"I'll admit it isn't easy."

"Tina, why do things have to get so complicated?" I implored.

"For me right now, things couldn't be simpler. Maybe you think they're complicated because you feel so responsible for everybody."

I took this in for a moment and then told her that I didn't know what she meant.

"I think you do know, Billy," Tina said.

The weather turned warm again. School let out for the summer and once again I accepted a job lifeguarding and teaching swimming. I loaded up my car and began driving home to my father's apartment. This time, I was doing an experiment: taking Tina's advice and trying to complete the trip without tranquilizers. I felt pretty relaxed driving along the backbone of Vermont, dazed by the sights and smells of new grass on the fields, the gentle towns with their country stores and flagpoles whose pulleys clanged in the wind. I was able to carve out four hours, dipping within two hours of New York City before I started to come apart. My breathing grew labored and my hands felt moist and clammy. My thoughts jumped randomly from subject to subject. Nearly forgotten scenes in the distant past bubbled my concentration like summer air waffling above heated asphalt. I put one hand over my chest: irregular heartbeats. I began noticing the sound of flying insects as they splattered against the windshield. Each time one hit the glass it made a "hupping" sound. I could feel the reverberations of this impact in my upper arms and in my cheeks. I tried to take a deep breath, but my lungs felt tight as a drum. The verdant landscape, the tall metallic silos on the passing farms, all conspired into a menacing blaze. Don't hyperventilate, I reminded myself. Find some distraction. I glanced at my watch, willing the time, the miles, to pass. I turned the radio up and tried singing along with the music, but that did little to calm me down.

I had just begun the dreaded debate of whether or not to take a tranquilizer, wanting so much to carry on my life without this dependency, when I happened to notice a sign: "Swimming 2 Miles — Open for the Season," with a directional arrow. I impulsively took the exit, figuring a grueling swim might quell some of my inner fire. I followed a narrow surface road with thick maple woods on either side. It was four o'clock in the afternoon, the sunlight fracturing through a tall dense network of evergreens. Tangles of larkspur and Queen Anne's lace flourished along the side of the road. Finally, I could see shivers of water through the trees.

Several miles wide, the lake featured a roped-off swimming area that enclosed two square wooden floats a good distance offshore. The place was quite busy. The narrow pebbly beach was thronged with sunbathers and small children darting in and out of the water, splashing in an endless commotion. I figured I'd swim past the ropes and continue along, hugging the shoreline. I parked the car, locked my valuables in the trunk and changed into my racing suit. I found a remote spot on the pebbly sand, spread out a towel I'd kept in the back seat. I dug a hole in the sand, in which I dropped my keys, then filled it, marking the spot with my tennis shoes. I grabbed my goggles, ambled carefully over the pebbled beach to the lip of the water and started limbering my muscles.

And then I noticed that the water was red. My head pounded

and my eyes teared; at first I thought it was a hallucination. A middle-aged woman wearing a white bathing cap adorned with rubber flowers paddled nearby in shallow water. I asked her tentatively if the water was red.

She regarded me warily. "Course it's red. Can't you see that it's red?"

"Why is it red?"

"Iron."

"Thanks," I said, diving in. I surfaced, sputtering. As it was early summer, the water was quite chilly. I don't know why, but something about the color kept bothering me. It also tasted strange, like liquid chalk. I swam out until I reached the rope line with its string of small white buoys attached to a net, slimy with algae, that dropped like a protective curtain down into the lake. Various bands of sunlight trolled the depths of the red water, making it look like the inner sanctum of a garnet. As I dove over the line I heard a whistle shrill in the background. The lifeguard had leapt down from his white wooden throne and was now gesturing at me to swim back to shore. I had obviously disregarded a cardinal rule. I poured on a sprint, showing him I was a strong swimmer, but the guard still continued to wave. I shortly rounded a bend in the lake and soon was out of range.

I could still hear the whistle, but it had grown fainter. Relief, being out in the water, totally self-reliant, unafraid of an element that most people feared. I continued swimming, passing quaint cabins built on the lake, wooden docks scaling down to the water where motorboats or sailboats were moored. But then a thought occurred to me, at first casually and then forcefully, that I was swimming in blood. But whose blood? My own? Yours perhaps? When I got out of the water would my skin be stained, as though I'd killed someone? Then I grew aware of the sound of my heart pumping. At first, I tried to ignore it, but that only made it grow louder and louder. Treading water with my legs, I covered my ears. But that only magnified the pounding until it grew as loud as a timpani. The water seemed to be turning a deeper red; maybe my heart was pumping blood into the lake. Frantically, I began checking my arms, my legs, my stomach and shoulders for ribbons of bleeding, but could find nothing.

I took a deep breath and dove down to where the water lost its ability to hold light, to where the ruby color bled into darkness. With my arms I propelled myself farther and farther until I reached soft slimy tendrils of weeds that grew out of muddy sand. I stayed there until my lungs nearly collapsed. I spun back up to the surface, gasped a few breaths, and suddenly it dawned on me that today was June 3, the anniversary.

In that moment I forgot everything I had learned about surviving, how to know where I was as opposed to where was safe. I surrendered the ability to swim to shore, I even forgot how to breathe. The only alternative seemed to be allowing water to enter my body, to let the red become my blood.

But then, close by, the surface surged, a whirlpool burst through the skin and gave birth to a slick mass. I screamed and the scream yanked me back. A young woman was laughing at me. Another hallucination? She had blond hair, darkened richly by the wet, freckles on her nose, a gold chain and locket glistening around her neck. The fabric of her bathing suit hugged her breasts and reminded me of your mother descending into the lake and how the fabric from her bathrobe slicked against her body.

"You swim here from the beach?"

I looked at her quizzically, not quite believing she was there. "Yeah," I stammered, managing to tread water.

"Do you need help?"

I whimpered.

She grew alarmed. "What's wrong?"

"Cramped," I managed to say.

"Where is it? Tell me where it is, I'll knead it for you."

I shut my eyes and groaned. The pain of you was now great. It couldn't be soothed; it lived in the bed of my body, a place that no one could ever touch. "My leg," I muttered, and she immediately reached for my calf. "No," I said. "It's okay, now."

"You sure?"

"This water is so *weird*. Why is it this color? I want to get out."

"It took me a year to get used to the color myself. Just don't look at it and you won't notice it."

I looked at her as though she were insane. "How do I do that?"

"Easy. When you swim, keep your eyes closed."

A simple solution. To everything. And then she smiled. Her eyes were a honey brown, small stones in a deep setting, the bones in her neck were prominent. I was suddenly embarrassed.

"My name's Sarah," she said.

"Billy."

"You okay to swim in?"

I peered beyond Sarah to the shoreline of evergreens, as deep in color as a charcoal smudge. Farther out a speedboat was cutting across at an amazing clip, parting the still water like a plow. "I guess so."

We swam side by side. Sarah was a steady swimmer, with broad, powerful shoulders. When we got to shore, I lay on the ground and stared up through the dense trees at blue shreds of the sky. My body was churning. I took deep breaths and tried to calm down. Sarah stood over me. "You don't look okay."

I shrugged.

"My family has a cabin nearby. Nobody's home. Why don't you come over and have something to drink." Sarah lent me a hand and helped me up. She was solidly built, like many swimmers I knew. As we strolled along a path in the woods, she explained that her family's cabin was once the bathing house to a large lakefront estate that had belonged to an aviatrix. I said little as we walked and she tried to make me feel at ease, joked and prodded me with her elbow.

"You're a good swimmer," she said as we came within sight of a house made of split timbers. "That ever happen to you before, these cramps?"

I shook my head.

"Did you eat before you went in?"

"No."

Sarah opened the door and I followed her inside. Everything in the cabin was white: white muslin curtains that matched a white muslin sofa. The walls, the color of ivory. The ceiling vaulted up to a skylight through which sunlight poured like milk. Once we were standing inside, Sarah came to within a few inches of my face and said, "Something's wrong, isn't it, Billy?"

"Yes," I said.

"Why don't you sit down and just tell me what it is."

"Okay," I agreed, because I knew it was no longer possible to keep this to myself.

"Do you want to come and see my fish?" I had asked you. To think that this question had altered the course of our lives. What had prompted me to make that offer? For up until then I had ignored you, who were so many years younger than I. Of course you were going to say yes; it was an honor being asked by an older kid to play.

And after all, the fish were beautiful. Orange carp with golden heads and silken tails, softly fanning water through their gills in the bottom of my shiny metal pail. You bent over and stared at them. I remember you so clearly, dark umber hair with its fine sheen, the blond down on the back on your neck, your smooth olive skin. You made soft gurgling sounds of pleasure as you reached into the pail and caressed the slimy dorsal side of a carp, which slithered away from you, until I said, "Stop it, Mark, don't do that!"

"Why?" you asked.

"Because you're scaring him."

"Scaring?" You repeated what I'd said, still bending over the pail. "And they go to sleep," you'd said. "And they don't wake up."

And with those words, you had actually turned to look at me. There was something in your face that was shaded and questioning. And I think this must have been the beginning of your leaving me. Perhaps by then you already sensed something imminent. Surely on the brink of such a transformation, people know. Why else would you mention sleeping and not waking up?

I remembered looking at you scrupulously, more scrupulously than I had ever looked at any human being; it was as though something had urged me to register your face forever in my mind: your small chest swelling with the excitement of seeing pretty fish and having an older kid pay complete attention to you, the glee in your large dark eyes, the blue vein pulsing quickly at your neck. I felt that we somehow knew each other, had been this close before, but didn't quite know how. And then a wind swept over the lake and ran its fingers through the soft whips of the willows. And as though possessed by that wind's disruptive energy, you grabbed my last slice of bread bait. You stuffed half of it in your mouth and tossed the rest in the water.

I got angry. I tried to send you away. Unfortunately, you'd been spoiled by my attention and refused to leave. I was so frustrated with you that, almost by itself, the fishhook I held gouged its way into my finger and my hand sluiced with blood. Hurting now, I was enraged. The afternoon seemed spoiled and you were its spoiler.

I paused in my story. Sarah and I were on a sofa. The place where each of us sat was surrounded by a halo of damp that had run from our wet bathing suits. "This is the part that I've never told anyone," I tried to explain.

"It's okay," she said. "I understand."

"No, you don't understand. I don't even know you."

"You can trust me, Billy. I promise you. I'll never tell anybody."

I scanned Sarah's face for a signal of possible betrayal and found nothing but concern. Having ventured this far, I knew I had no choice but to continue.

I pushed my bloodied hand in your face. "Look what you made me do!" I shouted. "Get away from me, you stupid idiot! Go home!"

You peered at me for a moment in surprise; you were frightened of me and tears sprang to your eyes. But I couldn't stand there and yell because I was bleeding. I ran back to Peter's house and asked his sister for a Band-Aid. I've told the police, my parents, Gita Romano, I've told everyone who has ever asked that when I went back outside, you were already in the water. But that's not true. When I returned, you were actually standing halfway up the bank, huddled over yourself, crying. I called out, "Go home, Mark, will you! Why don't you just go to your mother!" Suddenly, you screamed and started running, arms flailing, toward the water. Watching you, I felt as though I'd been flung into someone else's dream. At first I couldn't believe you were doing this. I finally yelled at you to stop, but you never stopped until you threw yourself in the lake. I ran after you, shouting for you to grab hold of the bank, but your arms continued to thrash wildly, pushing you farther from shore. Your head was fighting to stay above the water and I could hear you struggling for breath. And despite the fact that you were far beyond my grasp, I knelt down at the edge of the lake. I reached out for you, but could embrace only a body of water that had gathered so many years of rain.

After I was through telling Sarah what happened to us, she led me to the kitchen. She took these bulk carrots out of a vegetable bin in the refrigerator and made us fresh carrot juice in a blender. We stood there sipping from tall cut-crystal glasses, and then I kissed her, even before she'd finished her drink. "You're beautiful," she told me, kissing me back. "No," I said. "You're beautiful." We laughed at our tender stupidity, left our drinks on the white counter and went to a room where there

was a bed with a white bedspread. The sun was curling around
the edges of the drawn shades. We lay on the white bed and
made love until the light stopped coming through and the sky
was no longer visible. And it was afterward, when we were in
the shower soaping one another and laughing, when I made a
date to see Sarah on my way back to Burlington, I realized this
must be the beginning of my healing.

T H R E E   Y E A R S later, when Sarah and I were living together in Greenwich Village, my mother called to say that Tina had quit Mexico and showed up in New Mexico. "I hardly recognized her," my mother said. "She's lost the weight she put on while she was taking all that medication. She's very thin now and tanned and she wears all these silver bracelets on her arms."

"I'm amazed." I explained how during my last conversation with Tina, she had sounded reluctant to return to America.

"Well, I think her decision to come back began with that conversation," my mother told me. "Something she heard from you."

"From me? That's ridiculous," I said.

"Don't be so skeptical, Billy."

"Where is she?" I said. "Let me talk to her."

But Tina had just left for Galveston, to spend time with Rachel. Then she was coming back to Santa Fe, where she knew a dealer who wanted to handle the sale of the blankets she and her friends had been weaving, blankets which, according to my mother, would sell quite profitably in the Plaza.

"So how are you and Sarah doing with the new apartment?" my mother wanted to know.

"To be honest with you, Mom, we don't like it here anymore."

"How come?"

"New York has changed a lot since you lived here."

"It seems the same to me whenever Ravi and I visit."

During the last five years, on account of my resistance to traveling long distances, I'd only seen my mother and Ravi when they came to New York for twice-yearly conferences.

"I didn't even realize it until I started living here permanently again. The city is really dirty and you have to constantly fight crowds to get anywhere. It's depressing and ugly and it gets to us. Sarah particularly. She's used to New England. And with summer coming on, we're really dreading the heat."

"So what are you going to do?"

"We've actually been talking about coming out West.

"Really? And live where?"

"Los Angeles."

"Have you mentioned any of this to your father?"

"Of course not."

"I didn't think so."

Sarah, who was studying for a graduate degree in psychology, was interested in a child psych program at the University of California. I hated the recording studio where I was currently employed, the third one I'd worked for in the two years since graduating from college. My father had gotten each job for me through his entertainment connections and I was paying for the favor in spades: the people with whom I presently worked resented that strings had been pulled, my boss resisted giving me more responsibility than just assisting the chief engineer. Beyond this, I had collected a few outside introductions to recording studios in Los Angeles.

"You'd stop and see us on the way out, wouldn't you?" my mother asked. "Especially now that Tina will be close by."

"I'm sure we will if we drive. We just haven't decided whether or not to go by car."

"Billy, I hope you decide to drive. I think it would be good for you. But if you decide not to or you don't make it within the next six months, Ravi and I have a symposium in Albany at the end of the year. So at least we'll get to see you then."

Two days later, in the midst of getting screamed at for some faultily made cassettes, I flipped my boss the bird and was fired on the spot. In a way I was relieved.

It was a lot hotter in the streets than in the air-conditioned recording studio, and after hiking only a few blocks downtown toward my apartment, my whole body was glazed in sweat. The sun was pummeling me through a grimy haze and as I crossed Fourteenth Street, nearly choking on the fumes, I couldn't imagine how Sarah and I were going to weather another summer. The phone was ringing when I walked into the apartment, and assuming it was she, I picked it up and said, "I'm out of there, baby."

"Billy?" inquired an officious-sounding voice. "Is that you?"

"Yeah." I recognized the voice of my father's secretary.

"Hold for Mr. Kaplan," she said, which caused me to roll my eyes.

"Hello, Billy."

"Dad, why don't you ever call me yourself," I carped.

He ignored my complaint. "Would you please tell me what's

going on. I just got a call from Dick Saturn, who told me they fired you."

"They were treating me like dirt around there."

"That's the business, Billy. You wanted to work in it."

"Well, then, I'd like to find a job where people don't give me shit for using nepotism, not that I don't appreciate what you've done."

"In one way or another you pay for every favor you get."

"That's why I'll start looking in the trades and in the *Times*."

"Good luck," my father said sarcastically.

I peered across my living room at a poster of Jimi Hendrix, inherited with the apartment lease which Sarah and I had purchased for three thousand dollars from a saxophonist.

"You certainly don't sound too upset about what happened," he said.

"I guess it hasn't hit me yet."

"Billy, I don't know what more I can do for you."

"Dad, it's not your responsibility."

"But you'll have to find another job soon or you'll run out of money again."

"I'll get something."

"Meanwhile, I'll make a couple of calls."

"Dad, that's not necessary."

His outdated intercom buzzed and the receptionist announced the name of one of his oldest clients, a Broadway grande dame. "I have to run, Billy," my father said. "But I'm getting a haircut later. Can you meet me at my barber?"

"Where is he now?"

"The Pierre. If you stop by around five o'clock we can go get a drink somewhere and talk."

"A powerhouse of a kid, isn't he?" My father said to Dino, his haircutter, whom he had patronized religiously since I could remember and whose business had migrated among the lobbies of New York's established hotels. Dino was a strapping, middle-aged Sicilian with wavy pomaded hair and a face that had hardly aged in all the years I'd known him. He grabbed me by the biceps. "Jesus, you been working out?"

My father stared at me through the mirror, a glimmer of fondness in his eyes. "Nah, he's just built like that. God bless him."

Dino asked, "How long's it been since I've seen you?"

I shrugged. "Three, four years."

"You're bigger now than you were then. You work out?"

I shook my head.

"So how did you get that way without working out?"

"I swim."

"He does more than that," my father added. "He plays water polo with a club. I was never as big as he is. He must get it from his mother's side of the family."

"How is Susan?" Dino asked.

"She's fine," I said.

"A fine-looking lady, as I remember."

"Yeah, well, she's not so fine-looking anymore," my father told him. The last time my mother and Ravi had returned to New York, my mother had met my father for what had been described by both of them as an amicable drink.

"Come on, Dad," I objected.

My father waved me away as his eyes locked with Dino's in the mirror, man to man. "She would look a lot better if she'd stayed in New York instead of going out to Santa Fe."

"How's that?" Dino said.

"Would you leave her alone!" I snarled.

"Hold still," Dino said as he carefully manicured the line of hair around my father's ears.

"Okay, now they have this health craze out West, right?" my father resumed once Dino had finished his delicate clipping.

"Yeah, so?" Dino said.

"So these people, they get in shape, they get great physiques, while their faces and their skin go all to hell."

"It's very dry out there," I interjected.

"Precisely," my father said. "And always sunny. And people out there take a lot of sun."

"You take a lot of sun," I pointed out.

"Yeah, but do I look like a prune?" My father studied himself in the mirror. "Does Dino look like a prune? And we always get tan."

Both men were extraordinarily handsome, particularly Dino, who really looked ageless.

My father turned to Dino again. "I'm telling you, Susan used to look younger than all of her friends. She came to New York a couple of years ago to have a get-together with her Westchester cronies and by then some of them, maybe not figurewise, but certainly in the face, were looking a lot younger than she was."

"Dad, that's because they've all had face lifts. And she hasn't."

"Ah, come on," my father said.

"It's true. They all have face lifts and then they call up Mom because she knows about herbs and natural healing and they figure she'll be able to tell them something they can use that'll help them heal faster from all the scalpel cuts behind their ears."

I marveled at my father's obsession with appearance and aging. Perhaps he was growing all too aware of the slow failing of his own body. Although at fifty his compact frame had only thickened slightly with middle age, in the last few years his physiognomy had taken on a perceptible weariness. His shoulders had developed a slight forward slump, and his movements didn't seem as light and pantherlike as they used to. And yet, I felt the change had to do more with a withering within his spiritual constitution, a giving up on something, than with a calcification of bones or an inner aging of organs.

"God, is it gorgeous out," he said once we had left the wall-to-wall marble barbershop and were strolling down Fifth Ave-

nue. The irritably hot day had cooled into a lovely warm evening. The gentleness of the air and the ebullience of strollers
wearing new summer outfits momentarily assuaged whatever
strong feelings brewed within me.

"I've got to get my tennis racket restrung," my father said.
"So I can start playing again."

"You going to rent that house again in Salem?" I asked,
feeling guilty that if Sarah and I moved out West we would be
unable to spend any time at the summer house.

My father shrugged. "Don't know. Depends who's in my life
at the time." He had come to a recent conclusion that he would
never get married again. He claimed he was now content to float
from relationship to relationship. He said he had finally accepted
that his very particular needs would never be matched by the
needs of women he dated. This made me sad.

As we headed toward the Plaza, I said, "Why do you still
resent Mom so much?"

My father surprised me and said nothing in response.

"All that stuff about how she doesn't look as good, it's just
anger."

"So?"

"I mean, it's been fifteen years. Can't you let go of it?"

"I wasn't putting her down. I was just making a point about
the West and what it does to the skin. It's not only in her that
I've seen it. I've also seen it in many of my clients who live out
there. For whom looking good is far more important."

I waited for a moment and then said, "Sarah and I are actually thinking about moving out to Los Angeles."

My father swallowed the news without reaction and then
shrugged. "I can't stop you. You're of age to decide what you
want to do." He walked a few steps farther and then glanced at
me sideways. "On whose money are you expecting to move out
there?"

"We have some saved."

My father's look ripened into skepticism. He knew that, being a full-time student, Sarah presently had no income. "Really, how much you got?"

"Enough to live on for five or six months."

We had stopped at the corner in front of the Plaza and my father was peering up at the scrollwork of the architecture and the windows that were liquefying the late sun. "You'll get eaten up out there," he murmured.

"Don't say that."

The light changed and he crossed the street first, waiting for me at the far curb. "What makes you think it'll be any easier to hold down a job in . . . California?"

"I don't think it'll be any easier. It might be a little cheaper to live."

"Well, that's probably true. But I'll tell you something about that city, Billy. In some ways the business is a lot tougher than New York, mostly because it's so insidious when you're so busy thinking it's paradise. They go through human flesh out there faster than anywhere I've ever seen."

We strolled into the carpeted lobby and cut through a wave of expensively dressed foreigners: women in sleeveless silk dresses with bangles on their arms hurrying to fetch taxis, dark men in raw-silk suits suspiciously counting fresh denominations of U.S. currency, a strong smell of commingled perfumes that was as heady as church incense. We were now in my father's milieu; I could see how comfortable the atmosphere made him feel, how it became him. I felt disadvantaged, overwhelmed. I glanced back toward the doors through which we had just revolved. I wanted to break free from the discussion and walk home again.

We waited until a maître d' seated us at the Oak Room bar, where more chic-looking people swilled cold cocktails on what I imagined to be first dates or to ritualize the closing of major-league business deals. "You should concentrate on holding down a job and earning a steady living," my father said softly, almost distractedly, as he surveyed the crowd. "If you knew you couldn't get any subsidy from me maybe you wouldn't keep quitting or doing things to get fired."

I looked at him dismally. "That's why I should move to California. Not to have the temptation of having you to fall back on. I don't think it's healthy for either of us."

"Just because you're moving to California doesn't mean that I won't stop worrying if you're getting by. Money can be mailed, remember, funds wired between banks. At least if you lived here I could take you both out to dinner once in a while, make sure you got a good meal . . ." My father hesitated and then said, "Make sure you're feeling okay." The last comment, of course, referred to his continuing worry that I might plummet into a depression and end up doing myself in. He would always be haunted by the fact that he had caught me perched on the ledge of the condominium balcony in Palm Beach. "You're going to drive out there?"

I nodded.

"Will you feel comfortable doing it?" He also knew that I was still afflicted with a certain degree of anxiety when it came to traveling, the reason why, up until now, I had postponed a trip to Santa Fe. I suddenly realized that when Sarah and I visited New Mexico it would be the first time in five years that my mother and I would sleep under the same roof. It depressed me to face such a lapse in my relationship with her, but I realized I was partly responsible for it.

"I have to do it sometime," I said. "And Sarah will be with me. And we're going to stay a while with Mom and Ravi."

That was the wrong thing to say. Suddenly my father flushed scarlet. "You know something?" he said. "It really burns me. After she left you, after all this time, you're finally going to move far away from me, who hung in there for you, and go closer to where she is. I mean, I can't believe it." His voice boomed, attracting wary attention from nearby tables. Luckily, he realized that a hush was beginning to infect our small pocket of the bar and lowered his voice. "Your mother split on you and now you're going to live with her!"

He had to say it that way: my mother had left me. "I don't agree with you that she split on me," I said. After all, I had gone to college a year after she had moved to New Mexico. "And anyway, I'm moving to California. I'm not moving to Mom."

"Just tell me one thing," he intoned. "Where did you go when you came home from college all those weekends?"

"I went to your apartment, Dad. But remember, at the time I hated traveling. My life was more limited then."

"Maybe part of that limitation was that you really didn't feel like visiting her."

"Jesus, Dad, it had absolutely nothing to do with that."

The waiter arrived with two mineral waters on ice with wedges of lime. As my father settled the bill, I realized that he had bitten into a raw nerve. Maybe he was right. Maybe she did leave me.

"How long are you going to spend with them?" he asked once the waiter left us alone.

"A few weeks, a month at the most. I just want to see what their life is like. And then we'll go on to L.A. I've got some leads on a few jobs."

My father took a small swig of his mineral water and then stared gloomily into his glass. "So then you really are serious about moving away?"

"Yeah, Dad."

He looked at me tenderly. "If you go out there I'm not going to give you any money when you get low."

"That's okay. It'll be good for me."

He put down his drink and, looking away, shook his head. Even though he had now drawn the boundary, he suddenly seemed reluctant to abide by it. I knew that on some level he would enjoy the privilege of bailing me out of dire straits. It made him feel that he still had some sort of control over me. "I've told you about Donny McFee, the guy who comes to see me?"

Donny McFee, once a close friend of my father's, was a top recording engineer who had skidded out of the profession and now dressed like a bum and came to the office, reeking of booze, asking for handouts.

I groaned. "Dad, you must tell me about him damn near every time we get together."

"Well, maybe I've been trying to make a point."

"You're kidding," I said sarcastically.

My father continued sanctimoniously. "His life is a complete disaster. He has never been able to hold down a job. He just lives from hand to mouth. He's got a wife and kids living separately from him so they can be on welfare."

I stood up. "Look, Dad, we've been through this too many times. Believe me, I'm not going to end up drifting from job to job like Donny McFee. Stop playing this tape, or you're going to force me to leave."

"Sit down, I'm not finished," my father said good-naturedly.

"Only if we can talk about something else."

And then I spotted the thing in my father's eye that sometimes warned me when things were going too far. The expression was blank, opaque, a glaze of ice over a bay of agony and fury. "I said sit down!" He suddenly screamed.

A hush detonated in the room and everyone stared at us. I told him he was shouting. With a desolate feeling, I figured he had lost all touch with propriety and what remained to be played out was a terribly embarrassing scene. But then, miraculously, he got a hold on himself. His eyes lost their expressionless glint and now looked pained.

I now knew my father was afraid of my leaving. Without a steady girlfriend, he would be alone on the East Coast, alone at whichever summer house he decided to rent. He was looking at me expectantly. His drink was three-quarters full and he held it in his right hand. We had identical hands, which whenever I noticed it always made me feel strange. And suddenly, I felt the love brimming, such a love that it scared me, impeded me, shook me deeper and more profoundly than the love I felt for Sarah, who, at times, certainly drove me crazier, made me feel more desperate. This troubled emotion toward my father would burn on its own inexhaustible flame, for the rest of my life, no matter where I went, no matter how hard I tried to deny it. I collapsed into my chair.

My father leaned toward me. "What happened, Billy?" he groaned. "Why couldn't you hold that job?"

"Because, Dad, my bosses resented the fact that someone higher up told them to take me on. When strings are pulled, people in the middle can get pretty resentful."

And then suddenly, as in a bad dream, everything shifted into a terrifying gear. It amazed me, and perhaps part of our dynamic was that my father always managed to take me completely by surprise. "I thought you'd say something like that. And if you think that's what going on here you're deluding yourself."

"What do you mean?"

"Dick Saturn said they'd been dissatisfied with you from the beginning. He said you really don't have an ear for mixing and that they probably would have let you go even if you hadn't been disrespectful."

I glanced sharply at my father. "I could have lived without that bit of information."

"I'm sorry. I just thought you should know. Dick said you had . . . marginal talent as an engineer," my father told me flatly. "He told me you'd be better off getting a full-time corporate job."

Without a word, I stood and walked out.

· · ·

As soon as I arrived home, there were two messages on my answering machine: one from Sarah saying she was going to the library after her class and would be home late; one from my father, apologizing for what he had said and imploring me to meet him at the Four Seasons for dinner. It occurred to me that I must've wanted things to end badly. By letting my father do the wounding, I would feel less guilty and conflicted about moving away. Whenever I would feel a pang to stay in New York, I could remind myself of what my father said and how much it had hurt and that would make it easier to leave.

I got a beer out of the refrigerator and went back into the living room, which was filled with fairly decent furniture, most of it cast-off by my father when he moved from one river-view apartment to another and changed decor. There was a battered leather sofa, a tattered club chair. A white-and-taupe reproduction Persian carpet lay richly on the scuffed parquet floors. A tall, healthy yucca plant stood next to the bay windows that faced south. In the bedroom on my double bed lay the old rabbit bedspread—now worn pretty ragged—on which I lost my virginity and which my father had put in storage when he traded up for mink. All our friends thought it was the tackiest thing in the world, but I loved it. A penchant for fur bedspreads was something my father and I had in common.

Why had he been so hurtful? Why did he want to discourage me from pursuing something I felt I could be happy doing? What was he afraid of? It just didn't make sense.

The phone rang. I allowed the answering machine to pick up. My father's voice was nearly suffocated by all the restaurant clatter. "I'm here at the Four Seasons." Pause. "I'm waiting for you." Pause. He knew I was home, monitoring my calls. "Come on. Pick up!" In the background someone dropped a load of dishes and there was a concussive shattering. "Pretty lively here tonight," my father remarked casually, and then: "I wish you'd come here and let me apologize in person. I didn't realize what I was saying. You know how I get angry sometimes. Look, I was lying. Dick Saturn never said anything about your abilities or about finding another profession."

I picked up. "Dad, I don't believe you."

"Billy, I'm telling the truth. The whole thing was a complete lie. I was angry. And I'm really sorry I said what I said. Now please come here and meet me."

"Dad, you've overloaded me. I can't meet you right now."

"You have to come here and have dinner with me. I'm sorry. I'm sorry. I just said what I said because I'm scared . . . that you're going to leave me," he finally admitted.

I shut my eyes and fought back a sob. "I know, Dad. I know you're scared. Now why don't you just go home. 'Cause I'm not coming. I hurt. I need to be alone."

"Billy, let me ease the hurt for you. Just come meet me . . . How about if I come down to the Village?"

That offer stopped me for a moment, a real concession. My father never traveled below Forty-second Street.

"That's good of you, Dad, but I still want to be alone. In fact, when we get off I'm going to turn off my phone. So don't try calling back."

"Why are you doing this to me? What are you going to do —leave town now and not say goodbye?"

I finally broke down. And then in the background I heard my father join me. His sobbing sounded deep and treacherous and lonely. "Of course not," I managed to say. "You act like I'm leaving tomorrow."

"How will I know when you're going to leave?" he blubbered.

"I'll give you plenty of warning, believe me. I'll see you plenty before I go."

———————————— ◉ ————————————

Y O U   W E R E so much on my mind when Sarah
and I decided to give up the apartment, as we pared our
belongings down to the bare essentials—clothing, cartons of
books and records—and prepared to move to California. At first
I didn't understand why, but then I realized I was concerned that
in traveling beyond the boundary of where you once lived I'd
be surrendering my chances to finally seek the forgiveness of
your parents.

On the day of our departure, Aunt Tina called, wanting to
know how I felt about making such a long journey.

"A little shaky. But I'm not going to let it stop me."

"Well, listen, if it makes you bizarre, you can always call me and I'll remind you that I'm a helluva lot crazier than you are. That should make you feel better."

"Thanks," I said halfheartedly. "Where are you calling from?"

"Santa Fe." She went on to tell me she had just rented an apartment in town and was now only an hour's drive away from my mother.

"An hour? I thought my mother lived right outside Santa Fe."

"An hour is right outside town. Get ready, Billy, the spaces are a lot bigger out here."

I shuddered at this. Tina went on to say that she might not be in New Mexico when Sarah and I first arrived; in a few days she would be paying another visit to Rachel in Galveston. I recently heard that Rachel had completed a nursing program and had been hired by a good hospital.

"Sounds like Rachel is doing well," I said.

"She is. The best news is that she relies on herself completely. I guess she's had to a lot of the time."

"What about the stepmother? She still around?"

"Sure."

"Have you two met?"

"Once."

"How was that?"

"Pretty strange."

"In what way?"

"Well, for one thing, she happens to look like me."

"You might take that as flattery."

"I could, I suppose, if I thought about it enough. I'm just glad that Rachel's living on her own, so that we can see each other without having to deal with another party."

"A long time to wait for that," I said.

I heard Tina grunt and then she said, "I would have had to deal with their relationship any time I chose to come back."

I now brought up the conversation of a few years ago when Tina had called me in Vermont. Referring to my mother's comment, I asked her if I had said something out of the ordinary.

"No, Billy. I was just moved by how upset you got when I told you I wanted to wait before seeing Rachel again."

"That was before you explained your reasons, which I understood."

"Billy, you were right to be upset. What do reasons matter to a child who wants to be with their parent? After I talked to you, it dawned on me I didn't have to get completely well, that no matter what condition I was in, Rachel probably needed me. And I realized that I couldn't go forward unless I came back from where I was."

The conversation turned more casual, about packing and means of travel and how many days it would take for Sarah and me to reach New Mexico. Then Tina asked if I was ready for a new adventure. After an uncomfortable pause I admitted to her that I still felt the need to speak to your parents again. She said she was certain your parents didn't blame me anymore.

"How do you know?"

"Because it wasn't your fault—they must've realized that a long time ago."

"You can't be sure about that," I said, once again irritated by her presumption.

"Billy, after all these years, you're only purposely hurting yourself if you hold on to anything close to their blaming you."

"It's a lot more complicated than you realize."

"It doesn't make any difference how complicated it is. You have to let go of them sometime. Believe me, these things I know about. But how about this? How about if I forgive you for them?"

"No dice."

"Come on, Billy. You've gotten enough mileage out of this.

Why don't you just get in your car, drive out here and leave them behind."

"I just can't do that," I told her.

"Your aunt doesn't understand," Sarah said as she took the poster of Jimi Hendrix off the wall and began crating it in cardboard and sealing it with masking tape. I had just replayed for her the basic text of my conversation with Tina. Sarah now turned to face me with her warm eyes, her face wreathed with a painful smile. "Because she doesn't know everything that happened."

"Do you think that's important?" I now asked the only person in my life to whom I'd told everything about you.

"Important to nobody else but you. Because you've been living with it."

"But do you think they know?" I asked, referring to your parents.

Sarah spread her arms and hoisted up the crated poster. "Here," I said, "let me help you with that."

"Billy, I can do it," she said assertively with a toss of her burnished hair. Once she set the carton down and had leaned it against the bare wall, she turned to me, dusting her hands. "You'll never know unless you ask them and I personally don't think you should ask them. How could they know any more than what you originally told them? Nobody but you saw what happened. I think you automatically credit them with knowing more because there's more to know."

I looked at Sarah keenly. "I can't decide whether or not to go and see them."

"Billy," she said softly, "you know I can't make that choice for you. But I'll understand any decision you make." Sarah moved slowly forward, slipped her arms around my neck and kissed me softly on the mouth.

. . .

A few hours later, even after we had loaded up the Datsun with our belongings, dropped by my father's apartment to say goodbye and drove out of Manhattan, I was still unsure whether or not I wanted to contact them. "Let's just drive through the old neighborhood," I finally suggested to Sarah as we were heading up the FDR Drive.

"Fine with me." Her lips curled into a sly grin.

"What are you smiling at?"

She threw up her hands. "Nothing. Nothing at all."

This was not the first time I had driven Sarah past my old house, which had been sold yet again to another family, who had repainted it light gray with beige shutters. It now resembled tract homes built later on in the seventies, homes painted in pastel shades as opposed to the starker color schemes of the sixties. Leaving the car idling, I stared up at my bedroom. I spoke of the exhilaration of having school end and there being three months of summer vacation ahead, playing by the lake, catching frogs and fish, until, in the wake of the drowning, a shadow had passed over my life. Just as I was ready to put the car in gear and move on, my bedroom window cracked open. A small boy, not much older than I'd been when we lived there, although scrawnier and fairer, leaned out and launched a balsa-wood airplane. The miniature craft glided over the tops of the Japanese maples, captured a light swell of wind, nosed up for a moment and then softly landed in the middle of the flower bed, its wing catching on a spray of delphiniums that my mother had planted as bulbs so many years ago.

The lake was peppered with tree pollen, its dead-calm surface splintered by a pair of wild swans that had recently been imported. Once a predator of humans, the body of water, with years of drought, had been scaled down to the stature of a shallow reflecting pond. Except for two foreign compact cars lined up in the driveway, your house looked somber and uninhabited. In contrast to the freshly painted state of my former house, yours looked in sad shape. Blue paint was flaking off like scabby sores onto the shrubs, and the black shutters were cracked and warped. A single lawn chair with broken vinyl ribs was planted haphazardly halfway into the rhododendron bushes that ran alongside the front part of the house and whose underwatered leaves sickled inwardly. Disturbed by the obvious neglect, I pulled the car a half block down the street and parked. It was as though your reclusive parents had died years ago and the neighbors had yet to discover their recumbent bodies in an advanced state of decomposition.

Should I go and knock on the door? Or should I not? I glanced at Sarah with a look of perplexity and she squeezed my hand and said, "It's up to you, baby."

I got out of the car and for a moment listened to the evening song of the neighborhood, a discordant babble of children's voices intertwined with threads of Musak. I looked at the Freeds' house and found it relatively unchanged from when I used to visit. A swarthy teenaged boy with dark arms showing through a cutoff tee shirt burst out the front door, skipped down the steps and hurdled into the front seat of a red Corvette. He started the engine into a thunder, backed up and screeched out of the neighborhood.

As I strolled up the flagstone path of your house, I noticed a green garden hose coiled tightly and lying on the lawn just before the front steps, its brass couplings glistening with wet—a definite sign of life. Would they recognize me after so many years, or peer at me as blankly as though I were a stranger? The last time I came here was when my mother went berserk and dragged me into a dread deeper than any I could have ever imagined. She hadn't known what she was doing. By trying to confront the blame, she thought she was doing what was best for me. As I reached the front porch, Sarah turned off the car motor.

I listened for vital signs. I heard a few bars of music floating out from the upstairs window: Duke Ellington. I tried the screen door, but it was latched. I took a deep breath and pushed the doorbell. It was too late now, I had to go through with it. I heard someone hurrying down steps.

She answered. And because the house was not lighted and because it was nearly dusk and because she was peering at me through a screen, it was difficult at first for me to see her. I squinted. She was wearing a ratty housedress with short sleeve bands that held pale, saggy arms. She was clutching a green sponge, obviously having been caught in the midst of cleaning. Her face was even longer, sharply contoured, her nose more beaklike than it used to be. Your mother had substantially aged in the last few years. She was peering at me cautiously. I imagine that none of the neighbors would have stopped by without first calling.

"Yes? Can I help you?"

At last, I felt scared. Petrified. "I'm someone who used to live in the neighborhood," I stammered.

"Oh?" She was squinting at me.

"I'm . . . actually doing a survey. My name is Billy Rosen . . . I mean Kaplan," I corrected myself, rolling my eyes at this spectacular blunder.

"You should probably talk to my husband about this," she said, and turned to call for him.

She hadn't even noticed my name! Sure, I had stupidly given your last name with my own first, but when she had finally heard the name Kaplan, there was still no recognition. She left the doorway and I considered sprinting across the lawn to my car, as once, twenty years ago, I had screamed away in shame from her accusations. But then I realized that I had already told her my name, and if she didn't associate it now with the little boy who had last played with you before you died, she would certainly recognize it later when she told your father someone named Kaplan had appeared at the door.

Your father finally materialized, your mother standing just behind his shoulder. "Yes? What can I do for you?" he said, his eyes boring into me.

"She told you who I was?"

"No . . . wait a second."

He opened the screen so that we could see one another more clearly. Your father had held up better than your mother. Wearing a powder-blue golf shirt and seersucker slacks, he was still statuesque and strapping. His hair was snow white, his face flushed with good health, his eyes glacial. "I'm Billy . . ." I paused, afraid I was going to say Rosen again, to make sure I said, "Kaplan. I'm Billy Kaplan."

Your father's face underwent a spasm and his mouth lurched open. "Billy Kaplan," he muttered, turning to your mother, now barely visible in the depth of shadow beyond the porch light's orbit. "Didn't you ask who it was?"

"He said, but I didn't realize," she whispered.

Your father turned to me and said in irritation, "Why did you come here? After all this time? Can't you for once leave us alone?"

"For once?" I winced. "Don't you think I've left you alone?"

"Obviously not."

"I have up until now."

Your father recovered his balance, his features set in determination. "Look," he said more evenly, "there's absolutely no reason for you to be here. You're not in contact with us. You're not our friend. So please don't bring all this up again."

"Bring it up," I repeated in surprise. "But don't you think about it?"

"It's not your concern—"

"Of course we think about it," your mother interrupted. "He was our son."

"So it's not as though I'm bringing something up, if it hasn't gone away."

"What do you want from us?" she asked in a vanquished tone of voice.

"Don't ask him that, Harriet. Because I certainly don't want to know," your father said, stepping aside and preparing to slam the door.

"Well, I do," she insisted. "I want to know why he's come here like this to knock on our door."

"I would like to tell you," I said. "If I may come in?"

Your parents agitated for a few moments and then, without discussing it, stood aside.

As I stepped over the threshold I realized how terrible I'd have felt if your father had slammed the door in my face. To think it was your mother who had given me this opportunity. I breathed in the smell of your house, of their lives: furniture polish, cut flowers, something stewing or sautéing, laundry. There was a powder room off the foyer and as I passed it I sniffed rose water. I remembered myrrh-scented candles flickering the night we came, making the place feel like a chapel, and the horde of neighbors peering down at me, unable to hide what I felt had been their vague condemnation. It was different now. The house was less looming, yet in a way larger; for it was just the three of us. Your sister had grown up and moved away, and they now lived alone once again in the place where they had always lived, as if they never had children.

"Come into the living room," your father said. Now that I had come inside, he was forced to be hospitable. He motioned me to a beige love seat made of worsted fabric near the window, separated from the rest of the furniture—another sofa in matching fabric pushed against the adjacent wall, free-floating chairs upholstered in a textile that looked sun-trodden, a six-foot baby grand piano jutting from the far corner of the room—like a rock in the middle of a desert. On the black lacquer top of the piano perched three brass-framed pictures: one of a young woman in a maroon cap and gown, one of the same woman in a white wedding dress and veil standing alongside a heavyset blond man and one of a small boy grinning in a sailor's outfit. I tried hard not to look at your face, but couldn't help it, my scrutiny nakedly obvious to your parents. In the picture you looked quite different from the face that has crystallized in my memory. As I remember, you weren't so pale or plain-looking or cheerful, but rather darker, exotic, petulant.

Your parents sat close together on the long sofa, though far away from me. Your father said, "I don't think, I should say, I don't want this to be a very long conversation."

"I understand," I said. "I respect that." For a moment I was overwhelmed to have them sitting before me, waiting for me to speak my mind and then being forced to respond to whatever I said. My heart ached, thinking how I'd wanted this for so long, amazed that I hadn't tried contacting them until now. But then I grasped a sheet of panic. The whole situation seemed so real and yet so unforeseen that my breath darted and my head started to sing dissonant melodies.

"I'm sorry to be so abrupt and show up like this. Not calling or anything," I began haltingly.

"Yes, you should have called," your father agreed.

"Well, you see, I was on my way out West and I decided at the last minute that I needed to talk to you before I left. It was a spur-of-the-moment thing."

When your parents heard this, their faces drooped in distress. Later on, when I was thinking about their reaction, I realized that up until that moment they had assumed they were the only ones who had built vaults for you in their hearts, never realizing that someone else besides them had mourned you.

"I guess you know that we moved," I said. "We've been gone from the neighborhood for a long time. But ever since I've known how to drive I've been coming up here and looking at the neighborhood and the lake and trying to understand what happened."

"Oh, for Christ's sake," your mother said, momentarily surprised. "I think I've seen you. Down by the lake."

"No," I said. "I've never gone anywhere near the water. I've been careful to remain as inconspicuous as possible."

"Look, can you get to the point?" your father said sharply, beginning to fidget.

I had to remind myself that we were at odds over the issue. We had all suffered the loss, but were divided, and I felt this shouldn't be so. I should be sitting there like a family member, sharing grief, but instead I was sitting there like an outcast, a prodigal child.

"You seem angry," I said. "Are you angry at me?"

"We're not angry. It's just difficult for us to be reminded of what happened," your mother explained.

"Do I remind you of it, or do you actually blame me?" I asked.

They looked at me, astonished by such directness. Then they glanced at each other, their faces withering. "We don't have to answer your questions," your father informed me.

"You don't have to," I said, "but don't you want to?"

"Maybe we don't know what the answer is."

"You've had almost twenty years to think about it. We all have."

"Look," your father fumed. "Don't give me this 'we all.' It's not 'we all.' You're not in it with us. He was our son. We were his parents. And he died. The loss is ours. The loss is not yours."

"You're wrong," I said. "The loss belongs to whoever claims it, for whatever reason they claim it." I stopped, surprised I had uttered the words, which seemed truthful to me and yet completely unpremeditated. "And I claim it because I've felt partly responsible and I've always felt that you thought I was responsible and that you blamed me."

"We did," your mother said, her eyes flashing with tears. I felt breathless and crushed by what I had always suspected (and which my parents had repeatedly assured me was not the case). She glanced at your father. "Let's be honest with him, Larry," she insisted. "He came here. He wants to know."

"I do," I said, now halfheartedly. For I also knew that if the truth was as painful as it threatened to be, it might take many more years to embrace.

Your mother expired a sigh. "We blamed you because you had sense enough to take care of yourself. You knew how to swim, you knew how not to fall in, but you didn't have enough sense to think that Mark wouldn't know better, that he couldn't swim or didn't know the water was dangerous. And because you went away and left him there—"

"But I told him to go home. He wouldn't listen to me," I interrupted. "Even when I yelled at him," I added.

Your mother looked at me sorrowfully for a moment, and then continued, as if I hadn't fractured her monologue. "Mind you, we wouldn't have expected anything different from a seven-year-old child who met up with our son on the road. We wouldn't have expected another child to know that ours shouldn't have been outside unattended, not to mention near the water. It was our fault he was there at all and the nurse's fault for letting him wander. It was our fault that he drowned, but we still blamed you."

"Do you still blame me?" I asked.

Your mother bowed her head. She keeled over against your father, lowering her face into the crook of his neck. He now regarded me with the sorrow of a friend, no longer with the anger of an adversary. "It happened so long ago, Billy Kaplan." He pronounced my full name, as though emphasizing it would also emphasize his subsequent remark. "The pain is different now. It's become so much a part of our lives, of being alone, we no longer think in terms of blame. Even ourselves, we've stopped blaming. All we try to do is remember the short time we had with him. Which wasn't very much. Luckily, we have another child. A lovely girl," he added proudly.

"And you've had me," I whispered, "all along you've had me." But they didn't hear it. I stood up. When they made a move to stand also, I bade them to remain where they were sitting. "Thank you for talking to me," I said. "I'll show myself out," and saying goodbye, I walked to the door.

Outside in the dusk the summer air was warm, spiced with the fragrance of your mother's blooming roses. I wanted to pinch myself to fully believe that I had just survived a scene which I had attempted against the advice of everyone I knew, except for Sarah. I felt as though I had just crossed over a deep gorge on a rickety wooden bridge that, weakened by years of rain, had miraculously supported my weight. But your parents hadn't forgiven me; I hadn't asked for their forgiveness, as planned. In fact, they even admitted to having blamed me. So then why did I feel so relieved?

I walked to the car where Sarah was waiting. It was nearly dark and I could see her silhouette on the driver's side. She started the motor. Before I climbed in, I stood for a moment and looked at the lake. A distant cacophony of children's voices was interrupted by a shout of "Come home now!" I closed my eyes, realizing I would probably never know what home was.